THE THIRD DAY

Chochana Boukhobza

THE
THIRD DAY

Translated from the French by
Alison Anderson

MACLEHOSE PRESS
QUERCUS · LONDON

First published in Great Britain in 2012

MacLehose Press
An imprint of Quercus
55 Baker Street
7th Floor, South Block
London W1U 8EW

First published in French as *Le Troisième Jour* by
Éditions Denoël, Paris

Copyright © Éditions Denoël, 2010

English translation copyright © 2012 by Alison Anderson

This book is supported by the French Ministry of Foreign Affairs
as part of the Burgess Programme run by the Cultural Department
of the French Embassy in London. www.frenchbooknews.com

A CIP catalogue record for this book
is available from the British Library

ISBN (HB) 978 0 85705 096 0
ISBN (TPB) 978 0 85705 097 7

2   4   6   8   10   9   7   5   3   1

Designed and typeset in 11½/16pt Bembo by Patty Rennie
Printed and bound in Great Britain by Clays Ltd, St Ives plc

To my children
To Paul Raymond
To Michèle Chiche

Do you hear the violin's mournful song
Sighing notes of blood?
Already its heart calls the end of waiting
And plays the death tango
Be not afraid, my treasure.
        ANONYMOUS, *Das Todestango*

Author's Note

The characters in this novel, their names or personality, are imaginary, and their identity or resemblance with any actual person, living or dead, is purely an unintentional and involuntary coincidence on the part of the author.

FIRST SONG

RACHEL

I did not stay to unpack my suitcase. I went into Elisheva's room and told her I was going out. My professor went on hanging up her dresses, then she said in a neutral voice, "The rehearsal starts at 7 p.m. sharp."

I chose to ignore her warning.

"And you? What are you going to do?"

"Rest. Make a few calls."

"And the cellos?"

"I'll take care of them."

"But I can help you . . ."

"No. Leave it."

Elisheva handed me three tickets for the concert, and I put them in my pocket with a smile.

"They won't come," I said, thinking to myself that this woman was a witch. She knew where I was going without even asking.

"Invite them. That's what matters."

I picked up my jacket from the back of a chair and left without even stopping to slip on the other sleeve.

Blocking the hallway were two obese American women, decked in diamonds that shimmered against their pale skin. The fatter of the two was saying, raising the tone each time she repeated it, "Oh my God!" while her companion echoed, "Yes, yes!"

I hugged the wall and they went by, dressed in pastel chiffon that quivered with each jiggle of fat. I thought how glad I was to be me – poor, young and beautiful. I may not have the means to pay for a luxury hotel, but my body does what I tell it to do.

I took the elevator and walked through the hotel lobby as if I were in a dream.

Each step cost me a considerable effort. Jetlag and my night on the plane were beginning to get the better of me. If I did not want to screw up my solos during rehearsal, the best thing would be to go and get some sleep. But I needed to walk through the city, discover it street by street.

"I call you a taxi, miss?"

"I'll take the bus . . . Thanks."

The doorman in his brown livery, who must come here every morning in a collective taxi from a village in the territories, looked at me with surprise as if I were heading to my doom. I gave him a smile and ducked into the revolving door; its glass panes sparkled with sunlight.

And the hot breath of the *sharav* assailed me as I went out on the terrace ringed with oleanders.

I had not gone more than a few steps before I was drenched in sweat and sorry I had not listened to the doorman. The heat poured from the sky like a woollen blanket and there was not a single refuge of shade in sight. The trees were electrified by sunlight and offered no protection. The air was crackling with sounds from out of nowhere – crickets, birds chirping, engines purring.

I crossed the Plazza gardens, went around Kikar Tzion and down Rehavia. I felt like having a falafel and did not dare. How could I subject my stomach, at nine o'clock in the morning, to a pita bread stuffed with slices of onion, greasy eggplant and fried chickpea balls, all dripping in harissa?

But the more I thought about it, the more my mouth watered.

And I was about to buy one when I saw the 26 bus coming around the corner. I began to run like crazy to reach the stop. A soldier and a middle-aged woman also made a dash for it. The woman raised her arms, shouting, "*Atzor, atzor!*" and her chest was bouncing to the rhythm of her steps. The soldier sped on in silence. His kippa

4

was pinned to his hair and was flapping up and down like a little lid on top of his head.

The driver had seen us. He waited until we had boarded and then the woman, clinging to a rail, blessed him in a strong Moroccan accent: *Ti-ye bari, adoni!* I found a seat, wondering how to translate that expression – "Good health to you, sir" – then my mind went blank. At the intersection the driver accelerated abruptly to merge at breakneck speed on to the road to Givat Tzarfatit.

I clung to my seat and looked out of the dusty window at the dry, red landscape, the fields of olive groves, the roadside displays of earthenware jugs and pottery that had been in the same place for a decade or more.

Nothing had changed; and yet . . .

They were building a completely absurd new roundabout, and the Arab workers who were pouring the cement did not even look up at the bus as it roared around the bend.

How many more stops until mine? Two? Three?

I wondered how my parents would react when they saw me. I was looking forward to seeing them again, but I was apprehensive all the same. Our relationship is complicated, even if we do love each other.

I pushed the button for the stop. On the radio the speaker was announcing a record drought for the region. Then came the first bars of a song by Shlomo Artzi, and the rubber-lined doors closed behind me with a whoosh.

I walked down the gallery carved into the mountainside.

The heat was suffocating.

This suburb, eight hundred metres above sea level, sprang up in the 1970s. In the summer, it is cool at dawn, then the sun comes up and the heat settles in. At noon the furnace is at its hottest. Then the temperature goes shooting down again at night, and under a wine-red sky the mist wafts along the narrow streets in long white icy scarves.

My parents moved into the neighbourhood when I was six. They occupied an apartment on the third floor of the first building to be completed, and we began our life there among the ditches and the cranes, to the noise of pneumatic drills wielded by masons hired from the West Bank.

The buildings grew, the roads took shape, schools and grocery stores opened, but the hills seemed so vast that no-one thought they would ever be able to fill them.

Twice a month we went for walks on the slopes with my class. We would walk among the olive trees and thyme bushes; we went through Arab villages that lived off the fleeces of their sheep. Sometimes we would run into an Arab working the land with a horse and ploughshare. His plot spread over two terraces. He grew wheat and a few vines. Our teacher pointed out the low walls of dry stone, simple piles to combat erosion. He would caress the trunk of an olive tree and explain the secret labour of its roots as they branched out to create an immense latticework that would retain every particle of clay during the rainy season. The teacher swept the class with his gaze. We listened attentively. And we felt like crying when he added that we were like the olive trees. Our roots had saved us from destruction. Through books and prayer the land of Israel had spread its roots ineradicably into our thoughts.

The hills of my childhood had disappeared.

The cranes had been working relentlessly. Concrete had spread everywhere. Apartments were cheap, and the view over Jerusalem was incomparable. The mountain was covered with high-rise blocks. Beyond the blocks were the villas with red-tiled roofs, lovely houses without terraces, because they were Palestinian.

My parents live on a neglected little street. Six years ago the property manager ran off with the co-owners' funds, and the inhabitants no longer wanted to chip in to buy plants or heating oil. So the shared space is not well maintained and looks the worse for wear. In the winter everyone heats as best they can, which means poorly. When it gets very cold and the wind blows down the mountain, oil stoves and space heaters are not enough to heat the icy walls and you have to wrap up in shawls and down jackets. The people who are always cold even wear gloves. The year I left, my fingers got so cold that I could no longer play my cello.

Now it was mid-May.

I climbed the stairs, urging myself to be patient.

And I made the mistake of not knocking at the door, because it was slightly ajar.

I pushed it gently, a huge smile on my lips. I was coming home and, yes, I was happy to be there.

My father was all alone in the dining room with his ear next to the transistor radio. He was listening to a religious station that repeated year round that God loved Israel in spite of the errors of its people, that He had given this land on both sides of the River Jordan, and that one day the Messiah would rise to restore to us our heritage.

My father immerses himself in this commentary because it helps him to confront the harsh reality of life in Israel. There was a time when he would praise these programmes to me, and he wanted me to listen. He thought they would fill me with knowledge and wisdom, that they would put some sense into me. But it was not my thing. Any more than religious traditions were. My brother Avner was cleverer. He never refused my father anything, but he made him wait. My father would get a grip, keep a hold on himself, then he would completely lose it, calling us ungrateful and reciting the verse from Isaiah: "I have nourished and brought up children, and they have rebelled against me." He gave us everything, but we did not show any gratitude. That is the way it goes, *hatati, hatati ya Rabi,* "I have sinned, I have sinned, my God" and with a sigh he would slap his thighs.

When we were children, Avner and I, his sorrow was terrifying.

At the time, we did not know anything about the discovery of the Book of Isaiah in the caves of Qumran, which made the prophet world-famous, and the sect of the Essenes along with him. The Hebrew manuscript, written in fifty-four columns on seventeen leather scrolls, sewn together, prophesied the return of the "Master of Justice": for us it boiled down to the verse about the rebellious children.

I went to live in New York.

Avner paid the price of my departure by staying at home after his stint in the army. He supported my father and studied agronomy.

To complete his master's degree, he inventoried the diseases specific to wheat. In his conclusion he proposed fighting them by modifying the plant's genome.

Avner had already enrolled for a Ph.D. when he suddenly dropped his studies. He confessed to me over the phone that he was tired of hanging around the labs in the university and the kibbutzim. He wanted to earn a living, he did not want to have to keep track of every penny. My father was in despair when he signed a contract to be a truck driver, shuttling tomatoes and cucumbers from one end of the country to another.

If I had gone into the room ten minutes later my father might have blessed me. But I had shown up right in the middle of the news bulletin, worse luck. And for my father the news is as sacred as the prayer at Yom Kippur.

He motioned to me, his fingers together, to say *ashtana*, wait.

I had not seen him for five years.

In Arabic, French or deaf-mute sign language, that is the kind of greeting that will turn your blood to ice.

I had just spent an entire night on the plane, not counting the time in traffic jams to get to J.F.K. and the hour from Lod to Jerusalem. I had been dreaming of tears and tenderness. *Nyet.*

I collapsed on a chair and waited.

Finally my father turned the knob on the transistor and the radio fell silent.

"You're back," he said.

"Hi, Dad."

8

"Hi, hi. Talk about a surprise! How are you?"

"Fine, and you?"

"Your mother's not here. But she won't be long."

My father got up, tugging on his shirt and clearing his throat. In the old days that clearing sound warned us when he was coming. Avner and I figured we had one minute before he would open the door, and we would hurry to put away anything that might irritate him.

"How long are you here for?"

"Three days."

"Three . . ."

He was choking with indignation.

"How much was your ticket?"

I named a sum.

"You're wasting your money."

"I'm here for a concert, Pa. My ticket is paid for."

He smiled, relieved, then looked anxious again.

"Where is your suitcase?"

"At the hotel."

"Home isn't good enough for you?"

"It's just easier, Pa."

"We're not royalty, we don't live in luxury."

I shrugged.

"It's none of my business, after all. Besides, you never asked me! You just do what you feel like!"

"I do what people ask me to do."

"And who are those 'people'?" my father said.

"The organizers of the concert."

"Do they know you have a family in Jerusalem? A father and a mother?"

"I suppose they do . . ."

"And they keep you from your family? Some nice people you hang around with."

I thought he might use the opportunity to recite the verse from Isaiah, my childhood refrain, but he went off to the kitchen. I could hear the door of a cupboard squeaking, then the rush of the tap. Despite my absence, the sounds of home remained familiar.

My father came back into the living room with a glass of water.

"Easier for who?"

"What?"

"Easier to be at the hotel . . . Why?"

"For the rehearsals, for moving the instruments around."

I put the three comp tickets on the table. He picked one up and read it attentively.

"A masterpiece of exile," he murmured.

"It's the name of the event."

"You're only getting one concert?"

"Yes, on the third day."

"All this fuss for two hours of music?"

"Well . . ."

"What a waste! Why? Don't we have any talent in this country?"

"Elisheva . . ."

"She came with you?"

"She's my impresario, Papa . . . She arranges my contracts and she plays."

"And she came for free, too?"

My eyelids were getting heavy. I would have loved to sleep for an hour or so on the terrace or in my old room.

"Are you working a lot?"

I started, looked at my father, not understanding. How long had I been asleep? A second? A minute? My ears were buzzing and I could not move my hands any more. My father repeated his question. I was moved by the sight of his white hair.

"Are you earning a living?"

"I give concerts on a regular basis."

"But has your career taken off?"

"Not yet."

"And yet they invited you to Jerusalem?"

"Because I'm a local girl. And I'm following in Elisheva's wake. She's well-known here. They haven't forgotten her, even though she left."

"I see."

His head lowered, he registered the information. The last time I saw him we had quarrelled, and for over a year he had refused to speak to me on the telephone when I rang my mother from New York. We had a lot of catching up to do.

"You left so you could become famous. And you've failed," he said, sitting down across from me.

"I'm twenty-three years old. It's not too late, Papa."

I had promised myself I would stay calm and answer all his questions, even the ones that hurt the most.

"A few concerts. To live so far away from us for just a few concerts!"

"I have to play in Tokyo next year."

"In Japan?"

"Yes, Papa."

"Don't they have enough of their own cellists over there? They have to go and hire a musician who lives in New York? What's so special about you?"

I smiled.

My craving for a falafel had returned. Why hadn't I bought one? Why had I been in such a hurry to run after the 26 bus with my lungs fit to burst? Honestly, I could have waited for the next one.

My father picked up a ballpoint from the table, removed the cap, then put it back again.

"Incidentally," he said, avoiding my eyes, "I'm going to buy a studio for your brother."

"Ah!"

"Forty square metres . . . But to invest any more than that . . . I don't have the money!"

"That's already not bad."

"Get married! I'll do the same for you."

"Why, did Avner get married?"

"It's not the same."

"What's the difference?"

"He's a boy."

"You're right. Girls are worthless."

"If he moves away from home, people won't gossip about him."

"I don't live in Israel any more."

"Against my will! And anyway, whether you are here or elsewhere doesn't change anything. There's always someone who knows someone, my girl. They know who you're seeing, who you speak to, and how much you earn."

The conversation was beginning to take a dangerous turn, when my mother came through the door. She saw me and dropped what she was carrying. Boxes of medication fell from her bag and scattered over the tiles.

"Rachel?"

"Mama," I said, getting to my feet.

In a flash I could see the ravages of these last five years. Her face had withered. She was wearing glasses with heavy frames and she had put on weight.

She spread her arms and held me close.

"You should have told me you were coming. I would have come to meet you at the airport."

"I arrived during the night."

"Oh! I am happy! I am happy!"

My father cleared his throat to contain his emotion. He wandered around the room without looking at us then, soundlessly, he picked up the boxes of medication and went to put them in the medicine cabinet.

"Have you eaten?" said my mother.

"Yes, on the plane."

"I know all about their aluminum containers. They give you a little bit of omelette and a cake. You must be starving. I'll heat you up a plate of couscous."

"I'm not hungry."

"You don't need to be hungry for couscous."

She tossed her jacket over the back of an armchair and pushed me into the kitchen.

She rolled up her sleeves and drank a glass of water.

"It's hot out. What's the weather like in New York?"

"It's springtime."

She got busy, silently. She plugged in the electric kettle and opened the fridge. There was a sudden putrid smell. My mother went on rummaging among the shelves and brought out an assortment of plastic containers.

I lit a cigarette. My mother turned to me and said, "You still smoke? And your lungs?"

I shrugged.

"Don't start, Ma."

"I'm begging you, my girl," she said, pouring a thick red magma, where bits of potato and carrot were floating, into a saucepan. "How many do you smoke a day?"

She put her nose into the saucepan to make sure the broth had not gone off.

I watched her reheating the couscous in a scratched non-stick frying pan. She took a chipped plate from the dresser, put it on the crumb-strewn table, went over to the sink, grabbed a sponge, picked up the plate and wiped the table.

I was watching her movements with considerable interest, because I could understand why I too do everything backwards: I start off by painting a wall before I decide to protect the floor, I show up at a concert without rehearsing, but once I've greeted everyone, I attack the score and work like a maniac.

"Do you want a slice of bread?"

13

"Bread with couscous?"

"You can dip it in the broth."

"No, thanks."

"Just a crust?"

I did not answer.

When I am at my parents' house, I am no longer the same. I can no longer move or think or act. I go soft, empty. I no longer know my name, or whether I should crawl, or run away. Or whether I should shoot myself.

In the living room, my father switched on the transistor and the same shrill voice went on questioning the future of Israel, with quotations to illustrate his every point. I realized I had been there for an hour. I had just lost an hour of my life, but where was my life?

I ate four spoonfuls of couscous at ten o'clock in the morning to please my mother, who finally sat down by my side.

To encourage me to open my heart to her, she started telling me all about her life, a monologue punctuated with *baruh ashem*, "praise God", but when you are used to it, you no longer pay any attention.

Here's roughly how it goes: "I go to Bible class every Tuesday evening, *baruh ashem*. There are a lot of women who come, rain or shine, and *baruh ashem*, they are all friends of mine. I get along with everybody. After class, *baruh ashem*, we sit down, we eat, and we talk. There's a good atmosphere, *baruh ashem*, that's what you need, right? There was a pipe that burst and it flooded the neighbour's living room but, *baruh ashem*, the plumber found the leak, and he made a hole in the wall and repaired the damage. Oh, do you remember your friend Hanna? No? Well, she had her third child last week, *baruh ashem* . . . a fine boy. *Akbak lilak*, my girl, Shallah, may I sing at your wedding, amen and amen, may I ululate so loud they'll hear it all the way to New York, the day you marry an upright, kind, respectful, halal sort of guy . . ."

And then she raised her eyes and hands to the ceiling, to take the

God of Abraham and Moses as her witness, then fervently kissed her fingers.

"Amen, amen, amen. Say amen."

I said amen.

She took me by the neck and kissed me on the cheek as if she were biting me.

"Of course, amen! Why shouldn't *you* have the right to happiness, too? He'll come, your fiancé, he'll come, don't worry. Even if you're already twenty-three years old, he'll come."

I let go of my fork. I could not swallow another bite. And the little I had eaten was stuck in my throat like a stone.

I said to myself, I don't believe it, is it like this in every family? There must be some logic to what she's saying, but what is it? I must have lost the operating instructions at birth, or someone forgot to give me the decoder.

"Finish your plate."

"No, thanks."

"Some fruit?"

She opened the fridge and the same smell wafted out into the kitchen. I closed the door.

"What's in there?"

"Why?"

"It smells like dead cat in the fridge."

"A cat?" she said, so astonished that I could hear my heart begin to pound. "Oh! I must have forgotten the beetroot salad from Friday."

"*Only* the beetroot salad?"

"You're right, I'll clean it out. I haven't had time, I've been running around non-stop."

"Running where?"

"In town."

"What for?"

"I can't keep my head straight, my girl. I go to market, I take the bus to come home and can you imagine, once I get here, I see I've forgotten the noodles or the rice. So I dump my shopping bags and out I go again."

"You've got a grocery across the street."

"It's more expensive."

"And the ticket for the bus each way?"

"I don't pay for the bus," she replied triumphantly. "With my green card I can ride for free."

Basically, she needs the crowd, the people, the noise.

She puts on her lipstick, does her hair, takes her bag, and off she goes on the 26 bus, anywhere, wherever it happens to be going.

She moves, radiant, to the back of the bus. As she moves along the aisle she always runs into someone she knows with whom she can exchange a few words. She talks about the weather, *baruh ashem*, it rained this week, the level of the Kinnereth is going to rise. And they've been building some more, *baruh ashem*, housing sites between Talpiot and Mahane Yehuda, they say there are Jewish families about to immigrate to flee anti-Semitism. *Baruh ashem, baruh ashem*, the Jews are starting to realize that Israel is their refuge. Economic problems in the country, the price of milk has skyrocketed again, oh those poor people, and the ones with big families, pray God help the poor. And she adds, we've suffered too, we've been counting our money too, but, *baruh ashem*, we've brought up our children and made them into honest people.

Stop after stop, as the bus fills and empties again, my mother offers complete strangers her considerations on the future of the country, on the future of the Jewish nation, on the hardship of life.

When she gets home again she is drained.

She has to hang out the laundry, prepare the evening meal, tidy up a bit, wash the dishes.

My father refuses to pitch in and help. Housework is not his job. If he started, God only knows where it would lead.

She did everything she could to shake off her yoke, shouting, screaming, citing the example of dozens of families where the husband gave a hand, out of love for his wife, or just to have some peace around the house. My father would not budge.

He is prepared to accept weeks of silence, weeks of conflict, he would sooner leave altogether than stoop so low as to peel a vegetable or sweep the floor. "You think I'm some sort of female, or what?" he would shout in her face when we were little. "Each man to his own trade."

He relented on two points only: he would take out the garbage and go to the market.

As for the garbage, he still grumbles, but he loves going to the market.

He comes back loaded down like a donkey, fingers sawn through from the weight of the shopping bags. He buys everything – too much of everything – after squeezing the melons, to the annoyance of the vendors, and sticking his fingers into the pears, and lifting the apples to feel their weight, and pinching the ends of the cucumbers, and tasting a kilo of olives to buy a hundred grams, and asking for his receipt to check the total, and stopping in the middle of the crowd just to add up the purchases once again in his head.

He comes through the door all happy. No one has ripped him off. He has made some fine purchases for a price that defies all the competition.

ELISHEVA

The piano bar is lit by perforated metal wall lights, the décor is blue, and the atmosphere is hushed by a thick wall-to-wall carpet that stifles the sound of footsteps. Elisheva takes the measure of the place as she walks in; it is vast, full of cosy little corners, and behind a zinc bar counter a blonde is bustling about. There is a black piano right in the middle of the room in full view.

Elisheva, as a musician, is drawn to the Yamaha, fascinated. She lifts the lid, examines the shining keys. Her fingers glide silently over the keyboard. Suddenly she cannot help it, she needs to give birth to sound, to hear the soul of the instrument. She plays a few chords, discovers the instrument's clear timbre; she frowns, then decides to go ahead, plays a phrase from Chopin's *Impromptu*, the fragment where the melody is like a murmur.

The blonde looks up, attentive.

Their eyes meet. Elisheva's hands lift from the keyboard.

"That was beautiful," the blonde says, encouraging her.

"It's a good piano."

"I would so like to have learned!"

"You still have time," says Elisheva with a smile, closing the lid.

"Play some more. There's no-one here."

"I've forgotten the rest," says Elisheva. "That passage is all I remember."

The blonde does not insist. Elisheva heads for an isolated table over by a pot plant. The blonde does not come to take her order. She has started cleaning the mirrors.

Daniel arrives at last, ten minutes late.

He pauses on the threshold and raises his dark glasses to the top of his brow, big mirrored Ray-Bans reflecting the world. He is heavy, hairy, massive, wearing jeans, a white short-sleeved shirt, and a black jacket. He is the sort of man who electrifies people and who knows it. A man who likes to eat, drink and pursue his pleasure.

Daniel is drawn not so much to the piano as to the young woman busy behind the bar: he sizes her up like a connoisseur.

Finally he looks around the room.

He sees Elisheva.

Of course she is already here.

More's the pity.

He forces a smile and heads over to her, swinging a leather brief-case.

"Hello," he says simply, without apologizing.

"Hi," Elisheva says.

Daniel leans the briefcase against the table leg and sprawls on the chair. Then he removes his glasses, folds the side-pieces and hooks them into his shirt pocket.

He immediately turns round and snaps his fingers.

"Hey, gorgeous," he says.

The blonde looks up.

"Can we order?" Daniel turns to Elisheva: "What will you have?"

"Tea."

"One tea and a beer."

Elisheva and Daniel look at each other. She refused to meet him in her room, suggesting rather the piano bar, which is always deserted until evening. Having run out of excuses he eventually agreed, but her proposal sticks in his throat.

"I'm pleased to see you," he says.

"Thank you."

"Did you have a good trip?"

"It was endless."

He smiles.

"America is not exactly next door. And the jet lag? Is it bothering you?"

"I'm bearing up."

He gives her a sidelong glance. Her face is gaunt, her lips have grown thinner. Suddenly she seems old to him, far too old, even if her gaze is as powerful as ever.

She'll fuck up, he thinks.

For him this is now a certainty.

Even though he knows she is going to tell him to get lost, he must persuade her to abandon her plan. The woman listens to no-one; her indomitable will has got the better of all those who have ever gone near her.

As if she could read his thoughts, Elisheva stares at him so intensely that he blushes.

"And what else?" he says abruptly.

"Nothing."

"Are you ready for the concert?"

"More or less."

"And your little protégée?"

"Rachel?"

"Yes."

"She's fine."

"Has she made progress?"

"Impressive."

"Will she be playing with you?"

"Of course."

"Good . . . that's good . . ."

He does not know what to say.

Fortunately, the waitress brings their drinks. Daniel sits back and observes the young woman as she puts the beer and a tall glass down in front of him, and a steaming teapot with a cup and a small pitcher of milk for Elisheva. He feels like telling her that customarily one is supposed to serve the ladies first, but what would be the point? The girl is not even twenty, she is as cute as can be, he is not going to bother her with outdated rules about etiquette.

So he merely watches the movement of her hand as she tucks the bill under a little vase of flowers, and her hand is plump, white and delicate.

"Would you like anything else?" she says, finally looking at Daniel.

He relaxes into the armchair, arms spread, a blissful smile on his lips.

"What's your name?"

"Yael."

"Thank you, Yael. Everything is fine for now."

The girl's face lights up as she turns on her heels, holding her tray against her chest.

"What a treasure," murmurs Daniel, filling his glass of beer. "Did you see her eyes? Incredibly blue!"

Elisheva is no fool. He is playing for time.

"Have you brought me what I need?"

"Yes, but . . ."

"Thank you."

"Will you know how to use it?"

"You already asked me that. Yes, I know! Yes, I learned! With your father and mother and everyone of my generation."

"It's just that . . ."

"Enough, Daniel!"

"I'm not sure about this any more. It's not a good idea."

"It's not an idea, Daniel. And 'good' is not the right word."

Daniel moves restlessly on his chair. Suddenly, he grunts and says, "Don't go splitting hairs with me, Elisheva. You understand perfectly well what I mean. This is a ridiculous, dangerous plan . . ."

"Dangerous for whom?"

He manages to look right in her eyes as she submits, imperturbably, to his anger.

"For you."

"I don't matter."

"We love you. We need you."

"I *have* to do it."

"We can take care of it, quickly and without any blunders. Absolutely no danger for our men . . . and no risk for you."

"No."

He hunches over. His beer is going flat, he does not want it any more. This is a fucking burden, too heavy to bear. Will we never, ever get over it?

"I don't doubt your expertise," Elisheva says tensely. "But coming from you the gesture would have no impact. No-one would notice. Whereas if it's me . . ."

"They'll know it's us," murmurs Daniel hoarsely. "We will publish a communiqué."

"But you won't go bragging about it. And you know it. You might alarm your other clients."

Daniel looks down, so she hastens to whisper, "You cannot steal my revenge from me."

She says nothing more. She does not need to. She knows she has convinced him.

And she finds herself admiring his thick hair, his solid build in his nicely tailored clothing, the way he places his arms on the armrests, his large hands and neat, well-groomed fingernails.

He is a fine-looking man.

She would like to whisper that he is looking great for forty, that he has done very well in life, and with his family.

But now is not the right time.

He is unaware of her love for him, he is exhausted and unhappy, so he slips further into the armchair, crushed by a nameless sorrow.

All cheerfulness and tranquillity have completely drained away; he is burned out.

Elisheva pours the black tea. She lifts the cup to her lips, takes little sips.

They get to their feet at the same time.

He has not finished his beer, she drank only half of her tea. They leave the piano bar and Yael, behind her counter washing glasses with her hands deep in soapy water, watches them leave, astonished.

What could they have been saying to each other that was so serious that the man did not even look at her as they left, did not even thank her or say goodbye?

The young woman shrugs and goes over to their table with her tray, her step light. While she is clearing away, she looks at the banknote they have left and works out her tip. She did not expect that much. It has made her day. Strange people, all the same. The woman was surly and abrupt, yet she changed into a fairy when she sat down at the piano. And the man . . . half her age, all smiles when he came in, gloomy as could be when they left.

Yael is finishing her degree in psychology at the university; now

she walks away with her tray, wondering whether the elderly woman is the man's mother or his girlfriend.

She concludes that there is nothing between them.

The flash goes off just as Daniel leaves the piano bar.

Dazzled, he blinks, recoils instinctively, his heart pounding.

Who took a photograph? And why?

Then a jovial American wearing a plaid jacket waves his hand and shouts, "Sorry."

Daniel turns away and looks quickly through the lobby.

The entire space is being watched by security guards. In black suits, with an earphone in one ear and a wire spiralling down their cheeks, they are keeping an eye on everyone entering or leaving, and they pass on their information to each other with clenched teeth.

"What's the matter?" Elisheva says, behind him.

"A lot on my mind."

Daniel steps to one side. Elisheva starts to walk ahead then realizes what is going on.

They have to get to the lifts, with the briefcase. A hundred metres from there, perhaps a hundred and fifty at the most; they will have to go through the entire lobby and all the way down the corridor.

Daniel tightens his hold on the briefcase, slips his arm into Elisheva's and thinks quickly.

The security guards are not there for Elisheva. Otherwise they would have collared her when they came out of the piano bar.

But if one of them notices the briefcase and tells them to open it, they will find the pistol and there will be no end of trouble. Daniel has the right to carry a weapon, that is not the issue. But the man will not forget him, and later on he will find him again, in his memory. That would blow his cover. And the entire network along with him.

"Act natural," he says. "Speak to me. The lift isn't much further."

Elisheva steps closer to Daniel and smiles at him with her eyes, but he can tell she is trembling like a leaf.

"I forgot my key at reception," she says.

He glares at her, furious, stunned.

"What?"

"Let's go out. We'll come back later."

"We have to put the briefcase somewhere safe. Wait for me in one of the lounges, if you want."

"I'll come with you."

So he pushes her into the hall and leads her back to the front desk where a group of people have gathered. The receptionists are overwhelmed, running every which way.

"What's going on?" Daniel asks the man in front of him.

"A European medical convention."

"Are you attending?"

"I'm an emergency physician."

Daniel eyes Elisheva. She is very pale, standing very straight and tapping her fingertips against her skirt, and her lips are moving, reciting notes. The poor woman has taken refuge in her music to overcome her stress. If she cracks because of ten security guards, what will she do three days from now? Her operation is madness. Absolute suicide.

Daniel suddenly intercepts the emergency physician's gaze. The man has narrowed his eyes, is examining Elisheva, registering her emotion, her spasmodic breath. He must not speak to her: in the state she is in, God knows what she might say in reply.

Daniel tries to distract the man's attention.

"What brings you here?"

The doctor looks away from Elisheva, reluctantly.

"We have to establish a report on the health situation in the occupied territories."

"Hats off for the security."

The man smiles, scornful. He looks again at Elisheva, who has regained a bit of colour; only her gaze is bizarre, dilated, adrift.

"The Health Minister sent in all these guards. Given our convictions, he must be afraid of a terrorist attack."

"And what are your convictions?"

"That the Palestinians are not getting health care, the . . ."

"I suggest you go and have a look at our hospitals. You'll see that Jews and Arabs alike are treated."

"Are you Israeli?"

"I have that good fortune, yes."

The physician stiffens. Daniel continues to smile.

"Excuse me. I'm in a hurry," the physician says, embarrassed.

The front desk has cleared. The physician inquires how to ring London. Daniel asks for Elisheva's key and guides her in a zigzag through the crowd of tourists pouring off their coach.

"Europe hates us," Daniel says.

"I don't care."

"You're wrong. Did you hear that guy? He thinks we live in some kind of apartheid regime."

"Daniel, I'm not in the mood to discuss Israeli politics or anti-Semitism," she says, stopping short to look him in the eye. "Thanks, 'bye."

"I'll go up there with you," he says, forcing her to move ahead. His fingers close around her arm, his thumb sinking into Elisheva's tender flesh.

She is not up to resisting him in public, so she resigns herself to following him. They walk down the corridor with only one thought on their minds, how to part. He knows he is going overboard, that she is beginning to despise him. Never mind. Besides, if he were to take his own advice, he would just turn on his heel and leave her there, without a weapon.

She calls the lift and reaches out for the briefcase, which he refuses to give her. The lift arrives, he shoves her inside. Elisheva pushes the button for her floor. The doors close.

"I don't appreciate this, Daniel, not one bit!"

Her voice is gentle, even, but her eyes are sparkling.

"Take a pick-me-up. You need one."

"Thanks for the advice."

"Please just drop the whole idea."

"No."

Suddenly very weary, he says, "You've already made two mistakes …"

"I'll pull myself together."

"Do what you know how to do … Play your music!"

The lift stops. Elisheva takes the briefcase. Grabbing her by the shoulder, he ventures one last attempt: "Another question: where, and when?"

"That's two questions! The less you know, the better."

He tries to embrace her, but she steps aside and his lips meet only her grey hair. The steel doors slide shut. He is alone.

The light goes out, then comes back on. The lift moves up, stops at the floor above. People come in and he is pushed toward the back. He does not react; he seems hypnotized.

His mother had made Elisheva his godmother. They had been together in the same block at Majdanek; they had sorted gold teeth, carted corpses to the mass graves. And acted as guinea-pigs for Henker, the Butcher.

His mother had managed better, in the end. She had got married, had two sons. Elisheva, no. His mother was in the habit of saying those two dreadful words: Elisheva, no.

Never had there been a more attentive godmother. Elisheva did not miss a single birthday. When she was abroad, she had always found a way to come back for a few days, her arms laden with presents. A strange sort of godmother who did not know how to laugh or play or joke, but as Daniel gradually became a man, he came to understand her worth, and he fell under her influence, as did all those who got to know her. With Elisheva, every word, every gesture, every silence had weight and authority.

Suddenly he is sorry he did not finish his beer. He knows what he will do: go home, lower the blinds, get out a bottle and forget. The kids will be home late. He will have the house to himself.

Daniel leaves the hotel just as the Health Minister's limo pulls up at the entrance.

The car door is flung open.

"Daniel!" shouts the Minister, who has recognized him.

Daniel does not turn around.

Elisheva stares at the briefcase she has put on the desk. She cannot take her eyes off it. It is a fine case in black leather, with an elegant catch and a solid handle.

Daniel is right . . . She has grown old. She is not as careful as she used to be, she has lost her stamina. She no longer knows how to anticipate danger.

Should she drop the whole thing?

And then she sees the iron bed, the table with its instruments carefully laid out. And the Butcher, slowly pulling on his gloves, his ghastly smile.

Overwhelmed by her visions, Elisheva rocks from side to side, her arms across her chest. Fear rises, as liquid as the water of a bath.

Time has not passed. She is still there. Among the cries of the dying women that the strains of the cello could not hide. She sees herself playing: playing fit to tear her hands off, playing when she has been destroyed for ever. The women's naked thighs, their torn flesh, the blood and pus oozing from their wounds. They had gone to that place with their coloured shawls, with laughter and children at their breasts.

So few of them survived. Most died during "the session". Two prisoners would lift the victims like sacks of skin and cart them away in a wheelbarrow, then tip them into the mass grave.

Katya had survived . . . Renata too. But a few weeks later, with thousands of others, she . . . Elisheva sways, her skin sallow, all blood drained from her lips. Renata crumbles before her, her neck broken by a bullet; the S.S. are chasing them, shooting, killing, boot-kicking the bodies into the ditches; there is music. Elisheva can see the loudspeakers fixed to the watchtowers, but her memory has not recorded a single sound. Or has erased them all.

Startled by the creaking of a wheeled cart, she whirls around. A chambermaid is standing before her. The woman is morose, wearing a blue overall; she apologizes.

"May I change the sheets, Madam?"

Then the woman notices Elisheva's expression.

"Are you unwell?"

Elisheva is startled back into the present.

"It's the time . . . the jetlag," she says.

"I'll call a doctor."

"I don't need anything."

"You can't stay like that."

"I have tablets. I'm used to it."

Elisheva slips a banknote into the woman's overall and sees her out of the door, only to open it again at once to give her back her cart and hang the "Do Not Disturb" sign on the doorknob. She manages a smile, and locks herself in.

The briefcase.

Where can she hide it? It is too big for the safe. Under the bed? No, the hotel staff might find it. She opens the case, removes the pistol and the ammunition, puts them in the safe, chooses a combination and collapses on the bed, gasping.

The telephone rings.

She does not want a doctor.

It goes on ringing, in the silence.

It's Daniel, thinks Elisheva. He's trying to reach me, to warn me of danger. I have to answer.

She reaches out and grabs the receiver.

At the other end, a warm, laughing voice.

"Elisheva? Welcome home."

Her eyelids flutter; she does not understand.

"What?" she says. "Who?"

"Have you forgotten me, *mi bombón*?"

"Carlos, Carlos!"

He is moved as she bursts into tears down the receiver, and he says her name again, as if he were reaching out his hand in the darkness.

"What's the matter? What's going on?"

"Nothing ... I ..."

"I'll be right there."

"No. I have to go out. I'm stifling."

"Well, come and meet me."

"Where are you?"

"On the esplanade."

The esplanade! She will not have the strength to go that far.

"Don't stay shut indoors with all this sunshine."

"What are you doing?"

"I'm showing a delegation from the Vatican around."

"I don't want to disturb you."

"I'll have finished an hour from now. Take your time. Make yourself beautiful."

"Alright, in an hour."

"But you will come?"

"Yes."

"On the esplanade?"

"On the esplanade, in an hour," she says again like a robot. "I've got it."

"Perfect. I have a surprise for you."

RACHEL

My father came into the kitchen, took the chair, sat astride it and said, "Can you do me a favour?"

I thought he wanted to attend the rehearsal, to understand why I had been hired in New York to come and play with the Jerusalem Philharmonic Orchestra.

29

I soon found out that I was way off the mark.

"Can you come with me? Can you come with me to a money . . . to a moneychanger in the Old City?"

"A moneychanger? What for?"

"I withdrew a hundred and fifty thousand shekels from the . . ."

Now my father springs out of his chair to go and close the window. We have been speaking in French, but he would rather be on the safe side.

We had to put up with the heat. Sweat pouring from my temples, streaming down me as if I were a fountain.

The kitchen is tiny, not big enough for the three of us. My mother slipped away on the pretext that she had to hang out the laundry.

Leaning against the countertop, my father shoots me a glance, the glance of a man who is drowning in an ocean of words. I know I have to wait, be careful not to antagonize him, otherwise he will let fly about my "lack of respect". To respect my father means to accept that he does not respect me. To respect my father is to comply with his every whim, and this has been so ever since he began to suffer from speech impediments.

He might be hungry, so he will go and quickly make himself a slice of bread and butter. He might say, "Wait five minutes, I have to listen to the news," and I will just have to remain at his disposal while he listens to that voice shouting abuse at our enemies and the Jewish traitors who are trying to create closer ties with them.

My father does his best to hide his affliction.

Here is a man who used to speak three languages, and now he churns out this gibberish that exhausts everyone around him.

He begins a sentence in one language and finishes it in another. And in the intervals: hesitations, stammering, spluttering, as he tries to string together a semblance of a thought. "Uh . . . The . . . The . . . What's it called?" he says, looking lost. "The . . . It's awful, I . . . The . . ." He cannot find the word. "The thingy . . . thingy . . . You know what I mean? The *thing* . . ." No, I do not know. On the phone,

I stay patient, trying to find something to do. Sometimes my father just gives in. He hands the receiver to my mother or hangs up on me. Most of the time he persists, obstinately, in despair.

I admire my father, despite our difficult relations. He's a scholar who knows entire pages of the Bible and the Koran, and when he's in a good mood – which is rarely the case – he is capable of singing at the dinner table, dozens of psalms from the psalmody of the Tunisian Jews. At the synagogue he reigns triumphant. Every Saturday morning the rabbi calls out "*Bekhavod, bekhavod*", waving his hand, which causes his tallith to slip from his shoulders. The faithful turn to my father: "Go up to the Torah. Sing us a psalm!" My father loves to be begged: "I sang last week." "So? What's the problem?" cry the faithful. My father is stubborn: "The others have to take part."

We look at him tenderly and push him forward. Friendship is very strong in a group united by prayer. I have seen it everywhere, in churches, in Protestant temples and even in the Buddhist sanctuaries I agreed to visit, one day when I was utterly dejected. I remember carpets, candles, incense, and flowers placed before a golden statue, monks with shaven skulls, and draped in red togas, hopping and bowing, beating tambourines. They invoked the Buddha and looked insistently at one another. I stayed on my knees, my heart pounding. Me, on my knees. If my father had learned of this crime he would have rejected me, banished me, cursed me. His daughter among the idolaters, bowing down before a stone figure! Moloch, Baal, Buddha, it is all the same, as far as my father is concerned; abject creatures who distort the spirit of God on earth and repel his Presence to the far reaches of the universe. But fortunately my father could never suspect me of stooping so low. He imagines me smoking on Saturdays, eating pork, mixing milk and meat, and marrying a goy. That, yes. And when he is overwhelmed by such dark thoughts, he nearly goes mad. He tells himself that he has failed in life, that his daughter is a failure, that he will never deserve *ha-olam haba*, the next world. The fear that submerges him makes him break out in a rash. He scratches like mad,

31

until he bleeds. He scratches between his toes, grunting "ah"; he scratches his legs, his cramped fingers, and he moans, *ya Rabi, ya hanoun,* "Oh merciful God!"; he scratches his belly and his eyes cloud with tears; he scratches his arms; he leans against a corner of the wall and scratches his back, his teeth clenched fit to bursting his jaw.

I am my father's rash.

He did not manage to marry me off a virgin. He did not manage to get me shacked up with a *weld hahalal,* as he calls it; he has not found the relief that comes with knowing my future is in some other guy's hands. He sees how I gallivant around, still single. The years go by and I am not in a position to introduce him to my chosen one.

And this makes my father look pathetic, a poor schmuck who has been afflicted with a daughter who defies his authority, his protection, his upbringing, Judaism, maternity. So he scratches. He is so ashamed that he would gladly tear off his skin and burn at the stake.

All his tenderness he lavishes upon Avner. Avner is exactly the son he wanted to have, and he obeys him in everything: he has stayed at home, and in his old age, with a son like this, my father will be able to get up in the morning a happy man, and go to bed at peace. Avner is looking for a bride in Israel. And when my father cups his hands and blesses my brother, hoping that he will find a wife who will be gentle, tender and loving, my brother does not laugh. He does not say, I'd like a wife who's free, impulsive, and who loves sex. My brother merely replies, Amen.

I tried to broach the subject with Avner. One day I asked him, "What sort of women do you like?" My brother said coldly, "Any woman, provided she's not like you." I staggered under the blow. At least he was honest.

"And according to you, what's wrong with me?"

My brother broke a match into three pieces before saying, "You don't know how to pray!" Which means: you are an individualist, you have no sense of community, you do not know how to play by the rules, you do not know how to place the group and the group's interests before your own little self. You do not know how to govern your ego. Your ego comes across too loud, too clear, and above all your sense of timing is all wrong. That day I understood that prayer helps one to evade solitude and the fear of living; prayer is the oldest remedy in humanity, it came into being long before the drawings etched in the Neanderthal caves, before the discovery of fire, before the use of flint. Prayer allows you to return to innocence, to raise yourself, by degrees, toward the world of angels.

Every Saturday my father yields abruptly to the entreaties of the devout. He tosses the tallith over his shoulders. He walks past the rows of benches, humble and modest. He climbs the three steps leading to the altar, his eyes still lowered. He rolls the woollen fringes around his fingers and goes up to the rabbi, the president of the community, the cantor and other notables. He shakes their hands, lifts his fingers to his lips each time.

Once he has been around all the notables, my father stands before the lectern and it is time for his big show. My father's favourite singer is Farid El Atrache. "A golden voice," he says, peremptorily. "An ace!" My father croons the psalms like the great Farid. He becomes Farid. He is Farid, with tremolos in his voice, and he can hold a note for the longest time, his eyes half-closed. In his head at that moment he is a Jewish Farid, Farid is Jewish, Farid knows how to sing the Song of Songs.

In the synagogue, not a soul moves or breathes. Careful now! My father will stop if an old man coughs, if a child starts unwrapping a candy, if anyone shifts their foot ever so slightly. Ah, he does have his pride, my father. And in short, they all know this, and they grant him the consideration that he believes he deserves.

His memory, I fear, will vanish some day. You might say, like all memories. Except that we Jews of southern Tunisia have our own particular liturgy, we sing the way Arabs do, and you can count those who know our songs on the fingers of one hand.

There are times when I say to myself that I ought to record my father. But I am so involved in my struggle to free myself from his prejudices that I forget all about my desire to save our cultural heritage. You cannot do everything, record your father and at the same time fight against him to keep him from destroying you.

All these thoughts are whirling through my mind while I watch him peeling a mandarin orange.

"One hundred and fifty thousand shekels for your brother," he says again, his eyes shining with pride as he tosses the peel into the garbage.

"And you need me?"

"Precisely."

"What do I have to do?"

"You follow me."

"I don't understand."

"You walk behind me and leave about fifty metres between us. You keep an eye out for anyone suspicious. You try to protect me."

By putting all his snatches of sentences together, I manage to piece together the whole story.

My father wants to go to the Old City, to a Palestinian money-changer, in order to change one hundred and fifty thousand shekels into dollars.

He explains that he has carefully calculated his profit by harassing all the Jewish moneychangers in Jerusalem and by writing down in a notebook the name of each bureau de change and the rate they offered him. Then he hurried over to the Old City. He had a discussion in Arabic with the Palestinian moneychangers. He said, "*Houya*, what is the rate for the dollar?" He listened to their answers, then protested, "*Habibi*, your price is interesting, but it is still too low. I have a large sum to change. So, make an effort . . . We'll both come out winners." The changer gave him a penetrating look before quickly tapping on a calculator whose keys were so worn that the numbers had disappeared. And the answer was never given out loud, no, that is not done. The changer waves the screen before the client,

34

as if to say, this is my best price, my last offer, if you do not like it, go fly a kite.

It all hinges on one hundredth of an agora for every dollar, and that hundredth multiplied by one hundred and fifty thousand will only make my father richer by five or ten dollars at the most. A ridiculous profit. Who would want to carry one hundred and fifty thousand shekels around town for an hour just to make ten extra dollars? Answer: my father. Ten dollars, to his way of thinking, is ten dollars.

"Why? Do I find my money beneath the hoofprint of a mule? Did I not earn it by the sweat of my brow?" he says.

"But the risk . . ."

"What risk?"

"Someone could attack you and rob you!"

"Nonsense."

I see him smile, and venture a joke.

"Have you got an armoured car?"

"What do you think, that this is the first time I've ever made a transfer of funds?"

I am amazed. Transfer of funds. Very technical language, it seems to me, for someone who has minor memory lapses and stammers more and more.

"And when did you do it?"

"I don't owe you any explanations."

The kitchen is tiny and with the window closed the heat has become unbearable. We are sweating as if in a sauna.

I rush to the door to the veranda, open it, and let the air in. My father looks peeved. How dare I interrupt him when he is having a bad enough time as it is trying to speak? What is wrong with me, the way I constantly fail to show respect, and never give him any proof of love?

"Don't come, it's not worth it."

"Why?"

"You're not up to it."

"What have I done?"

"You're so annoying! Such a fidget! I can't think when you're around."

"It's too hot."

"End of the matter."

"Shit, this is silly, Papa, I . . ."

"What did you say? You're using swearwords now? What's the point of playing classical music if you talk like a fishwife?"

"I'm sorry. I apologize."

I have made him angry and there is nothing left to be done.

He grabs his books and goes to shut himself in his study.

My mother motions to me to be quiet, then suggests, "Shall we make a cake, Rachel?"

But I have no strength left. I will collapse if I move my little toe. I tell myself that I will never be ready to rehearse with the orchestra later on, that they have paid a lot of money to bring me to the country of my birth, for nothing.

I sit on my chair without moving and watch my mother making herself busy. She takes the box of sugar from the cupboard; the bottle of oil from the storeroom; and the almond powder and yeast from the shelf. Then she opens the fridge and chooses six eggs one by one.

"The size is important," she says mysteriously.

She closes the fridge. And opens it again at once to take out a pack of flour. I burst out laughing. Flour in the fridge. What a strange idea.

"You have to keep it cool to avoid weevils."

"Oh, I see."

"With the heat you can't leave anything out, you understand?"

My mother beats the eggs energetically and talks to me about the neighbours.

"They always ask how you're doing."

I shudder.

"What business is it of theirs?"

"You've been a topic of conversation in the neighbourhood ever since you left home. It breaks their heart, you understand? Do you understand me? A hundred million Arabs and four million Jews. If we don't stick together, we won't make it."

"I can't be responsible for the fate of the Jewish people! I don't want to sacrifice my life and my plans to this country!"

She goes as red as a beet.

"I know, my girl, I know. . ."

"And so? What do you tell them?"

"That I'm proud of you!"

"And you don't say anything else?"

My mother concentrates as she measures out the flour; normally she does everything by guesswork. "Your eye is your kitchen scale," she likes to say whenever she calls me on the phone.

"Yes! That you're the most gifted student in the *skoul*."

I burst out laughing and throw my arms around her neck.

"What did I say? What did I say?"

"Nothing. I love you."

"Did I say something silly?"

"Of course you didn't. You're fantastic."

"I'm not an educated woman."

"And so? You think that matters?"

"I'm so afraid you'll be ashamed of me."

"You're wrong, I promise you."

"Your father told me you're staying at a hotel? You're not going to sleep here with us?"

"Well . . . it's complicated. I have to be there to practise with Elisheva . . ."

"She's your true mother, isn't she?"

This left me speechless. Then I denied it, awkwardly. My mother was not looking at me. She seemed very busy greasing the edges of the cake pan; the butter was melting between her fingers. And the yellow smear created an opaque layer that veiled the transparency of the recipient. When she had finished she washed her hands, took hold of the mixing bowl, poured the batter into the cake pan and shoved it into the oven.

"There are days when I really resent that woman for taking you away," said my mother as she adjusted the temperature of the oven. "And other days when I bless her for having set you on to the path of a dream. I know it takes connections to get into your *skoul*."

This time, I did not laugh. But the name of my music school, the most prestigious in New York and maybe in the entire world, was ticking in my brain like a metronome: the Juilliard School.

"But it's not like I've ever broken my bonds with you and Papa, Mama."

She began to tidy the kitchen. I could hear the cupboard doors open, close, open again. The dirty dishes disappeared into the sink. I should have offered to help, but my head was nodding, my vision was blurring, sounds were muffled.

DANIEL

Daniel leaves his car in the hotel car park. He will not go to Tel Aviv today.

The scorching breath of the *sharav* veils the city in grey trains of cloud. The pavement trembles, the air as well. An agitation of engines, heat, roadworks. There is a traffic jam on Jaffa Road and accordion buses advance slowly and painfully to a constant bleating of horns. With each passing day the city's main artery becomes more congested with the rush of cars and pedestrians.

Daniel stops outside a kiosk. They sell everything here – newspapers, cigarettes, sweets, and bagels bobbing on a metal skewer.

"Are they hot?"

"Straight from the oven, my brother."

"The one you sold me last time was stale."

"It's your prick that's stale."

"And yours is fresh?"

It is a game between them, the time it takes for the vendor to wrap the crusty roll in a piece of white paper. The vendor bursts out laughing. He has four gold teeth in his mouth and he never misses an opportunity to flaunt his scrap metal. Every time Daniel sees those four teeth of his, he gets the shivers. God, he's ugly, he thinks. I wonder how his wife can kiss a mouth that doubles as a bank vault.

Daniel hands him a shekel. The vendor tosses the coin into a box. He presses both hands on his counter and leans out of his niche.

"What else?"

"Nothing."

The man can tell that under the veneer of their usual jibes Daniel's heart is not in it. He looks at his customer more closely. He knows he is an affluent man, with a happy marriage. If this guy is feeling down, what hope is there for the rest of humanity?

"Oh dear, oh dear! Eat that bagel, eat! It will revive you."

He shakes with laughter; his four teeth put in another appearance.

"Have a good day," Daniel says, moving off.

The bagel is perfect, dry and crisp on the outside, rich and moist on the inside. Daniel bites into the salt-stippled crust and greets acquaintances, who stop and shake his hand. Jerusalem is a village. They ask him how he is doing. He says he is O.K. And says, "And you?" Some raise their eyes to the heavens to take God as their witness. Others shrug. Still others joke: once this government falls, I'll feel better . . .

No-one complains. They do not know each other well enough for that. You only talk about your problems with friends and members of the family.

And no-one asks him for stock market tips.

Daniel would say outright, to anyone who dared: "I'm specialized in the Japanese market. I'd be the wrong broker for you. I don't want to ruin you or ruin our relationship. Ask your banker. He knows your portfolio, your retirement plan, he knows your needs. And he'll know best how to advise you."

If he did not make this clear from the start, he would never manage to get from one side of the street to the other.

They all want to get rich. It is human. But he cannot give advice to the entire city.

He smiles, picturing his neighbours, all drawn to him as if he were a magnet. Then very quickly he frowns.

He strides through the marketplace. Fruits, vegetables, olives, humus. Everything makes him hungry. He feels like stuffing himself, staining his trousers with dripping grease, burying his face in a *shawarma* oozing with hot sauce. He forgets his problems when he eats. When he fucks, too.

Suddenly he stops short outside a shop window. A woman's shoe, violet, ravishing, with a silk flower on the side, has caught his attention. Daniel pictures the woman's foot in that shoe, the divine curve of her leg. The merchant has seen him through the window and now comes to the doorway.

"Hey, Daniel."

"Hello, hello."

"Come on in."

"Another time."

"I've got some new styles in."

Daniel shakes his head.

"Shall I put a pair aside for you?" the merchant says.

"If you want."

"Violet, black, or green?"

Usually, Daniel would have said, all three. Now he merely shrugs.

"Daniel, are things tough at the moment?" the merchant says, tapping him on the shoulder. "Has the rate of the yen collapsed?"

"If only that were all of it!"

"What could be more serious for you than the rate of the yen?"

Daniel does not laugh.

"If you only knew, mate."

He shakes off the hand which is trying to restrain him and goes on his way.

"Come back, hey, Daniel, come back! I'll buy you a coffee," shouts the merchant, stunned.

Daniel shoves through the crowd without hearing.

RACHEL

A shout, *AAAAAnavim*, made me jump.

I had fallen asleep, my arms crossed over my head, and when I woke up, for a split-second I did not know where I was.

Dazed, I stared at the mouldy wall, the window so poorly constructed that the cement had formed blistered clots around the frame.

Was this another of those dreams about Jerusalem that I get in New York?

The images were fading, but one of them clung to my mind, clear and horrifying. I lay dead in the sand, stone dead, with two holes in my forehead. And suddenly I knew why. My mother's last words had followed me into my sleep.

"*Katel tini!* You killed me."

"You killed me, my daughter, when you left. You killed me, leaving me to face your father. You killed me, and deprived me of your company."

Words in Arabic have a mysterious power over me, a greater impact than Hebrew or French or English. They are the mark of exile, from the time before my lifetime.

It was unbearably hot in the kitchen. And there was the poisonous stench of something burning in the oven.

I staggered to the cooker, found the knob, turned off the gas.

I took out the cake.

It was completely charred.

The sight of the burnt cake filled me with distress. And I stood there in a kind of oblivion, my arms hanging by my side, my face streaming with tears.

Then I splashed my eyes with water and looked for an aspirin for my headache. When I opened the cupboard, the contents spilled out over my shoulders, an unbelievable mess, plastic plates, spice jars, medicine bottles and even a photograph of Avner at the age of eight. If it were up to me, I would have gone on a clean-up rampage and thrown everything into the garbage. But that is me. My mother has a different sense of order, she spends her life in the kitchen, and the kitchen, for her, means making dinners in order to freeze them.

I found some paracetamol and tried to put everything back in place. I made piles, pushed, shoved objects into the cupboard, but the door would not close any more. I swore under my breath and left a jumble of things on the countertop, then swallowed my tablet, telling myself yet again that the shock of seeing my parents would fade, and the jet lag would eventually disappear.

AAAAAnavim.

The shout was getting closer.

I walked all around the apartment, checked into all the rooms. My parents had disappeared, but my father's I.D. and chequebook were still on the table. So he had not gone down to the Old City; he must be no further than the grocery store, buying bread and milk.

But as for my mother – it was a mystery.

AAAnavim.

I unlocked the front door and went outside.

AAAAAAnavim.

A Palestinian woman in a heavy black dress was coming up the sidewalk, a basket of grapes balanced on her head.

I grabbed some coins from the piggy bank and went up to her. I wanted some of those grapes that grow in the red soil of Hebron. God knows how long it had been since I tasted any.

The woman saw me coming and interrupted her cries. I greeted her; she returned my greeting, unsmiling. She removed the burden of her basket and sat down on the kerb.

"*Anavim?*" she asked. Grapes.

Probably one of the six or seven words that constituted her vocabulary in Hebrew.

She held out her hand and told me the price per kilo, four fingers spread, her thumb curled against her palm.

I confirmed, *Safi*, admiring her neckline embroidered with red thread, her oval face framed by a grey cotton kerchief, her green plastic slippers open on her twisted toes, with broken toenails covered in dust.

The woman took a rusty metal chain from her pocket; to the end of it she hooked a battered tray.

She went across the street on to a vacant lot overgrown with brambles and strewn with abandoned objects. I saw her pick up some stones then toss them away one by one.

What on earth was she doing?

She was a strong, plump woman. Her black dress clung to her back as she bent over to the ground. She must have been my mother's age, give or take a few months. I thought they resembled one another, even if everything divided them.

I waited by the basket. The sun was burning, a thousand tiny fires, a yellow diamond in the sky. Silence reigned. The street was deserted, a vast geometry marked by the white cubes of buildings. At the heart of this bedroom-community architecture, the dome of the synagogue looked like an extraterrestrial space-ship.

We were alone, the Palestinian woman and I, separated only by the width of the road.

Suddenly I noticed her husband coming from the roundabout, tugging his mule on a rope.

His head was protected by a keffiyeh, but he had swapped the traditional peasants' djellaba of the Jerusalem region for a shirt and a pair of trousers.

When he saw me standing next to the basket he sat down on his

43

heels by the side of the road, not to disrupt the sale. His mule went off to graze what little grass there was next to the road.

The woman came back, waving a stone. A lumpy, chalky stone, bigger than her hand.

"Kilo," she said, to indicate that she was going to use it as a weight.

"*Aywa*," I acknowledged.

I smiled.

She did not respond to my smile. She looked at me as if I were transparent, as if I were nothing. She communicated with this transparency in order to sell her grapes. I had forgotten that in principle we were enemies. That between us there is the absence of peace, there are the burned tyres of the children of Gaza, our soldiers firing in Hebron, Jenin and Ramallah, masked adolescents throwing stones at anything wearing the uniform of the Tsahal and at any car, civilian or military, driven by an Israeli. I had forgotten. I had been gone too long. For me this land is simply what I call *Eretz*, Land.

The woman picked a bunch of pale green grapes and held it in the air so I could admire the tight, flawless fruit, the leaves, and the fragment of stem she had cut at the branch in order to preserve the fruit in all its splendour. As if she were saying, even though we were supposed to hate each other, that that was no reason to turn one's back on beauty.

"*Aywa*," I said again.

The transaction could begin.

The Palestinian woman held the chain up vertically. She threaded a pole through a ring. She put the stone on the tray and attached the grapes to the hook, her gestures full of grace, taking me to a place from long ago, to the homeland my family had left behind. And I was enchanted by the old-fashioned way she weighed the fruit, something that has disappeared with progress and which no doubt will not even exist ten years from now.

The woman added a small bunch to the one she had weighed, then she said, "Kilo."

I paid her first before reaching out with my open palms.

The woman put her green grapes into my hands. Her husband was still sitting on his heels at the end of the street.

What was he thinking about? What were his daydreams? Why does he follow her like that with his mule? Why does she carry that heavy load on her head while the mule goes around unburdened?

When the woman was about to put the basket back on her head, a neighbour rushed over. Despite her fat thighs she was wearing shorts, and her enormous breasts spilled like balloons from her bra.

The Palestinian woman did not even look at her.

The neighbour looked only at the grapes.

And each of them was judging the other in silence, one of them saying, Poor wretch, you're a prisoner of your jerk of a husband and your fucking tradition, and the other ruminating, You filthy half-naked miserable Jewish whore, the sight of you offends my eyes and pollutes my soul.

"Shalom," said the neighbour.

"Salaam," said the Arab woman, her voice placid.

The neighbour winked at me.

Beneath her white top I could see the straps of her bra with their lacy edging and even the little ribbon that decorates the gap between the two bra cups.

Her cleavage ran very deep and high, her breasts were not very firm, her skin was like fermenting dough.

"How are the grapes?" she asked me.

"I haven't tasted them."

"You buy things without tasting?"

"The bunches are beautiful."

"I'm not saying they aren't, but you have to be careful what you buy. You have to bite into one, see what it tastes like, and then you order."

"They haven't been washed."

45

"You do it like this, I'll show you for next time. Otherwise you'll get ripped off. It's harder to earn money than it is to spend it."

Without asking permission from the Palestinian woman, the neighbour broke off a grape, spat on it, wiped it on her arm, and popped it in her mouth. I could hear the grape burst beneath her teeth.

"Mmmm," my mother's neighbour said. "Nectar. How much did you pay?"

"Four shekels."

"That's robbery. At Mahane Yehuda the grapes are going for two shekels."

"They've just been picked."

"So what? Four shekels is too much. That's going too far."

"But . . ."

"If you let them, there'll be no more prices, only inflation. At the souk grapes cost two shekels. That's all there is to it."

The neighbour turned to the woman. She said, "*Shtayim*," two fingers in a V.

The Palestinian woman shook her head. No. But she did not pick up her basket. I realized she was refusing to lower her price because of me. I also understood, from the way she was waiting, her eyes narrowed, that she was prepared to negotiate. She might not let her grapes go for two shekels, but there was a good chance she would lower her price.

My mother's neighbour had got it right.

"*Shouf*," she said to her, "Give it to me for two shekels and I'll buy eight kilos."

She made the figure eight with her fingers. She kept her hands in the air to give the Palestinian woman time to understand her. A wise woman, this neighbour. But the Palestinian woman kept silent, bothered by my presence. She crouched down on the ground, her eyes on her basket. I was disturbing her. I was disturbing both of them. I had behaved like an idiot. I had forgotten the ritual of haggling, and I had not tasted the grapes, I did not understand a thing about the deep

46

flow that nurtured these people, the subtle balance of power, and the everyday transactions which, despite the bloodshed, attacks and arrests, went on day after day.

I walked away, carrying the grapes in my palm. I was carrying the fruit of this land as if it were a baby, I was walking over the olives that had fallen from the trees, I looked at the burning road, the empty lot, the squatting peasant. I sat down on the cement edge of a flower-box, put my grapes down next to me, and lit a cigarette.

I was trying to remember my neighbour's name.

When she went by, her arms held out with her eight kilos of grapes, her name came back to me: Shula. Short for Salomé, from Shulamit.

She saw me, and stopped.

"She's a tough one, that woman!"

"Did you get what you wanted?"

"I'll say. Her grapes are good, but no better than the ones from the Israeli growers."

I preferred to change the subject.

"What are you going to do with eight kilos?"

"My grandchildren love jam."

She laughed.

"I have two grandchildren now. Come over to the house, you'll see them."

"Perhaps . . ."

"Oh, you've got the right idea, I'm going to sit and rest for a second."

I did not especially want her to sit down, but I moved over to make room for her. She moaned with happiness as she put her butt on the flower box.

"This heat kills me. I can't stand the heat anymore. My feet swell up like tree trunks. And I used to love going to Eilat; well, for me that's all over now."

★

47

So Shula and I sat there on the flowerbox and smoked our cigarettes.

She fanned herself, waving her right hand in front of her cheek. She had crossed her legs and, seen from close up, her thighs riddled with cellulite looked humongous.

She was not in the least self-conscious about exhibiting her mottled orange-peel skin and her varicose veins.

In the neighbourhood, thanks to all her shouting, Shula has acquired the reputation of someone who vigorously defends her own turf. Her favourite sentence, which she says wherever she goes, has become her nickname: "*Ani lo mevateret*. I won't let anything go by!"

Not a thing.

One time, on the 26 bus, she went so far as to take off her sandal and threaten the driver because he had accused her of travelling without a ticket.

Another passenger would have said, "What is the matter with you? Are you in love? Just check! You punched my card!"

Not Shula.

She whirled around, her eyes popping out of her head, and aimed her massive body straight for the driver.

"You dare to call me a thief in front of my neighbours, in my own street? You think I'm that hard up I can't buy a ticket?"

The bus was overcrowded. People were grumbling, packed like sardines, in a hurry to get to their destinations.

The ones in the rear, who could not see what was happening, could not understand why the bus was still stopped. The people in front who did not realize how serious the situation was, otherwise they would have surrounded Shula like electrons to get her away from the driver. People were shouting: "*Yallah, nou, sah* . . . Come on, drive. Let's get going!"

Too late. Shula had already taken off her sandal and was screaming, "I demand an apology! Now!"

And the news spread through the bus. "It's Shula . . . Shula and the bus driver . . . We've had it." "May God protect us . . ." One passenger

began shouting, "Driver, put on the A.C. . . . We can't breathe in here
. . ." And another: "Go argue outside on the pavement . . . Leave us
out of this . . ." If there were other comments, they were lost in the
collective bus madness that flared up in no time. Two factions arose.
The first one came out in defence of Shula and grumbled their hatred
of the Egged bus company for refusing to put on more buses to the
suburbs, just leaving people stewing in the hot sun and making them
travel in horrendous conditions and subjecting them to the drivers'
impertinence. The other group shouted that the quarrel was none of
their damn business, and they should go and settle it somewhere else.
Then a rumour started going around the bus: Shula did not have
enough money to pay for her ticket, and all the passengers started
dropping coins into a plastic bag.

"Just get on with it!" they moaned.

Dozens of coins were collected; every passenger paid a tithe in
the hopes of bringing an end to the dispute. Their gesture of soli-
darity merely served to further enrage Shula's already wounded pride.
She began shrieking fit to snap her vocal cords: "*Busha, busha* . . . It's
a disgrace! This country is a disgrace! We give our sons, our lifeblood,
our strength and vigour – and they raise our taxes and treat us like
bandits."

After a quarter of an hour the cops showed up. They took Shula
and the driver to the station, screaming siren and all. The passengers
of the abandoned vehicle had to wait for the driver that Egged had
dispatched. A few of them headed en masse for the taxis. Others, in
the end, just went home again, abandoning any idea of going shopping: their morning had been ruined.

"What are you thinking about?" asked Shula.

"Your business in the bus."

"Aaaah . . . The cops kept me in a cell a whole day, but ever since
then all the drivers on the 26 line speak to me with respect."

And no wonder, I thought. The drivers are no different from the
rest of my neighbours. The entire street has had to learn to live with

her Greek music, every Friday. To psych herself up for Shabbat, Shula puts the music on full blast – *rebetiko* songs sung in Hebrew, as kitsch as they come, with words like: "Since you left, bitter tears flow through my body, my blood is hot and I'm dying of love."

Shula opens wide all her doors and windows, shoves the furniture up against the rear wall, splashes bucketfuls of water over her tiles, shakes her scrubbing brush, whistles and sings at the top of her lungs, and only falls silent the better to savour the sound of the bouzouki.

Neighbourhood families have sent several delegations imploring her to listen to her music more discreetly. Shula promises to turn down the stereo, and for a few consecutive Fridays the street is a haven of silence.

Then she forgets her promise and the nasal twang of the Greek singers fills the street again. "Without you I can't make it any more. Come back, my love."

My father nicknamed her Roula, the ogress, and he avoids her like the plague.

The moment he sees her he changes pavements and hurries his step. But for some reason, I do not know why, Shula adores my father. She runs after him, yelling, "Hey! Solomon, wait, *yekiri*, my dear."

My father's blood freezes with horror, and all he wants to do is make a run for it. But he cannot insult her in that way. My parents flood her living room on a regular basis with the plumbing from their kitchen. Every year they bring in the plumber and every year there is a new incident, as if it were deliberate. Shula is very patient about it all and reassures my parents, it's only water, she says, the walls will dry out over the summer. When it comes down to material damage, Shula is wonderful, she will tell you again and again that only death is a worry, that all the rest can be repaired.

So if you get angry with her, it means permanent war. But if you walk alongside this wild woman in her shorts with her boobs hanging out, and she calls you *yekiri*, it is fuel for the flames of the neighbourhood gossips and bigots.

My father rarely manages to escape her. Shula always catches up with him, sometimes at the last minute as he is scurrying up the stairs and thinks he is safe. "*Yekiri*, I've been calling you for an hour. Are you getting deaf or what!" she says with a laugh. "Forgive me, Shula," he stammers. "No problem, *yekiri*, I'm getting old myself." And she pins him against the handrail, her hot breath in his face. He blushes to the roots of his hair, does not know where to look. Her breasts, her naked thighs, are causing him to panic, *ya Rabi laziz*, he chants to himself, devastated, what did I do today that you leave me in her clutches?

I know that there are mornings where he opens the door with extreme caution. He listens, makes sure she is not outside sweeping or watering her plants. There are even times when he sends my mother out to scout, instructing her to distract our formidable neighbour so he can sneak past in peace. He feels sorry for her husband. "He's a good sort," says my father and, coming from him, it means that in his place he would have filed for divorce a thousand times already.

"How are you doing?" said Shula with a tender gaze.

"Just fine."

"You making a living?"

"I can't complain."

"If you don't mind me asking, how much is your salary?"

"I don't remember."

"How can you forget such a thing? You don't remember or you just don't want to tell me?"

"Both," I answered, at the risk of annoying her.

She burst out laughing.

"You don't mince your words, do you!"

I sat up straight, and she pushed me back on to the flower box, digging her nails into my skin.

"Where are you running off to now? Just hold it a while. Don't you have five minutes to spare for poor old Shula?"

"My parents will start to worry."

"What's a few minutes . . . Tell me, kid. New York? You like New York?"

"It's a beautiful town."

"They say it's expensive to live there, that hotels are exorbitant. If I buy a ticket, would you invite me to stay with you?"

"Uh . . . maybe."

"Then I'll come," she promised, stroking my arm with her damp fingers. "I'll talk it over with my husband. We'll write to you."

I shuddered, because I knew she would keep her word.

"You know, where I live is really small, a tiny room."

"We'll squeeze. I'll cook Greek food for you, you'll be licking your fingers."

"Fine," I said, appalled.

"Do you have a boyfriend?"

"Shula!"

"So? You're old enough to make love, no?"

"That's none of your business."

"Well, I really like making love. It's the only thing that relaxes me."

"Good for you."

"Let me give you some advice. Don't go out with some impotent guy. Find yourself a man who's well-hung."

"Hey, that's enough!"

The worst of it is that Shula does not realize she is being overbearing. In Israel, people will delve into your business with an incredible lack of consideration. The moment they meet you, they start bombarding you with questions. Where are you from? Are you a virgin? Do you have a lover? Why on earth aren't you married? You're not a cripple, are you?

I thought she might throw her sandal in my face, but she merely shrugged.

"You're very prudish, kid, aren't you. How old are you now? Twenty-five or twenty-eight?"

"I'm two thousand years old."

"So you think you can make fun of poor Shula," she said, furiously fanning herself.

Her agitation brought on a stream of sweat and the smell of her sweat spiced with cheap perfume assailed my nostrils. We moved into the shade, but the heat was baking our skin

I could not leave until I had calmed her down. My father would blame me for having destroyed in the space of one moment the good relations he has managed to maintain at considerable expense.

"I should get a move on and go and make my jam," said Shula, looking at her mound of grapes. "I will give your mother a jar."

I tried hastily to dissuade her.

"Keep the jam for your grandchildren."

"There will be plenty for them. Eight kilos of grapes and four kilos of sugar makes twelve kilos of jam. Dear Lord, I'm out of my mind. Twelve kilos! Even if I give away half the jars, I'll have six left to eat up. All at the expense of my hips. And the doctor has ordered me not to eat sugar. You will have to taste my jam!"

I relented, wearily.

I know where Shula's culinary gifts end up. My mother does not dare humiliate her by refusing any of her sweet or savoury dishes, so she always thanks her effusively. She invites her for a coffee, chats with her for a while, but as soon as Shula leaves my mother rushes to tip her offerings into the garbage. Shula's cooking is not kosher enough for my parents. They have no way of knowing whether their neighbour has one set of dishes for milk and another for meat, they do not know who her butcher is, and they suspect her of lighting a fire on Shabbat. So they would rather not eat any of her food.

I was already on my feet when Shula started moaning.

"That's my day gone with these grapes," she said, her eyes open wide. "And if I don't do something right away, they'll rot. As if I had nothing better to do. I didn't tell you! I bought myself a plane ticket for Salonika! I'm leaving tomorrow."

Naturally, I had to sit down again.

"Salonika! That's great!"

"No it isn't, not at all," she said feverishly. "Not at all. If you knew what it means. My entire family was decimated by the Nazis."

I lit another cigarette. I felt sorry for her. Her chest had gone beet red, but her face was livid. She was about to burst into tears, and this time she would not be acting.

Just then my father came along, slowly trudging homeward with all his shopping bags.

He saw us perched there on the flower box and he turned into a pillar of salt. Shula had not seen him. She was completely pre-occupied with mopping up her sweat. I could see in my father's eyes how badly he wanted to flee. If he turned immediately to the right into the stairs, maybe he would be able to avoid her? Too late. Shula saw him and called, "Solomon! Just who we were looking for! Come here, come here."

My father walked up to us.

"How are you, *yekiri*?"

"It's hot," said my father, his eyes lowered.

"Who are you telling? I'm soaked in sweat. Are you happy to see your daughter?"

"Very."

"When I finish my jam, I'll bring you a jar."

"Don't go to any bother, Shula," my father said, depressed.

"What bother? For you I would walk on my hands."

I leapt up to help my father with his shopping bags. He fought me off, saying, I'll manage, I'll manage, it's not heavy, but I was able to wrest the bags from his hands.

I reeled with the weight my father had been schlepping from the supermarket, almost twenty kilos, between the milk, potatoes, laundry powder and all the other good things he found on the shelves that he thought might make me happy, things he never eats – chocolate, beer, bourekas and sausages.

Shula gathered up her grapes. My father noticed the bunch I had left on the flower box.

"You've forgotten some, Shula."

"They're your daughter's."

"You've been buying grapes, have you?"

"Yes."

"How much did you pay?" my father said, so anxious that I stood there gaping.

I am twenty-three years old, I live in New York, and he was insisting on finding out whether I had been ripped off a few shekels ...

Shula had anticipated the problem and intervened.

"Two shekels a kilo."

I gave a cowardly nod.

"Well, that's alright then."

Shula winked at me.

I was so angry that I did not even manage to smile. Stumbling from the weight of the bags, I headed for the house.

They followed me, still talking. Shula was so pleased to have hold of the yarn that she unravelled the entire ball.

"Can you imagine, they wanted to sell her those grapes for four shekels a kilo."

"Huh? That's twice the price ... at the market ..."

"Exactly ... Your daughter refused ... She may not live here any more, but she still knows how to look out for herself!"

I knew I should have walked alongside my father to help him get away from her, but I was too angry with him. I left him at the bottom of the stairs, in a tête-à-tête with his Greek neighbour. He could manage on his own.

DANIEL

Daniel opens the door, kicks it shut, turns the locks and leans for a moment against the door, completely done in.

"Ava?" he says, to make sure.

Only silence in response.

So he crosses the hallway and goes into the living room splattered with light.

The flat has been tidied.

Ava goes round like a spinning top to put everything away before she leaves. She rushes from one room to the next picking up clothes, shoes, objects; she airs, dusts, loads machines, presses buttons, washes her hair, puts on her make-up, slips on a dress and at last, when she goes out, she is as ravishing as a doll.

On the table sits a chocolate cake, decorated with candles and waiting to be shared.

Today is the birthday of his eldest boy, David. He had forgotten. With all this business he did not even think to buy him a present.

He is not used to getting home before dark. He is never ill, and hates being idle. The only day of rest he gives himself is Saturday. If you can call it rest. The house swarms with kids who have overrun both floors, laughing and shouting, eating non-stop, play-wrestling out on the patio. He has only two boys but he seems to be providing a home for ten. And not just any ten. His boys have befriended the wildest kids in the neighbourhood. And the stickiest. If it were up to them, they would camp out there day and night. The racket persists until Ava loses her temper; she rails against their neighbours – aren't they only too happy to palm off their brats on her, so that they can have a quiet Shabbat? She ends up sending them all out into the street with their bikes, rollerblades and footballs.

Once the children are out of the way, Daniel jumps on his wife.

He has been waiting impatiently for this moment and does not intend to waste a second.

Ava laughs.

The angels in the sky are reciting Mincha; kids scrape their knees as they run along the streets; rabbis gather for prayer. While Daniel lifts up his wife's skirt and reaches eagerly for her sex.

Ava knows how he has waited for this moment, how scheming and ill-tempered he is.

He knows she has been making him wait, deliberately. To kindle his desire and his imagination.

Because over the last few months Ava has been complaining that he makes love too quickly. That he makes love to her the way Israelis go to war.

"Love," she says, "is not some commando operation! Take your time."

No-one will come back before six o'clock.

Ava works until four. Then she picks up the two boys and takes them to judo or the conservatory. The flat is all his.

For once.

Daniel leaves his jacket at the foot of the stairs. He tears off his sweat-soaked shirt, removes his slip-ons, and walks barefoot to the drinks cabinet. He takes out a bottle of vodka. You are supposed to drink vodka ice cold.

Never mind.

Daniel, standing in his living room at eleven o'clock in the morning with a bottle of alcohol in his hand, is a sight to see. Who knows when he will ever have the opportunity again. So he plants himself in front of the mirror.

He is a muscular man with a hairy chest, a flat belly, solid arms, and shining skin. His face, O.K. from his brow to his chin, is still holding up, but the actual structure is beginning to slide like a mountain of clay in the rain. It's all going to seed – the arch of his eyebrows, the bridge of his nose, his cheeks, his lips.

He mutters to his reflection, Stop the chocolate. Stop the fat, the olives, sugar, and cream sauces, you're getting fat. Words he says to himself a hundred times a day, without ever actually starting a diet. *Kibinimat!* you only live once.

And anyway, it is high time to taste this vodka.

He gives a quick twist to the top and tosses a glassful down his throat.

I went about it in the wrong way, he thinks, heading for the patio.

These words have been going through his mind ever since he left the Old Girl.

He has never called Elisheva by any other name: the Old Girl.

Even when she was young she looked a hundred years old. Forty years have passed. She has always had the same haircut, the same shoes, the same clothes. She must have bought the entire stock of a shop that was going out of business, he thinks with a laugh.

When he was a boy he used to spy on her, scrutinize her. He was fascinated by this grey woman. How had that greyness left its trace all over her? Why was she so opaque, so distant and serious?

The only time she came alive was when she was playing the cello. The moment she bowed her head towards her instrument, the greyness vanished, light entered her gaze and her body came alive. His mother said she had been through hell. That she had had plenty of reasons to do herself in.

At the age of six Daniel went through Elisheva's trunks. At ten he stole letters. At twenty he sneaked into her flat when she was away, awestruck at the thought that he might discover her secret, something about her life. He had decided that, if need be, he would obtain the hidden truth by force.

The patio is Ava's domain.

Twenty square metres, a cement floor, a wide strip of earth all the way round, an entire *parasha* where they could plant a few trees: lemon, lilac, orange and a few rosebushes that cost thousands of shekels.

He felt like smashing everything around him. He had been tricked, like a complete novice. And why had any of it even come about? For his mother's sake, out of respect for a woman who has become a vegetable. Daniel takes another swig of vodka. And the upshot of it all: he is still a little boy. A little boy who obeys unflinchingly. A brainless kid who does not think about the consequences.

The heat is crushing. A ray of sunlight falls straight on him: it is hard to breathe. The relentless, exhausting sound of a pneumatic drill in the street is hammering in his brain. How can those guys even work in this furnace?

He goes back into the living room and collapses into an armchair. There are a few paintings on the walls. In the centre is a portrait of his great-grandfather. An old rabbi with a white beard and smiling eyes.

His mother commissioned Abramovitz to paint it, which he did, from her memories. His mother had nothing else left, only her memories. She talked about the shtetl. The woods around the village. A violinist. A fountain. And the last time she saw the old man's narrow back as he walked away, in the wrong line. Disjointed memories, murmured hesitantly, her voice choking with tears. She added that he spoke Yiddish much better than Hebrew, that he had a few notions of medicine, that he owned two hats, one for weekdays and the other for holidays and Shabbat.

See if you can paint a portrait with that.

It so happened that the painter was talented. An exceptional artist. So gifted, in fact, that he left Israel to move to New York, where his paintings sell for millions of dollars.

But in those days he was a starving artist and he was willing to work for a modest fee.

When the painting was finished his mother went to pieces. Massive depression. Incurable. Those smiling eyes, the light the rabbi radiated – she could not stand it any more. Daniel is not even sure that the face on the portrait is the one she had known and loved. But the expression painted in the eyes stood for the expression of all those who had disappeared. Every time she passed the portrait she would turn her head to one side to keep from sighing or moaning or weeping. Until the day she wrapped the portrait in newspaper and brought it to Daniel.

That is how he inherited the painting.

He thought he would keep it wrapped up in the cultural pages of *Maariv*, but he had not reckoned with Ava's snobbery.

"An Abramovitz!" she said. "You can't leave an Abramovitz behind a piece of furniture! Abramovitz is our Gauguin, our Renoir, our Rembrandt! Have you any idea what this painter is worth? His fame is in-ter-na-tio-nal!"

Daniel tried to explain to his wife that this painting, which had destroyed his mother's brain, after all, might turn out to be dangerous for him as well. In vain. Ava went to fetch a nail, a hammer, and a folding rule. She chose a spot in the living room, right in the centre, the most visible place. And it had to be said that her choice was impeccable, because not a single visitor ever misses the portrait, the moment they come into the house.

From the threshold they cry, "Is it a . . ."

"Yes," Ava says, puffing herself up.

"I don't believe it! How did you do it? Your own Abramovitz?"

And so on and so forth.

Daniel raises his elbow, sucks on the bottleneck.

And bursts into tears.

He must have fallen asleep, because suddenly he starts, his eyes unfocussed, a taste of bile in his mouth. A musky animal smell has invaded the living room: whiffs of alcohol, sweat, feet.

He sits up straight, confused. The level of liquid in the bottle has drastically diminished.

He has knocked back more than half. *Ya'ani*, he is not a big drinker, he has just broken his own record. And in just three hours, he thinks boastfully, peering at his watch.

It feels good sitting there on the sofa, the only problem is he has to pee. And the toilets are far away. At the end of the earth. More than twenty metres from there. Can he even make it that far?

Of course.

Easy-peasy.

Easier said than done, that is.

Easy-peasy.

Clinging to the bottle, he leans on to his fists, collapses, starts over.

Someone – his mother, a friend? – once told him that vodka means "little water".

Little water, my arse. Strong water, more like.

He grunts, groans, laughs. Manages, finally, to stand up. The living room spins and reels.

Fuck, what a bender, he thinks between two hiccups. Ava won't like it. Won't like it one bit. But the kids will laugh. Those kids of mine always laugh. I've done a good job. I adore them.

He has taken only one step. The loo is definitely too far away. And the patio is not far at all. He will piss on Ava's plants.

It won't hurt the bloody plants. After all the time he's spent watering them, they're his plants in a way, too, no?

He has fought two wars, and made it through each time by the skin of his teeth. The first time was in '73, at El-Arish in the Sinai.

He had climbed down from the Merkava tank to go and take a piss. In the time it took to open his flies, the thunder of an explosion and a roaring flame hurled him to the ground. When he got to his feet, the Merkava had disappeared. His mates had roasted alive. Guys who were twenty years old. On leaving the base they had taped photos of their girlfriends to the gun turret, and all along the track leading to Suez and the front they had talked about how they would make their women come. He can still hear them. For months he had heard them talking and laughing. The minute I get back, you hear? I'll grab her breasts, I'll fuck her from behind, I'll lick her, I'll make her scream with joy. She'll be clinging to the bedposts. The bed base will collapse. The world will collapse. For a whole week, a whole month, that's all I'll do, mate.

And they died in a split-second.

He remembers how he sat down on the sand, stunned. The ambulance drivers came running. "Are you alright? Come with us, all hell is breaking loose." He had fought them off, got away from them to run over to the crater where the Merkava – or what was left of it – was burning. Ashes, more ashes, nothing but ashes. They had been pulverized, with their photographs, their songs, their youth.

Two hours later he was driving another tank. He had had no choice. No-one had a choice. It was war, they had to get on with it.

The second time, in '82, he had had the same incredible luck, this time on the road to Beirut. Three enemy rockets had destroyed the tanks at the head of the column, every single tank right up to his.

War, death. He knows it all. He has done his bit. More than enough. He does not talk about it to anyone. Sometimes he tells himself that he should go and see a shrink, just to unburden himself, to rid himself of all that shit.

Sometimes.

He has never gone through with it. For lack of time, and lack of faith. Basically, he cannot stand people who moan. Guys like that are washed up, he knows it; they're fucked. They've lost all their charm, they can't get it up any more.

And he wants to live. Live.

He is only forty. Which means? Ten more years to get rich? He swore he would slow down when he turned fifty. If he is not dead by then, in some attack or skirmish. In the meanwhile, he has learnt to live with the pressure. Or he thinks he has, which is exactly the same thing. He has two beautiful children, a wife who is hysterical but cheerful, and a house in the old neighbourhood of Mahane Yehuda that he has rebuilt from top to bottom. He let his wife supervise the renovation process. She loved talking with the architect, choosing the materials, tormenting the contractor to get the best price and the finest work. They lived in sand and cement, in the middle of rubble. They lived through their own sort of war – an interior, private, exhausting, ruinous war. He remembers the weeping and shouting, the endless arguments where the same questions surfaced again and again like a refrain: "Tell me when this fucking construction will be finished? When? How much is it costing us? I'm not asking you the exact amount, just give me a rough estimate. I want to know where I'm headed." Then one morning the workers packed up, a team of cleaners came in after them, and the tarpaulins, the supplies, the tools, everything vanished.

The house was magnificent.

Friends started coming over again for dinner, or to watch the football.

Every time they come into the house they are green with envy.

The wives above all.

The jealousy of an Israeli woman is something else.

They drip with envy as they murmur their praise and blessings. Their gazes linger on the whitewashed walls, the furnishings, the household appliances, the stereo, the television.

"Oh, and you got yourselves this fridge as well? *Saha lik.* To tell you the truth, even if you paid me I wouldn't want one like that in my house."

"Oh, no? Why not?"

"It's as big as a cistern. But it's true that *you lot* have room for it."

Daniel gives Ava a knowing glance. They figured it was better to arouse envy than pity. But just to be on the safe side, once a month Ava tosses salt into the flames on a gas ring to ward off the evil eye. From time to time, too, she and her mother, Emma, boil an egg in a saucepan and mumble magic formulas until the shell explodes. Daniel is glad he married a Moroccan woman. Thanks to her, to Emma, and to a few marabouts they consult on the sly, their house has been free of evil spirits.

But they have paid a price for this life of theirs.

He will probably drop dead of a heart attack on the motorway.

Like most of his friends.

Like most of the men in this country who manage to survive the fighting.

ELISHEVA

The taxi stops in the middle of the road, at Sha'ar Ha'ashpot, the Dung Gate.

Elisheva opens her wallet, takes out a note and is reaching over to pay for her ride when a violent thud shakes the car.

One of the drivers waiting for a customer on the pavement, his head broiling from the sun, has just slammed his fist on to the metal.

Elisheva's driver yanks on the handbrake, leaves the motor running and leans head and shoulders out of the open window.

"What? What?" he says.

He looks at the dark fellow walking up to him, dragging his slippered feet.

"Is that you messing with my car?"

"You think you're the king of the city? Park the way you're supposed to!"

"So you're in charge of traffic law now?" Elisheva's driver is fuming.

"Shut your mouth and get out of here."

Elisheva leaves the banknote on the roasting rear seat, opens the door, and dashes from the car. As does the driver, seething with rage. He lowers his head and charges at his adversary, who steps nimbly aside.

Snarling, canines showing, the two men start to punch each other as black exhaust fumes pour into the shimmering air. The other drivers, usually bored to death, now lean excitedly against their vehicles, arms crossed over their chests.

"Go fuck your sister, come on."

"I already did your mother."

Elisheva walks away, looking for a spot of shade. How can they find the strength to fight in this heat? It is beyond her.

64

She can hear the sound of a siren already.

She turns around and watches as the two drivers take to their heels, while their gleeful audience dissolves, hastily returning to their taxis. Sometimes a siren is enough to resolve a crisis; at other times it is not.

Elisheva holds her handbag out to be searched, then goes through the security barrier.

The usual crowd on the esplanade has scattered; the time for prayer has come and gone.

She sees Carlos conversing heatedly with a priest in a red satin cassock and a straw hat with braids and tassels.

Somewhat further back, to the intrigue of the soldiers, a dozen or so prelates in black robes, their hips cinched with a purple sash, are having an animated conversation.

I'm too early, she thinks, slowing her steps.

A boy bumps into her and immediately snaps open an accordion display of postcards. Elisheva gives him a coin, her eyes never leaving her friend, who is now bowing over the priest's hand to kiss his ring. The priest blesses him with a quick sign of the cross. And Elisheva thinks, Carlos is not yet done with the past; it's not as simple as he thought.

Children appear from all sides and surround Elisheva, waving glass bead necklaces, crosses and boxwood rosaries in her face. They shout, beg, hop up and down.

"Madame, Madame, Madame . . ."

She hands out the rest of her change and gently pushes them aside, never letting Carlos out of her sight.

Finally the red cassock goes to join the black robes and the entire group moves away towards the stairs that lead to the souk and the Damascus Gate.

When she goes up to him, Carlos is rinsing his head under a stream of water as it splashes into a stone basin.

"Carlos?"

The man raises his streaming face and roars, "*Mi amor . . . Oh, mi amor . . .*"

He lifts her up, whirls her round, puts her back on the ground and kisses her; he is laughing, suntanned, happy.

His long hair is gathered into a elastic at the back of his neck; it dances on the collar of a white shirt with full sleeves. With his grey canvas trousers and his soft cuff boots he looks like a hidalgo, even more so than when he first arrived in Jerusalem in search of his roots and an identity.

His exclamations arouse the curiosity of the faithful as they hurry to the Wall with their prayer books under their arms.

Elisheva would have preferred to curtail such effusive greetings.

But Carlos, with his pock-marked face, bushy eyebrows and large red mouth, has accustomed her to his exuberance.

He has a lean, vigorous body, a few wrinkles around his eyes, and a straight, strong, Spanish nose.

He is unmarried, a charmer who loves women, who return the sentiment.

"You look magnificent, Elisheva!"

"And you're in a good mood . . ."

"You're right, I am happy!" he says, with a thrust of his chin. "I've been showing a delegation from the Vatican around . . . A cardinal and some bishops. The dialogue has resumed between us, Elisheva. The pope is going to recognize Israel. He's a very good pope, this Karol Jozef Wojtyla."

And as she is staring at him, he shouts, "John Paul II, my dear friend. Pope John Paul II. Do you remember the fuss when he went to visit Auschwitz? I tell you, there's going to be another fuss, an even bigger fuss, when he comes to Israel. It's only a matter of months now."

He opens his water flask, takes a few swallows.

"I've been showing them around since seven o'clock this

morning. They wanted to see everything, understand everything. If you knew how carefully you have to handle these people. I'm completely, literally drained."

To illustrate, he sticks out his tongue. Elisheva smiles.

"When do you see them again?"

"Oh! Not before vespers, at the end of the afternoon. In the meantime I am all yours."

"And you won't have had a minute for yourself."

"How do you want me to get any rest when I'm participating in the reconciliation between the Church and Judaism! We've been waiting for this for two thousand years . . . Wait until my father hears about this!"

"You could write to him," Elisheva says, stroking his arm. "People do, you know."

Carlos cannot restrain a bitter laugh.

"I've never stopped writing to him. A letter a week. He never replies. He is ninety years old and he's as angry as ever."

He pauses for a moment with his head to one side and his eyes staring at the ground. She knows how desperate he is, even if his good mood hides his despair. His father banished him twenty years ago, and he will die without asking to see his son again.

"My sister sent me a photograph. He lives in a wheelchair. Not a pretty sight . . . he's all thin and twisted. Only his mind is working, and he uses it to curse me . . . He'll curse me until he's on his deathbed, until his last breath."

He throws his bag over his shoulder.

"Let's walk," he says, simply.

Carlos was thirty years old when he left Madrid, his old parents, his lifelong friends, and an enviable position in the tourist industry, to come and settle in Israel.

His metamorphosis, as he calls it, began after his grandfather died, and he was preparing to empty the house in La Serena which had been put up for sale. The furniture had already been taken away by second-hand dealers; bed linen and dishes were packed in cardboard boxes waiting for the van from a charitable organization. All that was left was the attic, which no-one had been through. His sister Mercedes suffered from asthma, so she had asked Carlos to take care of it, or to let the movers finish the chore. Besides, the floorboards up there were not safe. Their grandfather had told them time and again that they were rotten, and he had forbidden them from going up there.

And that, thought Carlos, is precisely why it's time to go and take a look. Then no-one could say they'd sold the house without taking a look at the forbidden place.

The floor was in perfect condition, covered in dust and cluttered with an assortment of things. Yellowed magazines, moth-eaten linen sheets, bits of old furniture, heavy armchairs gnawed away by mice, stuffed birds that looked alive in the pale light from an *oeil-de-boeuf* draped with cobwebs.

Carlos discovered wooden toys, doll's houses, tin soldiers, electric trains, coffee grinders. And a chest, hidden by cloth dress dummies. Inside were old papers, a few *grimoires*, rolled parchments. With Mercedes' consent, Carlos took the chest home with him.

The parchments he had found in the attic were in Hebrew. There was an entire collection, the Book of Esther, a Torah, a Haggadah of Pesach. The *grimoires*, embellished with drawings and calligraphy, contained incantations in Aramaic. A bookseller specialized in rare, ancient tomes, told him the entire collection was worth a fortune, and the man had removed his glasses and said abruptly, "Judío?"

He immediately made an offer. He knew collectors in Spain who were prepared to pay a top price for such a treasure. Then, when he saw Carlos hesitate and begin to put the parchments away, the bookseller suggested contacting the Americans. "Perhaps, why not?" muttered Carlos. He needed to think, to organize a family reunion before making a decision.

He had always known that the Montana lineage was an old one. Ramon, his father, claimed they went all the way back through the Middle Ages, but he had never given him any proof. Now the documents would speak.

Carlos had the oiled papers deciphered. Some of them bore the stamp of *conversos*. Others were *ktoubot*. Finally, there were letters; an entire cautious correspondence evoking the bloody nights experienced by the "brothers", and imploring the "sons of the shadow", if they did not want to disappear, to submit to the laws of the mighty and adopt the customs of the *"cristianos"*.

At last, the closing fragments of a secret rite made sense. The oil lamp his grandmother lit every Friday evening and placed in the windowsill; the Easter sausage that did not contain an ounce of pork; the glass of wine ready for a "visitor".

His ancestors were Marranos.

Ever since the Edict of Expulsion, ordered in 1492 by the Catholic Isabella, they had been going down into their cellars to celebrate their God and sanctify the wine on Easter night. They had clung to the soil of Spain in hopes of better days, praying with the same fervour to the Messiah who must come and liberate them and to Christ nailed to the Cross. Their ritual had been handed down from generation to generation, until Franco came and swept it all away.

When Carlos brought him the armful of documents, his father, Ramon, said, "The chain broke with grandfather." Ramon had raised his son in keeping with a hard-line Christianity, sending him to a Jesuit boarding school. For Ramon the matter was closed. And there was money to be made. Carlos must go ahead and sell the papers. They might as well get as much as they could for them.

Carlos had the papers appraised. They were worth, give or take a bit, his share of his inheritance. He proposed a deal to his parents: he would keep the papers, they would keep their money. His family saw nothing wrong with that, and they went to the lawyers' to make it legal.

Six months later Carlos went back to see Ramon. He was coming to say goodbye. He was going to live in Israel.

Mad with rage, the old man began to shout, hurling accusations at his son. That page of history was dead; they had broken the ties when the grandfather had made his choice; the Church alone was the *Verus Israel*. Carlos had tried to explain what he felt: although they were repressed and burned at the stake, their ancestors had not renounced their faith for all that; if they were to disown them, it was tantamount to condemning them all over again, and for ever. Overcome with anguish, Ramon stood before his son and pointed to the door: "I am not Jewish! I have nothing to do with all that! I am not going to pay for a thousand years for the right to be myself!"

Before he turned on his heels, Carlos looked for the last time at the white moustache of this man he had revered. Then he went along the corridor and across the patio, leaving the reception hall to his right, and he entered the kitchen where his mother sat sobbing, a handkerchief to her eyes. As he walked over to her, Carlos wondered if his father was not denying the past so adamantly to avoid displeasing this woman. Every year without fail, she attended the Holy Mass held in honour of the Caudillo at the Valle de los Caídos, the basilica erected in the Sierra de Guadarrama forty kilometres from Madrid, where the cult of the nationalists who fell in 1936 was perpetuated. Carlos and his mother shared neither a kiss nor an embrace; there was only the sound of her tears.

Carlos arrived in Israel with his paper treasure. He donated the scroll of the Torah to the museum of the Diaspora, sold the Easter Haggadah to a collector, but kept the Book of Esther and all the letters.

He prospered in no time. It did not take him even six months to find a position as a guide and less than five years to set up his own travel agency. He was a man between two worlds, and this was something the Vatican was looking for: they connected him with parishes the world over.

Ever since he had come to live in Jerusalem, Carlos had been telling anyone prepared to listen – and they were numerous – that his soul had been restored to him.

Sitting side by side on a bench they look at the Wall. High up, almost at the top, doves are flying in circles. At the foot of the Wall men are praying, bowing, dancing.

Carlos asks Elisheva if she would like to go closer for a few moments of silent meditation. She says no, in a hard voice, looking away from the massive stones.

He lifts his arms to the sky, exasperated.

"Make your peace with God, Elisheva."

"Never."

"God is not responsible for the fury of man."

"What is he responsible for, then?"

"The universe."

"And what is the place of mankind in that universe?"

"Mankind has its own place."

"Carlos, I adore you, but your sermons don't go very far."

"I have two religions . . ."

"And I have music."

He sticks a cigarillo between his lips and lights it.

"How can you be Jewish without God?"

"In the name of the dead."

"Elisheva, look around you. We are alive. It's a miracle."

"The miracle would have been to free us from Auschwitz. To send the Messiah to Majdanek and Sobibor and Treblinka."

At a loss for arguments, he says, "So what are we, here, all of us? The prolongation of chaos?"

"I didn't say that."

They have had this discussion many times. He knows what she went through, he respects her suffering, but he wants to restore her hope.

71

"We came back here after two thousand years of absence. In a way, a Messiah *has* come . . ."

"I walked on my father's ashes. Swallowed my sisters', inhaled my brothers'. For two years I was covered in smoke and ash. If God exists, why did he allow this tragedy?"

"I don't know."

"Then don't ask me to acknowledge him. As far as I'm concerned, the heavens were destroyed."

He reaches for her hand, their fingers entwine. She is on edge and he knows it. He must find a way to lower the pressure, otherwise their mission is sure to fail.

"Do you know Ravel's *Kaddish*?" she asks dully.

"Did he compose one?"

"In 1914. I authorize you to have it played beside my grave at my funeral."

"Because it's Ravel."

"Because it's Ravel, yes."

"Well! This is cheery!" He gives her a tight squeeze. And as she fails to react, he pulls a set of keys from his pocket.

" A present," he says, showing her the keys: one is small and modern, a shiny metal, the other is black, bigger than a man's hand, old and ornate.

"I don't feel up to it, Carlos."

"All the more reason, then! Let's see if you're equipped to go exploring."

He removes Elisheva's shoe and examines it, finds it is too flimsy, puts it back on her foot as if she were a queen.

"Cheap rubbish. You can't go walking around like that . . . especially in this country."

A faint smile, at last, lights up Elisheva's face.

"Carlos, be serious. We have a lot to talk about."

"I have to hand in the keys tonight. You can't miss this opportunity! Come on, get up."

He crushes his cigarillo beneath his boot and, ignoring her protests, leads her to the fence that restricts public access to the excavations, while still offering a view of the work in progress.

Carlos opens the gate and carefully closes it again behind them. The dig is thirty metres further along below them, a wide plateau strewn with stones and earth.

Hand in hand, they follow the stony path.

"You are about to set your eyes on something the entire country dreams of seeing."

Located to the south, and in the southwest corner of the Haram-es-Sharif, the excavations began at the time of Ygal Yadin and have been struggling along as best they can, against the wishes of the Palestinian religious leaders and under the strict supervision of the army and U.N.E.S.C.O.

In principle, only designated archaeologists have access to the site, along with a few rare privileged personalities – members of the Jerusalem city hall or high-ranking officials from the Prime Minister's cabinet.

The delegation from the Vatican had asked to see the cause of this dispute – yet another – between Israelis and Palestinians, and Carlos had acted as their guide. The delegation, for the time being, was withholding its conclusions. After the benediction, the cardinal told Carlos that he would have to talk it over with his bishops before he wrote his report.

Stones, carefully sorted and cleaned, lie waiting to be reassembled: fragments of arches, vaults, carved steles.

"Welcome to my world!" Carlos chuckles as he extends his arm to the site. "You see these relics? My memory is in the same state. Everything upside down."

They walk around 2,000-year-old slabs covered with inscriptions in Hebrew, a fragment of stairway from the time of Herod, tombs dating back to the era of kings, ruins of an Umayyad palace.

"It's beautiful," says Elisheva in a weary voice. "Let's go now."

"You haven't seen anything yet."

"Carlos."

"Are you ready for a major shock?"

He walks towards the thick bars of a grille dating from the Crusades which was brought back and sealed to ensure maximum security.

The fence along the esplanade can be cut. This one is impregnable. Carlos unlocks it with the big black key. He hands a torch to Elisheva, lights his own, sweeps the darkness below him.

"Señora! The heart of the sanctuary!"

She hesitates. Her rehearsal with the musicians is scheduled to start less than five hours from now. She should be preparing for it by resting on her bed with a black cloth over her eyes, going over the score in her mind. The jetlag has exhausted her. It is sheer madness, this escapade into the bowels of Jerusalem. If something were to happen to her – if she should twist her ankle, bang her wrist – then farewell to the concert. And her carefully constructed plan would be destroyed. In a way she has begun to suspect that Carlos is trying to put a spanner in the works, but then her friend whispers, "Trust me."

She has never seen him so excited, his eyes shining, his voice hoarse. Then she remembers how fascinated he has always been by crypts, cellars, underground places. A Marrano through and through.

The tunnel, propped up by metal structures, is damp and full of echoes. Out of nowhere a draught of cold air ruffles her summer dress.

She can smell the earth, the mildew, as they go through a series of vaulted rooms from the Roman era, old water cisterns, explains Carlos, that gradually filled with earth.

Every turn is indicated with an arrow: the blue ones point to Solomon's Temple, the green to the Omar and al-Aqsa mosques.

"There are other underground sites, but they haven't been cleared yet. Lack of funds. And the drilling is constantly interrupted. The

74

Palestinians are afraid the earth might collapse and bring down the two mosques."

Carlos holds a plasticized map up against a wall, pinning it with his elbow and aiming the beam of the torch on to it as he moves his index finger along a winding path.

"We are here," he says. "In this narrow passageway, which runs along three hundred and five metres, roughly, in other words the entire length of the Temple Mount – as the Jews call it – and the western wall of Haram-es-Sharif – as the Muslims call it. And this is the rampart. According to calculations, it continues to a depth of ten metres. And each stone weighs half a ton."

In the state she is in, between waking and sleep, the ogival portico, the alcoves, the deep vaults seem to be converging towards her, opening like an eye in the light of a lamp.

"It would seem our national identity does not suffice to justify the creation of Israel. Our right to return to Jerusalem is now being challenged. To prove our genealogy and our roots, the foundations of our past are being brought to light. Will this give us the legitimacy we are asking for? I'm not sure."

Carlos is trying to explain that the battle for Jerusalem does not exist solely on the surface but is also being waged underground.

But Elisheva is no longer listening to him.

Immobile, her eyes open wide, she is looking straight ahead of her. Something terrifying has emerged from the darkness, to brush past her, caress her.

She slumps to the ground.

Carlos, alarmed, takes her in his arms and carries her back to the light.

Outside, the sun streams dazzling rays.

Followed by a press of people asking questions, offering advice, urging they call an ambulance, the fire brigade, the army, Carlos walks diagonally across the esplanade carrying Elisheva in his arms. He lays her down on a stone bench and opens her bodice, murmuring her name again and again. Someone gives him a water bottle, a scarf goes from hand to hand, a bottle of eau de cologne and even a Bible, which some crank suggests placing on the sick woman's belly "to get the evil out". To a shower of advice, Carlos dampens a handkerchief and places it on Elisheva's forehead. Then he raises her head and tries to get her to drink.

The water dribbles into her dress, down her back.

Elisheva revives, her eyelids fluttering. She sees Carlos as he attempts to push away the curious onlookers. She sits up, tries to smile.

The sky that melted down on her like metal in fusion gradually returns to its place. She no longer knows why she fainted, or how Carlos brought her back up from underground.

Did he lock the door to the fence?

"Of course I did. Relax."

The guide's face is flushed, his breathing hoarse, his gaze anxious. And his hair has come loose from its elastic and frames his brow like the mane of a lion.

"Forgive me," she says, because she finds him handsome, because she is moved by his tenderness.

The onlookers finally scatter and they are left alone.

Carlos sits down next to her.

"Have you fainted like this before?"

"I'm not used to the heat any more."

"The heat, huh?"

He studies her, puzzled, worried.

"I think I was afraid of something down there."

"Of what, Elisheva?"

"Of the time that has gone by. Of how little my life is worth."

She recalls a weight upon the back of her neck, as if God . . . No. God was burned alive in the ovens. He died in the gas chambers with a naked people, their teeth chattering, their nails scratching the stone to try to find a mouthful of air. He died with his people who were expiring as they recited the Shema.

She looks at the crowd strolling along the esplanade. An old woman is praying, covering her eyes with a trembling hand, a beggar is holding out his cup, believers are gesticulating as they converse. What destiny awaits my people? she wonders. What star for Israel?

"Shall we go and have lunch?" suggests Carlos.

"I'm not hungry."

"Be reasonable."

"I want to go back to the hotel."

"Then I won't give you anything," he decides.

Their eyes challenge each other, and Elisheva relents. He's right. Lunch is what she needs. And something to drink, too. Drink. It is so hot that her dress has already dried.

"I'll just have a salad."

"We'll see."

Carlos jumps to his feet. His shadow is no wider than a thread.

They go through the Jaffa Gate and head along the footpath that winds down to the Pool of Siloam. Elisheva did not want to take a taxi. She says she needs the exercise, needs to get the blood flowing in her limp legs. Carlos agrees, somewhat annoyed. She is heavier than he had thought she was. And he is not as strong as he had thought he was. He nearly burst his lungs heaving her up to the esplanade just now. And he does not feel like having to sprint to the other end of the street to go for help.

To distract her until they reach the restaurant, Carlos talks to her about his pet subjects – onomastics, genealogy, the ties that are being forged between synagogue and church. This pope will come to the Wailing Wall, of that he is sure. He will come and ask forgiveness for the crimes committed in Christ's name. If only his own father would listen to his pope.

Elisheva listens to Carlos, as she stares at the Montefiore windmill.

"Carlos," she says suddenly, "if you stay with me you won't see the Pope enter Jerusalem."

"I know, *cariña*."

She falls silent. And they continue walking down Hativat Yerushalayim as if nothing had been said.

The restaurant is swarming with people, waitresses rush to and fro among the tables. Elisheva wants to leave again, but Carlos restrains her by the waist. They know him here, they will be served quickly.

A table, off to the side, is set at once, as if by magic. They sit down.

"You know how to win people over," she says.

"What good does it do? I'm forty-nine years old and have no children. I let all the important things pass me by."

Elisheva sits deeper into the cushions of the wicker armchair and says, distractedly, "What about your ladyfriends?"

"Which ones?"

"Myriam, Hanna, Joanne?"

"In bed, they are magnificent. In the morning, it all evaporates."

"Take a religious wife," Elisheva says. "She'll make a home for you."

"A home without the flames of love – that's not for me."

"I had an Orthodox student once. She wore a strict dress, with sleeves that closed at the wrists, and a skirt down to her ankles. But underneath, believe me, she was wearing a thong and fishnet stockings."

"Do I know her?" Carlos says, his eyes twinkling.

Their dishes arrive, bringing a momentary silence. The meat smells of cumin and chilli pepper. It is piping hot and grilled to perfection. Elisheva nibbles on a cucumber, Carlos drinks his wine slowly, little sips, never taking his eyes off her. He finds her gaunt, her complexion too pale, with shadows under her eyes. He cannot forgive himself for their excursion underground. He had only been thinking of the tourist angle. For her there was a mystical side. Her hatred of God, of men of religion, was all rubbish, so much blah-blah.

She answers with a shrug.

"I play Bach. It helps. Can we talk about the matter at hand, Carlos?"

"Finish your meat."

"I can't. I want some iced tea. And the documents."

He calls the waitress, orders an iced tea and a coffee. Then he opens his bag and pulls out a brown envelope which he pushes towards her across the table, delicately.

"It's all there," he says with a trace of a smile.

Her head to one side, she goes through the documents: a brochure for a tour of Jordan, a list of names, and a flier for a trip to Israel with the pompous, ambiguous title, in gilded Gothic letters: "Ascension in the Holy Land".

The sound of cheerful voices comes to them from the neighbouring tables. Bursts of laughter. Elisheva hears nothing, or next to nothing. She is carefully reading and rereading the papers she has spread across the table as if they were playing cards.

"He is on the tour? You're sure?"

Carlos nods.

"His name is fifteenth on the list."

"This list was drawn up before he left Venezuela . . ."

"He's been in Jordan for two weeks," Carlos says, stubbornly.

"Your informer has confirmed this?"

"Yes."

"Will he cross the border?"

"We'll find out tomorrow, Elisheva."

"When tomorrow?"

"Around noon. The priest I hired will use his break to give me a complete report."

"And until tomorrow what do we do?"

"We wait."

Carlos makes a rapid sign of the cross. A faint smile lights her face. She had met Carlos a few weeks after his arrival in Israel. Wearing a black coat and a *lavaliere*, he came to congratulate her in her box at the end of a concert. He said, several times over, speaking rudimentary Hebrew, "Such talent, such power in the cello." Sorry, sorry, he expressed himself poorly, especially in Hebrew. And as she answered with a smile, he told her his life story on one leg, as they say in Israel.

His gaiety and elegance, his life story – the Marrano Jew returning to the source – the way he had of uttering Jesus and Elohim in the same sentence, all captivated her. On the spur of the moment she invited him to the closing dinner given by the festival for the musicians.

They had quickly become friends. It was all or nothing with Elisheva, black or white, beautiful or ugly. When she liked someone, it was instinctive and everlasting.

One month later, she told Carlos everything she had never shared even with those who were close to her. Even the only true love of her life.

Carlos had grown up with the art of the Church, in the company of the great tormented Christs, and that night he listened to her, devastated. That night, she even told him about the Butcher. She knew the man was alive, and well-hidden. He had managed to flee with other war criminals, thanks to the complicity of Nazi policemen, extremist Christian groups, and money from the Vatican.

People the world over were looking for him. Jews, Christians, Gypsies, Protestants, Communists. An entire network of former deportees and spies; men from Interpol, Mossad, French agents, and even former SS who were trying to buy themselves a new life. Some of them shared their information, others worked alone. Elisheva had become part of a network where photographs were handed around, along with rumours and clues. She travelled a great deal. She had been contacted ten times in forty years. The Butcher had been spotted – in a town, a village, a hamlet on the far side of the planet. After further inquiries, it turned out not to be him. Sometimes it was his double, sometimes the suspect did not look at all like the man whose name she refused to say.

When Elisheva stopped talking, Carlos begged her to let him help her.

She remained silent.

Then she said, "You don't know what you're getting into." He knew. He had been born under a dictatorship, he knew how dangerous those people could be.

Time had gone by.

A fair amount of time.

Suddenly last year Elisheva had received a series of photographs taken with a zoom.

At last the Butcher had been identified.

She replied by letter, asking for more precise information about the bastard's habits, his relationships, his friends. She was about to go to Venezuela when her contact informed her that the Butcher had signed up for a trip to Jordan with some of the other members of his parish.

Jordan?

Elisheva had gone to find Carlos.

When she told him about her plan, her absolutely crazy idea, he did not say to her, you're off your block, it will never work. He was immediately enthusiastic for that very reason, because it was completely mad. She had given him a mission: convince the priest in Caracas to make a detour by way of the Holy Land.

Carlos smiled. He excelled at getting people to do things.

Carlos had the priest on the line that very evening.

The voice on the other end was young, smooth. A pilgrimage to the Holy Land? Juan de Dios, the priest, would like nothing better. But his flock had chosen Jordan.

Carlos put on his velvety voice.

Our Lord was born and suffered in Palestine, not Amman or Petra.

The priest could not agree more. However . . .

Carlos, breathless, waited for him to go on. The priest knew something, he would speak eventually.

"One of our members . . ."

He was hesitating again. How could he speak frankly to a stranger calling him from so far away? But Carlos's silence encouraged him to go on.

"One of our members hates Jews."

"I understand."

"You understand!" murmured the priest, astonished. "But the Vatican . . ."

"We are the *Verus Israel*."

They continued their conversation in hushed tones, whispering. The priest had tested Carlos, evaluating his faith, his political convictions, before asking him for the name of a priest in Latin America who might vouch for him. Carlos had acted as a guide for one once, a rabid anti-Semite, whom he had not attempted to contradict, knowing he might come in useful some day . . . Exactly how, he did not know, but the fact remained that Carlos respected him, in spite of his aversion.

By their fourth call, Juan de Dios had begun to tell Carlos about his parishioner, without ever citing his name or speaking about the past. The man, he said, was in need of spirituality. He knew he did not have long to live, and the Holy Land had become a constant obsession. However, there were all those Jews . . .

At the end of their talk, Carlos promised he would design a very short stay. The group of old age pensioners would have no dealings whatsoever with Israelis. They would lodge with Armenians and Christian Palestinians. Carlos would take care of the logistics – vouchers, guides, transportation and accommodation.

The priest had sounded pleased when he put the phone down. A month later, he called to give his consent. Carlos immediately asked him to forward the list of participants.

The Butcher had agreed to visit Palestine.

"I'm afraid, Carlos."

"I know."

"I don't want to go to pieces."

In silence Carlos observes her pale face, her feverish eyes. He knows only too well that the tremors have begun, that the quake is imminent.

"I'll take you back to the hotel," he says at last.

They go out into the hot street, to the scent of drooping roses; they are losing their leaves, withered by thirst.

DANIEL

That house in Mahane Yehuda was probably the best deal he had ever made.

When he bought that plot of land stuck like a hollow tooth between two loose hovels, the neighbourhood, never popular with young couples, was going to ruin. Given the feverish modernism that had seized the country, everyone was heading for the hills around Jerusalem, going into debt for life to stagnate in some hastily constructed block of flats. They thought they would prosper in those new urban developments, equipped with all the amenities – bathrooms, heating.

Daniel did not mind the fact the market was so near. The shouts of the vendors, the traffic, the drains of dirty water, the flies on the slabs of fish and meat tossed on to displays in the heat of the day – he liked all that. For him, that was the real Jerusalem. The heart of Jerusalem. He had never understood why these small houses seemed so charming to him, with their corrugated iron roofs patched with bits of zinc and scrap metal. A little corner of the shtetl? Perhaps. And yet.

The old people lived between their tiny garden and their synagogue, a library, a soup kitchen, a sculpture studio and a fortune-teller's parlour.

The deceased were taken away at dawn by a volunteer organization, then washed and buried the same day in the cemetery at Givat Shaul.

Daniel managed to convince Ava, and it was no easy matter, to invest their money in what remained of a potter's house.

The gate was rotting, a fig tree had poked through the roof, the three small adjoining rooms were dark, damp and smelly. At the end of the labyrinth a tiny room with a hole dug in the earth and a bucket of stagnant water served as a toilet.

Ava was pregnant with Yona. Her white cotton dress, sprinkled with poppies, was tight over her belly. Her feet in ballet flats, she stepped carefully over the dusty floor.

There was no running water. No electricity. The furniture had disappeared, sold one piece at a time to pay off the creditors.

"Please, Daniel, let's leave now. I can't breathe in here," Ava pleaded.

He did not listen, he was lifting the candle with its flickering flame to discover the vaulted stone ceilings, the walls as thick as fortresses. He would get a building permit, he thought; he could raise it by two more storeys.

The old man, with his parchment face and overripe body, followed them, taking timid steps, his gaze full of hope. He had worked hard in this place, the lead had eaten away at his flesh like a slow poison; his hands had become huge mitts from labouring the clay; his fingers were stiff and deformed, awkward. He dreamed of going to rest his old bones in a retirement home. If he were to stay on in this dilapidated house he would be doomed to join the host of the disinherited who could be seen at twilight scrounging through cardboard crates for whatever fruit and vegetables might still be edible. The old man's drooping mouth, peace to his soul, his hooked nose, the hump in his back . . . Daniel can still picture him standing there before him as if it were yesterday. They had begun to speak about the price when Ava cried out. There at her feet lay the dried carcass of a rat. She had nearly stepped on it.

The pathetic old man had mumbled an apology; the young woman did not hear him.

She was already out in the street, in the sun, struggling to breathe, one hand on her heart. They went back there three more times before making up their minds.

With each visit her aversion grew. The scrawny cats that lurked by the rubbish bins; the wild dogs that skulked along the alleyways of the souk; the noticeboards where black-edged obituaries were pasted one on top of another to dry in the sun until employees from city hall covered them over with electoral campaign posters, pamphlets, or calls to union meetings.

Daniel thought she would never get used to the idea.

Once the deed of sale was signed, Ava banished her repulsion. Yossef Caro Street became a breach in the honeycombed neighbourhood.

Now the deep labyrinth of the old quarter gleams beneath the sky. Captains of industry, bankers and artists have bought up the houses from the old people, obtaining building permits, hiring entrepreneurs from Kiriat Melahi or Haifa who sleep in their vans to be on site at dawn. Cranes, scaffolding, cement mixers have all invaded the area. Their heads protected by yellow hard hats, Palestinian workers picked from the checkpoints at Rafa and Jericho raise walls, lay electrical cables, bore into the earth, install drains, solder, drill, and embellish the maze of tiny streets which, bit by bit, are becoming home to palaces.

His sudden wealth, the house in Mahane Yehuda, his two sons – the apples of his eye – his position at the Tel Aviv Stock Exchange, ought to be enough for him to live his life to the full. He had fought two wars. He had given more to his country than anyone. He had a right to take a rest.

Yes, but.

There was the Abramovitz portrait; his mother had lost her bearings; Elisheva was ashen.

And the genealogical research he had started when Yona was born, his imperious desire to know his family tree and its multiple branchings, had triggered a chain reaction.

When "they" had contacted him, he had needed no persuading.

He had been seething with anger for years. On the list of relatives assassinated by the Nazis he had counted seventy-five people, including his great-grandfather. The tribe thus destroyed – uncles, aunts, cousins, grandparents – had been aged between three and sixty-nine. Thirty-eight people – and he knew their names, ages and professions – were slaughtered in 1941 by the *Einsatzgruppen*.

The others died in the gas chambers.

Daniel took part in two missions.

Both had been carefully prepared. Nothing had been left to chance.

The organization had its tentacles everywhere. Hundreds of individuals spread across the globe, devoted to the same cause. The moment a Nazi was identified and denounced, they began to hunt him down. It was long, difficult and unpleasant, and it could take months. Then one day the signal came. The members of the commando dropped everything, their friends, their work, their families.

Ava knew nothing of these activities. Nor did Amos, his own father.

But Elisheva did. How had she found out? It was a mystery. Or perhaps not. He suspects she may have been the one who recommended him to the organization, praising his discretion, his courage, his readiness for heroic deeds.

He hears the key in the lock. Then the door is shoved open with incredible force and bashes against the wall with a loud bang. That's Yona, thinks Daniel in the depths of his drunkenness. That's Yona coming home from school with his usual refined behaviour. With a flash of lucidity Daniel remembers his dark glasses, his magnificent mirror-lens Ray-Bans, which he forgot in his shirt pocket. Too late. The lenses have already cracked beneath his son's casual Nike step. Now the boy is tossing his school bag on to the tiles, and he has not even noticed the terrible crunching sound beneath his sole.

Yona heads straight for the kitchen, opens the drawers, grunts and says, "I'm hungry. I'm hungry, Ma."

"Just hang on a minute . . . I'll get you something," answers a light voice without an ounce, not an ounce, of reproach.

Daniel tries to sit up to greet Ava with some dignity.

She has paused on the threshold, motionless and tense, sniffing the air, seeking out danger like an animal whose territory has been violated.

"What's going on? Oh my God, oh my God. Yona, come here, Yona. There's a burglar in the house."

Suddenly Ava sees her husband's abandoned shirt and shoes and her cries become more shrill: "Dan? Dan?"

Daniel has managed to get to his feet, tries to smile, and murmurs in a high-pitched voice, "I'm here . . ."

Then he falls flat on his face.

Sprawled on the floor, his eyes on his wife, he moans and stammers, ". . . my darling."

And that is how Ava finds him, lying askew between two armchairs, stripped to the waist, with an utterly stupid expression on his face. Yona has seen him, too, and his eyes light up with a gleam of interest.

Father and son exchange a wink. Daniel loves the look of his kid, his jet-black hair, his coffee-bean eyes, his crooked teeth.

Ava marches over to her husband on her high heels, glares at the bottle of alcohol.

"What is all this?"

"Vodka."

"Vodka?" she says, grabbing the bottle from his hands. "You've been drinking? You?"

"I needed . . . a glass."

"You've drunk the entire bottle!"

"You're exaggerating, as usual," says Daniel, breathlessly, pushing her away. "It's been a long time . . . Very long time I . . . Long time I've been wanting to tell you."

Yona has begun to laugh, in silence. Shit, far out. Dad's drunk and Mum's losing it.

"Have you been having problems? Is that it? Problems at work?"

"No."

"The tax people? Have they sent you some adjustment? They want to confiscate the house?"

"Pfft! Bullshit. I'm spotless. I'm a patriot . . ."

His finger pointing to the ceiling, Daniel adds, dramatically, "I may have cheated now and then . . . But only tiny amounts, Ava, tiny amounts . . ."

The taxman. Daniel cheated on his tax return. And he has the nerve to confess as much, at the top of his voice, with no thought for the consequences. Ava turns around to make sure the door is well and truly closed.

She sees Yona snorting with laughter and she turns pale.

"Get out," she orders. "Go and play outside."

"I want to help you."

"I don't need you. Take your rollerblades and out you go. Do as I say. Right now."

"Mummy," Yona says, "I want to stay."

Ava can only handle one problem at a time. And in any case she has no authority over her younger son, who always does just as he pleases. The only person who has any influence over him is his father. Who for the time being is in no fit state to give orders to anyone.

Her hand in her hair, Ava tries to decide how to deal with the situation. A neighbour could turn up at any minute. People in the neighbourhood enter without knocking. And given the rubbish Daniel is spouting, raising his voice hysterically, they could get themselves into trouble. Ava has always been paranoid. She knows that their lifestyle makes quite a few people envious.

"You have to go and lie down," she says firmly.

She drapes Daniel's arm over her shoulder and tugs her husband towards the stairway.

Ava is a tiny little woman, no taller than a metre sixty. One metre sixty-four exactly, when she wears the dress shoes that Daniel carefully measures before he buys them for her. Because if he has a vice, that is it. He loves giving her high heels, mules, boots, sandals with straps; he has her try them on, he admires her foot, her leg straining with the effort, the way her muscles show. She bursts out laughing whenever she sees a new pair, and she slips them on with an expression somewhere between scorn and amusement. "Yet another pair for the *kalba*!" she says, looking at herself in the mirror. "And I thought our collection was complete." It took them months of negotiation and arguments to come to an agreement: when they went out, Ava would wear only heels that were an acceptable height, four centimetres at the most; her sharp stilettos were reserved for private moments at home, to be worn with airy negligees; her husband – and this is his second weakness – has given her an entire wardrobe of lingerie.

Her back bent, twisting on her heels, Ava tries to shift Daniel's big soft body, but he has only one thought in mind, to take her back to the sofa. She stumbles, narrowly escapes a fall that would have brought him down with her.

"Give me a blow job, darling."

"Shut up. Your son is here."

Daniel gives Yona a wink.

"How are you, son?"

"I'm O.K.," Yona says, laughing.

"School?"

"No problem."

"I'm proud of you. Stay with it."

"Get moving," says Ava again. "Go on! Go on!"

"Don't feel like it."

"Make an effort."

"But since I don't want to! Unless . . ."

It's a nightmare. And with her heels, she will never manage to go even a few feet.

So she takes her shoes off, and Daniel feels himself come down a notch, as if he were in a lift.

"I love you."

"I know."

"I want you."

"Enough," says Ava, indignantly. "Aren't you ashamed?"

"Ashamed of what? Loving you?"

"I didn't say that!"

"Yes you did!" shouts Daniel, stopping short. "Do you have someone else in your life?"

Ava says, "Have you gone mad?" which goes some way towards reassuring him.

"But have you ever cheated on me?"

"Never. Keep moving."

"I could forgive you . . . just tell me, and I'll erase . . ."

"I said, never!"

Daniel hunts for Ava's mouth with his own. She responds to his kiss, but her only thought is to get him to bed as quickly as possible.

What sort of news can have got him in this state?

Who is involved?

His mother? No, his mother lost it a long time ago. Daniel has become resigned to her madness.

Work?

He said no, and she believes him.

Did one of his mates die? A mate with whom he shared the bad days during the war? Perhaps. Yes, that is a possibility. It is plausible. It is the only explanation.

She ventures a question as they reach the stairs. And from one step to the next, breathlessly, struggling, she hoists him up the stairs.

"How is Mordechai doing?"

"He's fine. Just fine. He's finally left his wife."

He had not told her anything about it. She is mortified. How many other secrets has he kept to himself?

"Right. And Ilan?"

"Don't talk to me about that so-and-so."

"Fine, fine. Eleazar?"

"He's doing great. Saw him yesterday."

"Well, well."

"What d'you mean, well, well? Aren't I allowed to have lunch with my best friend?"

So the entire gang is doing great. If his friends are safe and sound, where is the problem?

Ava reaches the first floor landing, with Yona pushing his father from behind. Their bedroom is on the second floor. But she will never have the strength to drag him up there. Never mind. She will put him to bed in one of the boys' rooms. Yona's. She kicks the door open. The boy says: "Where am I supposed to do my homework, then?"

"Downstairs."

"Usually you don't want me to."

"So, for once!"

"All my exercise books are here."

"Yona!" she screams.

She is crimson, sweating, panting.

The room is a terrible mess. Books have fallen from the shelves, toys and clothes litter the carpet.

"Try and help. Clean up this bloody mess."

Yona sets to work, amazed that she has used a swear word. He will have some things to tell his mates tomorrow.

Ava watches him, impatiently, holding Daniel as he sways on his feet and tries to take advantage of the situation.

"You and me, hey," he murmurs lasciviously, "I'm tired of waiting for Shabbat."

He lifts her skirt, kneads her buttocks, and even tries to wiggle his middle finger between her thighs to . . .

"We never have time . . . We're always running like crazy . . ."

"Yona? Hurry up, will you?"

"Mum, I'm doing what I can."

"Faster, or I'll smash everything. I'm warning you, I'll smash your books, your exercise books, your toys. Faster," she shouts.

"Life is short," Daniel says. "Tomorrow we will be old. And we won't have lived our lives to the full . . . I'm mad about you, Ava! You're driving me insane . . ."

She positions her husband by the bed. He crashes with all his weight on to his back, and lies with his arms crossed over his chest. She looks at him, moved – his powerful torso, his golden, downy skin, his entire body completely relaxed there before her now. Daniel surprises her gaze, reaches out, grabs her dress and pulls her on top of him. In front of his son. She manages to get away, rushes over to Yona and shoves him out the door. Then she drives home the bolt, blessing the day her son asked for a proper lock.

Daniel snorts with laughter, gazes at her covetously. The bolt! Ha, ha! The kids won't be able to invade their privacy.

"My love, my love, my love," he croons.

Ava takes a deep breath, rolls up her sleeves, walks over to her husband.

"Now it's just the two of us," she says, in a halting voice. "So, tell me."

Nothing but a snore in response.

Daniel is fast asleep.

RACHEL

As I came into the room, I caught a glimpse of Nurit's hair before I actually saw her. It reaches down to her waist, like a curtain of silk. Thick and black, shining in the light of the torches on the wall that give this café a certain ancient feel.

Bedouin carpets, satin cushions and bolsters brocaded with golden thread cover the benches; the tables are in rough wood and the floor tiles are red flint from Judea.

This is where the city's youth congregate – poets, painters, gifted kids from Jerusalem. The girls wear jodhpurs and leather sandals laced up their ankles, the boys have prophets' beards, linen clothing and khaki haversacks they stole from the army at the end of their service and which they decorate, according to taste, with beads, charms, or felt-tip motifs.

The terrace seems suspended in a void, with a magnificent view overlooking the Sultan's Pool. The four tables out there are taken every night, reserved ahead of time, usually for lovers. But even from the back of the room you can still see the city walls. Grey during the day, washed with an ochre light at nightfall, they block the horizon and in their nest they enclose the Kotel, the Omar mosque, and the Holy Sepulchre. And, in any case, the secret of God.

Avishai, the boss, is passionate about music, the desert and women. Of course he used to try to charm me, but I managed to resist him. I explained to him that I loved his coffee more than his body, and he laughed, scratching his beard beneath his chin. He still tried to feel me up on the sly, pulling me toward him to put his hand on my hip and then trail his fingers along my spine. A real swine. Because I have to confess that his caresses did have an effect on me: I felt such a strong physical thing that I had to move away from him in a hurry.

But tonight Avishai is not there behind the counter.

There is only Esther, his slave, a good girl who puts up with his cheating, his tricks and his lies. He must love her in his way, because he always goes back to her.

She and I kiss each other on the cheek; I ask her how are things. She smiles, wiping a glass.

"Avishai?"

Her sigh is worth a thousand words.

She has lovely eyes, dark and liquid, but the rest of her is pale, as if the ink had faded. Her hair falls in a tangle down her back, her dress is shapeless, too big, and her fingers are tapering and endless. I do not linger.

I cannot stand her zeal and her cowardice. It gives me shivers to see how Esther accepts all Avishai's betrayals without saying a word.

And yet she could easily have her lover by the balls: if she left, the café would close. Avishai is too disorganized to make sure the orders are filled, to run the kitchen and manage the waitresses who work their butts off in the dining room. Most of the time he is off somewhere on the prowl, with some woman, or at the beach.

I make my way stealthily through the room and clap my palms gently over Nurit's eyes. She immediately raises her hands to feel for my face.

The sound of my voice gives her a moment's pause, maybe two, then she cries out, "*Bat zona!* You're back!"

My arms drop to my side.

She turns around and throws her arms around me. We kiss, jump up and down like two schoolgirls. I laugh, but I can see instantly that she has changed: she is wearing make-up and her gaze has grown harder.

I have known Nurit for ever. We played with the same hoops, swam together in the waters of Galilee, hitchhiked through the Sinai; and the image I have kept of her, God knows why, the image that stands out in my memory is her smile on a beach at Dahab. She is standing in the sea, her hair spread all around her like a black slick on

94

the water, and she is calling and waving to me. She is alone and isolated and she is calling, then she turns toward the open sea and moves away in the direction of Aqaba.

"You could have told me you were coming . . . Phoned or written . . . God, you're cruel."

I light a cigarette, exhale, step away for a second to fetch an ashtray.

"You look exhausted."

"I've just come from rehearsal."

"Are you giving a concert? With Elisheva?"

I nod, my eyes glued to the book forgotten on the table. *Essay on Mental Illness*.

"Who's conducting?"

"Haim Newman."

"They say he's very demanding."

"I'll say." My mind flashes back to the difficult hours at rehearsal. "Let's not go there. Your diploma? Did you get it?"

"I passed, yes."

"Have you found a job?"

"Yes, ma'am!"

We laugh again, for no reason, for the fun of it. We look at each other, trying to guess the thoughts we would share with no-one, not even the moon.

Esther comes to take the order: a cappuccino for Nurit, mint tea for me.

"Fill me in," she says.

"Let me start! Are you married?"

"No."

"Are you still with . . . ?"

A shadow passes over her face and I am filled with anguish. When I left, she was more or less engaged to this pretty spineless guy, but he was good at calming her when she went to see him, all out of sorts after the mental cases she had had to deal with.

"We split up. Two months before the wedding."

"Why?"

"All the wrong reasons: the pressure of the midterm exams, our families were opposed, money worries."

"And now?"

"He's got some passionate thing with a divorced woman in Tel Aviv, the mother of twins."

"But you, what about you?"

"No time to think about it. I work too hard."

"Do you still love him?"

"The heart is a muscle. If you don't use it, it gets weak."

What the hell did she mean by this dumb-ass answer? The sort of thing a fifty-year-old woman might say. And Nurit is twenty-four!

I examine her carefully, focusing on her expression, the inflexion of her voice. Nothing filters through. This girl protects herself with a steel shell. No way to find a breach in her armour.

I placed my hand on her head and smoothed her hair.

"I'm sorry."

"You shouldn't have left, Rachel."

"Why? Would you have stayed with him?"

"No," she says. "No."

Esther brings our drinks and a game of dominoes.

A game? When we have so much to say to each other? It's so absurd that we burst into uncontrollable fits of laughter. The room is filling, people come in and see us there doubled over, hanging on to each other just to stay on our seats. Someone says in a mocking voice, "*Sababa*, girls!" which sends us off into another fit until Nurit has to run to the toilets to keep from pissing herself.

I stay where I am, laughing to myself. I feel ashamed, as if I had been drinking. I sip my tea, avoiding the gazes of the people eyeing me, amused by my mirth. I do not dare look at the dominoes; I am afraid I will seem ridiculous if I start laughing on my own; then the laughter vanishes the way it came.

Nurit eventually comes back to join me, her mouth hidden

96

behind her hand. We begin talking about our friends and our teachers. She tells me that Raphaël died in a car accident; Merav committed suicide – he had simply lost it, who, what for, God knows! He was found in a pool of blood in his parents' kitchen, his wrists slashed with a razor.

"And you?" she says finally.

Just as I am about to reply, the walls of the Old City are illuminated. A crescent moon rolls into the sky like a celestial chariot. Finally I hear it, the music of Jerusalem, the city I have been watching all day long. With my eyes glued to the ramparts I wonder how sound is related to light, and why I feel reborn.

"Tell me about yourself, Rachel."

I smile, embarrassed. My memory is a void. If Nurit had questioned me five minutes earlier, I would have answered with a rush of words about my expectations, my studio in New York, my friends, my lovers . . . But the more I gaze at the ramparts, the cypress trees, the cubes of Arab houses scattered like Lego across the hills, the more I realize that, in a way, I am drained of words.

Nurit drinks her cappuccino. When she puts her cup back down on the table, I notice the line of froth along her lips, and I wipe it with a smile.

Our table has suddenly filled up, girls and boys, all former students of Elisheva's. Our group is constantly expanding and Esther brings more tables over.

I am delighted to see Elena and Tamar again; I kiss them. Elena's face breathes intelligence. She is blonde, very Slavic, and her good looks have made her very popular. She is not even twenty-five and she already has a Ph.D. in political science. I have always been jealous of her; I used to try to imitate the way she walks, her accent, her taste in clothes. As adolescents we were rivals, and I am not sure the competition is altogether over.

"I'm getting married at the end of the year!"

I congratulate her, but I feel an obscure pain in my belly – an unpleasant shock, a sadness so abrupt I could cry – as she begins to sing the praises of her fiancé. A marvellous young man, of course; a penniless student.

She shows us his photograph. I look closely at the falcon-like face staring smugly at the lens.

"Not bad," I say reticently.

"And you? Are you with someone?"

"Nothing serious."

"New York's not Israel . . . If we're not hooked up five years from now, we'll end up single."

Marriage is an obsession with women in this part of the world, whether they are Jewish or Arab. The Arab women are married off by their parents, practically by force. The Israeli women may be liberated and have their stripes from the army and occupy influential positions in civilian life, yet all they can think about is getting their lovers to make their affair official.

I turn to Tamar, her absolute opposite, a sort of belated hippie, with her rings and body piercing and gipsy skirts, and her layers of necklaces down her bodice. She comes from a modest family, Yemenites who have a souvenir shop near the Tahana Hamerkazit.

Her skin is like bronze, her hair is frizzy, her eyes are very dark beneath long eyebrows that extend to her temples. She speaks very quickly, waving her hands.

Tamar tells me she has opened a jewellery shop in a small street in the souk: intrigued, I look at the chains around her neck as if she were advertising her own shop.

"That's a lovely pendant," I say, lifting a blue heart dangling from a simple chain.

"Lapis lazuli. Someone brought it to me from Afghanistan, with . . ."

Tamar lowers her voice, and adds, ". . . you know what . . ."

Miming, she lifts two fingers to her lips.

"When are you going to stop getting high?" says Nurit with a smile.

"In Yemen we chew *khat*. Who'll come with me to Yemen to buy a kilo?"

We laugh, of course, at the idea of crossing the Israeli border with a cargo like that. Amidst our peals of laughter Tamar adds that we could tell the customs officers it is vine leaves. For stuffing with rice.

Then Michael and Gabriel arrive, wearing threadbare shorts, wrinkled short-sleeved shirts, their army satchels slung over their shoulders and filled with books.

They kiss my hair and say, "How's things?" as if they had seen me only yesterday, then they collapse on their chairs, legs spread.

We raise a first toast to talent, a second one to Elena's wedding, and Michael's eyes close for just a second too long. Tamar says that Gabriel, too, has something to celebrate. Everyone shouts, "What? What?"

Gabriel whistles under his breath, undecided, then he tells us he has bought a plot of land near Eilat. He wants to build a motel for ecologists. In his deep, measured voice he explains that Eilat, thanks to the peace agreement signed with Egypt, has become a free trade zone which will attract tourists from all over the world. I think of my brother Avner and the agricultural field station he has always dreamt of creating in the middle of the desert. That is the project he should be working on, instead of schlepping crates of tomatoes around in clapped-out trucks.

Everyone thinks it is a great idea. Gabriel protests, saying it is still in the early stages; to develop it, he is waiting to find out how much the government subsidy for setting up a business in the desert will be.

"You need some personal funds, too, right?"

"Yes," says Gabriel, blushing.

There is a moment of silence.

Gabriel's father has shares in the Élite company, and all through childhood we added to his wealth with our appetite for his cakes, chocolate, ice cream and sweets. There were rumours that his father was not just the manager, but the big boss, but Gabriel always claimed he was not, that the primary investors were American Jews. With or without a subsidy, Gabriel has the wherewithal to start his business.

"Kibbutzim are kaput," murmurs Michael.

Everyone turns to stare at him.

"Why do you say that? What made you think of that? Dammit! What does that have to do with Gabriel's project?" says Elena, intrigued.

"In the old days, the kibbutz was where you went when you loved nature . . . Now all the old structures are crumbling . . ."

"And so is our group," says Tamar, quick as a flash. "We've scattered in every direction."

"I'm still here," protests Nurit. "And what about you, Michael, do you think you'll leave?"

Michael peers over at Elena before announcing that he is going to Ethiopia.

We immediately bombard him with questions:

"Have you planned your trip?"

"Do you know anyone there?"

"The Falasha come here and you go there. Are you on a mission for Mossad?"

Time is flying by. The café has filled up, voices echo loudly amidst the clatter of dishes. Esther brings a new round of drinks and we did not even have to ask.

I feel good. As if I were safe.

DANIEL

The shells whistle as they rise skyward, turn, spin, and explode in multicoloured filaments. The Beqaa Valley is a stream of light and fire. As the tank advances the night is torn open, and the soldiers peer out, following the ballet of the fighter planes.

A rocket comes towards them, long and straight as an arrow.

Death is there, with its bloody lips and purple eyes. Death . . .

Daniel sits up, his hands outstretched, his mouth open on a shout. He meets only silence and the darkness of the room.

He is at home. Safe. It was just a dream. One more dream where he was about to die. A night will come when his heart pounding in his throat will leave him behind in the valley for ever.

He takes deep, deliberate breaths to forget about the pain throbbing in his temples. He sits on the edge of the bed, aching and exhausted.

What time is it? What day?

He stands up, crashes into the furniture, swears.

The door is slightly ajar, he can hear voices, but no laughter. Daniel goes down a few steps, leans over the banister, looks down through the stairwell.

Eight people sitting in the dining room, festive with coloured balloons, golden garlands and a huge white banner proclaiming, "I'm ten years old!" in red felt-tip letters. Ava, their two sons, David's best friend Jeremy, and the four grandparents.

The cake has been cut. The guests have been wolfing it down, scraping up the last crumbs.

David looks up and sees his father.

Then Ava turns and sees him: he is perched on the top step, bare-chested, acting the clown to cheer up their son.

All eyes converge on Daniel and there are bursts of applause.

"Ah, there he is!"

"About time."

"Hi," says Amos, Daniel's father, in his deep voice.

Legs outstretched and ankles crossed, Armand, Ava's father, leans back in his chair and slips his thumbs into the armholes of his waistcoat.

Daniel goes over to David, picks him up by the waist, lifts him up like a feather to his lips. The child complies, stubborn and sullen, to hide his pain.

"Is that any way to greet your father? Give me a kiss!"

David wiggles his legs to break free.

"Let me go!"

Daniel knows his eldest boy. A stocky child with puffy features and red hair, he is withdrawn, silent and resentful.

Daniel adores the kid, but does not know how to deal with him.

With Yona things are easy, fun, relaxed.

With David, every word, every gesture could lead to a scene. No matter what they do, the boy always thinks that his brother gets more of everything, and that they do not love him as much.

Which is absolutely untrue. Daniel is convinced that he is sharing his love equally between his two sons.

But here is the rub.

Yona is eloquent and quick, a little elf with a gift for charming adults, parents, friends and teachers.

David is glum and awkward; grown-ups do not listen to him. The child has spoken so often into a void that now he has finally fallen silent.

David has friends, to be sure, but he has chosen them among the bad elements at school, the losers and troublemakers; it is as if he were trying to draw on their strength just to exist.

"Happy birthday, son."

"You're never there. You couldn't even show up for my party."

"I fell asleep."

"You got drunk. Yona told me."

Daniel casts a menacing look at his younger son and says, "We have to talk."

In the room there is total silence. Daniel hugs David, wedges his head in his arm and drags him off to the living room, closing the door behind him.

Then he lets him go.

"I have worries. But I love you."

His cheeks wet with tears, the boy clenches his fists and looks away.

Daniel ruffles his hair.

"You're a man now. Stop that."

David does not look at him. Daniel's broad hand feels good, he could purr with contentment. He would like that hand to stay right there, so he does not move, not an eyelash, not a toe, the better to savour the thrill of it.

But all too soon, discouraged by his silence, the hand pulls away.

"Your mother wanted to give you a present. I was against the idea. At your age you should get money."

Daniel pulls out a wad of notes, counts out four bills of a hundred shekels each and slips them into David's pocket.

"Go and buy something you like!"

"Thank you," David says half-heartedly.

"Aren't you pleased?"

"Yes, I am."

Daniel has a headache. He hates conflict and needs to be admired.

"Why don't we go and have supper at the Kurd's place? Just you and me?"

Suddenly the door opens and Ava interrupts.

"This is no behaviour when you have guests."

"Just one more minute," says Daniel, who senses his son is slipping away from him.

"The kids have school tomorrow. They mustn't go to bed late."

She walks over, holding out a clean shirt and a glass where two effervescent tablets have nearly dissolved.

David uses the opportunity to run off.

"Couldn't you wait?" grumbles Daniel.

"What have I been doing all evening? Shit!"

They glare at each other. Daniel relents, saying, "You should have woken me up."

"Right. It's all my fault."

"That's not what I meant."

"I'm sick and tired of all your mysteries."

"Ava," sighs Daniel.

He puts on his shirt, reaches instinctively for the pocket.

"Don't bother. They're in a million pieces," says Ava. She hands him the glass and says, "You look downright scary."

The evening ends as it should have begun.

Ava has given Daniel his piece of the chocolate cake. Daniel asks for a candle. He shoves it into the wedge of cake, strikes a match, lights the wick and asks David to blow out the flame. David does not move. All the guests clap their hands, shouting his name.

"Da-vid! Da-vid! Da-vid!"

David needs coaxing. Then, shyly, he gets up from his chair and goes over to his father. Daniel hugs the boy closer.

"Da-vid! Da-vid! Da-vid!" they chant.

Daniel asks for silence. They all stop speaking.

"In Hebrew," says Daniel, "the number ten is represented by a yod. The yod is a great flame. This isn't a candle on this slice of cake, it's a yod. It's the number ten. Go ahead, son, blow it out."

David leans closer, holding his breath. He puffs up his cheeks and turns to his father, who is acting the clown. David bursts out laughing.

"Start again," Daniel encourages him. "No, wait, wait. Yona, turn off the light, please."

Yona does as he is asked.

The only light in the dining room is the flame of the candle, projecting shadows against the wall, of the grandparents, Ava, Jeremy and Yona.

David is over the moon and forgets to be sad. He blows on the candle. The flame goes out. Yona switches on the light.

Everyone gets up and goes to embrace the child, who is still hugging his father.

Daniel keeps David at his side, and when they all go to sit down again, he tells them about the day his son was born, how he waited for him, how many cigarettes he smoked, the nurse who was so tough with him.

He even imitates her voice: "'You're polluting the atmosphere. There are newborn babies and young mothers in here. Out, out.'"

"What did you do?"

"I tried to make myself as inconspicuous as possible. I said, sorry, sorry, good day to you, madam."

"I remember her," Ava says. "She had a hair on her chin."

"You're being too kind, Ava. That nurse had a beard. And the eyes of a werewolf."

"Really?" says Amos, playing along.

Daniel sits up in his chair, puffs out his chest and imitates the shrew: "She was formidable. She would sway her hips in front of me, with her huge chest" – the children burst out laughing – "and her enormous hips" – more laughter – "and her legs as thick as roof-beams" – peals of laughter.

Daniel collapses on to his chair and pulls his son closer.

"And then?" murmurs Yona, jealous.

"Then," says Daniel, "just as I was about to go out, I heard a cry. One long, lone cry. *Waaah*. And that cry was my own, in miniature. You know that cry, kids, when I'm angry. Well, when David was born, he let out my own cry, but it was weaker, of course, because I'm the father and he's only the son. And that cry struck the nurse, and she fainted away with terror. I stepped over her body and rushed back into the room. You had just been born, David, and you were magni-ficent. Your face was all red, and you were clenching your fists. Completely naked."

"I forgot to wear underpants?"

"Exactly. I'll never forget. Ever. I had given a king to Israel. King David."

The grandparents applaud. Jeremy shakes his head, terribly moved. Yona is biting his lips with vexation.

Daniel raises his fist and adds, "After the king, I needed a prophet. Ladies and gentlemen, allow me to introduce my second creation: Yona."

Ava declares that it is time to go and get some sleep. The boys protest: "Just one more minute ..."

But Ava will not budge.

Jeremy slips away. He lives on the same street and does not need to be seen home.

David and Yona kiss their grandparents and start heading up the stairs.

David's eyes are shining, his cheeks are red. He stares at his father and pats the pocket containing his four hundred shekels.

Daniel responds with a grave nod of his head.

RACHEL

We had been talking about the choices we have made in life when suddenly a deadly silence fell all around me. I looked at my friends, at their faces. They were petrified, as if they had seen the devil. I understood I was lost even before I turned around.

Eytan.

Standing on the threshold, leaning against the door, talking with a soldier.

My heart exploded like a bomb. The blood froze in my veins, my reason dissolved. I could not breathe. I could not think straight. The room began to spin in a blaze of lights and I was the eye, the centre, the tidal wave.

I think I nearly passed out, I think I may even have lost consciousness.

Eytan.

Eytan, my god.

All those years I had spent away, all the men I had kissed, embraced, all for nothing? To obtain only a thin film of forgetfulness, and can you even say there has been forgetfulness when pain and desire are still this intense and resonant?

When everything becomes raw again . . . eyes gazing, hands that cannot touch, breasts rising, so long bereft of caresses?

I was bleeding, just like before.

Eytan.

A fiasco lasting five years; a futile waste. It had never been anything else, just waiting. There, deep inside, deep in the place where I thought I might find my own self, in the end there had been nothing but mute, stubborn patience.

Eytan must have known I was looking at him. He moved his head. And the moment his eyes met mine, I understood that I had resolved nothing, that the equation was intact, insoluble.

I saw his eyes narrow. I thought, he's going to ignore me, he'll act as if I don't exist, and in a few moments he'll leave.

And I was hoping the opposite. With all the eagerness I used to have. With all the power of a damaged love.

Eytan.

My love had awoken, it was stretching, rising, huge, immense, like some angry giant laughing in my face, about to crush everything. Eytan's eyes, his smile, his skin, the dimple in his cheek, the mole at the base of his throat. And his voice, his laughter, the way he moved his hand, the way he ate, walked, all his gestures down to the most insignificant ones rushed up to me to subjugate me. Every dam, every dyke gave way. My heart was pounding, then it stopped beating, then it was beating too quickly, then it stopped again. I do not know how long it lasted, a minute, an instant, eternity. We were gazing at each other like two damned souls.

The people around me became shadows, the sounds in the room receded, the lights went out. I have dreamt of you so much and slept so little, my love, my love. I have spoken to you in my dreams, in my waking hours, when I was walking and composing my music; never for an instant did I let go of the thread joining me to you. I have remained faithful to you in spite of silence, in spite of distance. In spite of lovers.

Eytan left the soldier and began to walk toward us. I stood up like a zombie and all I could see before my eyes was the colour white, the white of his shirt, with its top buttons open, the white of his linen trousers, the white of the wall.

"Rachel!"

He had not changed. Still slim, tanned, his hair cut short, that powerful jaw.

"When did you arrive?"

A broken voice, not mine, answered, "Hello."

"Eytan, get out of here," said Nurit, coming between us.

He did not even pause to think. He took me by the scruff of the neck and shoved me into a corner of the room. I found myself blocked against a wall, so close to him that I could feel his breath; and when at last I dared to look up and managed to meet his eyes I understood that I was falling into him as if into a well.

Nurit tried again to separate us. She slipped between us and shook me to break the spell.

"Rachel, sweetie, come."

"In a minute."

"No, now!"

Eytan's hand fell on Nurit's shoulder. He shoved her away.

"Nurit, leave us alone. Don't get involved in this, alright?"

"Yes, leave us, I'm coming," I said, unable to take my eyes from Eytan's. I gazed at him and felt myself filling with delight, as if I had crossed a desert and I was able at last to stop by a stream of water.

Nurit gave a weary wave of her hand.

"You're crazy!"

"Three days," said Eytan, still smiling at me, and every one of his gazes was a caress. "Three days, that's some sort of joke."

"How are you?"

He shrugged.

"I'm fine," he said. "Now that I see you."

"You are expecting a child?"

"Yes."

"A boy or a girl?"

My voice was scarcely a murmur.

"I don't know. Liora didn't want to find out the sex of the baby."

"Bravo."

"Fatherhood is still too abstract for me. I don't get it, I don't know where I am. I'm afraid I'll be useless . . ."

"When's the due date?"

"In a few weeks."

He grabbed my wrists and we sat down across from each other. My friends sat silently at their table, looking over worriedly. I would have liked to have been able to reassure them: I do not love him any more, I have forgotten him, don't worry about a thing.

"How's the music going?"

"It depends on the day!"

"Are you successful?"

"Not yet."

"You haven't got your name up in lights?"

"No," I said with a laugh. "No, I'm afraid not."

"Are you happy?"

"I don't know. And you?"

"I don't ask myself that question. I live my life, that's all."

I looked at his chin, the dimple I loved to kiss. Did his wife put her lips there with the same fever? Could I allow myself to kiss him there, one more time? I did not want my lips to touch his mouth, just a kiss on his chin.

"Your life in New York?"

The space around us became stable again; faces emerged from the smoke.

"What did you say?"

"How are you getting on in New York?"

"It's tough."

He laughed.

"Well then, come back."

"To do what?"

"We could see each other."

"What the hell are you saying? You have a family now."

"Yes, that's true. I have a family," he said, as if he were realizing the extent of the problem for the first time. "I have a family, but . . ."

I knew what he was going to say, and I silenced him. What had happened to us once upon a time, and had brought us together, no longer existed. I got to my feet.

"I have to go."

"What? Already?"

"The others are waiting."

"And me? I don't matter any more?"

"Yes, but . . ."

"I have so many things to tell you!"

"What's the point, Eytan? We'd be talking in a void."

"I've been living in a void since you left. It's your absence."

"You have to move on."

"Rachel!"

I looked down: his fingers were circling my wrists. I had loved his sun-dark colour against my pale skin. And what if I were to stay with him, until the end of time? Then I saw the gold ring on his finger and I came back to reality.

"Which hotel are you staying at?"

"It's impossible, Eytan."

His voice broke as he said, "I'm not asking for a lot! Just to talk a little!"

"You're wasting your time."

He opened his fingers and let me go, as if I had been a butterfly or a bird in his hands.

I walked away without saying goodbye.

I sat down again between Nurit and Tamar.

"I'm going to go back to the hotel. I'm tired . . . I haven't stopped all day."

"What does he want?" said Nurit.

"Nothing!"

"Rachel," said Nurit, "stay away from Eytan . . . Liora is a great girl."

"She has nothing to be afraid of."

"Their relationship is fragile. And you know it."

"I'm not about to destroy their marriage in five minutes."

"Five minutes with you are worth a century with Liora."

"Nurit, you're starting to piss me off."

Elena interrupted: "Nurit is only trying to protect you. If she didn't love you . . ."

"Shit, are you retarded or what?" Nurit said. "What do you expect? What are you hoping for?"

"What am I supposed to do? Never come back to Jerusalem?"

"Maybe!"

"You haven't cut the cord," said Tamar.

"You're wrong!" I grimaced, and I knew my face was so pale it was frightening.

I stood up. I threw some notes on to the table. Gabriel put them back in my pocket.

"This is my round."

"I'll pay the next one," said Michael. "Sit down."

I relented, even though all I really wanted was to be alone, to wander aimlessly through the streets and try to lose myself by finding Eytan.

"You want a smoke?" offered Tamar, pulling out a joint.

"No."

"Just a puff, to decompress."

"I'd rather drink . . . something strong . . ."

"Well, I want a whisky," said Elena.

Esther brought over a bottle, an ice bucket and a tray of glasses. We helped ourselves. The alcohol went quickly to our heads, and the conversation became animated. Someone, I cannot remember who, Michael or Elena, began talking about politics. The discussion became heated, as they shouted and argued.

Our group is united by our shared childhood, the games we used to play, and our trips through the country, but politically we are diverse: Elena and Michael are militants with Peace Now, Gabriel and Nurit are for a strong Israel, Tamar does not care. Ten years from now, no doubt, our political convictions will have driven us apart. But for the time being our friendship is surviving everything.

I drank my whisky, feeling estranged from their voices, over-excited by alcohol and despair. I know the impossible dilemma inside out: Israel, Palestine, blood calling for more blood. All I could think of was Eytan. The way he had looked at me, the few words he had said, words resonant with desire.

Tamar went out on to the terrace to smoke. I followed her. The wind blew her dress. We put our arms around each other's waists and admired the sky. On the road below us the cars' headlights twinkled endlessly. There was a thin sliver of moon, but all the hills were bathed in a golden oil.

Tamar told me she missed the days when we used to go out exploring the country, scrambling down ravines, carried away by the sheer weight of our backpacks.

"Do you remember?"

"It's what keeps me on my feet."

One time in the desert of Judea we were caught in a rainstorm. In a split second the dried wadis filled with water and we would have drowned if it had not been for Eytan. He helped us hurry up a steep slope, and we turned to look back at the mad swirl of mud as it rushed after two ibexes, driving bushes and rocks before it, uprooting the acacias.

Tamar went to sit on the rampart. Below her, the void. She

stretched, her figure slim and elegant. I could see her fragile collar-bone beneath her dress.

She handed me her cigarette.

Time came to a standstill.

Tamar was talking. I nodded, I had fallen into complete oblivion. My drunkenness engulfed my distress and everything around it, my father, Eytan, the music.

Tamar began to walk along the rampart, her arms outstretched, placing one foot cautiously in front of the other.

"I'm so light," she murmured.

I was laughing, absurdly.

Michael came over. He grabbed Tamar by the waist and set her back down on the ground like a little cat.

"Rachel!" he said, his gaze full of reproach.

"That's me."

"Sit down and don't move. And you, Tamar, behave."

"He's afraid I'll end up in the ravine," said Tamar with a giggle.

"Take a deep breath."

"Some day I'll get my momentum and I'll take off and fly."

"Would you calm down?"

"I'm an eagle with powerful wings. The wind will take me away."

"Put my jacket on. It's cold."

"Leave me alone, Michael," she said, struggling to free herself from his grasp.

"When I finish getting some clothes on you."

"There's nothing you can do against two women," I said with a laugh.

Michael held Tamar and she wriggled like a liana in his arms, her eyes never leaving mine. He was afraid I might do something rash, because of Eytan. But I could not move. My head was wobbling. It was so heavy, my head. And the ground was so soft. I sank into it.

Our friends came out, surprised by our absence. They saw the three of us and understood the situation was urgent.

Gabriel took care of me.

"Can you walk, or shall I carry you?"

"I am going to tell you a secret. Can you keep a secret?"

"Get up, Rachel, stop acting like a child."

He lifted me up, and my legs were so weak I fell to the ground again.

"Slap her face," advised Elena.

"If anyone touches me, they'll be in trouble!"

Then everything went black. When I regained consciousness, I was walking down the middle of the road, leaning on Gabriel. I heard myself talking about the mist and the Goldberg Variations, about Jerusalem and Elisheva. About the concert I had not prepared. About New York. And all of it in a jumble, in a halting, ugly, shrill voice. I hated myself, but I could not help it. And before long I began to laugh and cry at the same time.

"What shall we do?" asked Nurit.

"Get a taxi."

"We can't take her back to her parents' in this state."

"Can you put her up?"

"If need be."

"I want to go back to the hotel."

"Later, sweetheart."

It was no later than ten in the evening, but the streets were deserted, as if the authorities had declared a curfew. In spite of its theatres, cinemas and cabarets, Jerusalem has all the restraints of a provincial town.

Tamar slipped out of Michael's grasp. She jumped on to the hood of a car. Then leapt to the car's roof, where she began to dance and sing an old Yemenite song. Her jewellery tinkled like bells.

DANIEL

The adults are alone now amidst the balloons and the garlands, and silence falls.

Normally, the four elderly people would get up and go home. It is past their usual bedtime. But they think that Daniel owes them an explanation so they are waiting, not taking their eyes off him.

Except that Daniel does not feel like sharing his story.

At a push, he could tell his father . . . he had transported arms, had fought in the Haganah. He would know how to keep quiet.

But he cannot trust Armand at all, he is a regular chatterbox.

Daniel loves Armand's daughter, but the man himself is incredibly pretentious, he talks too loud, bangs his fist, acts important and always finds ways to make himself look good. Daniel has nicknamed him "As for Me", without telling Ava, she would not like it one bit.

"You rescued the situation, but only just," Armand is saying now, smoothing the tablecloth with the palm of his hand. "Your son was really unhappy. We didn't know how to console him. As for me . . ."

"I know," says Daniel, suddenly finding the word to characterize Armand: he is overbearing.

Although Armand has just poured himself a glass of wine, Daniel goes over to the coat rack to fetch the old man's hat and anorak.

A rather sudden leave-taking. The erstwhile engineer is speechless, he frowns, and Daniel suddenly notices that the old man's face, oddly enough, is shaped like a light bulb. His hand trembling, Armand sets his glass down, and splashes wine on to the tablecloth.

"Where's the salt?" says Emma.

Salt? Does she not understand, the idiot, that they have been asked to leave?

No need to tell Armand twice. Annoyed, the old man springs to his feet.

"Get up, Emma!"

Leaning over the stain, Emma continues to pour salt on to the table.

"Are you deaf? I said, we're leaving."

"Don't be cross, Armand."

The salt has turned pink, the wine is nearly all absorbed. Emma smiles and leaves the table.

"We've saved the tablecloth."

She is his exact opposite. Devoted, silent, she goes to pieces, shrinking in his presence like a terrified chick. Whenever he needles her, she defends herself with a shrill laugh, waving her hand, "Oh, just listen to you!" to excuse him in front of others, to save him even when he is trampling all over her.

Sometimes she listens, her face white as chalk, to the rubbish he spouts, anecdotes where she is always made to look bad – the stupid, ignorant woman, the naïve housewife who cannot leave her kitchen without getting completely lost in the outside world.

She may not have had the good fortune to study, as he did, but what she does know how to do, she does well. Her kitchen is a little laboratory, sparkling with cleanliness, and she cooks, grills and roasts absolute marvels. There is no-one like her for salting food, simmering stews, or making honey cakes whose recipes were lost with exile.

Ava comes into the room with a tray of coffee and stops short, surprised.

"Are you leaving?"

Armand runs his forefinger over his neck above his shirt collar. He would love to say something nasty at his son-in-law's expense, but Amos, who is cleaning his fingernails with a piece of cardboard, directs his heavy, imposing gaze at him, warning him to be careful. Don't mess with my son, don't start a war between our kids, says Amos's silent threat.

Brought to heel, all Armand can do is shove his chair noisily against the table.

"Rub that spot tomorrow. Not before," warns Emma.

"What spot?"

"And be sure you don't use any bleach. It makes the cotton go yellow."

Ava suddenly understands. A tender smile comes to her lips.

"Mum, thanks for everything."

"Oh, my girl, what have I done? Not a thing!"

The words tremble in Emma's throat; her husband is hurrying her.

"Stop talking. You always find something to say. Come on, you can call your daughter tomorrow. That's all you do from morning to night."

Daniel opens the door, breathes in the cool wind that is whirling scraps of paper along the street.

Barefoot, in his shirtsleeves, he takes a few steps outside. The pavement is freezing. He shivers, filled with nausea. Vodka, chocolate cake, the cold pavement, all twisting his guts. He bends over, feeling sick with drunkenness and cold.

Ava kisses her mother, smoothes the fake fur collar of her coat.

"Cover up. Don't catch cold."

"My coat is warm, you know."

"Can you see them out to their car?" asks Ava, without looking at Daniel.

"Don't disturb *your* husband," says Armand, perfidious.

There it is. He has had his nasty jibe. At least he will not have it still bottled up inside on the way home, because he is bound to start ranting about his son-in-law, what a *sabra* he is, rude, aggressive and badly brought up.

"If only it would rain," says Daniel, peering at the stars, ignoring Armand's remark.

The two old people walk away side by side into the soft, white fog.

"He didn't even have a word of thanks for our gift. Did you hear him say thank you? I didn't!" says Armand indignantly.

"He was polite enough, calm down, Armand. It's bad for you."

"Polite? A drunk! My daughter is with a drunk!"

Ava goes back in, Daniel follows her and leaves the door open on to the night and the wind.

"What got into you?" says Ava reproachfully. "Making them leave like that."

"It's midnight."

"That's no reason."

"I'm tired."

He is wan. And he has to put his hand against the wall to keep from falling.

She has a moment of remorse, despite her annoyance.

"You're feverish," she declares, placing her hand on his brow. "Go and rest. I'll clean up on my own."

"I'll help you, you've been at it all evening."

He has forgotten about his parents. Now he sees them, side by side in the middle of the hall.

His mother stands there limply. With her silver hair, curled with an iron, and her fine porcelain skin, she looks like a precious, elderly doll.

Amos has arranged her thick blue woollen scarf around her neck, buttoned up her black coat, and slipped her little velvet bag on to her arm. Daniel is surprised to find that he envies Katya's indifference. The feverish years, when her life was a constant turmoil of too much activity, are now mere memory. A doctor has prescribed anti-depressants. She no longer speaks, or only rarely. She has escaped into a world where no-one can reach her. She does not even look at the Abramovitz painting. Who? she would say, in a distracted voice. Who, how, yes, are the rare words she still murmurs, her eyes staring into space, a smile on her lips.

His father has become a hunched little man, serene yet exhausted by a fatigue that never leaves him.

He does everything, the cooking, the cleaning, the shopping, the nursing.

He no longer has the time to meet his friends at the café to play cards.

He is afraid to leave Katya alone even for an instant. One time he came back to their flat in Rehavia and she was not there. He called the police. They found her in a square, twenty streets further along, in her nightgown, surrounded by a gang of dumbstruck adolescents. She was speaking to them in Yiddish, in a slow, ceremonious voice. Another time she turned on the gas. Enough to blow up the whole building. His father replaced the cooker with a new electric one. He puts appliances away as soon as he has finished with them, he locks all the drawers, not a single sharp object is left out.

"You can't manage on your own, Dad," says Daniel. He puts on his shoes, grabs a jacket. His head is spinning again, his vision blurring, his legs are wobbly.

"Go to bed," says Ava. "You can hardly stand up."

"Listen to your wife," insists Amos.

"Let's get going, Dad," says Daniel. He turns to Ava, waiting tensely. "I'll be right back."

They settle Katya into the passenger seat, fasten her seatbelt and slam the door. She let them, docile, murmuring, as obedient as a little girl. Now with her palms flat on her bag, and her eyes fixed on the luminous halo of the street lamp, she waits.

Father and son look at each other. The car is parked by the open space where the market is held, a long empty lane, the heart of Jerusalem where the poorest people come to buy their food to the concert of vendors' cries. On either side of the lane the shops are sealed tight with iron shutters. At this time of night, there is only a dim light in the alley, a garland of coloured bulbs, to save on electricity. The road sweepers have not yet come through. There is the smell of rotting fish and vegetables, of cats and urine.

"Is there anything I can do?" says Amos at last.

"No."

"Do you need any money?"

Daniel is quick to smile.

"Thank God, no."

"What happened this afternoon?"

"Nothing! I just had too much."

"That's not like you."

His father scratches his cheek and Daniel can hear the sound of his nail against the coarse white growth. He shaved that morning, and again in the afternoon, but it has already grown back, his beard grows at an incredible speed. Katya used to say, with her Russian accent, "Three days without a razor and your father turns into a yeti. When I met him at the kibbutz he was nothing but a ball of fur armed with a gun and two squirrel's eyes." And she would get out her proof: dozens of black-and-white photographs piled loosely in a shoebox, where Amos adopts a pose, with the wild hair and beard of a revolutionary.

Daniel has inherited the same tendency, as has Yona.

"I don't want to interfere in your marriage. Ava is a fine woman ..."

"Dad!"

His voice heavy with wine and fatigue, the old man continues, "Between a man and a woman, there are ups and downs. It's not rosy every day. It can't be. And you have two children. Family is important."

"Dad, you're mistaken ..."

Amos pulls out a checked handkerchief, buries his nose in it, makes a trumpeting sound to hide his emotion.

"I saw Elisheva today," says Daniel, and suddenly feels he is ridding himself of a weight.

"Elisheva?" repeats Amos, blinking in surprise. "What does that have to do with this afternoon?"

"I gave her a revolver."

"What?"

Amos loses his balance. Daniel reaches out to catch him, but fortunately the Renault stops the old man's fall.

"I'm O.K., I'm O.K. . . . I just stumbled."

Amos leans against the door, waxen, his forehead pearling with sweat.

"Does she want to commit suicide?"

"Not at all."

"A revolver . . . ! What for?"

"The Butcher is coming to Jerusalem."

"How can that be? The Butcher in Jerusalem?"

"She managed to entice him here."

"But how? How?"

"I suppose someone helped her."

Daniel tells his father what he knows.

All in one go, everything he has hidden from him for years. Nearby, behind closed shutters, a child is crying, and in another house the television is blaring, a love story that goes wrong or something like that.

Amos listens, stiff with cold, hostility in his eyes. He is looking not at Daniel but towards the end of the alley, distractedly letting his gaze follow a passing beggar, a couple walking with their arms around each other, soldiers eating falafel and slapping each other on the back. All around them against the walls are piles of rubbish, towers of cardboard boxes, crates, litter from the market.

It will end badly, it can only end badly. A revolver.

The road is black, the pavement is black.

Like life.

Daniel sees that the veins in his father's temples have swollen, and he is sorry he confided in him. Why did he have to go and tell him? This worn old man is not a hero any more. Daniel must let go of that image of his father in khaki shorts and shirt, smiling, leaning on his rifle, the desert in the background.

A long silence falls between them, and neither of them dares to break it.

When Amos finally turns to look at Daniel, his son sees how red his eyes are, as if he had been crying inside, silently.

Amos buttons up his coat. Now with this gesture Daniel recognizes the familiar image of his father. Haughty and nonchalant, his hair white as snow, and his eyes still full of confidence and insolence.

"You were right to speak to me."

"But I regret it."

Amos places his hand on Daniel's and, with a squeeze, conveys his love.

"Inshallah. Don't worry, go on home."

"Dad, forgive me. I've kept you out in the cold. And Mum is waiting in the car."

"I'll call you tomorrow. Will you be back at work?"

"Do I have any choice?"

"Let me think. Give me some time."

"Dad, in two days . . ."

"I understand. I'll go and see Elisheva."

"Don't tell her that I . . ."

"Of course not."

"She's completely mad."

"She's an artist."

"I know, but . . ."

Amos gets carried away: "How can I explain to you what a genius she is . . . She plays not only the cello, she plays the piano, the guitar . . . All she has to do is touch an instrument, any instrument, clarinet, saxophone, drums . . . She speaks to the instruments . . . and they answer her . . . Listen, I have a story to tell you."

Amos's gaze wanders off to the moon: "One day, after a concert, Elisheva told that young girl she trained, little Rachel, you know . . . ? She said, Lend me a finger. Which one? said Rachel. Elisheva said, Any finger. With my knowledge, and your suppleness, at last I will make music."

With the toe of his shoe Daniel taps the pavement, not daring to interrupt his father. His old man is not really with it. He is talking about appearances, about Elisheva's music, the admiration she inspires in him, and he is forgetting about the danger.

"Rachel," says Amos softly. "Yes, maybe she's the answer."

"Maybe!" answers Daniel, distractedly. "Go on home, Dad."

But Amos no longer wants to leave. He wants details, he even asks, "What is her plan?"

"I don't know."

"She must have one. She's never left anything up to chance."

Suddenly Amos shivers.

"I have to go, your mother is waiting," he says opening his arms to his son.

Then he moves aside and walks around the car.

He opens the door, settles inside and leans over to his wife. She is dozing; he murmurs a few words before starting the engine.

RACHEL

I only missed being born in Israel by a few months; then I would have been called *sabra*, prickly pear. But my father, although he had already decided to emigrate to Israel, could not yet bring himself to leave Tunisia behind. The Jewish community had fled a decade earlier to France, and only a handful of diehards stayed on in Tunis.

Some were too old to leave, and had no family. Their exile would have meant extreme poverty in France or elsewhere.

Others were very rich and would have become penniless the moment they emigrated. They owned houses, prosperous businesses, even factories, but the Tunisian state would not grant them the right to sell their property. Hostages of their fortune, prisoners of their estates, they could not resolve themselves to leaving, "one hand in front, one hand behind" as they used to say.

My father was neither old nor rich, but he was a grammarian. He was studying a dead language, a language which was written in Hebrew and read in Arabic. And as time passed, he became more and more isolated, adrift on a sea of signs and symbols, disconnected from reality.

My mother told the story of how the suitcases were ready, hidden

123

under the bed. Every week my father would say, "Get ready to leave", then he would breathe in the scent of jasmine and change his mind. "Things will quieten down with time. Peace will be signed in the Middle East. Let's stay. Soon the orange trees will be in bloom."

We speak French in my family, but all we know of France is the port of Marseilles, where we stopped off. My father, educated at a French school, was a product of colonization. The descendant of a line of rabbis, he owes his education to nuns wearing wimples.

Avner was four years old when I was born in the night of 1 June, 1967. My father was hoping for a second boy. He told me he was so disappointed the night I was born that he got drunk. But on 7 June, apparently he looked out the window at the stream of demonstrators down in the street, screaming their hatred of Israel and Jews, and he turned to my mother and said, "It's a good thing you gave me a girl. With these riots, we would never have been able to arrange the circumcision."

Barricaded in their apartment, they waited until the end of the Six-Day War. At the end of July they boarded a ship for France.

In Marseilles a messenger from the Jewish Agency led them to a photographer's. The identity photos which are on their Israeli passports date from that evening when they sat broken-hearted on a stool facing the camera lens. My father looks like a fugitive, or an outlaw. My mother, with her pale skin, shadows under her eyes, has something moonlike about her, but she was breastfeeding me and becoming anaemic, although she did not know it. Only Avner turned out nicely on the photograph, with his brown curls and round cheeks, his eyes shining like olives.

When all the formalities were completed, they had two hours to kill before boarding. My mother said, hesitantly, "Why don't we go for a walk? We're in France. I'd like to see what it's like here. If it's like in the schoolbooks, or different." My father replied, "What's the point? I don't want to have cause for regret!" He was afraid, in fact, that he was doing something really stupid. There, by the sea, two days' sail from that Promised Land his ancestors had been dreaming of for two thousand years, and which he had never stopped wishing for whenever he sang "Next year in Jerusalem", he suddenly realized what he was about to do. And he thought, "I'm not Tunisian any more, and not yet Israeli, but I do have cousins in Paris who have done well in textiles and dry goods and real estate."

He stared at the flashing neon sign on a hotel, and ideas started coming to him, things he had never thought about. He had only a few banknotes in his wallet, but they would be enough, all the same, to treat us to a week in the land of Molière. A week would be ample time for him to rest, reflect and clarify a few elements of the future into which, for the first time in his life, he was rushing at top speed. One week, seven days. The Israelis had fought a war in six days. He was asking for the same amount of time to see what might happen.

The messenger from the Jewish Agency must have sensed my father's reluctance. He was not a bad guy, just a convinced Zionist. He understood that this family would slip through his fingers if he did not shove them in the right direction. He pulled a bottle out of the hip pocket of his trousers and said, "*Yallah*, let's have a drink and then I'll get you settled on the ship."

"I don't drink!" my father said.

"Not even beer?"

"Just the Kiddush wine on Friday evening or Saturday midday."

"Well then, well then," the messenger said. "So you're a religious man? I haven't practised in a long time."

His confession left my father dumbstruck. How could a Jew live in the Promised Land and not respect Shabbat? He had heard of them, to be sure, but he had thought it was all lies. It was as if my father's soles had stuck to the pavement on the quay then and there. My mother sat down on a crate, covered me with her shawl, and breastfed me while keeping an eye on Avner, who was galloping around the containers.

"Wait a minute, just wait a minute," my father said.

These Jews! They're all the same. The messenger took his head in his hands.

"Now what?"

"When does the next ship leave?"

"You don't want to go any more?"

"I do, but with the next ship."

"It's full!" the messenger said, in an authoritarian voice.

"Then the one afterwards!"

"We're not discussing the Talmud here. We're talking about your life . . . Are you going or aren't you?"

Tears streamed down my father's cheeks. Last night he was still in Tunis; he had run away like a thief, but a man's heart does not respond to reason, a man's heart can remain attached even when all ties seem to have been severed.

"I know what you're feeling," the messenger said. "I went through the same thing when I left Morocco in 1955. I can't even count how many generations were born and died in Essaouira. I fought in the Sinai campaign and I'd never touched a weapon in my life. Soldiers died all around me, guys who'd been trained. And I made it out alive! *Mektoub!* I married a beautiful woman. I had kids. And on the sixth of June my captain came to get me at dawn to go back down to the Sinai. I've seen many things in my life, but I haven't forgotten Essaouira."

My father was deeply moved by the messenger's openness.

When he describes him, he is very brief, he talks about his sun-tanned face, his black eyes, his athletic body simply dressed in trousers and a short-sleeved grey shirt; and yet this man is as close to me as if I had met him. Unless the memory of a month-old baby was able to capture the features of a man whose mission it was to guide my parents to the land of the Jews.

"You fight for a Jewish state, but you no longer live like a Jew. Can you explain this paradox to me?"

"You can't get away from history," answered the messenger with a shrug. "History is stronger than God!"

"What you're saying is blasphemous . . ."

"It's been my philosophy ever since I learned about the extermination of the Jews in Europe. And we could talk about it for a thousand years and you'd never manage to convince me otherwise."

For years my father would tell me about this extravagant conversation, there on that poorly lit quayside cluttered with ropes, containers and machines. The dark contours of the ships blocked the view. You could hear the sea more than you could actually see it; it was lapping gently against cement and wood, and it was as if a huge body was breathing silently at your side.

That night my father must, in his way, have relived the exodus from Egypt, except that it was not the Red Sea there before him but the Mediterranean. He was waiting for a miracle to happen, for Moses to appear suddenly before him, with his white beard and the sandals of an Egyptian, the great Moses whose life he knew by heart, from the moment his mother had abandoned him by the Nile, laying him in a basket coated in pitch, to the moment God took his life from him with a kiss.

With a timid laugh, my father confessed that just for a fraction of a second he had hoped that the waves would part, that the great ocean liners would be washed away by waves higher than houses, that a passage would open to allow us to walk across the sea. He looked at the waves, waiting for the sign to come. Then he understood that the heavens would remain silent. He was master of his own destiny.

My father leaned over to grasp the handle of the suitcase, but the messenger was quicker.

"You look after your wife and children. That's already plenty. I'll take care of the rest."

"You're a good man," said my father, his voice hoarse with emotion. "You've been patient with me, you didn't try to crush me with guilt."

"It's only human to hesitate . . . Let me tell you a secret that you

127

should really have discovered on your own. The land of Israel is a toboggan."

"What's that, toboggan?" asked my father, who was hearing the word for the first time.

"It's a board on a slant and you slide down on it as fast as you can."

"And it leads where, this board?"

"To life, death, war . . . To the Messiah! What will be, will be."

My father had been expecting a great deal on leaving Tunisia, but not such a disenchanted opinion. It was all the more surprising given the fact that the messenger came from a country which had defeated a hundred million Arabs in six days.

The messenger from the Jewish Agency carried their two suitcases, my father grabbed Avner's hand, and my mother was holding me. One behind the other they went along a quay that seemed endless; the boat for Israel was ever further, even further, take heart, murmured the messenger, and my father was thinking, I have money in my pocket, why am I going there on foot, why didn't I take a taxi with my family, have I really lost my mind to this degree, Adonai?

"Let me give you a tip," said the messenger. "In Israel, take what you think you must take, don't wait for anyone to give it to you, or the Messiah might get there before you."

"Ah!" said my father, settling Avner on to his shoulders.

As far as throwing him a line went, this one was as good as any, and now was the time, or never, to impose his wishes. My father had the intuition that afterwards it would be too late, that once he got to Haifa he would no longer have the right to speak his mind.

"Since Jerusalem has just been conquered," he murmured, "I'm asking to live in Jerusalem. No other town will do."

The messenger walked faster.

"That's impossible!"

My father sat down on a cart.

"You give me Jerusalem, or I'll stay in France."

"I don't know what city they'll settle you in. Could be Haifa, Beersheba, Ashdod . . . But you'll have no cause for complaint. They'll give you a nice apartment, whereas when we arrived, we were put in tents, then in houses made of cardboard . . ."

"Jerusalem!"

"It's not in my power!"

"I think it is . . ."

They began to shout at each other beneath a streetlamp.

My mother was hunched over with the cold, it was a quarter past midnight, I had been suckling nonstop for hours, no sooner did she remove her breast from my mouth than I started to scream, clenching my fists. She needed a meal and a bed.

"You know what? Take it easy! Here are your suitcases. Get a hotel in Marseilles and do what you can to get a residence permit at the préfecture."

"May God bless you."

The messenger walked away. My father consoled himself with the thought that he would live for forty years in Marseilles, forty years and not a day longer, and that after that, if God still granted him life, then he would go and settle in the Promised Land. He pictured himself walking into a library in Marseilles and asking to see the Arab authors of the early Middle Ages, to compare their texts with those of the lesser-known Jewish rabbis of the Maghreb. He would some-how find a job as a professor of Hebrew in a Talmud Torah, while waiting to get a better position in a French school. He had enough diplomas, he would manage to feed his family. But the messenger had already turned around and was coming back at a run, and he planted himself in front of my father with his fists on his hips and his eyes blazing with anger.

"If you agree to spend a few months in a centre for immigrants, it can be done."

My father looked at my mother for her opinion and she nodded silently. The messenger slipped a blue card into my father's passport.

"Hurry up now, otherwise in twenty minutes that bloody ship will leave without you."

They hurried, hearts pounding, increasingly out of breath. At the end of the quay there was a mad bustle of activity, lights flashing, porters shouting, horns blaring. They were about to remove the gangplank. "Wait, wait!" My father was shouting, the messenger was shouting, it would be too much, wouldn't it, to think they had missed the boat because they had stood there debating the issue of Jerusalem.

But it had been ordained that . . .

By the time we got on board, the ship's horns had begun to blast. I started to wail with terror, nothing could console me, neither my mother's caresses as she hopped from one foot to the other, nor her songs, nor her flabby breast. My father always used to tell me, "You were one and a half months old, my girl, when you arrived in Israel. What do forty-five days of life amount to? Nothing. And yet you're not a *sabra* . . . You did not leave your mother's womb on Israeli soil. That is why you dream about the past."

And that is how my parents ended up in the first building constructed on the mountain of Givat Tzarfatit, in an unfinished street, where the earth was torn up by backhoes as they dug and excavated enormous plots of land to serve as the foundations for hundreds of buildings. And the forest of cranes was fed by an incessant coming and going of trucks, as they hauled sand, cement, breeze blocks and girders.

Later, I would peer at the black-and-white prints, or the handful in colour, and try to picture the neighbourhood in Tunis where I was born and that I will probably never see.

There is one photograph in particular that I like, where my parents are posing in a square courtyard, smiles on their faces. Behind them you can see a row of arches above marble columns, crowned with a green tiled cornice.

On some of the photographs there is a fountain and an immense palm tree. On others, with a good magnifying glass, you can follow the motif of the earthenware tiles that decorate the walls, inspired by a style which, I later learned, was not unlike the ones in Andalusia.

I could also get an idea of how the apartment was furnished. Everything had stayed behind, carpets, oak chests, tables and chairs. They left the key in a jar on the landing, and there were cupboards filled with perfectly ironed linen, perfumed with lavender sachets – excellent against moths, asserts my mother, with a sigh.

My father managed to rescue his books. He had arranged with his neighbour, Mohammed Larbi, to send them on to him *poste restante* in Marseilles: three boxes stuffed with worthless, yellowed books that cost a fortune in postage.

SECOND SONG

My nie chcemy ratować zycia.
aden z nas żywy z tego nie wyjdzie.
My chcemy ratować ludzka godność.

"We do not want to save our lives.
No one will get out of here alive.
We want to save human dignity."

Slogan by Arie Wilner,
Warsaw Ghetto Fighter,
Soldier of the Żydowska Organizacja Bojowa.

AMOS

Amos drives home as best he can, going through red lights or sitting at them for far too long. He heads down a one-way street the wrong way, compounds his mistakes amidst blaring horns and flashing head-lamps. At last he comes to the ramp leading down to the garage, which he always enters apprehensively at five miles an hour. Now he stalls just as they are half way down.

Amos steps on both pedals at once, chooses the wrong gear, sets the ballet of windscreen wipers in motion. He has forgotten how to drive, and the car jerks forward, stalls again, then slides, borne by its own weight.

By the time Amos manages to pull the handbrake, puffing, his face burning, the car has already collided with the sharp edge of the wall.

The shock has the immediate effect of calming the old man.

Katya is looking straight ahead. Once she would have thrown a tantrum. She would have jumped out of the car, screaming, "What the hell do you think you're doing? You've wrecked everything! It's a disaster!" Then she would have wasted untold time trying to put the damaged bits back together, only to make things worse. Now, nothing. Katya does not blink an eyelash. She is nothing but silence. Silence and smiles. The fire of her passion and her need for compen-sation have vanished.

Amos manages to move the car and park in his reserved spot.

"Here we are!" he says to Katya, not bothering to inspect the damage.

Step by step, they go together into their home, a comfortable ground-floor flat in Rehavia. He decided they should move there when he noticed the first signs of her illness – her memory losses, her aimless wandering through the town.

He undresses her. With the thin fabric of her pyjamas he covers her hips, marbled from needle marks, and the folds of her belly, and her thin legs, as he says, "Katya . . . I need to speak to you . . . I can't go on struggling by myself any more . . . Can you hear me, my darling?"

He gives her her tablets, puts her to bed, carefully tucks her in. He leans over to kiss her when suddenly she says, "Sir! I have a fiancé!"

Amos freezes, dumbfounded. Katya repeats her words, exultant: a fiancé, a fiancé. Her expression has completely changed. She is sixteen years old behind her aged face. Sixteen, her finest age. Nothing has happened yet. She is still intact, and her family are alive.

"What good news!" he says at last. And his heart is breaking at the sight of his wife's head with its sparse hair, her disjointed body beneath the sheet.

He kneels on the floor and looks at her intensely.

He was born in Jerusalem when it was colonized by the British, and he had had no childhood, but unlike Katya or Elisheva, he is not a survivor. He was not sold as a slave to IG-Farben, Krupp, or Siemens; he was not a terrified witness of the Aktion Erntefest.* Eighteen thousand Jews dragged from the camp at Majdanek and savagely machine-gunned to the sound of military marches blaring over the loudspeakers.

"Where is Mama?"

"She's not far," he says with a smile.

"Thank you, sir."

Her last words are lost in sleep and a trace of drool.

Amos kisses his wife's hand and gets to his feet. He leaves a light on at the bedside and, limping on his stiff leg, leaves the room.

Korsakoff's Syndrome, according to the neurologists. A disease

---

* Aktion Erntefest: Operation Harvest Festival, in German. Code name for the mass killing on 3 November 1943 where ten thousand Jews were shot in Majdanek. A similar slaughter occurred in the camps of Poniatowa and Trawniki.

that alters memory and executive functions. Amos has another hypothesis: Katya cracked up when she became immersed in reading the accounts of the trials at Nuremberg.

He should have known what might happen, given her fragility; he should have tried to discourage her. What was the point of reading forty-two volumes, thousands of pages, words like knives turning in wounds still raw? Did she not already know it all? He did not feel he had the right to warn her. And anyway, when Katya got an idea in her head . . .

She never managed to read as far as the minutes of the sentencing. A letter from Bayer, the German pharmaceutical and chemical company, to the commander at Auschwitz had set her on a path of deep, irremediable anxiety. He had read the letter so often that he knew it by heart: ". . . would you be so kind as to place at our disposal a certain number of women on whom we may conduct our narcotics trials. The fee of two hundred marks for each woman seems excessive. We will offer only one hundred and seventy marks per head. We have received the shipment of one hundred and fifty women. Although they are in a state of advanced deterioration, we believe they will suit our purposes. The women sent in the last parcel have died . . ."*

The ringing of the wall telephone shatters the silence. Amos reaches out, picks up the receiver. Daniel is on the line.

"Papa? I was waiting for you to call. Did you get home alright?"

"Yes. Go to bed."

"Papa, I am so sorry to have got you mixed up in this business."

"If I can help."

"You have enough to do with Mama. I know Elisheva is your friend, but . . ."

"We'll talk about it tomorrow," Amos says firmly. "Goodnight, Daniel."

* Excerpt from "Nuremberg Document NI (Nazi Industry)-7184".

"Papa, what I mean is that you and Elisheva weren't all that close . . . She won't listen to you. It's pointless going to see her, it might jeopardize the trust she has in me. I'll find another way, alright?"

Amos says, "Yes, yes," and hangs up.

Not all that close?

He sits down in the kitchen, his eyes on the bars he had installed on the window.

And a smile comes to his lips, a sad, infinitely bitter smile.

Not all that close?

What do you know about me, son?

He met Katya at the kibbutz in August 1948. She was dancing the hora, wearing a yellow dress that buttoned up the front. He had just arrived with his brigade for a surveillance operation in Galilee, and he had paused, fascinated by that yellow dress whirling like a sun around the campfire. Thirty or more boys and girls were dancing in a circle, holding hands and singing. Someone, off to the side, was playing a guitar, the notes did not match the dance, it was another melody altogether but this disturbed no-one, the dancers did not even notice.

That yellow dress is the fable of his life. The myth on which he founded his marriage.

As if he were looking through a zoom lens, the image of that night grows larger, closer. He sees again the cart piled with wheat, the old donkey resting by the shed, the young people coming and going to set the table, their stifled laughter, the joyous exclamations. Like his mates from the brigade, he placed his rifle against a wall and went to wash his hands at the fountain, where a tin bucket had been placed to save water. He splashed his face hastily, and slicked his hair back with the comb he kept in the gun pocket of his Bermuda shorts. His friend Shapira, who would go on to become a judge in the Supreme Court and who, in those days, was a renowned womanizer, was bristling with impatience. Wherever he went – buses, stations, army bases, *moshavim*, kibbutzim – Shapira would chat up the girls. He had an insatiable need, a need that still beleaguers him even today, as a grandfather.

Amos can still hear him rejoicing, this kibbutz is a real gold mine, yes, there were more girls than boys, survivors who had been in Cyprus before they obtained permission, upon Independence, to sail for Israel on board the *Medinat Israel*. The girls are from Poland, Russia, Romania. They speak several languages, and Hebrew badly, but Yiddish should help smooth over any difficulties, Yiddish and caresses.

"Have a good time," called Shapira, before going to join the circle of dancers.

Shapira found a partner within the hour. The moment dinner was over he headed off into the fields with the young woman, where the wheat, still high, swayed to the breath of the wind.

As for Amos, he had his eye on the yellow dress, and when the dancing had stopped, he went over to her and offered her a glass of water. He was pleased when he saw that she was as lovely close up as from afar.

"Your father rushed up to me with a jug of water," Katya liked to tell the children.

"With a glass, my dear," corrected Amos.

"With a jug. I know what I'm saying. And you looked as if you'd lost your wits."

"What did he say to charm you?" Daniel or his brother, Ruben, would say ecstatically.

"Nothing. Absolutely nothing. He followed me around all evening, never saying a word, just feasting on me with his eyes."

Amos does not remember it like that, but so what, is it so important, in the end?

Katya, with her dark irises and full lips, has completely subjugated him. She is wearing a kerchief over her head, tied at the back of her neck: he would like to remove it and touch her hair. She is beautiful, wild, her hands raw from working in the fields. She can see the boy looking at her blisters and the scratches disfiguring her skin up to her elbows, and she explains in her halting Hebrew, with her Russian accent that rolls like a handful of pebbles, that there are not enough gloves for all the girls. As she has to tear out the nettles, they take turns. The girls who have no gloves wrap their hands and arms with rags, but the rags slip off, and besides it is too hot, and your skin eventually gets used to pain; the marks remain, yes, and your flesh bleeds, but you do not feel the pain any more. With no transition the young woman says, "My name is Katya."

"Amos."

He will stay by her. It is true. He admits as much. He follows the volatile young woman into the press of young people settling around the tables for dinner, he hurries, pulls up a chair, and offers it to her; she is charmed, and shoots him a look filled with emotion, her eyes brimming with tears and gratitude.

After all she has been through – the camps, the march through the snow, the ship packed with immigrants, the harsh life of the kibbutz – here is a gentleman who is fussing over her, who finds every way he can to be attentive, who tries to make her comfortable. Such a man must be a Martian.

She feels her heart begin to beat, waking from a long sleep.

Life is made of little things.

This brings them together: for him it is the graceful movement of a yellow dress, for her the courteous gesture, reviving memories of her once-happy home, her father the doctor, her mother who loved poetry and the theatre.

A few girls are on duty. They bring salad and bread, put everything down on the table, and head off again to fetch the water and the fruit juice from the kitchen. There the staff, who will eat later on, dish out great ladlefuls of pasta, sauce and beans into the salad bowls.

The kibbutz is young and poor, the work in the fields is exhausting. People have to be fed. There is not enough fruit, not enough vegetables. The orchard has only just been planted. They had to invest to build the stable where five cows are sleeping. Three years from now they will have oranges. In the meantime, they eat starch.

Amos listens, nodding.

The entire country is on the verge of famine. Immigrants keep arriving, from eastern Europe, Yemen, Iraq. Milk is rationed. People improve their daily fare, thanks to the black market. He could tell her about the camps where people are crowded together, without resources, the lack of doctors, children sick with malaria, the hastily built wooden huts, but he cannot get a word in, Katya talks and talks. A flood of words in Hebrew, Yiddish, Russian and Polish.

"And your dress?"

"I bought it from a second-hand vendor in Tel Aviv. A lady who fled at Independence and left him her wardrobe. He has cupboards full of peignoirs and silk."

Katya suddenly stops the girl who is serving.

"This is my friend, Elisheva."

Amos sighs impatiently, he wants no intrusions. He looks absently at the girl's graceless figure in her shapeless blue shirt, faded skirt and worn sandals. Her legs are spindly, her knees protrude, her hips are as flat as a boy's. She must be twenty, she looks like a nun and yet her face, which he sees as through a cloud, this face consumed by burning eyes is one of those you do not forget. He can feel her strength, her strange, spectacular energy, a mixture of violence, intelligence and irony.

"Did you hear her playing the guitar?"

So she was the one playing that solitary instrument, unheeding of the others, and yet as if in unison?

He finds something polite to say.

"You play well."

The young woman is amused, raises an eyebrow.

At the time he did not know, really, what music was. He had grown up without it; rather, he had grown up with the songs from the synagogue that his father and grandfather used to hum, Italian style, with quavers, their voices soaring. He also knew a few English tunes. That was as far as it went, with Amos and music. When would he have had the time to learn anything? The war filled his days, it was all he knew. He was twenty-four years old; he had enlisted at the age of seventeen in the troops of the Palmach. In seven years he had known nothing but skirmishes, ambushes and sentry duty. True, there had been the cabinetmaker on the far side of the courtyard when he was a boy, he suddenly recalled, who used to practise a few tunes on his violin, but Amos would have been hard put to say what his repertory was, the violin playing a cascade of notes for hours, as if the man were possessed by a *dybbuk*. Later, much later, Elisheva would explain to him that this cabinetmaker, whom everyone thought was *meshuga*, was playing Mozart, Liszt and, above all, Paganini. She made him listen to recordings and he discovered, to his amazement, that he had etched entire fragments into his memory.

"She is a great musician," Katya says indignantly, rolling her r's.

"So great," Elisheva says, "that no-one listens to her."

"But I heard you!"

Elisheva bursts out laughing, looking away at the darkened fields.

"Music isn't much use here. There is too much stone, too much sand, it's an elemental world."

She moves away, they're calling her, they need bread and pasta at the other end of the table and the diners are joyfully banging their knives against their aluminium plates.

"Elisheva, Elisheva!" they chant.

Amos had not grasped her name when Katya first said it. But now, with the young people chanting, her name pierces his heart. He knows he will never forget it, just as he cannot erase her dispirited words, music isn't much use here. Music serves a purpose, of course it does. Some day they will be out of this rut of poverty and war.

He ruminates for a moment, then asks, defiantly, leaning over to Katya, "Have you known her for a long time?"

A shadow passes over Katya's face.

"Yes."

"Is she Russian?"

"Polish."

Katya has lost her gaiety. She replies monosyllabically and ever more hesitantly.

"You met each other at the kibbutz?"

"Before."

Oblivious of the danger, Amos insists, persists.

"On the boat?"

"Before," Katya says.

She is ready to talk about everything – the kibbutz, the work in the fields, Cyprus, her childhood home. Everything, except the camps. Especially to a stranger.

Amos hands her a fruit; she softens.

"How I love to eat!"

He is about to reply that he has the same weakness, that he has become little more than a rumbling stomach, when Katya says that it is getting darker and darker.

"I can't see your face."

"I'm not good-looking."

She laughs. "I saw no-one else once you arrived."

"But you were dancing . . ."

"What do you think? You can dance and notice what's going on around you."

He is amazed by her confession. He saw her. She saw him. The candles are smoking, the wicks have burned down. He takes her hand, hardly touching her rough, injured fingers, and asks her to come with him for a walk. Tomorrow he will be leaving at dawn, for the border. Katya does not reply. It is too dark now to see her features. He does not know if she is smiling or thinking, or if he bores her. He thinks she will probably say no. But suddenly she gets to her feet.

"Come," she says.

★

Amos stops to listen.

A long moan is coming from the bedroom, and he hurries down the corridor. No. He is mistaken. His wife is sleeping peacefully. Her breath rises and falls, deep and regular, with a smile at the corners of her lips, not unlike the smile of an infant replete with its mother's milk. Their children used to smile like that, too, as if an angel were whispering a fairy tale in their ears.

Amos leans against the doorway and observes his wife affectionately.

They had set off together that night, the two of them, they did not know each other and it was to be for the rest of their lives.

Amos was not like his friend Shapira, flirting with women, loving them for a night, then forgetting about them.

Even when he realized that Katya was not the right one, he stayed with her. To spare her the pain. Not to betray her. To be true to his word.

He had missed his chance, and Elisheva's.

He goes back into the kitchen, opens the fridge, pulls out a bottle of fizzy water, takes a glass from the shelf and gulps down the cool, invigorating liquid.

He will not be able to sleep tonight. He has to find a way, do whatever he can, to protect Elisheva.

RACHEL

When I stopped outside my door, I saw the light beneath Elisheva's; it went out when I turned the key in the lock.

She must have stayed up all night waiting for me, worrying herself sick.

In five years we have had only one falling out. And one hour later I was on a bus for Miami.

When I called her a week later she was careful not to ask me a single question – where I was, who I was with. She only talked about music, the way that I loved, and when I got back to New York we started rehearsing again without ever mentioning my running away.

I was thinking about it when I phoned reception to ask them to wake me up at eleven. It would not amount to a lot of sleep, but I had promised my father I would go with him to the Old City to change his money, and I did not want to let him down.

I did not even manage to get undressed. I collapsed on my bed. I was not proud of my behaviour at Avishai's café, but Eytan's smile led me into sleep.

AMOS

He had left Katya the following morning, whispering in her ear, "See you later."

He had thought he would be able to get back to the kibbutz for Shabbat, but the brigade received the order to stay on the border.

While he waited for the enemy, playing cards with his comrades, walking through the sand dunes, oiling his rifle, he thought about what Elisheva had said. The little she had told him became an obsession. "Music isn't much use. An elemental world." The woman was a defeatist. An elemental world, and then what? What choice did their people have? After Auschwitz, Treblinka, Sobibor, Birkenau, sand after ashes was something of a miracle. He had to stop thinking about her. But while waiting for the enemy, Amos went on mulling over the odd thing she might have said, or an expression; he went on assembling, building, adding depth to the meaning of the few moments he had spent with her. Until the more he tried to banish her from his mind, the more attached he became, mysteriously.

By the time he was released from his obligations, two months had gone by.

The war was coming to an end. Ben Gurion had organized a regular army and veterans were sent home.

Before returning to Jerusalem, Amos went out of his way to stop off at the kibbutz.

He had not received a single letter from Katya.

So he thought that their story had lasted the time it takes to dance the hora. He did not feel sad.

He was coming back for Elisheva.

He wanted to understand why this ugly woman, who had said all of three sentences to him, had made off with his heart.

He climbed down from the rattling bus. The wind was whirling gusts of ochre dust along the ground before him like a regiment of djinns. What the hell am I doing here, thought Amos, as he headed towards the buildings of the kibbutz, simple cubes with openings draped with mosquito nets.

A few hens were pecking along the ground that was hard as cement.

The threshing floor was deserted, abandoned to the sun. Oil drums painted bright colours were planted with cacti. A tyre dangling from chains served as a swing.

The fields covered only a limited area of the dry, ancient landscape that vanished into the warm, shimmering mist. There was still so much to do. And it was madness to do it. Nature could only close again like a trap over these pioneers who dreamt of taming her. A giant ogress crushing them like ants with all the weight of her dug-like mountains.

There was no-one at the kibbutz.

No-one? Yes, there was, a woman coming out of a house with a basket of bread.

"Elisheva!"

She had recognized him, too, and she held her hand to her brow like a visor: "Katya's working."

"Hello."

"Hi."

She had nothing to say to him, nothing at all, and he did not know how to resume the conversation about music. So he played the only card that might justify his presence there. Katya.

"Where can I find her?"

"Follow the road. Or cut across the fields. They're right over there at the far side, way down at the end of the plain."

Silence again. A dull rumble of tractors in the distance throbbing in their ears. He did not know what else to say, he had never been any good at chatting up girls. He was silent and passive, and he would wait for them to take the first step, a charm tactic as good as any other.

This time he ventured to whisper, his heart pounding, sweat trickling down his back, "Can you come with me?"

"If you want."

"But if it's an inconvenience . . ."

"No. I've finished my day."

"And your music?"

"It's too hot. The strings get soft. No matter how often I tune them, they don't hold." Looking at him with her shadow-coloured eyes, she said, "I hate when it's off key."

They began walking, slowly. The air was acrid and dusty. Elisheva took mechanical, somewhat twisted steps, not at all elegant, as she swung her over-long arms. He immediately told her that her words about music had deeply troubled him. That he had come back to talk to her about it.

"You didn't come because of Katya?"

"Yes, of course," he said quickly, realizing he had even forgotten his lover's features. His only memories were of a yellow dress and her raw scratched hands. "Don't you have faith in this country?"

"That's not the problem."

A sparrowhawk was gliding above them in the sky. And he wanted to see this as a sign, as if a presence were following them, keeping watch over them.

"We are building a world of brutes," she continued. "Without a spirit. Without culture."

147

"Was it culture that saved you from death in Europe?"

"Nothing could prevent our destruction. Not books, nor music, nor men. Not even God. And yet . . ."

"Yes?"

"That's not a reason to stop thinking."

He paused to look at her. He smiled for no reason, overcome with emotion. They sat down by the side of the road on two flat rocks. The mountain range in Lebanon rose before them, blocking the horizon. He picked up a handful of earth and crumbled it between his fingers, unconsciously. Where had she learned to speak such pure Hebrew? At the *ulpan*.* But did she speak any Hebrew before that? No. Who was this woman, dear Lord? He stared at the number tattooed on her forearm, the scar on the back of her neck, another one that ran across her temple. She did not try to flaunt her knowledge, but responded simply, her knobbly knees pulled up under her chin without an ounce of feminine grace. And he could not help but be stirred by her gaze, when she turned to him.

The day was fading. Clearly no-one came along this road. By cutting across the fields, people could gain twenty minutes – twenty minutes less out in the hot sun, which was already something.

Then he saw them in the distance, walking in single file, all the young people who had been working in the fields and were now heading home, singing as they walked, with their tools over their shoulders and their guns in their hands, and Amos suddenly understood that Elisheva had been trying to keep him away from Katya rather than help him get closer to her.

He waited until the dark, tranquil column had disappeared into the setting sun before he said, "Are you going to stay at the kibbutz?"

"Why not?"

* *Ulpanim* are educational frameworks run by the Ministries of Immigrant Absorption and Education and the Jewish Agency, for learning the Hebrew language. (Translator's note.)

"In town, you could go to concerts."

"I'll leave when I'm ready."

They should have got up, but they stayed on, talking in hushed voices, about deep, secret things; and he did not dare to break the spell by turning to her to take her in his arms. He had never wanted a woman like that. He had never felt such desire. He grew hard. Something emanated from the woman at his side, something sensitive, alive and sorrowful, something which drew him to her yet filled him with fear. He would have liked to cry out to her, Marry me, marry me, but his throat was dry as his gaze swept over the darkening night that was engulfing them.

Elisheva leapt to her feet, dusted off her skirt, and said they had better go back.

He had to control himself when they were back at the kibbutz and Katya rushed over to him, her arms outstretched.

"Amos, Amos."

Katya's curves had blossomed. Her breasts were swollen beneath the taut fabric of her dress, and he could feel them when she pressed up against him, warm and breathless and happy.

He turned to look for Elisheva. She had vanished.

"I wrote you dozens of letters. But I didn't know where to send them! I've been waiting for you for so long, Amos!"

She smiled, flung her arms around his neck, kissed him and led him away from the others and from the buffet they were preparing for the evening meal.

"Letters?"

"I have to explain. We have to talk. I've known for two days. Even Elisheva doesn't know a thing . . . It's the first time I've ever hidden anything from her . . ."

Daniel was on his way.

Amos did not know how to say to Katya, we've been too hasty, alright, I know you're pregnant, but there are ways to get ourselves out of it, I know a backstreet abortionist in Jerusalem.

It was not the way you did things back then. The prevailing mood was one of gravity.

ELISHEVA

Elisheva devotes half an hour to her gymnastics, as she does every morning: arm lifts, upper body twists, foot flexing and extension, abdominal contractions. Breathing deeply, she observes every movement, every difficulty.

She takes a quick shower and gets dressed.

Then she looks after her hands. She is developing arthritis. Her hands — these hands that once had wings — have become an obsession. A feeling of numbness in her left hand was already unbearable, and then the right hand began to go to sleep. She will have to think about having an operation, or stop playing. Elisheva spreads a dollop of cream and slowly massages the surface of her palm and all her fingers, dwelling on her thumb and tendons. She clenches her fists, releases them, crosses her fingers.

She wants to be ready for the concert, for she knows it will be the last one.

Suddenly, a gentle knock on the door.

Elisheva listens, then walks across the room wiping her hands on a handkerchief.

A couple is standing in the corridor, shyly, on the verge of leaving again. Amos is freshly shaven. He is wearing his best suit, blue with black pinstripes. Katya in her pink silk suit looks like something from a sweetshop.

"Katya . . ."

Her arms spread wide, Elisheva goes to her friend and holds her close, rocking her backwards and forwards, all tenderness and love.

"*Kinderlekh dort . . .*"

For a split-second her words seem to act as a lever, as if they are prising Katya from her darkness: she rounds her lips, her body trembles.

"*Kinderlekh?*" she says in a childish, sing-song voice.

As he watches, fascinated, a heartbroken smile on his face, Amos grabs at a gleam of hope. If only Elisheva could get through. So many doctors have failed. So many psychiatrists, specialized in the afflictions of the soul, the ills of persecution.

"*Kinderlekh dort gelakht**... Don't you remember, sweetheart?"

She hums the lullaby, caressing Katya's hair, kissing her again and again.

But the disaster lies too deep. There is nothing to be done. Katya's face has retreated into absence.

And it is up to Amos to pull them apart, gently, firmly, placing his hand on Elisheva's frail wrist, for she has begun to shake her friend like a plum tree, and now she turns to look at him with moist, seeking eyes.

"Stop," he says simply.

Elisheva steps aside, exhausted.

"Come in," she says.

They enter the room, gingerly, to the rhythm of Katya's small steps and the squeaking of Amos's brand-new shoes; how old I have become, he realizes. They have nothing in common any more. Elisheva has become a great lady and Katya and he are mere relics.

Amos, Amos, say Elisheva's eyes; she has recovered from the shock, they have gone to such trouble to come and see me. Remember our kibbutz in the north; how little we had.

The room is light, spacious, pleasant.

An immense bay window fills an entire wall.

There is only one painting, a copy of a modern canvas, with zigzags superimposed upon circles, filling the space with its enigma.

Amos sees the shining wood of the cello in its open case on the bed. Scattered on the floor are piles of sheet music; now Elisheva gathers them up quickly before she goes to close a door. She does

***

* *Kinderlekh dort gelakht*: the children were laughing there (fragment of an old Yiddish lullaby entitled *Belz, mayn stetele belz*).

not want to disturb Rachel, who came back early in the morning.

"Were you about to play?"

Every time he sees her, Amos asks her the same question; he has the same stage fright, the same infinite, hushed respect for her music.

"I was getting ready to. But I have time. I'm glad to see you, Amos."

He pushes back the strands of white hair, tries to sit up straight so that he will appear taller, less worn.

"And so am I, Elisheva, so am I."

To begin with, Amos wanted to ask a neighbour to look after Katya and come on his own. Then at the last minute he reckoned that his wife, in spite of her illness, might be a precious ally.

He settles Katya in an armchair, with her empty gaze, and tries to control his emotion, turning to look towards the window.

"She's slipping in deeper, isn't she?"

"Yes."

"I admire you."

"Me?"

"What you are doing for Katya . . ."

"I have no choice, Elisheva."

"You could have thrown in the towel."

"It's my fault, entirely."

"What are you talking about? Have you gone mad?"

"I didn't know how to reassure her . . ."

"You mustn't blame yourself. She was destroyed."

"She had children, she . . ."

With the back of his hand he roughly wipes away a tear, bites his tongue to silence his complaint. His mouth fills with blood. But that is not yet enough, for the mental suffering he has so carefully suppressed comes in a sudden wave, breaking down all the dykes, all the walls so stubbornly constructed to silence his love. He would like to go up to Elisheva and shout, I will lay down my arms, I want to rest with you, there is so little time left, let us make the most of it, my beloved, come, come, can't we go away together? But she will say no. He knows that. He senses it. It is too late. This love does not exist. Has it ever existed, anyway? A woman like her could never love a dark, ignorant man like him. No, he will not say anything. He will go down with his ship, that is all that is left, to go down with his head held high and his heart sinking.

"Happiness cannot erase despair. It is written over the top of it. It is written with the stories of the past."

"That is terrible."

"Amos?"

"Yes," he says with an effort, his mouth bleeding.

"You were her good fortune."

Never before has he felt such stress, such oppression. Now that the armour of resignation has burst open, he sees himself as if he were naked, prey to his demons, staring at his choices.

Elisheva falls silent. Amos waits for the terrible moment to pass, calls to his rescue the faces of his sons and grandchildren. Why should he be feeling sorry for himself? He has not lived in vain. And yet, in a way he has. Distractedly, with one hand he lifts a corner of the net curtain. All the light over the city now floods into his retina.

The houses set like dominoes on the hills, the colossal city walls: it is in this landscape that he has found vigour and consolation, every day. He sees himself as he was in 1967, in the human tide swelling, running towards the city of David. All over the country there was the same dazed commotion, the same immense jubilation: Jerusalem! Jerusalem!

Elisheva picks up the telephone and, never taking her eyes from Amos's back, she orders some coffee and pastries.

"Don't go to the trouble," Amos says, turning around at last. "We're not staying. I just wanted to . . ."

She sees his bloodshot eyes and, with false gaiety, says, "I just feel like a good coffee. Don't you? By the way, I'm giving a concert tomorrow."

"I know."

"Your names are on the guest list. I was going to call you today."

"I've already asked them to hold tickets for me."

"I'll have them cancelled."

"But . . ."

"It's my pleasure."

He bows his head to thank her.

He is ill at ease and he knows it. He is about to talk about the reasons for his visit when the bellboy arrives, wearing black livery. He rolls a breakfast cart into the middle of the room, his eyes riveted on Katya. A nutter, in this suite, one of the most luxurious in the hotel? The man sets out a glass tray heaped with crispy pastries. Elisheva shoves a note into his hand and sends him away.

"Israel has changed," Amos says.

"Hasn't it," Elisheva says distractedly, unscrewing the lid of the thermos. "A little luxury doesn't hurt."

Unhurriedly, she pours the steaming coffee into the cups. Amos serves Katya to begin with. He gives her a coffee and a croissant, and covers her lap with a little white napkin of thick well-ironed cotton.

Elisheva pulls out the chair that was tucked under the desk, lifts it, and sets it down next to Katya's armchair. She sits down. Amos has no choice but to take the other armchair. He is immediately embarrassed. How can he talk to a woman who is sitting at a different height from him?

"Croissant?"

"No. Thank you."

"A *pain au chocolat*, then?"

"No."

"They're delicious."

"I don't doubt it."

"Give this raisin bun to Katya. She likes them so much."

"I came to ask you . . ."

He stops himself in time. Their gazes grow troubled, foundering.

Something passes between them, a flash of understanding, regret, the certainty that they are bound by something indestructible, stronger than anything, stronger than sex or the irremediable passage of time.

"Amos," she says.

He chokes on a sip of coffee. He coughs, pants, takes his handkerchief out with one hand, holding the coffee cup with the other as it rattles on its saucer. His entire body is trembling.

"When are you going home?"

"In two days."

"Go now! Please! This evening!"

She stares at him, bitterly, silently.

"I'm not driving you away," he stammers, confused.

"I didn't really think you were . . ."

"I know you're not here for a concert . . ."

"So why am I here, then?"

"I'm your friend. Talk to me."

He is still waiting, hoping she will open up to him and he will not have to betray his son. But she is distant, and she thinks their meeting has gone on long enough. Right, she needs to get back to work. Next time she will come and have dinner with them. Promise. And anyway, she has had enough of this exhausting travelling, she has to make room for others, give young people the chance they deserve. Rachel will take her place. Does he know that Rachel is exceptionally talented? That she is music itself? Not just a virtuoso?

She smiles with every sentence, her tone so tender that Amos understands the transfer she has made: Rachel is the daughter she never had.

"Daniel told me everything."

Elisheva's face grows hard, the look in her eyes dark as night.

She finishes her coffee and puts the cup down on the cart.

"He can't be trusted."

"That's not true and you know it. He got drunk yesterday. He was in such a state."

"Why?"

"He loves you, Elisheva. He cares about you."

"Who else has been informed?"

"No-one, I swear, no-one."

"Let's hope not."

She gets up, sends the delicate chair flying; it falls noiselessly on the carpet. Amos bends over and picks it up.

"If I hadn't needed a weapon . . ."

"I know."

"In addition, let me point out, just to get things straight and just in case you didn't know: Daniel belongs to the Organization. He has . . . he has already eliminated one bastard . . . who was living in complete impunity in a villa with swimming pool, servants, privileges . . . It was Daniel's team who took care of him. Two bullets in the middle of his forehead. After a trial in due form. Because we're not like them, after all. We give them a lawyer for their self-defence. A lawyer who justifies their crimes, who thinks up all sorts of attenuating circumstances: war, obeying orders, the chaos of the era, personality dissociation. Yes, that's what we do," she concludes, clenching her fists.

She paces back and forth across the room, with her long strides, her shoulders shaking, full of a fury she can no longer control. And Amos shrivels in his armchair, hunched over, his eyes down while he waits for the storm to end.

Suddenly he looks up and sees Katya. She has her tongue out and is licking her finger, again and again. For once he blesses her madness which makes it impossible for her to question, which spares her so much pain.

As if she had read his thoughts, Elisheva plants herself in front of him: "Would you like me to tell you how Katya was tortured?"

"No."

"How I was, then?"

"No."

156

"About the women who were eviscerated, or sterilized, or the women who . . ."

Amos is hardly listening. He keeps hearing Daniel's words: "She can prepare her plot at the cemetery . . . If she attacks him, it's as good as setting a bird down in front of a cat."

"You're the one I want to protect. Not the Butcher. I don't want to lose you."

"A little more, a little less."

He feels dizzy and croaks, "Let justice take its course . . ."

"Justice!" she says, thoughtful. "You come to speak to me of justice? Where is the justice that lets such criminals go on running around scot-free?"

"Katya has gone mad, and you've lost all common sense. I'm not asking you to forgive, but to live."

"His eyes haunt me. His gestures. I have not had a moment's respite in forty-five years. Night and day. He has invaded my music, the most beautiful melodies . . . Everywhere I go I can hear his clipped voice. I want him to die and I want him to die in Jerusalem."

"I'll call Shapira. We'll have him arrested. He'll be judged."

"They'll let him go within the hour. He has a new identity."

"Mossad . . ."

"Neither Mossad, nor the Organization can act against him. Go home. Take Katya with you and pray for me."

They have woken Rachel with their raised voices.

The communicating door opens.

A brown-haired young woman appears, dishevelled, her eyes swollen with sleep, her body wrapped in a bathrobe which she hastily closes over her breasts before reaching for the belt and tying a knot.

"Why are you guys shouting?"

Elisheva freezes. One finger on her lips, she motions to Amos to be silent. Then her face is immediately transformed, and it fills with light.

"Did you sleep well?"

157

"Not enough. Hello, Amos. Did you manage to make Elisheva angry?"

Rachel kisses the old man, looks over at Katya, embarrassed, then heads towards her cello.

"Did you hear us?" Amos says.

"No," Rachel says, plucking a string. "Should I have?"

Amos reaches out to Katya.

"Let's go home, dear."

Katya goes up to the cart and stuffs the pastries into her handbag. Amos lets her, too overwhelmed to react.

Elisheva walks over to the door and yanks it open, briskly.

"*Kinderlekh dort gelakht*," says Katya as she goes by. "Kill him!"

RACHEL

It seemed like I had barely closed my eyes when I heard the telephone.

I reached out, picked up the receiver, and in a thick voice thanked the receptionist. I glanced at the clock and realized that I had had the phone ringing in my ears for half an hour without managing to emerge from sleep.

Avner taught me how to fall out of bed by rolling on myself, with my hands behind my head to protect myself from the shock on landing.

I followed his advice, but landed badly. I dragged myself over to the bathroom, cursing my clumsiness, then turned the tap on full blast and let the cold water gush over my head.

My teeth were chattering, I was shouting, and I saw again before my eyes Eytan and Tamar walking along the edge of the void, and the panicked expression in Michael's eyes.

I wrapped myself in a bathrobe and went into Elisheva's room.

There with my professor were Amos and Katya; Katya has gone mad. Elisheva looked like she was in a bad mood and Amos, dressed as if he were going to a wedding at the synagogue, was like an old, wounded beast.

I think I interrupted their conversation. Elisheva does not realize that I know how she feels about Amos. I ate the croissants Katya was kind enough to leave for me on the cart, drank a lukewarm coffee and went back to my bedroom.

I took a pair of white trousers and a tank top from my suitcase then changed my mind. These were the wrong clothes for the Old City. Jews and Muslims both would think they were too provocative. And my father would call me an exhibitionist. Fucking religion. I grabbed a blue cotton shirt and a skirt.

Elisheva came to sit on my bed.

"I have to get dressed."

"Go ahead."

Since she refused to leave me any privacy, I went to take refuge in the bathroom.

When I came back out Elisheva had not budged an inch.

"You look weird."

Elisheva did not say anything, she just sat there with her chin on her fist.

"Is it because of Amos?"

She did not react.

I sat down opposite her and all I could think of was my father who must be stamping his feet with impatience.

But I could not get away until I had spent a few moments with Elisheva.

"You want a coffee?" I said.

"No, thanks."

I opened the window. The sky was blue. The breeze caressed my face, burning like a lover's kiss.

In the distance a crane was moving blocks of concrete; from here they looked like sparkling lumps of sugar. Among the trees there were walls topped with barbed wire, balconies covered with flowers, television antennas. Jerusalem, your stones, whereon there hang a thousand bucklers. Rings of green adorn your ears. Your slow, religious, inspired crowds, ever cautious, as they walk over your saints.

"The *sharav* is still blowing," I said, and felt as if I were talking in a void.

Elisheva did not respond.

"I'm not used to this heat any more."

"And a lot of other things as well."

I turned around, instantly alert.

"Such as?"

"Your self-respect."

"A big word," I murmured through my teeth.

I bit into a roll and started looking for my sneakers. O.K., so they were under the bed. Shit, that meant I would have to get down on my knees in front of Elisheva to reach them. And that was absolutely out of the question. Fortunately, I remembered I had a pair of sandals that I had slipped into the pocket of my suitcase just as I was leaving. They were as old as Methuselah, but they would do.

In no time I had fastened the straps.

"See you at the rehearsal, Sheva."

"I have to talk to you."

"I'm late now."

"We have a concert."

"Oh, really?"

"Spare me the irony. Haim Newman was not pleased, yesterday. He said you were coming in late."

Late? And so he went to complain about it to Elisheva instead of discussing it with me?

"I wasn't coming in late."

"You were. By a note."

"One note in the entire piece?"

She nodded. "I told him it was the jetlag, the trip . . . But be careful."

"Newman can criticize my playing, my interpretation. But to say that I came in late by one note . . . That's absurd."

"I asked for a recording of the rehearsal. Do you have your cassette player?"

I nodded.

"Here's the cassette," she said, handing me a box. "Listen to it carefully. I would have preferred to work on it together, but since you can't . . ."

"My father needs me."

"Yes, yes . . ."

I dropped the cassette into my handbag, took my tape player and headphones. Giving me an icy look, Elisheva said, "Far be it from me to tell you what to do—"

"Great . . ."

"—but there's a rumour going around."

She went to get her tape player, a heavier device, not as portable as mine, and she pressed *play*. The music from *Don Giovanni* filled the room, at the very spot she had chosen.

"He's not like that," I said, collapsing in a chair.

"You're going after other women's husbands, now?"

"I'm not going after anyone. I am incapable of keeping anyone."

"Don't underestimate yourself."

"We spoke all of three minutes."

"He'll be back, all the faster. What do you think? He's a man!"

If she had said *kelb*, or *kelev*, or dog, her tone would have been identical.

"His wife is due to give birth a few weeks from now."

Elisheva stood up tall, as thin and long as a conductor's baton. And then flung at me, mercilessly, "He didn't choose you. He chose the Lipschitz girl! Get that into your head."

She was still speaking when I slammed the door behind me, my eyes swollen with tears. If anyone had met me in the corridor, I think they would have called the police. I was groaning like some sick animal as I ran toward the stairway and hurtled down the steps four at a time.

I do not know how I was counting the floors, but I could not find the way out.

I ended up in the laundry room, then the boiler room, and the kitchens. Surprised employees watched me go by but no-one stopped me.

I shoved open a service door at the back of the hotel and got out into the delivery yard, where swarms of buzzing flies were attacking the garbage spilling from the green iron cans.

On the bus I slipped the cassette into the player, wedged the headphones into my ears and pressed *play*. My playing exasperated me. I was not good enough, I had not mastered my performance. There were places where I should have emphasized the rhythm, others where I should have faded to a murmur, or held back, the better to release my energy rather than dissipating it throughout the piece. I took off my headphones. Newman was right to find fault with my transitions. Do you call that work? Might as well go on stage with a saw.

I had to correct my position when holding the cello, sit up straighter, allow my right arm to be more supple. Work. I put the headphones back on. But no matter how I concentrated, I just was not in the music. What did Elisheva want, exactly? Did she want me to relive her tragic love affair with Amos for her? And besides, who went and told her that I had seen Eytan? Nurit? Elena? The boys?

Shula and her husband were sitting on the sidewalk on their suitcases, waiting for their taxi to arrive. She was wearing a purple dress and shoes the same colour.

"When will you be back from Salonika?" I said, stopping for a moment.

"In a month. The time it takes to buy a bottle of ouzo for your father."

I managed a smile. What was it with Shula, always going on about my father?

162

"He doesn't drink, you know that."

"He does drink," said Shula, "I guarantee you." She turned to her husband, who nodded. "Once a year, at Purim. I'll keep the bottle for him until Purim."

I wished them a good trip and went up the stairs. I found my father standing by the door, his jacket on, all set to go.

"Oh, finally . . . I wondered if you'd ever get here," he said. Then he frowned. In a hoarse voice, almost too low, he added, "What's wrong? Have you been crying?"

"No."

"Something worrying you?"

"I'm tired."

"*Aïsh benti* . . . Look after yourself. Sleep. Eat."

I put my forefinger to my temple: "It's all in here . . . I have stage fright, over the concert."

"*Ma tehafish, rabi maak*, don't be afraid, God is with you," answered my father in Arabic.

I shook my head; our eyes met. "God helps you when you work . . . But I haven't done a fucking thing."

At that point my father lost his temper. He pounded his fist on the table and shouted, "If that's your reason for not coming with me to the Old City, well then, I'm not about to take my hat off to you."

ELISHEVA

Elisheva enters the Church of the Holy Sepulchre. Gold, paintings, mosaics, candelabras, statues, dome of the rotunda. The site was a pagan temple devoted to Venus before Constantine ordered Helena to build a church on the spot where Jesus had been crucified.

The Arab conquest destroyed it. Then the Byzantine architects managed to save the rotunda, and the Crusaders rebuilt it, in the Romanesque style, in the shape of the Cross.

Elisheva goes up to the aedicule housing the tomb of Christ.

Candles are burning in glass tulips and candlesticks. People bow, murmuring prayers, sobbing in silence, desperately confiding.

She does not know why she came here. Or why she is walking down the aisle, taking tiny steps, feeling a need to hide.

RACHEL

My father lifted up the mattress and stacks of banknotes appeared. I had never before seen so many fifty-shekel notes stockpiled in someone's house.

"You've been sleeping on them?"

"The best bank vault is my bed. This way at least I'm O.K. during the night."

"Your dreams are priceless."

"Vanity of vanities," said my father. "Wealth is in the hands of God. And I'm not doing this for myself, but for your brother."

I wanted to test him, to see whether he would give his son and daughter equal importance.

"And me?"

"What about you?"

"Are you going to do something for me?"

"Come back to Jerusalem and I'll give you my eyes."

"That would be more than enough."

"A manner of speaking."

"I know, I know . . . And if I stay in New York?"

"Then don't count on me."

"I just wish that you would accept my life the way it is!"

"Never, you hear me," he said, spluttering with fury. "There's more than just music on earth. *Mashub*, music, big deal, sure! Look at Elisheva! She never had children. Without you she'd be all alone. She'd live like a dog! You call that a life?"

"Stop right there."

"Either I have to agree with you or shut up, is that it?"

"Just take your money and let's go."

"We have to count it first."

My arms by my side, I looked at my father. He shoved a stack of bills in my hand and told me to recount it.

"Whatever for?"

"There might be a note missing from a bundle. I want everything in order. I don't want the moneychanger to think I'm some sort of thief."

"And who would have taken a note from you, Papa?"

"*Yazi ad!* Either you help me, or you get out of here."

I obeyed, despairing.

Why does this religious man, who has so much integrity, use only the sort of irritating language that drives you mad? He has his own idiom, so scornful that it invariably ends in conflict – and then he is the first one who is hurt and puzzled.

The love he feels for people is never in sync with his speech. His heart feels things that his lips cannot express. My father's language is utterly lacking in charm.

One day I transcribed his sentences in musical notation. I imagined a saxophone, and percussion, and pizzicato notes for the cello; the vocal parts were like singing exercises, rising to the upper scales to echo the sort of emotional shock he produces in the people close to him.

Two opposing themes incarnate my father.

The first is boom boom boom, a low, dull sound, when he says, "Get out of here!" or, "What am I going to do with you?" or "You and your opinion don't make any difference to me!", a pounding, disjointed rhythm, to a tight drumming sound.

The second is long and slow and gentle, and it represents his relationship with God. It is played by a flute, on two notes, E and B, which if you sing them in his musical French tongue, you get *Messie, see me, mais si, miss me,*[*] over and over again, to suggest a prayer-like

[*] Messiah, see me, but yes, miss me. (Translator's note.)

rhythm. Two notes to describe the way my father blesses the bread, two notes to express his joy at the synagogue, two notes when he is chanting his psalms.

I counted the banknotes and looked sidelong at my father. An old man at sixty, who has never given himself a break, who has "bled himself dry" for his children: how could I help but be moved?

When we had finished counting we had one hundred and fifty thousand shekels. There was one note too many. My father went hysterical. He ordered me to start counting all over again. I wet my thumb with my lips and did as he asked.

Finally he put everything into a rectangular blue cloth shoulder bag, a bit dirty and very ugly, then he zipped it closed and said, "Off we go!"

"I'd like to speak to Avner. Do you have his number?"

"What do you want with your brother?"

"I'm not going back to New York without seeing him!"

"You promise not to say anything about the apartment?"

"Yes."

"He has a pager in his truck for emergencies."

"I'm leaving in two days, isn't that an emergency?"

My father gave me the number.

Avner's voice came on the line.

"Rachel?"

There was interference on the line and we could hardly hear, but we managed to make an appointment for eight o'clock that evening in Romema, at the entrance to his building. My father stood there in front of me, inspecting my every word.

We took the bus, of course, a taxi was out of the question. When I told him I had an expense account, he gave me such a scornful look that I blushed. The state of Israel was suffering, and I, a musician, had come to suck its blood like some filthy parasite. To regain his trust I gave a hollow laugh and said I was only joking, and my father said, "That's more like it."

He sat behind the driver and began chatting with the passenger next to him about trifles. I was sitting three rows further back and I could see him laughing as he turned toward the window; I was touched by his suntanned face, his wrinkled neck. I thought, That is my father, he brought me into the world. I don't know how to define the feeling that binds me to him. I don't know whether I love him or whether I'm just trying to stay connected because I'm supposed to, so that I don't turn into a monster. Sometimes I even forget he exists, and sometimes I miss him so much I could die.

At King George my father got up and I did likewise, in silence. Fortunately there was no-one we knew on the bus, otherwise what sort of impression would that have made, a father and daughter not sitting side by side? But in fact there has always been this distance between us. My father behaves in a strange way when he is away from home. He walks quickly, on his own. He will not wait for anyone, not even my mother. She has got used to straggling behind. I think she must have protested when they were first married, but my father was not going to change his habits. When she has something to say to him, she leans up against the wall and she waits. She knows that sooner or later he will turn around and see she is not there. He always retraces his steps and he is always fairly annoyed, I must say.

"What's going on?" he will say, as soon as he is within earshot. "Why did you stop?"

Passers-by turn around, wondering what all the shouting and waving is about. My father does not give a damn. They want to look at him, well, let them look at him. If people like wasting their time spying on other people's lives, that is their problem, not his. In short, my mother stands there, placid and mute, and watches him coming back to get her. She waits until he is right there next to her to point to a dress she has noticed in a shop window, or a pair of shoes, or some item for the house. "What do you think?" she says with a smile, to soften him. My father starts grousing, "You always want to do too many things at once. We're going to be late." My mother does not

167

budge an inch. She wants his opinion, she will get his opinion. She does not shout, she does not get carried away – what would be the point?

My father relents, he gives a quick look at the object of her desire. He sighs, sniffs, focuses more on my mother's pointing finger than on the object itself. "It's too expensive!" is his initial reaction, which he then tempers by adding, "But if you want it . . ." which he then corrects by saying, "It's not reasonable, we have other plans!" My mother nods, she knows what to do. The next time she goes into town, she will stop off at the shop and ask to see the dress, the shoes, or the item for the house. Three times out of four she decides not to buy it. And if she does go ahead and decide to treat herself, she immediately feels guilty. She never uses it right away. She lets it age on a shelf, she will pass her purchase without touching it, without daring to enjoy it. Sometimes it takes her months to start using it.

My father and I walked to the Lions' Gate, with him in front and me behind. When we got close to the ramparts I felt my heart melt. Every time I come to the city of David my head begins to spin, and I think in music. Music fills my being.

The silence of the souk astonished me. The narrow little streets were deserted, and there was very little merchandise out on the sidewalk. The intifada had dealt a blow to commerce, and business did not seem to be thriving. Worse than that, a sort of lassitude reigned everywhere. The iron shutters on the shops were lowered, blue and green against the grey walls. In the centre of each shutter was a black spray-painted slogan in Arabic; it was like an immense shout.

My father headed with a sure step down a small street, his thumb in the strap of his bag that he continued to carry as carelessly as if it contained only a pile of worthless paper. I felt feverish; I even had goosepimples, I confess, every hair on my body standing on end. And what if we fell into an ambush? What if some young kids began to throw stones at us? How could I save my father's skin, and my own? The money was the least of my worries. My father's life was worth more than a hundred and fifty thousand shekels. And all this fuss so that Avner could become a property owner! Not to mention the fact that the money had been put aside at the cost of merciless savings on meat and sugar. Who would ever believe me if I told them that my father walked around the Old City right in the middle of the intifada just to convert his money? Avner could go fuck himself. I wanted to run over to my father and shout, Stop it right there, stop right now, you're pissing me off with your stupid ideas, let's go home, right now; but all I did was follow him, the way he had ordered me to.

And besides, he seemed to know where he was going, as if he had been born in this souk, and nothing in his attitude betrayed the slightest fear. Even when he saw soldiers standing guard at the intersections, their machine guns at the ready, their fingers on the trigger, even then nothing could dampen his determination.

On he went, my crazy father, deeper and deeper into the tiny streets, heading straight for the Damascus Gate. Suddenly we came upon a crowd of people, pilgrims with radiant faces returning to their hotel after a visit to the Holy Sepulchre. Their eyes shone, strangely dilated, as if they were on heroin.

My father followed the cluster of people and I felt the vice around my chest loosen. As long as we were near a crowd, we would not be in danger, nothing could happen to us.

But my father let the pilgrims get ahead of us. He slowed down, walking more calmly, for a reason I failed to grasp. I did not dare go up to him. He had said, "You follow me and don't speak to me under any circumstances."

Finally he stopped outside a small shop. The owner was sitting on his doorstep smoking a water pipe. Above him hung a sign that said in Hebrew, Arabic and English: "Foreign exchange".

The man had a pot belly and his backside was wide as a barrel. My father was talking and the changer did not let go of the pipe of his narghile; pinching his lips, he went on sucking. From a distance I could see him gravely nodding his head. Then he began shaking it from right to left, *no, no, no*. No what? What was my father saying to him? Asking him for a better rate? Asking him for the same rate as when they had had their previous discussion, even though the shekel had plunged?

My father was standing up, the moneychanger was sitting down, his legs crossed below the stool, his narghile in his mouth.

Time stood still.

I told myself that they would notice me if I suddenly stopped walking and just planted myself there; I absolutely had to find something to do.

To while away the time as I was waiting, I went over to a stand selling scarves and stencilled T-shirts, all glorifying Jerusalem. Loud colours, hideous designs . . . Who would ever wear this stuff? Americans? Asians? The few Israelis who ventured into the souk?

At last the moneychanger pressed his wide palm against the side of the stool and stood up. While I unfolded a scarf, I saw that he was stocky and squat. He held his hand out before my father to say, Stay there, wait for me. My father complied, biting his lips, a tic that I recognized and which with him is always a sign that he is upset, either physically or emotionally.

Just then the shopkeeper came up to me. He greeted me courteously, his hand on his heart. He asked me what I might like, and could he help me. I said that I had not made up my mind. The man smiled. With a nod of his head he gestured to me to come into his shop. He had lovely things in his baskets, Have a look, have a look, he said, in English. Years ago, he would have spoken to me in Hebrew. He would have been proud to show me that he had learned to speak the language, that he had adapted to the Jews.

I stretched my neck, looked closely at the fake bronze candlesticks, the mother-of-pearl chessboards, the olive-wood rosaries, the hand-painted plates.

"Please, go inside . . . Please . . ."

I hesitated, took one last glance over toward my father. The street was perfectly quiet. My father stood there with his thumb in the shoulder strap of his bag.

I went into the shop.

"*Tfadal . . . Shu . . . Inta min oun?*" said the shopkeeper, following closely in my steps.

My heart pounding, I bought a few simple things, the cheapest ones, fish made of coloured glass, a jewellery box and a painted bowl. When I took out my wallet my hands were trembling like leaves. The shopkeeper noticed. His eyes narrowed, he gave me a sharp look. Why was I afraid? What of? He wrapped up my purchases in newspaper printed in Arabic, slowly, meticulously, folding down the corners and holding them in place with Scotch tape. Then he took my money and handed me the change.

I went back out into the street.

My father had vanished.

The moneychanger had lowered his iron shutter.

Where was my father?

If he had finished his transaction, he must be wandering around with thirty thousand dollars in his bag. Or else . . .

My heart in shreds, I hurried down to the end of the street. No-one. I retraced my steps. No-one. Neither to the right, nor to the left. My father had vanished into thin air.

And suddenly I panicked.

Where had he gone?

"The Ride of the Valkyries" carried me away at a frenetic, implacable pace: the brass in ascending thirds, the rapid violin arpeggios, the blaring horns. That immense blaring of horns to express the fall, then the theme starting up again in a new tonality.

It was a trap.

I would never see my father again.

They had robbed him and cut his throat.

I figured that if I ran like mad to the intersection I would eventually come upon one of the patrols that policed the souk.

But how much could I tell them? That my father had risked his life for a few extra dollars?

And I had nearly decided to go and pound on the moneychanger's shutter when the iron rods began to move up with a creaking sound. My father's shoes, then his trousers, then his torso came into sight, and the shutter was still rolling when at last I saw my father's laughing face appear.

A brief, cordial handshake with the moneychanger, a last salaam, a blessing.

It abruptly occurred to me that my father was a nutcase and that his madness was of a very particular kind, the consequence of his birth in an Islamic country. The fact that he was a confirmed Zionist changed nothing in his case. He carried inside him a stubborn, secret territory, a territory where Jews and Arabs could get along, do business together, and go on speaking to one another.

My father gave me a fleeting gesture of recognition and headed off again toward the Jaffa Gate.

He was now carrying around stacks of dollars instead of stacks of shekels, and he was buoyant, I could see it from the springy, almost bouncy way he was walking. On he went, then he paused by a stand of spices, lingered over some pewter plates, carpets, djellabas. He was strolling along as if all danger had been brushed aside, as if there were nothing to fear from anyone at all.

I would have liked to say a few words to him, to tell him how afraid I had been of losing him, how sorry I was for all these years of misunderstanding. I could not say a word. I was still walking right behind him, beneath the arcades of the souk, and I was afraid I would annoy him if I went up to him on such a futile pretext.

Then I saw the Jaffa Gate, which the Arabs call Bab el-Khalil, the Gate of the Friend, there before us against the sky.

My father could choose between two passageways. The most ancient, decorated with machiocolations and arrow slits, was built by Suleiman the Magnificent. The other portal, six metres high, had been carved in the wall so that Kaiser Wilhelm II's carriage could go through. My father chose the Kaiser's gate, no doubt in homage to Theodor Herzl who, in this exact spot, had had the audacity to inform the Kaiser of his plans for the return of the Jews to the Promised Land.

We were right on time.

My father had an appointment with the lawyer at two o'clock to sign the deed of sale.

MEIR

"It's such a pity!"

Through the open window, behind the closed shutters with their movable slits, the rumble of the buses rises and falls with the flow of traffic.

Every three minutes you can hear the whooshing of the bus doors opening at the station, the moaning of pistons, the purr of their accordion joints.

The poor soundproofing is clearly the only thing wrong with this brand new building in Rehavia. It has been built like a palace, with steel turrets, porches and garden plots, and it seems to have sprung from the pages of a picture book. As if the architect had wanted to convey something to those people who, like himself, had stayed behind in their childhood. An excellent design project, which had made a lot of money. All the flats had been sold off plan to the companies whose bronze plaques shone at the entrance to the stairwells. Everyone in Jerusalem rates it a prestigious address.

The room is vast, square; there is a heady scent of vanilla. The lawyer has furnished it tastefully: a bench decorated with cushions, an oak desk, two cane chairs. The dim light dissolving into the walls gives it a warm, intimate atmosphere. Only the background noise of the buses is nerve-wracking. But in the long run you get used to it and eventually you no longer hear it.

The lawyer straightens the box of pens on his desk, scratches his hand and neck then leans down to scratch his leg.

Meir Tropmann has a disease of the lymph which has made him monstrously obese. But his head, which has kept its proportions, is still handsome. Silky chestnut hair falling in waves on his forehead; eyebrows drawn as if with a brush; a small, pleasant mouth and a lively gaze in brown eyes rimmed with thick long lashes. When you see his head, you find yourself thinking that all it would take would be a sharp pin to deflate the black-clad balloon on which that head sits in order to recover the lawyer's true body. Alas, his illness is incurable and will only get worse with time.

Tropmann knows his days are numbered. He lives with it.

His wife continues to love him, his two children are charming, his clients have remained loyal. The hideous fingers of disease have not affected his intelligence. And he has set out to prove there is no better lawyer, no better negotiator in the entire country. The two luxuriously framed photographs on the wall will certify his worth to anyone who, upon meeting him for the first time, might find him slumped in his armchair, dropsical and repugnant.

In one of the photographs he is in the Knesset shaking hands with Begin. In the other, he is at Camp David, in the foreground next to Shamir, who looks like a dwarf next to him. Tropmann led the team of jurists and finalized the text which was brought to the negotiating table.

"A pity for whom, Meir?" Elisheva says, ironically.

Meir Tropmann lifts a cup to his lips and takes a swallow of tea.

"For me, for everyone who used to enjoy meeting at your place. Your house on Rehov Haneviim is a symbol."

"I need the money."

The lawyer nods, still scratching. He remembers the old house with its thick walls, the balcony overlooking the street, the big, airy, red-tiled room, constantly echoing with music.

When his parents took him to Elisheva's he had just turned ten:

he was thin, too well-behaved, and he lived through books. He was fast becoming unpopular with the other children, who bullied him. His mother spoke to Elisheva at length. Such an extraordinarily bright child, who was withdrawn, who needed company. She had the notion that music could transform him into a happy adolescent. Tropmann was sure that his mother was confusing classical music with the tango, and cellos with accordions. Music lessons would put a big dent in the family's income, but they had only one child, they could make sacrifices, and bring him up to be a deputy, or a president.

Elisheva did not laugh at the joke.

Finally his mother fell silent, somewhat lost. She had said things in jest, but deep down it was her dream, her sensitive spot. She cared for her son as if it were her mission to bring him up to be above others. Her son was going to be someone. And music was part of the programme.

Elisheva listened patiently.

In those days, she was still poor and she lived from the lessons she gave. But she had built her walls, she would not take just any child solely to eat her fill. She wanted only those children who were motivated. Mo-ti-va-tion was Elisheva's great creed.

She went up to Meir, and as he would not look up at her, she crouched down before him and whispered, trying to get him to look at her, "Meir? Who is it that wants you to take music lessons? Is it you, or is it your parents?" The parents looked at each other, disconcerted. Meir remembers he did not dare reply and she was obliged to repeat her question. Given his silence, Elisheva eventually asked the parents to leave. "Let him stay alone with me for half an hour. Go for a walk. When you come back, I'll tell you whether I can take him on."

Elisheva handed him a bow. "Wave it. Make it dance . . . Good. Now, go and sit behind the cello. Pull it towards you. Touch the wood. See how much it weighs. Tell me how you feel."

Elisheva probably does not remember that first lesson she gave him. So many pupils went through her living room on Haneviim

Street. "If you don't want to play, no-one can force you. You are the one who will be learning this instrument, not your parents. I don't want this to be a source of pain between you. You must know that your life will be bitter for many years. Your parents will harass you and tell you about the money they are throwing out of the window. They will say, 'Practise, practise' . . . You will obey them, and hate your cello. That is not the way I see music."

He had listened to her, gravely, even though he did not understand everything she was saying. Since his mother wanted him to study music, he would study. Where was the problem?

"But if you are motivated," said Elisheva, "your life will fill with light. You will never be alone again. Your instrument will go everywhere with you, in joy and in sorrow."

Meir leafs through a thick file, pulls out a sheet of copy paper and reads it out loud.

He has taken care of everything over these last four months. He sold the house to some rich Americans, paid the last instalments and capitalized on the sale by investing the money at a profitable interest rate. Elisheva had been calling him from New York and dictating her mysterious orders: book the Binyanei Hauma for a single concert, use her money to hire the Philharmonic Orchestra, send an astronomical amount of money to a travel agency in Venezuela.

He complained, at every assignment. Her money was vanishing. Had she lost her mind?

From New York Elisheva merely repeated that this was what she wanted. She had become rich in the United States, so now she could behave like one of those wealthy donors who, thirty years earlier, had made it possible for Israel to have its classical concerts.

"Israel, O.K. But Caracas? What have you got to do with Caracas?"

"There is a debt I must repay."

He eventually did everything as she requested.

They are meeting today as a formality and, he hopes, out of friendship.

176

"The balance is in this account at the Bank Leumi," he says, handing her a paper on the bank's letterhead.

"Because there is still some money left?"

"Good Lord, I should hope so. Your house was worth a fortune, Elisheva. I took my commission . . ."

"You did well," she says, indifferently.

"7 per cent instead of 10."

"There, you were wrong."

"What is the matter with you? Do you know what 3 per cent represents? People here will fight over ten shekels."

"That's just what I mean. You were wrong."

They fall silent.

The lawyer's bare arms are as red as lobsters. Elisheva watches with growing unease as his wide, rounded fingernails scrape against his skin, back and forth, mechanically, faster and faster. Meir is in discomfort, that much is obvious. She has a tube of cream in her bag that she brought from New York; it might provide him some relief. She opens her bag to take it out, then thinks better of it. Finish with the paperwork first, sign the powers of attorney, close the accounts. She will give him the tube of cream just before she leaves.

"Could you take care of the . . . um . . . balance?"

"Right. If I remember correctly, in dollars it comes to—"

He does not finish his sentence. With the back of her wrist Elisheva brushes off the amount: "I want to leave half of it to Rachel . . ."

Now he gets it: she must be ill, doomed by cancer. She is preparing her will.

"What is the matter with you?" he cries. "Tell me the truth . . ."

"Meir, you are not to worry."

"Have you seen a doctor?"

"There's nothing wrong with me."

"So this concert, it's just a charade, and the sale, it's all . . ."

He is on the verge of tears.

If he owes anything to anyone, it is to this woman. Without her

177

he would have become autistic. Again he sees the music room on Rehov Haneviim, the clutter of instruments, old keys, music stands, piles of sheet music. Where did she buy her cellos in the 1960s? She told him one day that she came to Israel with a guitar that an English soldier had found for her. Very quickly she started her collection – harmonicas, saxophones, tom-toms, clarinets. And she attracted energetic young teachers who convinced her to open a school.

"Meir, can we continue?"

"You're keeping secrets from me!"

"You are my confidential adviser, what more do you want?"

These words of praise restore his serenity; the smile returns to his face. Elisheva uses the moment to get him back on track.

"So, 50 per cent for Rachel."

"And the rest? Are you keeping the rest?"

"I want to give it to charity. Sick children, handicapped people, the elderly, the blind. And preferably in that order."

The lawyer nods, dismayed. His breasts, as voluminous as a woman's, jiggle whenever he moves. His bad feeling has been confirmed. You just do not go around getting rid of everything in such a casual way.

So, at the risk of seeming like a damned nuisance, he insists once again, his handsome eyes staring at the cellist; she remains implacable.

"And what are you going to live off?"

"I don't need a great deal."

"You're no longer young."

"I have some money put away in the United States."

"My heart is shouting to me that that's a lie."

She gives a sigh.

"Do you need my signature, Meir?"

"Yes," he says. "But I have to draw up the contracts for the transfer of property."

"Just write a simple note, the way you always do."

Tropmann is about to add a final warning, when a sudden gurgling rises up from deep inside him, as dreadful as a sewer. The lawyer goes tense and tightens his buttocks, looking painfully towards the silent window in hopes of a certain miracle, one that occurs a hundred times a day: to hear a bus come rattling along with all its metal shaking, or the exclamations of passengers disembarking, the miracle of the cacophony that will hide the explosion of his intestines. But there is only stubborn silence. The street remains empty. The gurgling spreads throughout the room and there is nothing to attenuate it, no birdsong, no child's cry, no mother's shouting. For ten, twenty, thirty seconds, his face burns with shame, and the gurgling roars like thunder.

Elisheva looks down at the handbag in her lap. She now knows why there is such a heady smell of vanilla in the room. And when at last the rumbling sound stops, the lawyer is out of sorts, at a loss for words. With his eyes on the white sheet he has only one thing in mind, to be left alone with his illness. He wants to purify his hands, spray perfume all over his body.

He takes a sheet of paper from the drawer and quickly writes up a draft agreement, while the sweat dries on his forehead. The sweat, but not the shame.

"There we are. This restrictive clause gives you one month to consider your decisions. In case you change your mind."

"Thank you."

Elisheva leans over and puts her signature to the document without bothering to read the lawyer's spidery scrawl.

"Have we finished?"

"I think so."

"Will you come to the concert?"

"I have reserved three seats for my family and two others for my old bones."

Elisheva gets up.

She adjusts her dress, loops the handle of her bag over her elbow. The lawyer pushes back his armchair, designed especially for obese people, in order to keep his spine straight, a sort of black leather swing: he had it imported from the United States.

"I'll see you out."

She does not dare tell him that there is no need, she knows the way. The lawyer heaves his massive body out of the chair, pressing with all the strength in his arms on the armrests. She catches a glimpse, beneath his trouser leg, of the bandages around his ankles; his socks, as wide as boats, have fallen down.

They walk to the door, Elisheva as frail as a reed, Tropmann waddling like a penguin.

"How are your children?"

"They are magnificent."

"And their music?"

"They are so lazy!" he says, stopping short.

Elisheva bursts out laughing when she sees how crestfallen he looks.

"Meir, my little friend, have them listen to records. That is just as good. Did you keep the list of performers I recommended? It hasn't changed."

He holds out his hand. Lightly, she shakes his thick podgy fingers, with a smile.

"Meir, thank you."

Elisheva goes back out into the street and the dazzling sunshine. She sits on the bench in the bus shelter, and from the inside pocket of her handbag she pulls out a pair of old-fashioned sunglasses that stay, more or less, on her nose. Then she takes out her notebook and pen and ticks off Meir's name. And realizes she forgot to give him her miracle cream.

RACHEL

I left my father outside the lawyer's office and went back into the Old City, despite the danger, the intifada, the stone-throwing. I do not know why I did, something seemed to beckon me, a desire stronger than I was. Perhaps I was headed towards disaster, but I could not help it.

Outside the Lions' Gate, reservists were sitting on their kit eating sandwiches. They had a casual way of wearing their uniform, their tunics open on their undershirts, their boots loosely laced. Men in their fifties, with beer guts and greying hair, a weary air about them. They were sprawled on the ground, listening distractedly to the lively blonde girl who stood before them, her finger pointing to the Montefiore Windmill, telling them the story of the wealthy, devoted English philanthropist who, at the end of the nineteenth century, built the first Jewish quarter outside the walls of the Old City.

She could have been giving them a maths or physics lesson, the men would have listened with the same indifference. All they could think of was having a rest before it was time to go and get on with their security duties around the Esplanade of the Temple; they did not give a damn about history, they were in it up to their necks.

The girl saw me slip under the arch and she shouted, "*Mesukan!* It's dangerous."

I answered with a nod that I knew, and went on my way.

As soon as I began to walk through the narrow streets, I heard the Song of Songs. *Shezaphani hashemesh,* "the sun hath looked upon me: my mother's children were angry with me; they made me the keeper of the vineyards . . ." As I walked, there were tears in my eyes. I did not know why I was weeping, no doubt because of the flute that I heard briefly as I walked past a school, a flute accompanying a children's choir. In any event, once I heard it, the sound of the flute did not leave me as I walked past the Christian quarter and entered the Via Dolorosa. I could sense the soft skin of Jerusalem beneath the powerful rough white stone of the walls. A soft skin beneath the bone of the city. Hundreds of men have died for this sanctuary. Thousands of young men only twenty years old have been wounded here. But in the city nothing has changed. An incredible paradox, the terrible paradox of a civilization that will not allow a single stone in the city to be moved, but which will let people die for it.

I hurried through the tiny narrow streets of the souk. Sights and sounds burst in my head, while my sandals slapped against the steps. I think I was running, my intestines in a knot, as if I were in Vietnam, or deep in the jungle. There was not a single soldier in sight, all the small shops were closed now, the sun was weighing upon the green canvas awnings and there was no-one, not a soul to be seen, no old people, no women or children. I had to get out of there, I had to get back to a busier neighbourhood, no matter what.

And yet like a sleepwalker I continued on my way toward the Esplanade of the Temple. I was thinking, what does death matter, here or elsewhere, now or later, what does it matter, I see no point to my life, no reason to stay alive, and if I have to fall, I would rather it were here than in America. Another sound, another music was prevailing, muted this time, consisting solely of strings; a music, dear Lord, played by a viola, two violins and a cello.

The Old City was terribly still, silent and devastating.

I was looking right into Jerusalem, as if it were a jewel, and its light was blinding. Notes came to my lips, and vanished instantly, notes that were like drops of water falling from a fountain, and the violin took up the theme of the drop of water with the cello, and gradually I heard the sea.

From street to street the music pursued me, mingled with noise and words.

I went past the arch of the Convent of the Sisters of Zion, I went through Bab al-Hutta, and for the pleasure, looped up through Rehov Habustanim before going back down toward Sha'ar HaArayot. Hassidim went by; they looked like flying fish. It would soon be time for the Mincha prayer.

An Armenian priest in a black robe with a white silk stole around his neck was sitting in the shade of an archway.

"Young lady?"

I turned around.

The priest beckoned me over, waving his hand.

"Who are you?"

I smiled.

"Why do you ask?"

"I saw you coming from far away. Sit down next to me, I have to speak to you."

I sat on a stone. I looked at the priest's hands on his knees. Fine white hands, well cared for, his nails filed and transparent. On the ring finger of his left hand was a finely wrought silver band.

And that is when I noticed that the priest was handicapped. The folds of his cassock hid the little wheelchair that enabled him to get around.

"I am listening . . ."

The priest looked me in the eyes. He had big blue eyes, set symmetrically on either side of a straight nose with flared nostrils, eyes that sparkled with silver and light.

"You are a garden."

"Me?"

"You."

"I don't understand," I said, stammering, after a long silence.

"You don't have to understand things the minute you hear them."

I gave a little laugh, but I could feel the sobs that were shaking me from head to toe.

"I don't understand, but it's a nice compliment. Perhaps I only came back to the Old City to meet you and hear those words."

"Perhaps, indeed."

"What do you mean by a garden?"

"It is a place where there is water and sap."

"Thank you."

Our gazes met again and I had the impression I was dancing with this man with his dead legs.

"Don't let anyone cut down your trees, or pull up your plants, or tear up your earth."

I nodded. This priest was mad, but he was harmless and generous, a poet.

We began to speak quietly and slowly. The priest quoted to me from Jesus and then said, "Do you have the strength to push me?"

"I hope so."

He lifted either side of his cassock and two wheels appeared. He put his hands on the wheels and gave a gentle push with the flat of his hand.

I stood behind the wheelchair and we set off on a walk.

"Do you have a bit of money on you?"

"Yes."

"Have you ever eaten at Abd el Hakim's?"

"No."

"I can teach you his best dishes."

"Teach me?"

"Do you know the meaning of Abd el Hakim?" he said, waving his hand to dismiss my question.

"The servant of the judge."

"Very good. How do you know Arabic?"

"My family comes from Tunisia."

"A good point for you. I like Tunisians. They are gentle. And kind. I have never regretted the time I've spent with them."

I thought that the priest could not know my father. But I kept quiet.

"Turn right. Now, listen to me. Whenever we come to a cross-roads, you must systematically choose the path to the right. It's a bit long, but this way we won't run into any steps. Is that alright with you?"

The priest spoke Hebrew with an Armenian accent. All through the Kahn el-Zeit souk he sang Ave Maria in a tenor voice, while I pushed his wheelchair as if I were in a dream. And all through the narrow streets his voice spun the impression of an enchantment.

When we came to a blackberry bush the priest stopped singing. I walked on the purple berries that had fallen to the ground. I could not avoid them. They covered the ground the way the olives in September spill along the pavement in Givat Tzarfatit.

We went into a dark restaurant. The owner came over to us. He kissed the priest's ring. A Muslim honouring an Orthodox priest: this I had never seen. But then perhaps I have more than my share of preconceived ideas.

Abd el Hakim took the priest's wheelchair from my hands and whirled it in and out of the tables as if they were dancing a Viennese waltz, guiding him into a quiet corner far away from the bar.

In a flash our table was covered with a paper tablecloth, whereas the other customers were being served in a simpler fashion. People immediately began to look at us, surprise and envy in their eyes. Why such a display of respect? Who was this priest, with a Jewish girl, that the owner went so far as to spread his table with a cloth?

"How are you, my friend?" asked Abd el Hakim.

The priest merely smiled mysteriously.

"This priest is a rare man," whispered Abd el Hakim when I got up to go to the toilet. "You are lucky to have met him."

"How do you know him?"

"My child! My dear beloved child! I was born in Jerusalem. I know every stone, every man, every cat in this town."

"Really? But you didn't know me until today!"

"That is because you live in one of the new neighbourhoods. Are those neighbourhoods part of Jerusalem? No! So I'm not obliged to know them. But don't let me keep you. The toilets are in the court-yard, behind that brown door. I'll give you the key to the realm. You'll see how vast it is. Just don't get lost."

I laughed, while Abd el Hakim took a flat key from a chain and handed it to me solemnly.

"Go in peace."

Behind the brown door was a space of three feet by six, painted lemon yellow. The toilets were Turkish style, reeking. I hurried, and splattered my sandal with urine.

When I got back to our table, the priest was rolling the boxwood beads of a rosary between his fingers. Abd el Hakim set down the glasses and cutlery and then, like a magician, he pulled a pencil from behind his ear where it had been hidden.

"What would you like?" he said, preparing to write on his palm.

The priest ordered lamb chops, and I chose humus and tahini. I realized I would have liked to have had lunch with my father, and that because of his business with the money I had been deprived of his company.

"I didn't ask your name."

"Rachel."

"Are you married?"

"No."

"What are you waiting for?"

"I don't know."

The priest leaned over to me.

"You must not grow old without love."

"No?"

"No."

Our dishes arrived and the conversation paused. The priest picked up a chop that was still steaming and began to nibble on it. Large pieces of rare meat disappeared behind his teeth. When he had finished gnawing at the chop he picked up another one and devoured it just as quickly. As he ate he informed me that he came from a long line of merchants. His father had sent him to the convent at the age of fifteen and in those days he had been tall and strong and, above all, he could walk.

"I was a giant. I was a full head taller than my classmates. And the women looked at me with desire."

"And you? How did you look at them?"

"I am attracted to women. I am a man before I am a priest. I love women and I love God. Sometimes I love God more than women. And some days women more than God. I would have liked to be able to pray to God and love women. But that, alas, is totally out of the question. That's why I fell ill."

He explained that he had prayed and prayed, but his prayers had no effect on his illness. No matter how often he knelt on the icy tiles of the convent floor, or stretched out his full length on the carpets by the altar, his illness got worse and worse. By the age of thirty he had lost the use of his legs. And he became resigned to being nothing but a body that others would lift by the armpits, that others would carry to the bathroom or toilet or bed.

I listened to the priest as I dipped pieces of pita bread in my humus. He was unstoppable and my silence did not seem to bother him, on the contrary.

"I'm a priest, an invalid, and I'm in love with beauty. It's not just one cross that I carry, but many, and they overlap. Did I say they overlap? No, the proper expression is: they are superimposed upon each other."

I laughed. The priest's appetite was incredible. After the lamb chops he ordered a cake made of cheese and honey, then a bowl of ice cream. Eating was enough to make him happy.

"Rachel . . ."

"Yes?"

"Children will come from your womb to drink the milk of your breasts."

"That's a prayer that the Jews sing, isn't it?"

"Perhaps . . . I like to mix up prayers. I tell myself God will know what to do with them."

I paid for our meal and said goodbye to the priest. I had just enough time to go back to the hotel for a shower and change before the appointed time for the rehearsal at the Binyanei Hauma.

Abd el Hakim followed me out into the street.

187

"Young lady, I'd like to give you a piece of advice . . ."

"I'm listening."

"There are rioters heading towards Mount Scopus. The Old City is dangerous."

"Thank you. I'm going home."

"My son will go with you to the Zion Gate. You'll be safe with him."

I wanted to refuse, but Abd el Hakim called out. A six-year-old boy came to us, dressed in white trousers and a plaid shirt, his head shaven, his eyes black and shining and deep. His father spoke a few words into his ear. The child took my hand, but without smiling, and led me on.

"You know what," said the boy when we came to the end of the street, "I hate the Jews."

"Then leave me here."

"I'm obeying my father. He said Bab el Yahud and I'm taking you to Bab el Yahud."

"Don't bother, I know the way."

"You hate me, too. I hate you. And you hate me. You'll kill me. Or I'll kill you."

"You're wrong there. I want you to live. I don't want anything bad to happen to you."

"You're Jewish."

"So?"

"So we're enemies."

I stopped.

"You're being stupid. I'm fed up with you. Let go of my hand. I'm cross. Very, very cross. Your father is nicer than you are. And more intelligent. And stronger."

The boy began to laugh.

"Some day I'll be just like my father."

"You have to learn how to talk to girls, first."

"*Yallah.* Let's go. *Yallah, yallah.*"

"Tell me your name."

"No."

"I'll never be your babysitter."

As I left the gate behind, in the southwest corner of the wall, where the border had divided Jerusalem from 1948 to 1967, I saw a woman in a white dress with polka dots and ran after her.

"Elisheva!"

My teacher turned around. When she saw me her eyes filled with rage.

"Are you spying on me?"

"What?"

"I didn't think you were like that," she said.

I looked at her, dumbfounded. Her eyelids were ravaged, her cheeks gaunt, her hair dishevelled. Suddenly, as if she were overcome by nausea, Elisheva took a handkerchief from her pocket and held it against her nose.

"How long have you been following me?"

"You're crazy! Why would I do such a thing?"

She threw me a suspicious glance, then smiled. She took my elbow, muttering an apology to justify her anger, then in a wink she was once again the level-headed woman I knew. And I believed her, preoccupied as I was by the day I had spent.

We melted into the crowd, always thick on Yaffo Street. Elisheva plied me with questions. How was my day? How were my parents? I told her about the moneychanger in the Old City, and my lunch with the handicapped priest, and the six-year-old boy who wanted to kill me. Elisheva listened, her expression grave. She stopped off at a pastry shop and bought me some cheese pie. A bit further along she offered me a can of Coke.

"You need your strength," she said, affectionately. "The rehearsal may well be exhausting today."

"So let's take a taxi."

"The distance is nothing. No-one would agree to take us."

All along the sidewalk there was a jumble of dishes, fabrics, shoes, crates full of ripe fruit swarming with flies. Live hens in cages beat their wings, trays of eggs were being sold at auction, and handcarts pushed by skeletal boys with knotty muscles wove their way past a pair of buses.

I found a driver who agreed to let us off outside the Binyanei Hauma. I offered the guy a sizeable tip, and he was willing to navigate the traffic in the market. It was the time of day when the vendors marked down their wares to get rid of them, and all the poor people in town hurried to do their shopping.

By the time I realized I had not asked Elisheva a single question about her day, we were already right outside the concert hall. The musicians were settled behind their music stands and one by one were trying to tune their instruments in the spotlights. Strings rasped; the winds hissed softly; there was a thrumming of percussions, a tinkling of triangles.

Two sound technicians were bent over, quickly checking cables, microphones and amplifiers, and they connected the sound system to adjust the balance between the bass drum and the alto; the interference blasted our eardrums.

Newman and the stage manager hurried over to Elisheva. They exchanged a few words, then the conductor went to his place, leafed through his score, and raised his hands.

We set to work.

Time flew by. I played the way Elisheva had taught me, my body tense and straight, feet apart, all the weight of my body spread on my thighs. The scroll of the instrument light against my shoulder, I plucked the strings and attacked with the bow. My name, my origins, Tamar on the stone rampart, and my father's white temples, all exploding before my eyes while the music entered through every pore. Vanity of vanities. The angel of death was watching over us, implacably. It was watching over the soldiers running behind their

Jeeps, the civilians who scurried to catch a bus, the financiers, the politicians, and the rest of us, poor us, who so proudly thought that we could control things for a thousand years.

Newman interrupted me.

"Play that measure over again."

I played the piece again, according to his instructions.

"No," he said, consulting his score. "That's no good. Shorten your left hand."

I shortened it, but it still did not suit him. The other musicians were waiting. The rehearsal was dragging on. Newman was hard on everyone, despotic with me. He saw I was tying myself in knots and, instead of reassuring me, he started nitpicking, harassing me relentlessly. Faster, forte, allegro, allegro, he said, tapping his baton on the podium. No, vivace now. Tempo, tempo. My technique was up to scratch. But the soul of the piece eluded me. I was crimson with shame, sweating profusely, my hands slipped, I made one mistake after another. Newman lowered his arms, sighed, looked at the orchestra as if to call on them to witness my incompetence.

When he began to roar that we were not in some tea room painting our fingernails, I nearly laughed in his face to retort that he was mixing up his venues, had he never been to a nail salon?

Fortunately, Elisheva caught my eye, and her dilated irises helped me to get my wits about me again. I swallowed my sarcasm and thrust the bow against the strings.

At the end of the rehearsal Newman took Elisheva to one side. I figured they must be talking about me. The conductor had not let me off lightly. He did not like the way I was playing. He thought it was frivolous, too rhythmic, probably too modern. Elisheva, with a forced smile, nodded her head without protesting.

She came back over to me, frowning.

"What did he say?"

"He doesn't like your placing. He thinks you're not emphasizing the phrasing enough."

"But you're the one who . . ."

"That's what I told him."

"I can let someone else take my place. I don't have a problem with that."

"You're kidding, I hope?"

I was at the end of my tether, my back was killing me, my face was gaunt. My hair was soaking with sweat, sticking to my cheeks. We had been playing for over four hours without a break. My arm was so leaden that I could no longer move my shoulder. I tried to lift a cigarette to my lips and it rolled on to the floor.

"I think you're very tired, Rachel."

"That has nothing to do with it."

"You haven't slept a wink since we left New York."

"That has nothing to do with it," I said again, harshly.

She took the match and the box from my hands, and the match flared with a cracking sound. I took a puff, while she pushed me over into a discreet corner. All we needed was for the stage manager to catch me smoking. Elisheva repeated her offer to work with me during the evening. Not long. An hour. Just those passages that Newman had referred to.

"What do you think?"

"He's worn me out. I'm fucking fed up."

"Rachel!"

I preferred not to answer. They were turning off the spotlights. In the fading light, the musicians hurried to see to their instruments one last time, changing a string, fixing a screw on a cymbal, placing their clarinets and oboes in their cases. They were chatting in hushed voices, happy to have finished.

When I went back on the stage, I came upon Newman. He was telling the viola player off, and the poor guy was muttering incoherently in reply.

Elisheva helped me to put the cellos in a safe place. Newman left, along with the stage manager. The musicians disappeared one by one.

"You need to trust yourself a bit more," Elisheva said. "That's what he wants."

"I don't like the man. He doesn't know how to conduct."

The wrinkles at the corners of her lips deepened, and she slumped as if I had been attacking her and not him.

"He's one of the best conductors in Israel."

"He doesn't like the way I play, and I don't like the way he conducts. So we're even."

"Play the way you feel. Give more of yourself."

I gave her a vague nod and turned on my heels. Elisheva ran after me: "Where are you going, Rachel?"

"I'm supposed to meet my brother."

"When are we going to rehearse?"

"Not tonight, no way! We won't rehearse. I won't be able to charm Newman. And I need a breather."

I found Avner waiting at the foot of his building. He parked his truck and jumped nimbly down the three metal steps from the cab. It was an old vehicle with metallic slatted sides like a cattle truck. Avner came over to me, wearing a pair of army fatigues and a faded T-shirt full of scorch marks and holes. His hair was greasy, his cheeks unshaven. He kissed me on the forehead and shoved me in the back, into the stairway. He had been driving all day, he had to take a shower. And then if I felt like it he would take me out for some grilled meat.

As soon as we went into the apartment he left me to lock himself in the bathroom.

I walked around the three pleasant, sparsely furnished rooms. In one of the rooms I saw a stereo and a big mattress right on the floor. In the other there were pouffes and a copper tray, piles of books, notebooks, pens and a grey telephone. The third room was completely empty, white walls and tiles, a smell of whitewash still lingering in the air. In the kitchen I found a table and a few dishes on a shelf, an electric stove with two hotplates and a tiny fridge. Avner's apartment was just a place to stop off. Just a place to put his feet up when he came back to Jerusalem. I opened the fridge, and there was nothing on the racks but beer bottles and a stick of butter. No vegetables or fruit, not even any salami.

I was closing the fridge when my brother came suddenly into the kitchen. He was wearing a blue towel tied around his hips, his hair was wet, and at last a smile lit up his face.

"Help yourself to a beer."

"Are you having one?"

"Why not?"

"Don't you ever eat at home?" I said, removing the caps from the two bottles of Macabi.

"Never."

I followed him out into the corridor. He went back into the bathroom, but this time he left the door open.

"Whenever I try to cook I burn it. And besides, I don't really have time to go shopping."

"Doesn't Mum bring you any little meals any more?"

"She stopped, since I wasn't eating them."

Avner plugged in the electric shaver and the noise made it impossible to talk.

With my beer in my hand I went back into the living room. I looked at his books – no novels, no non-fiction, all agronomy textbooks. A sliding door gave on to a south-facing balcony the width of a footbridge. The sun was dipping low behind the roofs, splattering the laundry lines and television antennae with red. On the left-hand side of the balcony I saw a mattress with folded sheets and a blanket. Neatly arranged planters filled the rest of the space. So my brother was still growing things. The strangest species grew alongside each other, cacti and rose bushes, tomatoes and marigolds. A few pots contained nothing but gravel, but the plants were sturdy and prosperous. Other pots filled with soil were home to plants that were withered or dried out. In one row, despite the sand that filled up the pots, dwarf orange and lemon trees had borne their fruit, and they shone in the light of the setting sun.

Avner came up behind me in his underwear, his trousers in his hand. I glanced at him quickly. His body was flat, finely muscled.

"What are these?"

"Experiments."

"What for?"

"To understand which plants protect themselves and which ones kill each other. To define the exact volumes of earth and water they need to survive. To check which ones manage to adapt in sand and gravel . . . Stuff like that . . ."

"Mum said you've dropped agronomy."

"She's right."

"But what about these experiments?"

"I'm having fun."

"You want to go on being a truck driver?"

"Why not? The pay is great."

As always, my brother is skimping on words and emotions. You have to ask ten questions to get one satisfactory response.

He put on his jeans and a shirt with a wing collar, then he rubbed his hair with gel to give it shape. When he turned around to face me, I thought he looked splendid, with his thick black eyebrows; he looked like me.

He drank his beer from the bottle, slipped a wallet into his pocket, took his keys and grabbed a leather jacket.

"Let's move it," he said.

In a restaurant painted in brown gloss, yellow sofas with pink peonies added a cheerful touch. Groups of young people were smoking water pipes. My brother led me to a small courtyard with a dozen tables or so. People were dining by candlelight. A television protected by an awning was blaring the news amidst the pervasive smell of grilled lamb. A girl came over to us. She gave me a dirty look before kissing Avner on the lips. He returned her kiss then said simply, "Penina, my sister, Rachel."

The girl, visibly relieved, gave me a broad smile. I thought she was pretty, domineering and vulgar. Her protruding eyes were rimmed in kohl and she had loud red lipstick on her thick lips.

"We want to eat," said Avner.

"The boss will be here soon."

"So let him be here."

Penina gave him a bored stare. She went over to the awning, clumping her platform shoes against the tiles. She picked up a folded iron table that was leaning against the wall. Her back was completely naked. Two straps tied at her neck and waist held her top on. Her black trousers were so tight that you could see the outline of the cleft between her buttocks. His hands in his pockets, Avner let her struggle with the table, open it and set it down. The girl was strong, her muscles bulged on her white arms. I hurried over to help Penina with two iron chairs. I noticed her worn fingernails, her flaking nail polish, her hands reddened from dishwater. She smiled to thank me.

"Is there a problem with the boss?"

Penina glanced quickly at my brother, who was greeting people.

"He doesn't want him to come here any more."

"Why not? Because of you?"

"Because of Ahmed."

"Who's Ahmed?"

"The dishwasher."

"What happened?"

"Your brother has been stirring up trouble because of the people from the territories. He says they're badly paid and mistreated. I'm ashamed when I hear him talking. I'm going to drop him. I don't like traitors."

"Avner's a traitor?"

My brother walked nonchalantly up to the table. He pushed the chair closer with his foot before sprawling on to it. Then he said to

Penina, waving his hand: "Bring us kebabs, grilled heart, liver and olives for two."

He tilted back on his chair and began rocking back and forth, staring at me.

"Come closer. I feel like talking to you."

"Well, I don't. We'll eat and smile at each other. That's more than enough for me."

"I haven't seen you in five years."

He lifted his hand and pointed to the stars.

"I don't want to argue with you. The weather is fine, life is beautiful, and you're going back to New York. Enjoy! Let's not go making a *parasha* out of the past."

"Who is Ahmed?"

He let his chair drop down to the ground, his face tense.

"Penina spilled the beans!"

"I don't know what you did, but the girl is terrified."

Avner put his elbows on the table and told me that for a month now he had been putting Ahmed up at his place. I remembered the mattress on the terrace, the folded sheets, the blanket.

"Why are you doing that?"

"The West Bank was closed off because of an attack. I offered him a place to stay. Ahmed is a good kid."

"And?"

"I don't feel like talking about it, Rachel."

"But I do."

"People found out. I had trouble with the military police, the civil police, at work. They called me every name in the book. Eventually I managed to get Ahmed a residence permit. He's legal, but there are people in Jerusalem who have turned their back on me."

"You did right, in my opinion."

"I don't give a fuck about your opinion," he said, furious. "I live in a three-room apartment and most of the time I'm not even there. I can help someone out, no?"

Penina filled the table with salads, hot peppers, flatbread and grilled meat that was tender and fragrant. My brother took a healthy serving and sprinkled hot sauce all over his meat. From time to time he clapped his hands together to kill a mosquito.

"I thought you voted Likud."

"I am for a strong Israel, and for giving the territories back."

"All the territories?"

"All of them. Except Jerusalem."

"That's not Likud's programme!"

"You're wrong there. Only a right-wing government would be capable of signing a peace agreement with our enemies. The Left is spineless, sick and subservient to foreign governments."

For a moment I thought that my brother had gone mad, but it would have been absolutely pointless to try and make him listen to reason.

"Is he a nice guy, this Ahmed?"

"Very nice."

"So why is he sleeping on the terrace?"

"He went where he felt like going. I offered him the room. He refused."

We went on eating to the rhythm of the buzzing of mosquitoes and Avner's hand-clapping. Suddenly I saw a huge guy with the head of a walrus, a shaven skull, drooping moustache, and a flabby body, charge over and stand right next to our table. I said to myself that all hell might break loose, that the walrus was about to tip the table over on to us or something like that.

"You pay and you get out of here," said the fat man.

My brother was not expecting this. He dipped his bread into the sauce and licked it unhurriedly.

"And you take your slut with you."

The slut was me. This I realized the moment my brother leapt to his feet and grabbed the fat guy by the collar with one hand, while with the other he picked up a knife from the table. Conversations instantly broke off. Everyone was staring at us. Men left their seats and surrounded us as if my brother had gone mad. I stood up, frightened.

"Avner, stop it, calm down."

"Apologize to my sister."

The fat man melted like sugar.

"I . . . Sorry . . ."

"My sister is a great musician. Not a slut."

"I'm sorry. I didn't know."

"Watch your words. Next time I'll rip your guts out."

My brother loosened his grip. He sat down as if nothing had happened. He tore off a piece of bread, but his hand was trembling. I no longer recognized him. Before me sat a stranger who inspired a mixture of admiration and amazement. In five years, the Avner who had always obeyed my father in everything had turned into a wild, irascible man.

"Let's go, Avner."

"Where? This is my town, my country, my people. I have no intention of running away like you do the minute there's a problem."

"I didn't run away."

"No?"

"I'm studying music."

Avner's eyes filled with hatred and sorrow.

"A fine pretext. You're ashamed of our parents, of me, of Israel. Go on scraping away on your cello, acting as if we didn't exist."

ELISHEVA

Carlos has come to see Elisheva in her hotel room. She opens the door, he bows slightly, she responds with a faint smile and goes back to lie down on her bed. Carlos puts his bag on the desk, walks over to the curtain, finds the handle and opens the window to air the room. The breeze lifts papers that fly up and drift down again.

"He's here," says Carlos. "It's started. He's on Israeli soil."

Elisheva does not answer. Instead, she places a black mask over her eyes as if she wanted to shut herself off from everything.

Carlos collapses in an armchair.

"You have nothing to say?"

"I'm thinking."

"What about?"

"The rehearsal was tiring," Elisheva says wearily.

"Don't you want to talk about the Butcher?"

"No."

"Or your plan?"

"No."

Carlos gets up.

He has no intention of leaving her alone tonight. He is afraid she might do something stupid, for no reason, out of despair. He knows he has to keep an eye on her. He knows he must make sure she eats and drinks, water, a lot of water, so that she does not become dehydrated. He also knows he must be patient, that it might take him hours before he can bring her out of her shell. In the meanwhile he plays with time, opens the minibar, takes out a tiny bottle of J & B and drinks it down in one.

"Where is Rachel?"

"Gallivanting around."

"Are you having trouble with her?"

"Newman made some remarks that she could not stand."

"Deserved, or unfair, his remarks?"

"Both. But he went too far. She's the baby of the orchestra. With diplomacy he would have got better results."

"Newman is no diplomat."

Elisheva sits up on her elbow and her eyemask falls off; Carlos smiles at the sight of this touching face, a face that never tries to please or to cheat.

"He's a great conductor."

"Would you like to drink something?"

"I'm already washed out," Elisheva says, flopping down again on the mattress.

On the desk he finds a bottle full of white pills: he tips one on to his palm and licks it cautiously.

"And how was he with you, Newman?" he says, recognizing the taste of the sleeping tablet.

"The way he ought to be. He has no choice."

"Can I lie down next to you?"

He stretches out on the bed, in his boots, without waiting for her reply. He takes her in his arms and holds her against him, kissing her on her cheeks, her neck.

Elisheva, with her eyes closed, accepts his embrace. These are the caresses of a friend who is overcome with admiration, of the brothers she would have liked to have saved. But they died, all three of them, she did not manage to keep a single one alive. All three entered the mouth of Moloch and all three of them stayed there. She never forgave herself for having shouted at Moishe, or for having snubbed Isaac, or for having failed to console little Elie, whose frail spindly legs threw him in the way of every obstacle – stones, the sharp corners of walls or furniture. He would scream with anger and hold out his arms to be carried. She would run off to the neighbour's to play her music. If only they would shut up and leave her alone, leave her in peace at last so she could practise her cello. Mendel Rajchman, her father, covered in white powder from head to foot, just laughed. "Why on earth did we sign you up for music lessons, *voy*, come and help your mother, you'll practise later." Her father was a baker. With his hands he fashioned rye bread with caraway or flax, and oat bread, and white loaves. When he began to make pastry, they became rich. Thanks to their strudels, to their cream and prune *pączki*, their fruit babas, their poppyseed or cheesecakes, their iced fruit cakes, the family was able to move to the centre of town. Her mother, Gisha, bought herself a buffet, curtains, crystal glasses and a fur coat. The cello entered their home one Purim night, along with Moishe's bicycle and Mendel's camera. For two years the cakes went on selling as fast as their breads, and Mendel had hired two shop assistants to help him. He went to buy his flour at a mill in Pruszkow, fifteen kilometres to the southwest of Warsaw. In Germany Hitler was bellowing and Mendel kept saying that God would send him cholera, frogs, leprosy, darkness and the death of firstborn children.

When the Germans attacked Poland, Mendel fell silent. But his faith did not waver. God was preparing a punishment. God was searching for a Moses. God would send a seraph, an angel, a messenger. The news from the queue that grew ever longer outside the bakery dashed his hopes. Danzig had fallen, there was fighting in Kraków, Jews were being murdered in Lublin. Stalin had signed a pact with Hitler. The two ogres, Gog and Magog, had formed an alliance. The end of the world was near.

In the rubble of a bombed-out Warsaw, they suddenly appeared. A multitude of black insects with helmets, boots and weapons. They emerged by the thousands from among the ruins, insects that spoke German. On her family's sleeves Gisha sewed white armbands decorated with a blue star, and Mendel took his children to the banks of the Vistula. We will leave one day, he said as he walked, we will leave for Eretz Isroël.

Was it Rosh Hashanah or Kippur?

Again she sees the Jews turning their pockets inside out to toss the sins of the year into the river. She is sure of one thing, it was in October 1939, the tenth or the twelfth, in any case right in the middle of the *Tishri* holidays.

Driven out by the S.S., they left their flat and the bakery behind, both confiscated, to follow the crowd heading into the ghetto. A wall three metres high was put up to divide them from the others, a wall topped by barbed wire.

Mendel found a room on Grybowska Street, in the south of the ghetto. And while all the other Jews had cause for lamentation, Elisheva saw an opportunity: Welwel Rzondzinski, the greatest cellist in Warsaw, now lived on the same landing. He had been driven out by the very people who had acclaimed him, and now he was penniless and his instrument served no purpose. He would give no more concerts, he could not even hope to survive on lessons. What madman would waste his money when corpses littered the streets, when children and old men were begging for bread? She was twelve years old, he was thirty-eight. She asked him if he would play for her, but a neighbour interrupted: "Music! *Oy vez mir* . . . He hasn't eaten for three days."

Welwel laughed.

"Don't listen to her. My belly is full."

"Make a fire with your cello," said the woman. "That's all the good it will do you in the end."

Elisheva had begged her father to find some work for Welwel, anything. Mendel had found him a job as assistant at the bakery in the heart of the ghetto. The musician was now carrying sacks of flour. She can still see him dragging the sacks from one end of the bakehouse to the other, reciting notes from Bach. Every evening he gave her a lesson.

In Majdanek, it was thanks to Welwel that the Butcher spared her life.

"Tell me about Welwel," Carlos said.

"How did you know I was thinking about him?"

"You think about him before every concert."

"I owe everything to him. Music, life, and my love for Bach."

"What became of him?"

"He was deported before the Uprising. There were no more than forty thousand Jews left, 10 per cent of the four hundred thousand who'd been penned in there in 1939. Moishe, who belonged to the Żydowska Organizacja Bojowa, the Jewish Combat Organization, tried to save him. With a few other combatants he slipped in among the Jews whom the Nazis were taking to the Umschlagplatz. My brother led Welwel to a safe place. The next morning the Nazis came back, in greater number and better armed, to look for more prey. The only Jews remaining before the Uprising, six thousand in all, were taken, and Welwel was rounded up with them, to the blows of the S.S. truncheons.

The Spaniard caresses Elisheva's hair and listens to her in silence. She describes Welwel's thinning hair, his light eyes, that air he had of an aristocratic tramp. But no matter how she tries, she is elsewhere, with the naked skeletons falling by the hundreds into the trenches they had to dig, skeletons rolling over each other to the shouts of the kapos and the clatter of machine guns. In a street deep in mud that clung to her shoes, a street squelching with blood.

Majdanek.

RACHEL

After his tirade, Avner did not say a word. He stared at the knife on the table, and I think he himself could not get over the fact that he had threatened the restaurant owner. I was afraid the owner might call the police, but Avner said the man had too many things to hide, he could not risk it. The narghiles? No. Other kinds of trafficking. Penina brought us some wine, fruit and cakes. She shot Avner an angry look. He was smoking and drinking, slowly, his features tense. The diners next to us left their table and walked round ours, their scorn visible, and I could see my brother start every time someone he knew went by without saying a word. Before long we were all alone in the little courtyard beneath the lanterns.

My brother was ready to pay the bill. He went up to Penina; she looked away. I saw them exchange angry words. My brother shoved her; she went right ahead and shoved him back. The owner remained invisible despite their loud voices. Then my brother shrugged and went out into the street without even motioning to me. I got up and said goodbye to Penina. She grabbed me by the arm.

"If you love your brother, help him."

"And what am I supposed to do?"

"I don't know," she said, her eyes misting over with tears. "I think he's losing it."

"Because he's got a Palestinian staying at his place?"

Penina stared at me for a few seconds, intensely.

"He's violent."

"Has he hit you?"

Again that strange, hunted look.

"You don't know your brother, do you? He's got a lot going for him, but he's frustrated."

Then she began to pile up the plates and forgot about me.

Outside on the sidewalk Avner was pacing angrily back and forth.

"What were you up to in there?"

"I was saying goodbye to Penina."

He snorted.

"Why are you laughing?"

"It's none of your business. Are you going back to the hotel, or do you want to have a last drink at my place?"

"I'd like to stay with you."

"Suit yourself."

"Do you like that girl?"

"I fancy her, but she's stupid."

"Stupid in what way?"

"She's racist," my brother said, kicking a cardboard box.

A man stepped out of the shadow. Small, bow-legged, with raisin eyes, olive skin and a protruding jaw, wearing a velvet vest and fake leather sandals on his feet.

"Salem," he said.

"Ahmed, Rachel, my sister," said Avner.

I shook the rough hand he held out to me.

We began heading silently toward Romema. The boys were walking side by side, not speaking, and I could sense a strong complicity between them. We went past a garage filled with old wrecks, a crater surrounded by a fence, windowless buildings slated for demolition by the urban planning division but where you could still see satellite dishes.

At Avner's place the Palestinian offered us some tea. From his pocket he took a bouquet of fresh mint and a small bag of roasted almonds, and my brother smiled when he understood that Ahmed had pinched them from his boss. We sat down on the cushions. Avner turned on the radio. The water was taking for ever to boil in the saucepan, in the living room was the sound of jazz, and I did not know what attitude to adopt. My brother was increasingly tense. He smoked non-stop. I thought again of Penina's warning, but I could not see any way to help him, not a single one.

Finally Ahmed came back into the living room and told us that the tea was ready.

He filled the glasses and served us courteously before sitting down on a cushion.

"Avner, I'm leaving tomorrow," said Ahmed.

"O.K."

"The boss fired me."

"I'm sorry."

"Me too. I've brought you nothing but trouble."

"And I only made things worse."

"Forget it. Sooner or later he would have fired me."

"What are you going to do?"

"Go back to Ramallah and help my father. But I'll wait until Friday and stay with cousins in East Jerusalem. I want to go to prayer at the al-Aqsa mosque."

I took a sip of tea. This guy Ahmed seemed like a good sort. He held himself straight, both hands around his glass, his feet together, his face implacable. Despite his weary gestures, he radiated an inner strength.

"You'll hate us now," said Avner in a hoarse voice.

"I don't know. My cousins in Ramallah are real heroes. They've learned how to shoot and make bombs."

His words froze my blood.

"Don't do that," said Avner.

Ahmed said nothing.

Avner went into the kitchen. He came back with a bottle of wine. We drank, my brother and I, not looking at each other. And the jazz spilled into the room, a tenor sax solo with the same resonance as the Yom Kippur shofar.

I had paid for the taxi and was about to go up the few steps into the hotel lobby.

I was drunk and I think I was not walking straight.

I was trying to make my way into a revolving door, and there seemed to be two of them, when I heard Eytan calling me.

"Rachel!"

I turned to face him; he took my breath away.

We said nothing for a long time, our eyes riveted on each other, as if the world had stopped, as if we had entered another expanse of time.

How often, in New York, had I imagined our encounter?

It was always the same scenario, only the setting changed. Sometimes I ran into him on Ben Yehuda Street, and other times it was the crowd outside the Mashbir that propelled me in his direction.

In my dreams we were old, he and I. Eytan's hair was grey, and we were surrounded by our children. We stood there looking at each other, but just when I was about to shout out that I loved him, that I had never loved anyone but him, a shadowy figure came between us, dark and vast. His wife. She took his arm and led him away from me. I heard his children chirping, "*Aba, Aba*," while he disappeared into the mist.

When I reached this point in the dream I woke up with a start, oppressed by tears.

Reality overwhelmed me.

I would get up and go over to my cello.

I tried to empty my mind as I played a fragment from a sonata, softly, but I would think about his marriage to that girl Liora, the daughter of a prominent family from Ra'anana, and the little I knew about her would spin through my mind and would not leave me alone. Liora's father, Mathias Lipchitz, was famous all the way to the United States. He was an outstanding physicist who got invited several times a year to the University of California at Berkeley to give lectures to future weapons engineers.

I had known the man's name ever since I was little.

Everyone in Israel knew who Mathias Lipchitz was.

He was the leading light of the élite scientists who were the prestige of our nation.

When the Egyptian soldiers beat their hasty retreat from the Sinai in 1967, they left Soviet weaponry and tanks behind.

Tsahal took over the lot, and ordered its engineers to improve their performance.

Mathias Lipchitz took a tank apart piece by piece, found the secret mechanisms and adapted the turret and tracks for desert warfare.

Before long, thanks to him, a little factory opened somewhere deep in the Negev desert.

Israel began manufacturing a limited series of the Lipchitz tank.

The factory expanded. It created hundreds, then thousands of jobs.

Israel is doubly grateful to Lipchitz: he gave greater mobility to the tank crews and brought wealth to the Negev region.

Eytan and Liora's wedding had been all over the Israeli newspapers. The Friday editions, that weigh over four kilos and give all the country's gossip in detail – they really cashed in on the wedding.

"You are beautiful," said Eytan with a smile.

I was so moved that I burst out laughing.

"Have you been waiting here for long?"

"Yes."

"You're crazy."

"I have to talk to you, Rachel."

I laughed again, a bitter laugh. My eyes could not leave his, and they cursed him and implored him to leave.

But no matter how I tried to harden my gaze, he did not turn his back on me, but even came a step closer.

A sort of tension arose between us, like the one between two magnets with the same pole.

I knew I should have left him and gone on into the hotel, but I just stood there on the white marble outside the lobby.

All Eytan would have had to do was touch me or graze my skin with his fingertips and I would have fallen into his arms.

"Why are you laughing, Rachel?"

"Would you rather I cried?"

"Invite me to your room."

I clenched my jaw and recoiled so quickly that I felt the oleander branches scratching my back.

I have never been fooled by the so-called reasons why it did not work out between us. The shadow of my parents' marriage had shattered me. I loved Eytan, but I was afraid to commit. And instead of trying to hold me back, he became lost in my own darkness. I had sown the wind, and reaped the whirlwind.

"I have a few things to say to you, Rachel. You have to hear me out."

I merely shook my head, from left to right.

With his fists rammed into his pockets and his head tilted to one side, he looked magnificent. Even taller than I remembered, as thin as a rail but with powerful shoulders and a sturdiness to his body, a density, an existence.

"Let me come up."

I heard myself saying in a low, hoarse voice: "That's impossible."

"Why?"

"Elisheva."

"Are you sharing the room?"

"Yes," I hissed, hoping he would believe me.

"I'll rent one."

"The hotel is full."

"We can go somewhere else."

"I don't want some sort of secret affair."

"We love each other. We can't help it, either of us."

"You forget you're going to have a child."

"I'm not forgetting anything."

"Just go, Eytan."

"Don't make me!"

"Just go," I said again, my voice faltering.

He came up to me and put his forehead against mine, but he did not kiss me. I stood there, not moving, my arms hanging at my side. I could not leave, and I could not make him leave. I was drinking in his breath, inhaling him and the perfume of his cheeks.

I thought: I'm not doing anything wrong. What harm can there be in breathing in my love like a flower? Who could reproach me for these miserable moments I'm stealing from his wife? How could these few seconds possibly damage their relationship? Liora will have him by her side all her life. She sees him in sleep, she sees him as he eats, and she shares her morning coffee with him; she is carrying his child. These moments I'm stealing from her don't carry any weight at all.

But I knew that was not true. I knew that life is a succession of ordinary gestures that set us on one course or another.

"I thought I could forget you," he said.

We stayed for a long time with our foreheads touching, and the porter standing next to the revolving door must have wondered what we were up to.

Then the door swung round and he came out, determined to make us leave.

He had strict orders. No kissing outside a five-star hotel.

"*Hevre*, comrades," he said in a voice full of outrage, "you should be ashamed. There are foreigners staying in this hotel. They've paid a fortune for comfort and silence. Go do your snogging somewhere else."

I stepped back into the shadow.

Eytan raised a conciliatory hand.

"We're on our way."

"Good. That's more like it."

Eytan took me by the elbow.

"We can't talk here. Come with me."

I tried to resist, but so limply that he did not have to make much effort.

In less than a minute I was standing by a brand-new green Nissan, very stylish for Israel, a present from Lipchitz, I thought, unspeakably chagrined.

He noticed how I recoiled, and he opened the door and pushed me in, then walked around the car to flop on his seat and start up the engine in a burst of anger.

In no time we were on Yaffo Street, deserted at this time, then we drove out of Jerusalem to the motorway.

The road wound ahead of us, taking us to Tel Aviv.

At every bend the powerful headlamps lit the hills which, according to the Bible, will rise some day to meet the Messiah.

I could hear the verse running through my memory, from one bend to the next: *Medaleg Al hearim, mekapetz Al hagvaot, Kol dodi, kol dodi, iney zey ba.*[*]

Shafts of tall cypresses, dishevelled crowns of olive trees, bouquets of tamarinds rose for an instant in the light of the headlamps, six million trees planted all around Jerusalem in memory of the six million victims of the Nazis.

Among the trees were rusting tanks that had witnessed the fighting in 1948, during the War of Independence.

---

[*] The voice of my beloved! behold, he cometh leaping upon the mountains, skipping upon the hills.

I rolled down the window and leaned out to clear my head.

But among the trees I caught glimpses of the ghosts of the adolescents we had been. How we marched with thousands of others beneath the blazing autumn sun, sunhats on our heads, as we took part in the twenty-five kilometre march organized every year before the *Tishri* holidays.

So many people used to join in, in those days.

Corporations carried huge banners proclaiming the name of their business or company. Electricity. Gas. Bank Leumi. Histadrut.

The military sent delegations: infantry units, paratroopers, tank crews, the Golani Brigade, all of them striding in step. The men were streaming with sweat in their uniforms, their weapons over their shoulders and their berets tight on their brows. When the path narrowed the soldiers would break rank and scramble up the rocky hillside before regrouping and taking up the square formation.

When we arrived we were given cheap little medals.

Every year the medal was a different shape and colour.

The veterans would pin them on their chests before they left again, as if they had been decorated for bravery.

My eyes filled with tears as I thought back on this lost page of youth.

Eytan was driving like a maniac. Around every bend the wheels grazed the edge of the ravine. Gravel splattered beneath the tyres, into the void or to bang against the chassis.

I did not ask him to slow down. I merely whistled to myself.

"What's the matter?"

"It would seem we're less afraid of dying together than of living together."

"Could be."

"Don't you think that's strange?"

"If it's our fate."

"It's all your fault. You can go on accusing life until you're blue in the face, but that's the way it is. You had no balls."

"As if it's not your fault we failed, my dove."

"I didn't get married."

"If you hadn't left . . ."

"Fuck you!"

"Don't shout. I hate it."

"It makes me feel better."

"Fine. Go ahead."

And he stepped on the gas, flashing me a smile.

"One more shout and we're dead."

"May I smoke?"

"Wait until we get there."

"No."

"The ashtray is in the glove compartment."

"Strange place for it."

"We don't smoke in the car."

We!

When I pressed the latch I came upon a lipstick, hairpins, and a photograph. I leaned over and took out the print. Eytan and Liora, staring at the lens: they looked happy. Their heads were close together. And they were holding each other close, by the waist.

"Is this her?"

He shot me a furious glance and the car swerved.

"Yes."

"You make a fine couple."

"Enough, Rachel."

I put the photo back, closed the glove compartment, and lit my cigarette, my fingers trembling.

If I died, I might stop suffering. But I could not even be sure. The Kabbalah says that souls must accomplish their mission in order to find peace. *Gilgul neshamot*. And my mission, since the dawn of time, had been to seek union with this man, to know pleasure with this man.

And if he was there next to me, driving like a lunatic, with the speedometer hovering at a hundred and eighty, it must have been because he was thinking the same thing.

I was in the last year of secondary school, not yet eighteen, when two men came into the music room. They sat down against the wall at the back, crossed their arms, and listened to us play.

Irina Bachalom was accompanying me on the piano, a piece by Schumann. I thought my cello did not sound right, that I was not developing my arm sufficiently.

At the end of the piece the men went up to my teacher. Elisheva stood there stiffly, her arms by her side, as if they were the bearers of bad news. They went off together down the corridor.

Irina left the piano, the score in her hand. She said, and this I remember because I had been deeply shocked, that the men had come to fire Elisheva. Then she burst out laughing. Several times over she said, "It's a joke, I'm joking, no-one will touch your guru." I answered that I did not give a damn about her bullshit. Then we calmed down and in hushed tones we began to discuss the passages where the nuances were still problematic.

Irina wanted the cello to be played more smoothly, whereas I insisted on giving it a harsher tone, but I agreed with the notion that I had not yet found the right movement to link each note to the next. I had to reduce the silence, precipitate the rhythm. And the tempo was not right yet, either.

An hour later Elisheva – pale, weary and smiling – motioned to me to come over. I had been selected to represent Israel in the United States.

After that everything happened very quickly. I had to convince my parents, who were against my leaving. My father kept saying that I did not have my matriculation. He reminded me that without a diploma I would not get far. I replied that his studies had not got him anywhere. He was a grammarian, but he had spent all his life working as a teacher. He had dreamt of writing a treatise on the relationship between Hebrew and Arabic, but he had not. He had dreamt of translating fragments of the Bible into Arabic, but he had not. He had dreamt of composing pages of the Koran in Hebrew, but he had not.

My father listened without moving an eyelash. If I hurt him that night, he did not show it. He merely said, "That could be, you're absolutely right, but it doesn't prove that I'm wrong for wanting to encourage you in your studies."

He opened his hand, folded his little finger and murmured his prophecies: without a diploma I would end up as a sales assistant in a supermarket or a waitress in a bar. I would never make money with my cello.

Elisheva let him talk. She did not look at my father. Her eyes down on the coffee she had not drunk, she seemed to be probing the black liquid to find the answer to my destiny.

When at last my father fell silent, Elisheva opened her bag and took out a paper. "You have until tomorrow to sign this power of attorney. After that it will be too late!"

She hugged me and left.

My father, with tears in his eyes, went to shut himself away in the synagogue. I took a bus and went to meet Eytan at the Jaffa Gate.

As soon as he heard the news, Eytan turned pale. I was holding his hands in mine. "My love!" I said to him, looking at the line of his eyebrows, "my love."

Eytan stood up abruptly. He said, "Leave, if you want, go to New York. But if you do, it's all over between us."

He began walking toward the ramparts. I shouted his name: Eytan, Eytan. The sound of the cello burst into my head, notes streaming like water. I could understand at last the vital strength of the piece, the importance of each bow-stroke. Twilight was seeping into the sky, the west was bathed in a light as red as blood. Eytan's figure stood out like a shadow puppet against the crenellations of the fortress that Saladin built.

I followed him up on to the ramparts. "Why are you against my leaving?" His head deep between his shoulders, not even looking at me, he said, "You won't come back. I'd rather break up now than wait for you."

He shoved his hands in his pockets and turned away with a brusque jerk of his shoulders. I grabbed his jacket. "I'm only going for a week. Let me go in peace. I need your support." He shook his head, furious, wounded, inconsolable. "You won't come back. You're too talented."

"I love you, I don't . . ."

"Your only ambition is to conquer the world."

"Help me become a great performer. If you are there for me I can go a long way."

"I can't live in your shadow. I can't waste my life running from one concert hall to the next. I don't want to wait for them to finish applauding so that I can take you in my arms."

I looked at him, sobbing. "I have only two passions: music and you. You have no right to ask me to choose between you and the cello." He shot me a dark look. "You're right," he said. "I have no right. We are two strangers."

I followed him. I was walking on his heels, calling out to him fit to lose my voice. Eytan played deaf, and the soldiers we met along the ramparts laughed and made fun of me. "Hey, girl," they said, "didn't your father teach you about life? Girl, stop crying. Come talk to us. We'll know how to make you laugh."

My step was getting heavier and heavier. I could see the tufts of grass growing between the gaps in the walls, the fur *streimel* of an Orthodox Jew, the blur of a nun's wimple as she hurried to her convent. It would be dark before long. The streets were getting deserted. If Eytan did not come back to protect me, I would be at the mercy of anyone passing by. Eytan. Eytan. I could feel a pebble in my sandal, grinding into my heel. The time it took for me to remove it and look up again, Eytan had disappeared. I decided to head off to the left. A stairway led to a round square. No-one. I retraced my steps and took the path to the right. The street was narrow, two people could hardly walk side by side. Where was I? In the Armenian quarter or the Muslim quarter? I no longer recognized the place, my heart was pounding fit to burst. I was afraid of dying, afraid of the shadows of the night.

Suddenly a man blocked my way, his arms outstretched. "Good evening, gorgeous." I stopped. "Let me by!"

"Then give me a kiss . . ."

"You're crazy. Get out of the way!"

The man's lips on my neck: on certain dark nights I can still feel them, and I wake up screaming, crazed with terror. I can feel the man's hands tearing my dress, grabbing my breasts. I can feel his teeth sinking into my flesh, insulting me.

When I regained consciousness I was lying on the ground. Eytan was bending over me, looking at me, his eyes full of worry. I folded my arms over my breasts. My cheek hurt.

"Forgive me," he said.

I got to my feet, avoiding Eytan's gaze. My aggressor lay on his stomach, knocked out. "I heard you cry out. I ran back. Please, speak to me!"

I took a few steps holding to the wall, my legs wobbly. "Can you walk? How do you feel?" Step by step, I made my way down the little street. I was not crying. It was as if there were no more joy in the world. Five minutes earlier we were just two children. Quarrelling like two children. How I would have liked to go back. But it was no longer possible. I collapsed on my knees.

"I was angry . . . Forgive me! Forgive me!" Eytan picked me up. I struggled against him, and my fists were as devoid of strength as two rags.

"Take me to Elisheva's place, Rehov Haneviim."

We stopped a taxi. My teeth were chattering to a strange rhythm. The driver gave Eytan an odd look. "Are you hurt?"

"I fell off the ramparts," Eytan said.

217

"I'll drive you to the hospital!"

"I'm alright. My mother will look after me." The driver hesitated. "Your little friend, did she fall off the ramparts, too?" I nodded. The driver bit his lips. "Get in! I believe you."

I heard Eytan ask the driver to stop in Davidka Square, at the corner of Jaffa Street. He was trying to confuse the issue, just in case the driver began to think twice and went to the police to give them our particulars. When the taxi dropped us off Eytan turned to look at me. "It's ten minutes on foot. Will you be alright?" I nodded. I thought of my father. If he found out what had happened, he would not let me leave. To make sure I was safe he would watch my every move and never let me go out alone. And I had only one desire: to live elsewhere. Eytan took off his shirt and helped me put it on. He stayed bare-chested and people stared at us. We began to walk faster and faster, cutting through the back streets and passageways, making dozens of detours before we were ready to go into Elisheva's building.

We walked through the small courtyard filled with plants. Eytan pressed the buzzer and did not remove his finger until my teacher had opened the door, exasperated. "What do you mean, ringing like this, little hooligans?" Then she saw us and her face changed. "Rachel? Eytan? Come in, children, come in . . ." She put her arms around me and led me into her living room. I lay down on her yellow sofa, an antique she had brought back from one of her trips and which she was very proud of. She would stroke the silk and insist that princes used to sit there to rest, and she would give a sigh at the thought that she was placing her buttocks on a seat that had welcomed royal derrières. And as Elisheva did not share her pleasures, she had formally forbidden her students to sit on her sofa.

She removed my sandals, her gestures gentle. She went out of the living room and came back with her first aid kit, a glove and a bowl of water. "How do you feel, sweetie? Are you hurt? No? Then I'll take care of you first, my boy." Blood was streaming from Eytan's head.

The gash was deep but not serious. And his ear was torn. "Tell me everything. Don't leave anything out."

I heard Eytan describing the attack to her. He had hit the guy with a metal bar. "Is he dead?" Elisheva said.

"I don't think so, no . . ."

"What did he do to Rachel?"

"Nothing . . . But I feel responsible, Elisheva."

"Be quiet, now. Get some rest."

In Hebrew, Elisheva means several things. But the most beautiful translation is, "my God who is arriving".

"My God who is arriving" is a tall, dry, ageless woman. I know she went through a place where, upon entering, you had no hope of ever leaving again. Her father, mother and three brothers perished there. They have no graves. Their ashes were scattered, sifted with the ashes of hundreds of thousands of others.

Thanks to the grace of her bow-stroke, Elisheva had met a different fate. For three years, behind the barbed wire, she played for the barbarians.

Elisheva never talks about that time. We found out about her past from people who were in the camps or on the death marches. Sometimes when I hear her play I try to imagine this drab person as a young woman in full bloom; I try to imagine her, famished, her eyes splattered with horror; I try to find her in the rows of deportees who scrabbled, one step at a time, for a few more minutes of life, who went deep into the snow, resisted, resisted until finally they fell to the sound of barking dogs.

And I cannot.

I just cannot, ever. For me she is nothing but silence and music. Wherever she goes, a thick space is created where anxiety, anger and conflict cannot go. When Elisheva says, "It doesn't matter", we know for certain that she is speaking the truth. And we feel calmer. Or we go and find somewhere else to scream.

Elisheva usually wears long-sleeved shirts that close at the wrist with a button, but that evening, when we knocked unexpectedly at her door, Eytan and I found her in a bathrobe, a cotton piqué with loose sleeves that with every move revealed her arms up to her armpits. She was surprised by our sudden appearance, and did not think of going to get dressed, and on her marked skin I could read, for the first time since I had met her, a series of digits that looked like an ordinary phone number. A number that, inexorably, connects her to those who disappeared.

Elisheva sat down across from me and asked me if I wanted to go back to my parents'. I shook my head in silence. She pursed her lips, ran her hand over the back of her neck, then said, "I suppose this is one chore I'll have to deal with." She picked up the phone and called my father. Her voice, normally so neutral, became as sharp as an axe and I understood that in order to silence him, she had to speak briskly and firmly. All it took was three sentences to get my father to agree to let me stay at her place overnight. Then Elisheva was silent for a long time. She was listening to my father. What did he say to her? Was he complaining? Was he accusing her of taking me away from my family? Elisheva's features remained impassive. She only spoke again when it was time to end the conversation. She said, "Fine. Thank you very much. That's a good solution," and then she hung up.

She stood by the telephone. I did not dare move. Nor did Eytan. He had met her several times in the corridors of the music school, and he was always careful to greet her, even if she hardly seemed to notice him. He heard her play once, I dragged him to a concert, and Elisheva's face was twisted and tense, as if inhabited by a ghost.

Eytan, who speaks only Hebrew, was so moved by her performance that he memorized the German title of the piece: "Der Tod und das Mädchen", "Death and the Maiden", by Franz Schubert. I did not need to explain to him the brutal attack in the first movement, the pizzicati of the cello over the lament of the violins during the second movement, and the fourth movement, hard and implacable, announcing the end of the *danse macabre*.

"Your father will meet us at Lod tomorrow with your passport, your cello and a small suitcase. Anything you're missing we can buy in New York."

Elisheva withdrew into the adjacent room and when she came back she was wearing a long skirt and a blouse buttoned up to her neck.

I only found out later, much later, where she was about to go.

That night I could think only of the joy of spending an hour alone with Eytan in a safe place.

Elisheva summoned Eytan into the kitchen and I heard them whispering for a long time. Then Eytan came back with a forced smile on his face. Elisheva went out almost immediately afterwards.

Eytan took me in his arms. He kissed my lips, I could feel his breath in my mouth. I could smell the perfume of the cigarette he had smoked, the beer he had drunk.

But what I experienced was an extraordinary dizziness.

Elisheva was gone for more than two hours. When she came back, her eyes were neutral. She urged Eytan to leave, saying mysteriously, "They are waiting for you!" I would subsequently hear those words echoing in my head for years. Sometimes I told myself I was an idiot, and reproached myself for not having understood what she had meant. Sometimes, too, I thought I had understood perfectly well, but that I was in no fit state to connect the word "police" to the matter.

Eytan held me in his arms. He called me his little flower. He asked me to forget everything he might have said against my leaving for New York. He told me again and again that he was sure I would come back to Jerusalem covered in honour and glory. Finally, he urged me to practise my cello, to devote every ounce of strength and intelligence and musicality I had to it. Then he slipped away.

Elisheva lent me a pair of pyjamas and gave me a new toothbrush.

I got ready for bed. I switched off the light and lay there with my eyes wide open in the darkness.

A new life was waiting for me. I wanted to win this competition. I had decided I would win first place. If I managed to qualify, my whole life would change. I would be able to stay in the United States, I would be admitted to the Julliard School.

Eytan drove on to the ultramodern motorway leading to Tel Aviv.

The city sprang up before us, streaming with lights.

"It's magnificent," I said, stunned.

"You haven't seen anything yet," he said, driving easily along the busy arteries. "The city council is restoring the old neighbourhoods. There's work planned for the old docks. If you want to make a good real estate investment, now's the time."

"I don't have the money."

"Borrow! Or get your father to do it. In ten years he'll have multiplied his investment by a thousand."

"How do you know?"

Eytan did not reply and I understood that he must move in circles of developers and politicians.

"Do it, Rachel. Please. Right now, this neighbourhood is worthless."

It was well past midnight and young people were still sitting outside in cafés. The music that came in waves from the sea was a sign that the bars on the beach were packed with soldiers on leave.

Eytan offered to take me on a complete tour of Tel Aviv, and I accepted, recalling that both times we had been here before we had got lost.

The only landmark we had had back then was the bus station, baking in the heat, black with the exhaust fumes from the buses.

We drove for a long while along the waterfront where skyscrapers have sprouted – cubes, triangles, bursts of concrete straining toward the sky.

"Do you know the new slogan for Tel Aviv? *Ir le lo hafsaka*. The city that never stops."

In Jerusalem the bars, cafés and restaurants had thrown their customers out long ago, and locked their doors. But Tel Aviv was still dancing, eating and drinking, as if the night did not exist.

Suddenly Eytan braked and parked next to the sidewalk.

The lounges in the Hotel Dan were deserted. The dimmed lighting seemed yellow, as if it were wartime.

At the front desk the man dozing behind the counter followed us with his gaze as we walked through the French doors to sit on the plastic chairs by the swimming pool.

Tired after the driving, Eytan flopped into the chair, his back round, his arms crossed over his chest.

I tilted my head back and looked at the sky. The air was warm. Only the lapping of the water and the purr of a generator broke the silence.

There must have been a garden behind the swimming pool, but it remained plunged in darkness, as if the starlight illuminated only the water, the closed parasols, the chaises longues and the tables.

Eytan broke the silence.

"The air feels good, doesn't it?"

"It's humid."

He responded to my irony with a patient smile. He knew me well enough to realize that this was my only means of defence in life, and above all, against him.

"You have never liked Tel Aviv."

"Why did we come here?"

"To get away from the gossip."

I shot him a quick look.

"I have nothing to hide."

"I want to kiss you."

"No."

"One kiss won't change the way of the world."

"It will change my life."

"Do you still love me, Rachel? Please, answer me."

"Where would the pleasure be, huh, if I stopped suffering because of you, Eytan?"

"Because I love you. I still love you. I'm not ashamed to say it. When I saw you yesterday I realized I'd been living like a dead man for years."

"You're making up stories for yourself."

My voice was becoming shrill and I hated the way it sounded. What had come over me, to try to lecture him? What did I know of the man he had become? Of his world, his likes and dislikes?

"The main thing is that you are doing well, Rachel."

"I didn't say I was doing fine."

"Why not? What's wrong with your life?"

"What do you want to know, Eytan?"

"The truth!"

"Forget it. There's no one truth."

I got up and pushed back my chair roughly.

"This conversation is pointless. I want to go back to Jerusalem."

"I don't feel like going back with you."

"Who asked you? I'll order a taxi."

"You are going to sit there and calm down, Rachel. Is that clear?"

I shrugged.

I went over to the pool.

The moon was swimming on the water like a broken plate.

And suddenly I saw again the urgent letters Nurit had sent me, telling me that Eytan had changed. She had said he did not go out any more, that he turned down invitations to dinner and parties.

In another letter she told me he had signed a one-year contract with the army. He had asked to be sent to the north front, the most dangerous.

"Do something, Rachel. Get him out of his rut."

I had written dozens of letters to Eytan. I told him to come and join me. I told him about New York. I described the city, the fine sand on Long Island. "Come. I'm waiting for you. I need you!"

He did not reply.

Then one day the letters I sent to him came back to me in a box tied with string.

Not one of my letters had been opened.

On a sheet torn from a spiral notebook Noga, his mother, explained that she had decided, for the sake of her son's "happiness", to put an end to our relationship.

"You want to decide everything, be in charge of everything," she wrote, in her long downstrokes. "You love my son? Then come back and marry him, if you can. You are not going to make him waste his best years with fantastical promises. A woman must obey her husband. Whereas you only think about yourself. *Yesh gvul!*"

Yesh gvul. There are limits.

The formula was ridiculous.

I did not smile. I sobbed and sobbed like a lost soul. I should have hated Noga. The thought did not even cross my mind.

Because I had loved Noga Azoulai.

She had been a friend to me, practically a mother. She had curly blonde hair, and round shoulders, and was full of a tranquil, smiling cheerfulness. In Katamon they said she had a green thumb. She would put a root in a spot of earth and a plant would grow. Her balconies had more flowers than any other in the building. Noga grew lilacs in a jerry can, rosemary in the bottom half of a sawn-off plastic bottle, and a rose bush in an aluminum pot. She would go off on a walk with a bag and a pair of scissors and come back from her escapades with little branches she would hastily stuff into a flower pot before going off to hunt for their Latin name in a dictionary.

Her nursery prospered, she had many friends, her sons were happy, and her sons' friends were treated like royalty.

Noga conferred a sort of grace on everything around her. When Eytan brought me home she welcomed me with open arms. She stuffed me with chocolate cakes and pies. I enjoyed her company, her conversation and her laughter.

Eytan's father was also a good guy. Gershon was sturdy and hospitable. He had left his *moshav* near Beersheba, where his parents grew melons, to open a boutique in Jerusalem selling costume jewellery: it was a great hit with all the young people in town.

When his thick, lined fingers held earrings and bracelets, they seemed finer, more delicate.

Gershon gave us special prices. And credit when we could not pay up front. He had a notebook he kept under the cash drawer. On every page there was a girl's name and the amount she owed him.

Our debts grew ever larger, as if they were in some devil's cauldron.

Gershon would wait for months to get paid.

He knew he had to be patient until Purim and Hannukah. But no sooner did we pay him than we hurried to run up new debts for ourselves.

On Saturday evening Noga and Gershon would slip some money into their sons' hands and urge them to go and have a good time.

"Life is short," they said. "Enjoy your youth."

And every time, I would open my eyes wide, full of envy.

My father said, "Money is hard to earn and even harder to hang on to. Learn to do without."

Or even, more than once: "People who bite off more than they can chew never amount to anything in life. Save your money! Save it!"

Avner and I were always broke. No pocket money. Starving for trivial things that could be had for a few pennies. We lusted after cheap junk, some fashionable clothing, something good to eat.

Eytan's family was as poor as we were, but they lived better. They did not seem to be haunted by a fear of the future. They took life as it came.

And then one evening in February Gad, the elder son, was killed in an ambush in Lebanon.

Ever since, Noga has been depressive.

She began to behave strangely, and people would talk, and sigh, and pretend not to notice, but it was getting worse by the day.

One year after Gad's death, exactly a year to the day, she stood outside the offices of the Tsahal in Jerusalem. She took off all her clothes – her jacket, her dress, her bra and her underwear – one by one, and went naked into the huge air-conditioned hall full of young recruits.

Dismayed, aghast, the young soldiers – men and women alike – stood there speechless. Someone rushed up to Noga to hide her nakedness with a blanket.

A moment later an ambulance from the Magen David Adom took her to the Shaare Zedek hospital.

Eytan was called urgently to her side, and he explained to the psychiatrist that that day was the first anniversary of Gad's death.

The psychiatrist asked if Noga was receiving treatment.

Eytan said she was, both she and her husband.

And where was Gershon? At the cemetery. At Gad's grave.

"Try to reach your father," said the psychiatrist. "Your mother won't leave here without him."

Noga did the same thing a year later, in another army office, this time one day before the actual anniversary of Gad's death.

Since then, the family had been on its guard.

Cousins, aunts, brothers-in-law didn't let her out of their sight all through the month of February.

They tried to distract her from her sorrow, they locked all the doors and windows. They never left her alone, even in the toilet, for fear she might try to take her own life.

The eleven other months of the year Noga behaved quite normally. Or almost. For while she had always given her sons a tremendous amount of freedom, now she was terribly demanding with

Eytan. She would harass him when he wanted to go out. Where was he going? When would he be back? Why wasn't he married? When did he plan to carry on their name and give them grandchildren?

When I learned of all this, I was filled with sadness.

I could not stop thinking about Gershon, that giant of a man, showing his bracelets made out of the stone from Eilat; his delicate gestures.

Nurit told me that he had shrivelled up like an autumn leaf, that he had lost his imposing *moshavnik* stature. Nothing interested him any more. Not even his shop in town; his stock was no longer in fashion.

And suddenly there came a letter from Nurit: Eytan had been seen around town with a girl.

I reread the letter several times, wondering how to react.

My vacation was still two months away; if I left Julliard before my exams, I could kiss all my good work goodbye.

Not one of my professors would accept the reason I would give. You do not drop a whole school year, a year of music, because your boyfriend is waltzing around cafés in Jerusalem with a young woman.

I wrote back to Nurit and begged her to give Eytan a letter as soon as she saw him. I specifically instructed her not to leave the letter at Noga's, because Noga would send it back at once, but to hand it to Eytan in person.

I was unbelievably confident when I mailed the letter. In fact, I thought all it would take to get him back was one letter.

That girl could not separate us.

Two days later I got a card from Nurit, which had crossed my letter, informing me that Eytan was engaged to be married.

"Jump on a plane and get back here," she concluded. "Nothing has been finalized. As long as they haven't been to see the rabbi, you still have a chance. I beg you, come back. Don't let him make this mistake."

I did not reply to Nurit.

Mektoub.

Fate had spoken.

Eytan had made his choice.

Go back – to do what? Throw myself at the feet of a man who had chosen someone else?

Suddenly I saw a shadow dance across the water of the swimming pool and as I turned around I saw Eytan coming toward me.

"Would you like to have a swim?" he asked.

"I don't have my swimsuit."

"Use your bra and panties . . ."

I laughed.

"Are you crazy?"

"There's no-one watching at this time of night."

"I would never do such a thing!"

"You're chicken?"

"Absolutely."

"You had more nerve when you went into Noah's orchard to steal oranges."

"You gave me a leg up."

"You were ready for anything to eat oranges. Even walking on my head."

I took out my pack of cigarettes and lit one. When I struck the match, Eytan's face emerged from the shadow for a fraction of a second, and I saw his eyes staring at me, filled with such desire that it was like a fist in my guts. No-one, ever, had looked at me the way he did. What would our life have been like if we had stayed together?

"Tell me about your wife."

"Well, what?" he said, his voice harsh.

"Isn't she going to wonder where you are?"

"Yes."

"And?"

"Nothing."

"She won't tell you off for leaving her alone?"

"No."

"No?" I echoed, surprised. "This is not the first time you've spent the night away from home?"

"No."

I ruminated over this information, wondering what to ask next, before taking the most direct route. May as well cut to the quick.

"Are you cheating on her, Eytan?"

"Fuck off."

"O.K."

"Stop saying O.K."

"O.K."

He burst out laughing and I could feel his tension ease somewhat. But I was not able to relax. I felt oppressed, and I had the impression that the dull wheezing sound we could hear intermittently was coming not from the generator but from my own chest.

"It's good to see you, Eytan, anyway. How is Noga?"

A waiter emerged suddenly from the shadow. We had not heard his footsteps, and only the yellow stripe down his trousers betrayed his presence.

"What will you have?" asked Eytan.

"A Coke."

"One Coke and a whisky."

"No, wait. I'll have the same."

"Two whiskies," said Eytan.

The waiter went away as he had come, his steps muffled.

"So you drink alcohol, now?"

"Sometimes."

"And what does your fierce doorkeeper say?"

"You mean Elisheva?"

"She was watching over you like a diamond."

"I'm not kosher, and she knows it."

Once again he laughed, a happy laugh.

"I've tried. I made rules for myself. But it doesn't work."

The waiter came back, but this time we saw him because of the little lamp he was carrying on the tray between the drinks.

He placed our drinks on a low table before asking if we could pay right away. Eytan handed him a bill and told him to keep the change. The waiter put his hand on his heart to thank him, then quietly went away.

We moved closer to the table, raised our glasses, and I took a swallow of whisky.

"So it's true," said Eytan mockingly, "you're all grown up now!"

"You thought I was going to stay a little girl for ever? Five years have gone by, Eytan . . ."

"Four years, four months and seventeen days . . ."

"You keep count?"

"Yes."

Eytan drummed lightly on the table. The waiter came back at once. He must live hidden beneath a folded parasol, or he was keeping watch on us with infrared binoculars.

"I'd like some olives, chips and crackers," said Eytan, looking at me. "This young lady mustn't get drunk on an empty stomach."

We began to speak in hushed tones, the way we used to, talking about everything, his work, my life in New York, Noga, Gershon's jewellery shop. I told him about my brother's problems, and he nodded without comment. We were speaking ever more slowly, our voices more and more intimate. We were floating in a sort of ecstasy, refuelled by the waiter who came running at the slightest gesture, as if he had been mandated by the hotel to soak us with alcohol.

By the third drink, the man stopped asking us to pay right away. He merely changed our glasses and went off to hide in his lair somewhere on the terrace. He understood that we had decided to stay there until dawn. No doubt he too had once known a feverish, forbidden love.

Then we began to lose it, Eytan and I. Impossible to recall a single word of our conversation. But one thing was certain, Liora was no longer there between us. Even if it had hurt me to see her face at last, on that photograph.

The day rose, pale and grey.

The hotel came to life. The water in the pool took on the colour of the sky.

Eytan paid the bill; it must have been exorbitant.

The waiter said, "It will work out, kids. Life is full of resources."

"No," said Eytan harshly. "Life is a puff of air."

"If you knew what I know," replied the man.

"And what do you know?"

"That there is no life without pain."

Eytan handed him another bill to thank him.

"So what?" he said to me, opening the door to the hotel. "That man watched over us all night."

I wanted to go home alone, by taxi, to Jerusalem. Eytan refused.

I do not know how he got me back.

No sooner was I in the car than I closed my eyes and fell asleep.

THIRD SONG

In the night there is you
And in the day.
Robert Desnos

RACHEL

When I woke up at noon, Elisheva had already gone out. She had left a note advising me to be at 7 p.m. at the Biyanei Hauma for the run-through. The concert would start at eight o'clock sharp. I had nothing planned for my last day in Jerusalem, and I was depressed at the thought of all the hours that lay ahead of me.

I got dressed and left the room.

As I arrived in the lobby I saw Eytan waiting for me, at the far end of the front desk, leaning on his elbows. He was wearing the same clothes as the night before – jeans, black shirt, sandals – and, with his wallet sticking out of his back pocket, his tangled hair, his air of a tired wolf, he was nothing if not desirable. The girls who walked by shot him glances or even smiles, but he pretended to ignore them, his eyes riveted on the mosaics on the floor.

I stopped to get my breath. He had not seen me yet; I could try to avoid him by heading through the kitchen, that would be the best thing. In a flash I recalled the way I had gone the day before, the complicated labyrinth that eventually led to the service entrance. Stand back, stay deep in shadow. But the temptation to speak to him was too strong. Besides, this sign of his love went deep into my guts.

"Good morning," he said, with a sad smile.

"What do you want, Eytan?"

"A coffee, for the time being. Would you like one here? Or shall we go out?"

"We said everything we had to say last night."

"Everything? Are you sure, Rachel?"

In a flash I understood that my resistance had nothing to do with my will, that it depended solely on his good graces. He was the master of the game.

In silence I turned round and headed to the piano bar. A blonde girl served us our coffees. Eytan gave me time to surface, then filled me in on the situation. He had not gone home after leaving me. He had tipped the doorman and slept in his car. And he had thought it all through: he would rather live life as a runaway with me any day than a dog's life with his wife. He no longer had the strength to lie to Liora, to go on having one affair after another in his effort to forget me. Their life together could not go on.

I looked at him. In his eyes I read that same exhausted expression as on the day they told him about Gad's death. I was there when his father collapsed in tears in his arms; I was there for the funeral and for shiva. Eytan had remained silent and absent throughout.

If he had cried . . .

Shoulders hunched, he went on with his explanation in a hoarse voice. He had never hidden from Liora how he felt about me. Their affair had started one night when he was drunk, during his military service. He had gone after her to punish me and make me come back. Only I had not come back. Months had passed, life had gone on its own sweet way. He had tried to leave Liora, dozens, hundreds of times, but their marriage had lasted in spite of his disappearances and the strife between them.

I got up and he made me sit down again.

"Hear me through. Then you can decide."

"Your story makes me sick."

"Is yours any better?" he said.

"I don't owe you a thing."

"How many guys have you been with since we broke up?"

"Dozens," I said, hotly.

My words were like a slap. What a pleasure to see the blood drain from his face, more delightful than any lover's confession.

"Dozens, really?" he said, tearing a packet of sugar that scattered all over the table. "Dozens?"

"So what? What business of it is yours?"

"How many?"

"Go fuck . . ."

His jaw clenched, he grabbed my wrist and almost twisted it: "How many?"

I could have told him that all I had done for months was go from the school to my room, from my room to the school, and nothing more. That it had taken me almost a year to accept an invitation from a boy to go to the movies, and another year to have an affair. That anyone who dared declare his love to me would get a sharp reply, and that there had never been anything but one-night stands, deliberately.

"Let me put the question another way. Did you . . . did you love them?"

"Let me go!"

"Answer me first."

"Eytan, I'm warning you, if you don't let me go I'll scream."

"You really are a filthy bitch," he said, staring at me furiously. Then he let go, pushed me away, and collapsed against the back of the armchair, breathing heavily.

A long silence fell between us. I massaged my wrist; it was aching. Then I said, turning my head to one side, "I've set my standards too high."

"Why?"

I knew he wanted me to say it was because of him, but I preferred to sidestep the issue: "Because of my music."

"You really have sacrificed everything for your music. Me. Israel. Your parents. Any man who dares go too near."

"It's better to be on my own than in bad company."

"Any other clichés up your sleeve?"

"It comes of being well-educated."

237

We were beginning to get annoyed with each other, and the blonde, from behind her counter, was looking at us with curiosity. Eytan said I was a cock-tease. With a heart of stone on top of it. He said I was the daughter of Attila. I imagined my father as King of the Huns and flail of God, galloping along and shouting, "Where my horse has trodden, no grass ever grows again!" and I was overcome with irrepressible laughter. Eytan calmed down. Our anger began to wane, even though we knew it was not gone completely, that it was still lurking in our presence, along with its sidekicks, desire and resentment.

After a moment, I asked, "Why did you get married?"

"For my mother's sake."

I was again tempted to humiliate him. A mama's boy. That's what he was, a softie, a coward. But it would not have got us anywhere, and I wanted to know whether this was just another fib or whether Noga really had manipulated him.

Without looking me in the eye, he told me he had not seen things that way in the beginning, that he only really understood the consequence of her behaviour when he spoke with Gershon on the night before the wedding. The old man must have seen that the two of them were not suited to each other, that they argued over the least little thing. His father had shoved him into a room, closed the door, and said, "Are you sure of what you're doing; is this the woman you love? This woman and no other? Because if you are trying to sacrifice yourself to make your mother happy, believe me, you still have time to back out. I have nothing against Liora. She's pretty, she has a good heart, she comes from a good family, she'd make an ideal daughter-in-law. But my aim is not to have an ideal daughter-in-law. My only desire is for my son to be happy. Your life belongs to you. You don't owe us anything. So answer, son. Is she the right woman for you?"

He asked his father how he could think such a thing, did he really believe he was trying to compensate for the loss of his brother? And

Gershon had staggered over to the armchair: "You think I don't know what is going on in my own house? You think I haven't noticed the sort of man you've become? You have nothing to prove to us. You can't live for two, you can't be valiant or joyful enough for two. Gad was taken from us; we can't change our fate."

Eytan had barged out of the room, away from his father, as if he had been released from a burden, as if he were recovering from a shock, from amnesia. Gershon had sworn he would stand behind him, that he was prepared to deal with the Lipschitzes' hostility. But only on condition that Eytan go and speak to Liora. He could not just toss her to one side like an object. She had done nothing to deserve that.

Eytan went to Ra'anana.

He enumerated all the reasons he thought they should break off their engagement. He had expected shouts and insults in return, but instead Liora threw herself at his feet. She begged him to think it over. Her face ravaged with tears, she eventually proposed a bargain, astonishing to say the least: if he saw me again, and realized that there was a chance of winning me over again, she would give him back his freedom. No questions asked. And she swore it to him on everything that was dear to her on earth. The day was dawning, Liora was exhausted and Eytan was moved by her sorrow.

A few hours later they met again under the canopy.

It did not take him even a month to realize that for an imaginary couple like them, there would be no way out.

"We're not in sync. The more Liora keeps her eye on me, the more unfaithful I am. And the more I make her suffer, the more I feel indebted to her."

My heart was breaking. For the first time in years I felt close to her, to this woman who was carrying his child, to her solitude.

We drank a second cup of coffee. Then a third one. I finally said, "In Mozart's *The Magic Flute* the two priests who guard the iron gate to the underworld tell Tamino what he should expect.

239

Do you want to know what they say?"

"I'm listening," said Eytan, beside himself.

"'And on you, too, Prince, the gods will impose a salutary silence, for otherwise you shall both be lost. You will see Pamina but at no time will you have the right to speak to her. The moment of your trials has arrived.'"

"Translation: you and I, there's no way?"

"I really don't know."

"Why the quote?"

"Maybe we're not meant to live together."

"Say it again and I'll go. I'll walk out of your life and you won't hear from me again."

He would never do such a thing, and I knew it. I slid lower in my seat and put my head on the armrest. "The moment of your trials has arrived." The words whirled in my head like an expanding tornado, hurling everything away. Eytan might be a coward, but I was not much better. For five years I had been living locked away in staves and the key of F and the key of G, and bar lines and silences and cadences and half-cadences, at the mercy of crescendi and diminuendi, and vivace non troppo, allegro, andante.

"Marriage, I can understand. But a child? Why have a child if your relationship is a failure?"

He could tell I was about to relent, no matter how weak his excuses might be, and I saw hope reborn in his eyes.

"To consolidate our union," he said in a low voice. "To give ourselves a second chance."

As I sat up straight again in anger, and sent my cup spinning on to the carpet, he said: "Feel sorry for me, criticize me, judge me, but don't reject me. Please, don't reject me."

Without warning I wanted his saliva. I wanted our tongues to mingle, I wanted my mouth at the curve of his armpit. To breathe in his male odour, to curl up in his arms. If I had to move heaven and earth for our bodies to reunite, nothing else mattered at all.

"Where are you going?"

"Take me away from here, Eytan. Take me to the Dead Sea."

It took us an hour to reach the kibbutz of Ein Gedi. A torrid sun poured its rays on to the road. The air was roasting. The windscreen was a dazzling pane of light. We did not say a single word during the whole trip, we just looked straight ahead. And that was already a lot.

We left the car behind and began walking along the path through the rocks.

The road to the kibbutz was splendid. Borders of shrubbery surrounded the fence around the buildings, underground pipes irrigated, drip by drip, plants which, deprived of water, would not have survived a night in the desert.

Further down, the swimming pool was a beehive of activity. Children were jumping in the water, shrieking, and I thought about the Essenes who had hidden themselves away in caves and holes in the rocks to resist the Roman invaders, saving their meagre resources. Their ghosts that roamed through this land must have been startled by all the puddles that grew beneath the swimmers' impatient feet as they emerged, streaming, from the pool to hurry again to the diving boards.

I looked toward the mountains, searching along the paths and promontories for the outline of those literate warriors who had buried their texts in earthenware jars before taking their own lives. Their descendants had returned, two thousand years later, to their dried-out lands; the desert had blossomed again, water sprang in fountains toward the sky, but who, in the present day, remembered the weight of their sacrifices and their torments?

At the front desk they told us that all the rooms were taken. There was a little bungalow available, but the price was exorbitant. We began to argue over who would pay for it, in front of the receptionist who was waiting, key in hand, for one of us to hand him a credit card.

I took Eytan to one side.

"I don't want Lipchitz to pay for our afternoon."

"Who do you take me for? I earn my own living."

"So do I."

"I can give you a present."

"So can I."

"Don't spoil these few hours, Rachel. Don't start a fight over a trifle."

"Deep down, we don't know each other."

"It's now or never."

"Let's go halves."

What I did not tell him, but he had understood perfectly well, was that I did not want to be his whore. He reasoned patiently with me, determined to have the last word.

"For once, just obey. Let the others take care of things. Let others love you. If I had wanted to buy you, I would have looked at your teeth."

I relented.

We found ourselves in a comfortably furnished bungalow with windows looking out on the mountains. We had only three hours to enjoy it. Eytan let down the blinds and we sat on the bed.

"Rachel?"

"Yes?"

"Do you still love me?"

I did not even know if I loved myself. I no longer knew who I was, or what I hoped for. What I was doing there in that room in the desert was a disgrace. I was satisfying my desires, savouring my revenge, I was measuring the power of an old love that refused to die: but was this really love? And yet I refused to listen to the voice of reason, because that voice spoke with the words of my father, and Elisheva and my friends.

"And you?"

"Are your family Talmudists?" he murmured, his eyes shining with mirth as he brought his lips close to mine.

We continued in this jesting tone, the way we always had whenever when we were aroused, but I could tell that there was a tragic note of truth in everything we said. There was still time to go back, Eytan to Jerusalem and me to New York, snails in our shells. Perhaps what we knew best was how to love each other from a distance.

"I'm obsessed with you, Rachel. You haunt me."

"Remember the priests at the iron gate."

"Priests, huh," he said angrily. "Let them prepare their punishment."

Suddenly I felt his hands on my breasts, his mouth in my hair. Suddenly, after all these years, I placed my head on his chest to hear the beating of his heart.

I walked toward danger, toward the priests who stood motionless, observing us in silence.

I awoke, exhausted. The room was dark as ink. There was not a sound. I hurtled out of bed; I switched on the light, began to hunt for Eytan's watch. It was ten minutes past seven. "Wake up, wake up!" I said, pulling my clothes on as fast as I could.

Eytan opened his eyes.

He put on his shirt and trousers, picked up his shoes and began to run barefoot along the path, as if this were some army training. The run-through had begun. Without me. The concert was set to begin in an hour and only a miracle would get us there in time. Eytan started the engine and, without switching on the headlights, pulled out into the road. Suddenly we saw before us the enormous mass of a truck glittering with lights, and my scream of terror was lost in the squeal of the tyres.

It all got mixed up, the road, the sky, the façade of the mountains, in the halo of lights and the dance of the vehicles. Eytan's car went waltzing over to the left-hand lane. The truck driver swerved the wheel to the right. The two vehicles missed each other, but if another car had been coming in the opposite direction, we would not have made it.

Eytan managed to get the Nissan back on track and drove straight ahead.

For two kilometres the truck followed us, furiously blaring its horn. The guy refused to let us go and kept trying to ram our bumper to teach us a lesson.

Eytan swore and pressed his foot on the gas, in spite of the fact we were going downhill.

At first the car refused to respond, then it surged forward and we began to put some distance between ourselves and the truck.

I was slumped against the door, overwhelmed with fear, staring at the tail lights ahead of us, while Eytan tried to reassure me: "We'll get there, I promise you we'll get there, trust me."

The speedometer was climbing, climbing. Eytan passed all the other cars, taking all sorts of risks, forgetting the turn signal.

I saw drivers giving us the appalled look you give to murderers, others panicked and swerved to one side, practically on to the hard shoulder. And in the yellow beam of the headlights, which Eytan had finally switched on, the asphalt seemed to shrink under our wheels as we zigzagged to overtake the other vehicles.

In my pocket I found a pack of half-crushed cigarettes and I began to smoke like a maniac, my eyes riveted on the clock.

At 8 p.m., the scheduled time for the concert, I realized that I was fucked. We still had three kilometres ahead of us before we got into Jerusalem, and a military convoy was slowing us down, four trucks full of drowsy soldiers led by a Jeep covered with a tarpaulin that was flapping in the wind. I could picture the packed concert hall, Newman in a rage, Elisheva at a loss what more to say to excuse me.

When he heard me sobbing, Eytan said, "Stop moaning, for God's sake!"

He made his way past the convoy at a breakneck speed, swerving back between trucks every time there was an oncoming car, and the drivers shouted insults or stabbed their fingers at us.

And suddenly, when I no longer believed it was possible, I saw the central station, swarming with people, then the building of the Binyanei Hauma and, finally, one minute later, as if in a dream, Elisheva waiting for me at the stage door. At the same time, Eytan jammed on the brakes, pulling the handbrake.

"Knock 'em dead," he whispered.

I looked at him one last time before I reached hurriedly for the door handle. No sooner had I put a leg out than Elisheva rushed over. It took her only three strides to reach me.

"Where were you? Have you seen the time?"

She grabbed my arm and pushed me into the corridor, and as I turned around I saw Eytan's eyes shining behind the windshield. His face was pinned in my memory; part of me was walking down the corridor, and another part of me had stayed behind in the parking lot.

Eytan tore out of the car. He followed us, shouting, "Rachel! I'll see you at the airport tomorrow!"

I did not have the strength to turn my head, tears were distorting my vision, the corridor was nothing but a swirl of blurred lights.

"I love you. I love you."

Elisheva made me run, and he came running behind us, saying again and again, "Rachel, I love you. I will always love you."

"Enough!" said Elisheva.

I found myself in the dressing room we had been assigned, and made to sit on a wobbly stool. Elisheva slammed the door in Eytan's face.

She picked up a hairbrush.

As she brushed my hair, twisting it into a chignon, jabbing in the pins too hastily, too harshly against my scalp, her hands expressed her disapproval.

I was late. My neck was marbled with Eytan's kisses. At last she was discovering who I really was, a worthless girl, the kind who throws herself at a married man, a man who is expecting a child. I risked destroying my career, everything she had been trying to build for me from the very first afternoon I entered her class to take lessons with that cello that was just my size.

Elisheva yanked at my hair and I saw myself again at the age of six, a sort of strange beast who carried a shape hidden by a black case on her back. Even then, there was only one thing I wanted, one thing I dreamt of: to be one with my instrument. Almost seventeen years later, I can still feel the hand my teacher had placed on my shoulder, as if she were dubbing me, like a knight. She told me one day that she knew the moment she set eyes on me that I would make music the way my father had studied the Torah – without ever noticing the time that passed or how tired I got, without expecting anything in return, without a thought for having fun.

Elisheva added that she recognized my devotion because it was the same thing she had felt.

One minute later I was dressed in a gown of black velvet. It was a cheap dress, but in the spotlight it would create the illusion, that I knew.

Elisheva dropped my high heels on to the floor. I slipped them on and ran a lipstick over my mouth, while with her foot she kicked aside the clothes I had scattered on the floor.

"Stop! You are beautiful enough like that."

"Your collar," I said.

"What? Oh . . ."

She gave a quick look in the mirror and fixed it. I thought she looked beautiful in her flowing dress, with the flat pleats she had arranged against her neck, covered by a caraco jacket studded with jet beads on the collar and sleeves.

"Let's go."

We ran back out into the corridor.

The stage manager, a little man with ginger hair, stood there twisting his hands.

"Quick, quick, hurry up."

Behind him, the musicians in their penguin suits, pale and nervous, had stiffened, at attention, ready to go on stage.

When we walked on to the stage at last, the entire hall got to its feet to applaud us. There was no end to the homage. The audience was shouting Elisheva's name and I looked at her, fascinated, and realized I had underestimated her fame and prestige.

She was very pale; she inclined her chignon and greeted the public, but they went on with their thunderous ovation. Then the spectators sat back down, and sporadic applause continued here and there until silence fell and we went and took our seats.

Haim Newman did not look at me once. He was so indignant that it took him over a minute to pull himself together. And the musicians waited tensely on their chairs, holding their breath, staring at him as if he were lightning in the sky, waiting for his signal.

Music.

Music.

Newman could not bring himself to raise his hands. Music. Everything depended on him raising his hands: the group's momentum, the strength of the performance, the strength to draw the notes out of the brass, the strings, the wind instruments, the percussion.

I knew that Newman would refuse to perform with me in future, that he would do whatever he could to destroy my career, that he would not leave me the slightest chance of going on stage in Israel or in the United States.

My hands damp and trembling, I watched as the lights in the hall dimmed, then went out.

A few impatient whistles punctured the silence. The audience had melted into the darkness, six hundred people preparing to commune together, all of them middle class, Ashkenazi for the most part. The Iraqis, Moroccans, Algerians, Iranians and Egyptians who also inhabited the state of Israel were busy doing other things. They were at the café, or having dinner, or at the cinema, or nibbling sunflower seeds in front of the television. Their idea of music was something else, something livelier, noisier. They were few and far between, the ones who might be crazy enough to go and buy tickets for a classical concert, where not a sound, not a cry, was allowed.

The division between the Hebrew people was there, in the Binyanei Hauma, and I would have wagered three years of my life that in that hall you would find only new Russian immigrants who had just arrived, thanks to the fall of the Berlin wall, or the children of Germans, Poles, Czechs. In short, the country's elite. And the head of government, to start with: I had been told, at the first rehearsal, that he would be trying to postpone the elevated tasks of his office to honour us for a short while with his presence. No-one knew when the Prime Minister would make his appearance – at the beginning, middle or end of the concert – but that appearance, however brief, would be an event in itself. And the Philharmonic Orchestra, aware of the honour, was all the more febrile.

Newman picked up his baton at last.

The moment he raised his arm, my last thought was for my parents. And I fervently hoped that they were not sitting in the front row, in the seats that had been reserved for them, for I realized just then that the concert would be a fiasco, that I had done everything I could to ruin it.

Adonai, sphatai tiftah. God, open my lips . . .

No sooner did I make this wish than I heard the opening measures of Dvořák's Concerto for Cello in B minor, modulated by the oboes and the clarinets.

We were off.

And I was flung into the void.

The violins responded, the horns and trumpets clamoured. It would be my turn in a little while, after each instrument had spoken its phrase.

For over a year I had carried in my fingers the notes of this work written by an innkeeper's son, a child of Bohemia who had gone into

248

exile in America to try his luck, and who had returned to Prague covered in glory only to die of a stroke three years later. I had practised and practised the score, listened carefully to the performances by Casals, Rostropovich and Yo-Yo Ma; I had acknowledged their virtuosity, admired their fingering, but the work itself had not touched me.

Dvořák was too sentimental, too lyrical for me. I found his composition uneven, because I loved Bach, his rigour and tempo.

Elisheva merely countered, "We are entertainers, we are at the mercy of a contract in order to survive. You know the deal! It will be a wonderful opportunity to go to Jerusalem. What more do you want?" Nothing, of course. Elisheva was right, as always.

I brandished my bow, and waited for the exact moment, staring at Newman's profile. He was in a trance, working himself into a sweat. Would I be able to soar the way he had? Become one with my cello? I could feel the still silent wood of my instrument against my knee, its weight, its volume. Its contours were more familiar and more beloved to me than a man's body. I prepared my left hand on the strings, rounded my right arm.

The countdown was beginning.

And something triggered me. I suddenly understood that I was in Jerusalem, that I was performing for Jerusalem. This city that had known me as a child, this city where I had cut my baby teeth and felt my breasts budding, where a lover's kisses had ignited me for the first time.

Newman turned his profile to me. In the same instant, my bow took off.

And the concerto's melancholy was revealed – spellbinding, but too late. I could hear the composer's secret voice, his last farewell to the woman he had loved. It was music that had no framework, no structure, the music of a man in exile speaking of the fragility of existence, the fleeting nature of happiness. Welded to my cello, humble and human, I performed this hymn to disaster for Jerusalem. So many things came back to me – my mother's "*katel tini*", Tamar's sleep-walking steps, my father's crackling transistor radio. Narrow and almond-shaped, Eytan's green eyes seemed to be everywhere, a foliage of olive leaves that had somehow penetrated the empty space of the Binyanei Hauma.

At the end of the solo I refused to stop and let the orchestra speak. It was nothing premeditated, I had not thought about this new phrasing for the cello, but I knew that I had to make an incision in the music, tear off its skin, bury myself in it and pierce its heart.

Haim Newman shot me a stunned look.

His hand raised, he tried to impose silence on me. I did not obey. I was rebelling, in some hallucinatory state; I was playing mutely, *poco espressivo*, to a tempo that restrained the brass and opened space for the strings. I wanted each note to be born as a murmur, without emphasis, even in the crescendos.

Newman, in despair, tried to take back the reins of the orchestra. But it was too late, far too late.

Like a herd hurling itself into an abyss, the musicians accepted the change of conductor. They modulated the accentuation, softened the theme until it became a funeral oration, and a prayer seemed to rise up, bitter, dark and fragile.

Newman obeyed.

Did he even have a choice?

His baton signalled a new beat to the violas and violins, and he constantly turned to me to find out where I was going, to guess at my intentions.

My madness that I had always managed to hide, my madness born of my father's tattered sentences, of losing Eytan at the top of the ramparts, now showed its face, clinging like a monkey to my back. I knew I would never see Eytan again, that it would not be granted to us to run away together.

A mortal silence fell upon the hall. The final note had been played, and yet the silence lasted.

Then booing and hissing burst upon the speechless, stunned audience. A smattering of applause, too little, quickly drowned by booing. If anyone cried bravo, I did not hear them, the catcalls dominated everything.

I did not move from my seat. I did not even manage to bow my head. I saw the floor moving, coming up to meet me. The curtain fell. Light flooded the concert hall. Elisheva came running to catch me. I slid into her arms. One of the musicians rushed over to rescue my instrument from a fatal fall.

They carried me backstage.

Someone, to reanimate me, pinched my cheeks until they nearly bled.

I charge you, O ye daughters of Jerusalem, by the roes, and by the hinds of the field, that ye stir not up, nor awake love, till he please. I charge you . . .

In the hall, the outcry was getting louder.

"This girl is crazy," said Newman, as he walked by me.

A few minutes later my parents burst in. Silent and dazed, I waited on my wobbly stool, what for, I do not know, maybe for them; and when they found their way into the dressing room I was overcome with shame.

My father had made an effort to dress up. He was wearing a black jacket over a beige shirt, but his feet were shod Israeli style, in socks and sandals. My mother had put on a dress of royal blue, tight at the waist, with a little round straw hat of a lighter blue.

They stood before me.

"*Ya kebdi*," said my mother, stroking my cheek.

My father remained silent. He knew nothing about classical music, but he knew what the stormy, divisive uproar in the hall meant. At the synagogue, if one word was mispronounced, if there was the slightest error in the liturgy, the audience would explode.

"What happened?" my father said.

I shrugged. "I made a mistake."

"Did you play badly?"

"Worse."

"What could you do that is worse?"

"I drew attention to myself . . ."

"As if to say, *shoofooni ya nes?*" said my mother candidly, which, when translated from Arabic, means roughly, Look at me, people!

I nodded.

"Yes, that's right."

"And why?" my father said, upset. "Why did you do that? They paid your ticket and your hotel! And you had to go and make such an *ashooma*? That's not right . . ."

"Never mind the money, Papa . . . Who cares about the money?"

My mother, devout as ever, wanted to bring out her theories based on magic and occultism.

"It's the evil eye," she said. "Someone put a spell on her."

My father looked daggers at her, then turned to Elisheva.

"I don't get the impression my daughter is sorry for what she did," he said, clearing his throat.

"That's Rachel," said Elisheva with weary resignation.

"What do you think?"

She shrugged.

"What does it matter, now?"

What my father really felt like doing – for I know him – what he really wanted to do was strangle her. He pulled himself together.

"May I have your . . . whatsit . . . your thing . . . your analysis?"

"Rachel has lost Jerusalem. I doubt they'll ever invite her again in future. She has ruined the conductor's reputation and he'll be out to take revenge."

"Rachel, Rachel," my father said. "Rachel, why do you always saw off the branch you're sitting on?"

"On the other hand, Rachel's interpretation of the concerto was unique. Debatable, perhaps, but unique, completely out of the ordinary. Something happened this evening . . . And it took daring to do what she did."

"But . . .

"Youth is creative . . . Do you understand, Solomon? Youth needs new interpretations, at the risk of being lynched."

"Are they going to ask her to reimburse her flight and her hotel?" asked my father, staring at the ground.

"No."

My father pointed at me with his chin and his voice was clear as he said, "Tell the organizers that I will vouch for her, financially. I'm prepared to cover all the costs. I have thirty thousand dollars . . ."

I raised my head. My father was not looking at me, he was staring at Elisheva, whose face had lit up.

"I have thirty thousand dollars, I will place it at your disposal. And if it isn't enough, I'll get more, I'll take out a loan to absorb . . ."

"That won't be necessary, Solomon," interrupted Elisheva, gently.

"She's my daughter . . . my soul," my father said, his voice hushed. "If I don't do this for her now, today, when will I do it?"

I am the daughter of a grammarian and my father's research irrigated my life. His hypotheses, his proofs, his arguments, his linguistic and philosophical approaches of the biblical text fed me in my cradle almost as much as my mother's milk did.

My father loved to talk about his work. When I was a child, he gave me lessons. From him I learned of the miracle of Hebrew, a consonantal language whose words, depending on the vowels with which they are paired, can lead to one meaning or another. *Shin*, *lamed*, and *mem*, for example, can spell not only the word *shalom*, peace, but also *shalem*, wholeness, or *shulam*, paid. And my father came to the conclusion that peace in Jerusalem will only come if the city is whole, integral and paid.

And what debt he was he referring to?

It remains a mystery.

These grammatical games entertained my father, but they were not the vital crux of his work. The primary sphere which sapped all his strength and consumed his life was the *vav consecutive*. When placed before a verb, the letter changes the tense of the sentence. Past becomes future and vice versa. Long before my birth, my father launched an attack on the *vav* the way a climber dreams of conquering the north face of Everest. He wrote dozens of texts on the enigma: the biblical tense of the story transformed by the power of a single letter, from past to future. My father said that the *vav* proves that the history of humanity has not begun. And that, at the same time, it is being repeated. If you were to believe him, Moses was born, but has yet to be born. King David reigned, but he has been called to sit on the throne of Israel. The Philistines, the Ammonites, the Amalekites have all disappeared and yet they will appear again.

Who knows what to make of it?

The *vav consecutive* has been intriguing Jewish and Christian thought for millennia.

Dozens of grammarians the world over have struggled to explain the enigma, comparable to a time machine. My father is in touch with some of them, the best ones, he claims. They write to each other. They meet for symposiums. They publish tiny texts in university journals, translating the effort behind their ideas. My father follows their progress closely. He reads every one of their rare publications with admiration and envy, and when he responds to them it is always with quotations, ready to back up his arguments. I have seen my father weep more than once, with his head between his hands. Because the further he ventures into the land of the *vav*, the more stubbornly he believes that it holds the secret of prophecy and writing. That he will never, all alone, be able to express how vast it is. For my father, *vav* is the most elaborate linguistic sign, the absolute letter. For a long time I believed he was confusing fiction and reality by putting them on the same level, until one day he objected: "In the end, perhaps time does not exist!" "And death, birth?" I said, thinking of the heartbeat in music. My father brushed aside my remark: "That's not time." "And history?" "Nor is history. We are the object and the subject of history because we are the ones who write it." "Then what about God?" "Perhaps, but we can't be sure." "Then tell me what time is?" "Hope. Messianic hope."

In the dressing room at Binyanei Hauma, I understood that my father's ideas about time had inspired my relationship with music.

I started to light a cigarette, but Elisheva stopped me.

"Try not to smoke in the dressing room. We are in enough trouble as it is."

I met her gaze.

Her irritation was becoming anger.

I crushed out my cigarette.

"Get changed and let's get out of here," said Elisheva.

She picked up her raincoat before she led my father, still crushed, out into the corridor. My mother looked at me with infinite tenderness, then she walked sideways over to the door to avoid offending me by turning her back.

I stayed there, not moving. I was alone at last and my teeth were chattering. What had I done? And why? What would my future be? I could see the consequences clearly now. I had compromised myself for a long time. No conductor would be willing to work with a rebel who turned a concert into a battlefield.

I took off my gown. I got changed. I put on my jeans, shirt and sandals. Behind the door my father and Elisheva continued to whisper together.

I was ready to leave, then retraced my steps. I picked up my bow and snapped it in two over my knee before ramming the pieces into my bag. There, it's really over now, I thought. The end of sound has come.

I can still feel the quick gaze Elisheva gave me when I came out into the corridor.

We walked along the corridor and our steps rang out on the

cement. Hundreds of people should have been waiting there to congratulate us, and all I had created was an immense desert.

When we left the building, the sky was coal-dark, shimmering with stars. The *sharav* had dropped, leaving a long-awaited coolness over the city.

A car was parked outside the stage door: Elena was at the wheel.

Tamar was sitting next to her, and in the back were all my friends. It was then that I was struck by my brother's absence. He had not attended the concert. Where was he? Why had he let me down?

Gabriel opened the door. He got out, came up to us.

"Rachel, come on."

I hesitated. All I wanted was solitude, silence and darkness.

"Go on," said my father, surprising me again. "You need to have some fun."

"Yes, go on, go on," Elisheva said

We were due to leave Jerusalem the next day at noon. We still had to pack, and our instruments, carefully cushioned in bubble wrap, had to be registered and shipped with extreme caution, according to the insurance requirements. I could not leave her alone with all those chores.

"It's no trouble," said Elisheva. "Don't worry about it."

And as I did not react, she turned to Gabriel: "I'm leaving her in your hands."

I looked at her gratefully.

"I let you down."

"Don't talk nonsense, sweetheart."

"I've brought you nothing but trouble. If you only knew how sorry I am."

"Forget it. Go have fun."

"What time do I need to come for you at the hotel?"

"I've ordered a taxi for eleven. Come when you want."

"And what about us?" said my mother. "Will we see you before you go?"

"I'll stop by the house between seven and eight tomorrow morning."

I felt that my mother was tempted to cry out, What, is that all? but she swallowed back her reproaches and kissed me.

Before climbing into the car I glanced at the three of them one last time. Elisheva was waving her hand, friendly. She had her beige raincoat over her concert gown. Her mica eyes were warm, her face serene. And yet it was as if I could see something or someone near her, in any case a terrible presence, seeking to warn me about her fate.

I felt a shock of emotion. Elisheva looked worn, vulnerable. I could not abandon her. I had no right. This concert was to have been the apotheosis of a career she was ready to leave behind, that I knew.

"Leave me here, Gabriel, I want to stay with Elisheva."

"I don't think so, no."

"She needs me."

"What you need above all is a change of air."

I tried to fight him off, but Gabriel shoved me on to the back seat with the others. We squeezed together. The door was closed.

In the front seat, Tamar waved her index fingers.

"Step on it," she said to Elena. "Time to party."

We headed for Ein Karem, taking the back streets.

EYTAN

Eytan dropped Rachel off over an hour and half ago. He parks outside his house, but at the thought of confronting Liora, he pulls out of the parking space and drives off again, aimlessly, listening to a programme of Israeli rock on the radio.

He knows what he wants: to leave Liora and live with Rachel. He knows what he does not want: to hurt Liora and the child she is carrying.

257

The entire problem consists in extricating himself without causing any damage, which is an absolutely impossible proposition.

Liora will get over it.

But the child?

What sort of future for his child?

He is completely worn out, exhausted by the mad dash from Ein Gedi to Jerusalem, and the only thing he feels like doing is sleeping. His movements are pure reflex. He is in danger and he knows it.

For the third time in five years he is faced with a choice: follow Rachel or let her go. Twice already he chose spontaneously to break it off. The first time out of spite, the second time he left it to fate. And today he knows that the circle of time that has brought him to Rachel once again is offering him one last chance.

In Ein Gedi he was sure of what he wanted. Now he does not know, or he no longer knows, he has reached an impasse.

The child. The child. The child.

The word is swelling in his brain.

He told Rachel the truth just now. Even if it is not an exact truth, even if, when he thinks back on his words, he despises himself, calls himself a good-for-nothing, a scoundrel, a bastard. In his mind he goes back over everything he said, and his heart pounds at the thought of this underhand story, the way it casts aside his feelings for Liora.

If Gad had not died, if Noga had remained the mother he had always known, if Rachel had not left, yes, if none of these things had happened, he would have lived a calm, flat, painless life.

He has tried in every way possible to go beyond himself, has thrown himself body and soul into the army and work. But no matter what he does, there always comes a time when he finds himself face to face again with his limits, and he hates himself.

He has loved his wife, stopping himself all the while from loving her. And he is the only one to blame if his marriage is a failure, if he has found no serenity in his home life. For he has been sincere in one thing only: his marriage is an unhappy one, and he and Liora are not in unison. Except in bed. There, something happens, something exceptional and flamboyant, which justifies, to put it crudely, the deeper thrust of their union. For the rest, in their everyday life they are as mismatched as a bird and a fish. They have no shared tastes. They cannot get a single thing done together. Liora is a child. A little girl dominated by her father. She lives under her father's influence, tells him everything, obeys him in everything.

Eytan goes through town, slows down as he drives past the cafés, then speeds up abruptly, repelled by the laughing couples he can see outside his window.

He loves two women, one for her talent and the other . . . The other because he said, in front of witnesses, as he slipped a ring on her finger, *arey at mekudeshet li betabaat zot*, "with this ring you become sacred to me". And this oath, whether he likes it or not, has attached him to her, mysteriously. He has been unfaithful to her, to be sure, he has gone with other women, spent the night out, he has wanted to leave her, and yet he agreed to give her a child, the child is no accident, the child is something he wanted with her, night after night.

The thought of the child brings with it certain questions he has not considered. What will he do with his life in the United States? Far away from his parents, far away from Gad's grave?

He hardly notices the sprawl of the university campus, he has already turned back to the city centre, accelerating with a skid in the direction of the central station.

Lights, music.

Gad, up there, is watching over him.

Gad who will never grow old, who will always be twenty.

"You left me on my own . . . Why did you leave me, bastard! Why did you die? Why? Fuck you! FUCK! I loved you . . . ! I need you. I can't stop needing you."

He drives on and on, like a madman, his throat tight with sobs, his gaze blurred with tears. In an altered state, he drives all the way to the

Arab village of Abu Gosh, just as he always does when he is down or he has had a fight with Liora, when his brother's absence becomes unbearable.

These neon-lit, greenish cafés have become a haven for Israelis. Young people slumming it; divorced women looking for a lover, far from Jerusalem gossip; families with children, who wolf down generous portions of *shawarma* and share stories in loud voices.

Eytan does not mix with anyone. He will drink and stare into the void until he figures he has the courage to drive home.

Tonight the village seems calm, almost asleep. Eytan walks over to a table against the railing on the terrace. A Palestinian comes up to him and vigorously shakes his hand with both of his.

It's Djamel, the son of Abu Shukri, the boss.

He has a sharp eye, a mocking smile, a perpetual *"inal a bouk"* at the ready on his lips, and he speaks perfect Hebrew. After years at university Djamel has taken over his father's business, and amidst the fug of oil from the frying vats he serves humus and falafel. A handful of people know why he does this. Others assume the father pressured his son, to force him to earn a living.

Djamel and Eytan exchange a few words about the weather, the *sharav* that is scorching the fields, scorching the men, *aywa*, other than that, things are fine, things are fine, *ham dullah, aywa, habibi*, what can I tell you, it's dead here this evening.

They eventually fall silent, allowing their gaze to wander over the valley and the jumble of fig trees and bramble bushes and olive groves.

They will not venture into a discussion of the latest news – the soldiers deployed in the West Bank, Fatah's terrorist threats.

Eytan is perfectly aware of Djamel's political activity, how he is involved in Birzeit in recruiting the best elements for Arafat's ranks. And the political agitator knows Eytan's rank in the army, his belief in the fight. But life is life. Each thing in its own time. While waiting for the day when the confrontation will be merciless, the day of chaos and attack, the enemies spend time together, talking, supporting each other.

"*Kawa?*"

"With pleasure."

Djamel comes back a moment later, a round copper tray balanced on his palm. He sets a tiny white porcelain cup and a coffee pot down on the table and rearranges the ashtray. Finally Abu Shukri's son leans close to Eytan's ear and suggests, "Narghile?"

Eytan declines, not tonight, no; in the state he is in, he is not sure he would be able to drive.

The coffee is syrupy, lukewarm.

He takes a sip and nearly chokes when someone shakes the back of his seat, laughing loudly. Ariel Rapoport is a friend of Liora's, and he has a gift for turning up at Eytan's feet like a bad penny. Now he propels him from his chair. Eytan hides his bad humour and slowly stands up. He has always viewed this scheming arriviste, whose prime intelligence consists in turning up everywhere, as a potential threat.

"Lay off, man!" says Eytan.

The two men shake hands.

"Have you lost your sense of humour?"

"You've made me waste my coffee and you want me to be pleased?"

"Djamel," shouts Rapoport, "bring my friend another coffee."

Ariel is a bureaucrat at city hall, in charge of planning. His body is soft, his face doll-like, and his thinning hair reveals a pink skull. He is ugly, but that is not the problem. Eytan reproaches him for granting construction permits to rich people while refusing the same permits to people who do not bring him anything, who are nobodies. And he suspects Ariel of accepting backhanders. Eytan asked Liora to stop seeing him. His wife pointed out that they needed him. Their flat in the Mamila district, bought off plan, was far from finished. The baby's birth was drawing near. They weren't about to risk complications and get stuck in their rented bungalow in Moshava HaGermanit?

Rapoport sticks a toothpick in his mouth and cleans his incisors.

"I'm inside, with a group of friends. You want to join us?"

Eytan does not move, says no, gloomily.

"How's Liora?"

"She's fine."

"She's not with you?"

"She's tired."

"I know. I spoke to her on the phone this morning. She sounded awful."

The toothpick dances between Rapoport's lips. If only he would impale his own tongue.

"By the way, I've found a buyer for Mamila. An American. He'll give you a good price, above the market price. Will you tell your wife?"

"Are you talking about my . . . our . . . ?"

"You didn't know?" says Rapoport perfidiously.

"Yes . . . yes . . ."

"That's more like it. I just wondered if there wasn't something going on between you and Liora. You've made us all jealous, you know . . ."

A woman comes up behind them, wide as a mule, wearing a clinging black muslin dress. With her lipstick, her swollen feet in tight heels, and her cigarette dangling from the corner of her mouth, she has the strange beauty of women who have been around and who know all there is to know about men and desire and then some.

She is looking for a light.

Ariel deftly fulfils her request. He strikes a match between his palms and holds out the flame. With a dreamy, sexy air, the woman leans over and lights her cigarette, never taking her eyes off Eytan.

"This fine-looking lad is expecting a baby . . . There's no hope for you," Ariel says.

The woman supports her elbow with her hand, exhales a cloud of smoke, then says in a supple, sensual voice, "*Mazel tov*. Boy or girl?"

"I don't know."

"Are you superstitious?"

"Could be."

The woman bursts out laughing and for a brief moment Eytan feels a powerful surge of desire. By her very presence she has set something in motion, the way only whores or very free women who have seen it all can do. Her teeth are small, set well apart. Her skin is dark, her eyes blackened with kohl. She has a strange, almost obscene way of smoking: her nostrils quiver, the tip of her tongue is visible through her lips.

"When's it due?"

"Two months from now," sneers Ariel. "And he leaves his wife on her own to come to Abu Gosh."

Eytan slowly closes his fists.

"The seventh month is a critical time," says the woman. "I was pregnant twice and both times I thought I wouldn't make it past the seventh month. I could feel the baby's head pressing between my legs as if I were about to give birth."

She illustrates her words, placing her fingers on her groin. Eytan is gobsmacked. He is aroused, and at the same time an image springs to his mind, of Liora, contorted on an armchair, massaging her belly and complaining that she has a backache.

When he comes back to reality the woman is crushing her cigarette under her shoe, and she says, "If the doctors hadn't forced me to stay in bed I would have lost both babies."

Eytan catches Djamel's eye, draws a circle with his index finger to indicate he is paying Rapoport's round, and places a banknote on the table.

"Don't forget to tell Liora about Mamila. Otherwise I'll kick your arse!"

Eytan goes back to his car. He turns around in time to see Ariel nibble the woman's earlobe, then lick her ear.

Eytan drives off, heading for the motorway, eager to get home, suddenly anxious. Liora. The baby.

These last few weeks his wife has been complaining she was in pain. So it was not just airs and graces?

"It feels tight," she said, breathlessly. "You think that's normal? Feel."

She took his hand, laid it on her belly, spread her legs, pulled up her skirt to reveal her sex, and made him feel her groin.

"There, there," she said, "you feel how hard it is? It hurts ... And there, on my pubes, I can't feel anything any more, it's all cold, it's bizarre ... When you touch me it's as if I were made of wood."

He urged her to go to see her gynaecologist, true, but he did not offer to go with her, and he never looked her in the eyes, because he was irritated by her swollen face, and the way she would doze off, and her nausea.

He could tell she was finding it hard to carry the baby, that she was anxious about her imminent motherhood, but the more she needed him, the more he shied away, tense and distraught.

Embryo, uterus, umbilical cord: words that stifled his libido and quashed any desire to screw her.

He would lie down next to Liora and mop up her sweat with a towel. Unpleasant gestures. Eytan despises intimacy.

"I love you," Liora would murmur, then add, "Caress me," and as he said nothing, she hounded him into a corner with her reproaches, her tears, her threats. And when he agreed to make love to her, it had to be ever so cautiously, taking her from the side or doggie-style, always mindful not to thrust against her belly, and he was daunted by the mass of life imprisoned in that smooth bluish egg – it could hear them coupling, its mother's cries, his own jerky breathing.

The doctor had confirmed that it was good for the baby and good for Liora, that she needed tenderness, that they needed to nurture a carnal environment and loving moments; neither of them must deprive themselves of anything. He had buddies who were roused by it, their wives' pregnancy. But not Eytan. Maybe if it had been Rachel ... He would come all of a sudden, and collapse, drained, dreaming of a fresh, young, elegant woman, whom he could see only from the back.

The next morning Liora would maintain that she too had come, and he pretended to believe her, staring at the wall, thinking dark thoughts. What was that happiness that refused to enter their home, that the slightest gesture caused to disappear? He went off roaming again, to Tel Aviv or Abu Gosh. He started picking up girls again. He abandoned his wife, who turned for comfort and support to her father.

Eytan pulls up outside the villa in Moshava HaGermanit.

All the spaces are taken, so he starts driving around to park. Down one side street, driving at a snail's pace, speeding up, then back into the Bakaa neighbourhood, crawling along for the third time in front of the house, where the lights are on and everything seems peaceful and normal.

He is tempted to double park, to hurry inside to make sure that Liora is alright and there is nothing the matter with the baby.

Then he remembers that he has not been home all night, that he has not shaved or washed, and so he had better take care of the car first before he goes to face his wife.

At last he finds a space at the end of the pavement. He parks with the wheels overlapping half the zebra crossing; never mind. If he gets a fine he will give it to Lipchitz; he will pay.

He locks the car, and heads towards the house, staring at the green shutters, the stone, the balconies. He has to pack his bag, buy his ticket for the States, find his passport.

Is this really the last time he will see her? The last?

He goes through the gate, past their little garden that has run wild: Liora is not interested, and he has no time.

Mathias tried to set them up with a gardener, but Eytan has been learning to say no recently. And the engineer gave in, with an incredible remark: "You like your gardens spontaneous – I see, I see. When you've had enough of wild grasses, you can come and enjoy my lawn."

Eytan is tired.

He climbs the three levels of the stone stairway. He puts his key in the lock. The house is silent. Almost too silent. Again he sees Rapoport's insinuating gaze, hears him referring to the sale of the Mamila flat, and suddenly Eytan's belly knots with fear.

Liora has left.

She has taken her things and she has left him.

She has finally decided to let him live his adolescent love story.

He goes into the hall, calls loudly, "Liora? Liora? Answer me, Liora! Liora, are you there?"

RACHEL

Gabriel put on some disco music and began to clap his hands and dance, knees bent, rolling his shoulders. Tamar turned up the volume and the neighbour on the landing took no more than all of three minutes to burst in.

I thought there would be trouble, but the girl had a radiant smile on her face.

"Gaby, this is great . . . I was fed up to here with studying."

Gaby introduced me, but another neighbour was already making his way into the living room, his eyes shining with excitement.

Michael made some tea. The building was full of young people – roommates, students, a few single army officers, three or four girls in vocational school.

Before long there were people everywhere, some dancing, others standing around talking, leaning against the door frames, still others who sat on the floor in the kitchen and got in everyone's way, and you had to step over them whenever you wanted to fill the teapot with boiling water or grab some glasses from the cupboard. There was such a press of people in the apartment that couples went out on to the stairs just to be able talk normally.

I realized that my friends were part of a circle I no longer belonged to. I had left it behind long ago, and I had not wanted to admit it to myself. They still tried to include me, but the distance between us was ever wider. A day would come when they would no longer miss my company. When we would have nothing left to say to each other, our lifestyles totally irreconcilable.

I opened beer bottles, smiled to newcomers, gave my name to those who asked, and I felt as if I had become a stranger.

There was a knot of dancers in the middle of the living room. Hands above their heads, three steps forward, three steps back, they were singing, *Young man, there's no need to feel down, I say, young man, pick yourself off the ground, I say, young man* . . . They spun round, jumped with their feet together, raised their fists.

When the refrain came around, they all screamed in unison, *YMCA*.

Someone took me by the hand.

I refused his invitation with a laugh.

I braced myself against my chair. No, I did not want to dance, sorry, some other time.

The boy would not listen.

Suddenly he flung my arms around his neck, practically picked me up and carried me into the middle of the dance floor.

I fought him off.

My partner spread his hands, and called on the others as witnesses, as if to say, what's wrong with me? What can I do?

Abruptly it came to me, *Kibinimat*, he's right.

My hermit's life makes no sense, I have been digging my nails into my music, perfecting my instrument, working like a maniac, only to come to Jerusalem and be a total flop. There it was, the rationale behind all my doggedness. To be a flop.

I joined the circle of dancers. I screamed in unison, *YMCA*, and there before my eyes I could see the tower on King David Street, forty-six metres high, a three-sided phallus, the work of the architect who designed the Empire State Building.

EYTAN

Eytan walks through the living room, which is filled with furniture belonging to the owner, a guy who spends his time travelling all over Europe making his pile, selling microprocessors.

He starts up the stairs, taking the steps two by two, until he reaches the first-floor landing. The bedroom is empty. The bed bears the imprint of a body, the pillows are rumpled, the bolster has fallen on to the rug.

He goes into the bathroom, checks the guest room which will soon be the baby's room. The cradle is ready; a dresser with toys has been placed below the window; layette has been piled on the scales; frames decorate the wall, photographs of bears, a giraffe, a lion king. A lavender-blue changing table in a plastic cover awaits the infant's arrival.

Liora is nowhere to be seen.

Eytan switches off the light, perfunctorily.

Then switches it on again, instinctively.

That fetid, cloying smell. My God, what is it?

The door to the dressing room is open.

He goes over and his heart jumps, shatters in pieces.

A foot is blocking the way.

Liora is lying on the floor in her blood. She is holding her belly and she looks up at him, a silent gaze, a gaze that turns him to ice.

RACHEL

The *shalom* changing to *shalem*, the peace you can find only if you have wholeness – I could not stop thinking about this as I was dancing.

For two thousand years, from the time of Rabbi Akiba, men had

268

been devoting their lives to carving words, to filling words to over-flowing with meaning, to establishing connections between phrases. And this fathomless perspective became complicated the moment the Kabbalists began to deal with the notion of God, whom they called *sovev ve mesuvav*, who surrounds and is surrounded, a metaphor to define the transcendent nature of YHWH, his invisible greatness. With a few words the wise men described the god of Moses as the point and the circle, the origin and the void.

One day my father explained to me – in a private conversation, because I am a girl and these questions, as a rule, are discussed only among men, between the walls of a schoolroom – that the name of God reappears every forty-nine words in the biblical text.

A recurrent measure in a symphony?

Talented composers took up the challenge: Haydn, in his Symphony number 96 in D major, *The Miracle*, caused a third from the adagio to reappear in the finale; Bach hid the letters of his name, like a keystone, in his last *Études*; and Beethoven, in the *Pathétique* sonata, amused himself with making the major theme appear and disappear.

FINAL SONG

"When we hear that music, we know that
our comrades outside in the fog are walking like robots.
Their souls have died and it is the music
that drives them onward, as the wind
drives the dried leaves."

Primo Levi

Ilan Bar Tzion reaches for the blue file that has been on his desk since the previous day and which he has had no desire to examine, despite the tag stamped "Urgent", and above all because of the word "Nazi", which he can no longer tolerate.

What more is there to be said about that era, thinks the head of Shin Bet, leaning back in his office chair. What can be so urgent that I have to read it, when the country is in a mess, with the Palestinians growing restless in the territories and the everyday fear of some scud missile falling from the sky to wipe us off the map?

Bar Tzion opens the folder and finds three white sheets, typed by a girl in the information division, a set of thumbprints and two series of photographs bound with paperclips.

A pretty thin report, thinks Bar Tzion as he looks again at the cover to check the name of the agent who sent it. The stamp with the initials "A.L." decorating the corner of the document does not give him the slightest clue, but the number after the letters, yes. 17. He takes a quick look at the chart tacked to the wall.

17, Venezuela.

"Better and better," he thinks, studying the thumbprint, whorls with two centres, cut down the middle by a thin spiral, a scar from an old gash.

It is one minute past five and Ilan Bar Tzion yawns fit to dislodge his jaw. He woke up at three o'clock and did his fifty laps in his swimming pool before setting off for Jerusalem. Forty-five minutes to get here spent listening to the news, to get into the swing of things. The night was calm on the borders. No-one wounded, no-one killed. An excellent result. The feast of the Ascension can get underway without incident.

But Bar Tzion knows better.

There is no peace. Far from it. And anyone who thinks otherwise is out of his mind. Information gathered in the territories has indicated an alarming increase in militant activity. Weapons getting in to Gaza from everywhere – Egypt, Lebanon, and by sea. Hamas is increasing its strength in men and munitions. Commando operations have been put on stand-by, the better to make Tsahal's attention wander. Bar Tzion is the only one – and all of Shin Bet along with him – who is still worried.

Only yesterday he tried to reach the Prime Minister, who no longer wants to speak to him on the phone. The cabinet leader agreed to speak to him, but no more than five minutes, by the clock.

"I've got a zillion problems, Ilan. I know you do too. So give me the facts, briefly, and then let's get back to our own business."

If that jerk had been within reach of his fist, he would have floored him with a right hook. But he was only on the other end of the line, and Bar Tzion knows that the man has the power to hang up on him. If he pisses him off he will never be able to speak freely and directly to the Prime Minister again.

So he smothered his pride, suppressed his irritation, and gave him the rundown of the situation.

It's quiet on the borders, that's true. But they've been stockpiling weapons. A very large quantity of weapons. The P.L.O. and Hamas leaders are respecting the ceasefire in order to organize a major operation.

Both he and the jerk know what this means. Some day, when the swarms are ready, they will join forces to attack the Jewish State.

The cabinet head reacted in a flash:

"We have to respect the status quo. As long as the borders are quiet, we don't move. Destroying the Palestinians' arms cache is out of the question. The Americans and Europeans would say it was deliberate provocation, the left wing would say it was harassment, and the Palestinians, yet again, would be seen as martyrs."

And the cabinet head ended his long-winded speech with a sigh: "Everything nowadays has to go through diplomacy. Don't piss me off, Ilan. Unless there's the risk of an attack. In that case we'll take the necessary action."

It is cold in the room and Bar Tzion has kept his jacket on. He picks up the blue file, but cannot concentrate. The lines jump up and down before his eyes, the photographs blur. An overpowering desire for nicotine blows his will to smithereens. He had promised himself he would wait. He had sworn he would not smoke the first cigarette of the day until six o'clock sharp. Fifty-six minutes to go. A century!

Suddenly he can stand it no longer.

He shoves his chair back roughly, its metal feet scraping against the concrete with a sinister sound, walks around the desk and switches on the electric kettle.

He will die if he does not have a coffee and a cigarette.

If you remove the oil and petrol from a car, it will not start. Well, it is the same with him. No coffee or fag and he is good for nothing, as snappy as a cur. He thrusts a spoonful of instant coffee into a mug decorated with a red heart, pours the hot water, adds sugar, stirs. His cousin had an operation last week for throat cancer. Bar Tzion is not afraid of death. Life and death, in this country, are in constant balance. But he is terrified at the thought of being butchered on an operating table. The hole in Josh's throat, the gauze veil rising and falling with his breath, have persuaded Ilan to wean himself off the fags. The problem is that no-one believes him, no-one tries to help him. Not even his wife, Myriam.

When she heard the news she groaned and looked up at the ceiling.

"God help us. As if you weren't nervy enough already as it is."

"Would you rather I got cancer?"

"I would rather nothing at all. But you won't last ten days. And we're in for a rough ride, Elohim!"

"We?"

"The girls from the office and me!"

"Go right ahead. Make me feel good," said Ilan, exasperated.

"You see? You're starting already! I can't say a thing!"

He lasted two days.

During those two days he swallowed down everything he could get his hands on – chocolate, slices of meat, peanuts, baby rusks – and he drank two or three bottles of mineral water which sent him to the toilet to relieve his bladder every twenty minutes. That was the hardest thing, in fact, rushing off to the toilet before he could even finish a sentence, then go back to the conference room until it was time to go off and piss like an elephant yet again.

The third day, at the end of his rope, he smoked one before bedtime, hiding like a thief behind the big eucalyptus tree. Myriam acted as if nothing had happened, but she got the picture.

On the fourth day he smoked four cigarettes. Spacing them out. Stuffing his face. Constantly looking at his wristwatch.

And as he had only slept a few hours the night before, he understood the moment he opened his eyes that this was one war he had lost. The urge for a cigarette had completely swamped his night. He wrapped himself up in his sheets, and dreamt that he was smoking in a room full of scantily clad she-devils who excited him with a whole range of cigarettes and cigars to choose from. She-devils or whores?

He did not even try to get to the bottom of it. One problem was enough.

The minute he got up he ran to the pool and swam until he was out of breath. He even hurt his back when he was on his last lap.

He came out of the water thinking, I'll resist, I have to resist, I can resist.

And anyway, he could not smoke in the car. Myriam had strictly forbidden it because of the baby. And with the work waiting for him to secure Jerusalem for the Ascension holiday he will not have time to think about it.

Except that it turns out he can think of nothing else.

He takes a swallow of coffee. Five forty-seven. Shit, anyway! He grabs his cigarettes and a lighter. Shit! Who gives a damn!

The first puff of tobacco goes straight to his brain, strikes his neurons, spreads through his blood. He can feel the rush of well-being. He is off. He is himself again, Ilan Bar Tzion, thirty-five years of age, colonel in the Tsahal, Golani emeritus, head of Shin Bet and next in line to be fired after the Prime Minister.

He has everything against him: young leftists who dream of pacifism, and war-weary veterans. Jerks. As if you could kiss your enemy on the lips and say, *habibi tfadal*, go ahead, mate, help yourself to whatever you want. Gaza? No problem! The West Bank? No problem! Jerusalem? By all means! And Tel Aviv? Don't you want Tel Aviv and Haifa and Ashdod? Arad?

Bar Tzion pictures an entire Palestinian family relaxing on his plastic chairs around his swimming pool, the women in their head-scarves and the men all standing around the barbecue to grill their kebabs: his heart skips a beat.

He crushes his butt on a sheet of paper, since he removed all the ashtrays from his office. Then he lights another cigarette right away.

Bar Tzion has spent a great deal of time in the territories. He knows the Palestinians well, he knows the eyes of their children which can scare you to death, even when you are armed to the teeth. He used to stand in front of them, during the intifada. He saw the stones flying, the tyres burning, the smoke that swirled in great black clouds into the wind. He has not forgotten the masked adolescents who rush at the roadblocks screaming *Allahu Akbar!*, ready to die right there before the soldiers who are trying to gain control over them, soldiers who retreat, then crouch, take aim, fire; soldiers who then break down, and ask to be transferred, because they cannot take it any more, the stoning, the fighting against children.

The uprisings have been curbed; but what about despair? As long as the living conditions in the camps don't improve . . . As long as the men cannot find work in their own land . . .

For this is the paradox: because they have to go down into Israel to earn their living, because they cannot find any work in Gaza or Nablus, their hatred of Jews has been growing. They leave at the first glow of dawn in collective taxis with their bread in their satchels; it takes them an hour to get to the checkpoints; they have to wait three, sometimes four hours to find out whether they will be taken. Most of them are sent home again, rage in their bellies, no money in their pockets. Those who are chosen are searched. There is nothing the soldiers can do. Their orders are strict: search the men and the vehicles to ensure that no arms or bombs come into the country. The solitude of the soldiers, the solitude of the Palestinians. If there is one thing that unites the two peoples, it is solitude.

Pensive, anxious, he turns his cup in his hands, then stares at the ordnance survey map tacked to the wall of this windowless room in a very ordinary Jerusalem building. The building is home to a branch of a citrus import–export firm who employ a hundred or more people, and to everyone from Shin Bet, obviously, whose job is to protect Israel, no matter the cost.

The basement – four rooms protected by bullet-proof doors – is a veritable fortress.

Access is through the underground car park. A fire door, signalled by two yellow flashes, bars entry to any curious onlookers.

The door leads to a little corridor where another door, perfectly nested in the wall, slides open when you insert a magnetic card into an near-invisible slot.

The entire personnel was subjected to a thorough background check. For months, reports came in listing their tastes, their relations, their reading habits, their degree of patriotism, and not only their own but also that of their families.

Bar Tzion opens a drawer.

Rummaging through papers and paperclips and pens and rubbers he finds a clay pot, a souvenir a subordinate officer brought back from Greece. Ilan will use it as an ashtray until he can buy one at the bazaar.

RACHEL

At seven in the morning Gabriel dropped me off in Givat Tzarfatit. We hugged for a long time, silently, in the day that was becoming blue.

I left him, feeling oppressed, that we had not had time for anything, that life was nothing but frustrations.

"Take care of yourself," he shouted as he drove off.

I went into my parents' building. I had one hour to give them, that was all, and so much love to show them.

Halfway up the stairs I saw that the door to the apartment was propped open with a chair against the wall.

I climbed more slowly. Now what? I wondered.

My mother was in the midst of a conversation with Daniel Luzzato.

If my father is absent, my mother cannot receive a man in the house. No tête-à-tête conversations are allowed in religious families, no matter the age of the man or the woman.

The fact that my mother is twenty years older than Daniel Luzzato is irrelevant. The clerics believe that desire is more powerful than will, commitment, age or beauty.

They claim that all it takes is for two people to be alone together for them to feel desire and throw themselves at each other.

Orthodox Jews have abandoned the use of chaperones, but two young people are not allowed to meet alone before marriage. They can only meet in public places.

You often see them in the luxury hotels – the Hilton, the Sheraton or the King David – shy young couples leaning toward each other and smiling, terrified, when their eager encounter dissolves into silence.

Not an inch of their body ever touches. She wears fine clothes, he wears his best suit. You walk past them and, automatically, you say *shiduh*, arranged marriage, it is so obvious they have nothing in common with the country's noisy, liberated youth. They are meeting for the second or third time, and they have to decide, quickly, whether they can marry.

I stepped into the apartment, on the alert. Daniel was sipping a coffee, with an air of constraint. Sitting opposite him my mother was trying to keep the conversation going. Daniel, at my parents' house? Their worlds are as far apart as the moon and the sun, even if they do share the same sky.

My mother, crimson with confusion, leapt up from her seat when she saw me.

"Do you know Daniel Luzzato?" she shouted, as if I had gone deaf.

And in her haste she knocked against the table. Daniel slowly stood up, too.

"Hi, Daniel," I said, putting my bag on the floor.

I stole glances at him, astonished to see how pale he looked, and he was unshaven, with dark rings under his eyes. He was a proud man, with a sharp sense of humour, but now he seemed to have been crushed by a steamroller.

"Hi, Rachel."

"You want a coffee, some tea?" my mother said with a forced smile.

"Don't bother. Where's Papa?"

"At the neighbour's. They need a tenth man to recite Kaddish."

"Who died?"

"No-one. Well, yes, last year . . . The old man who lived on the corner."

"Will he be long?"

"I don't think so. He'll be here in ten or twenty minutes."

"Fine," I said.

We were standing, all three of us, ill at ease, bored. I observed Daniel, who was jiggling from one foot to the other. His eyes wandered over the walls, the curtains, the furniture. Visibly he could think of only one thing, to talk to me and get the hell out of there.

"Daniel came to see you," said my mother, waving her arm.

Daniel confirmed the fact with a flutter of his eyelids; for some reason, God knows why, it made me want to laugh. I have always found him funny. I like his self-effacing reserve and the gallant way he behaves around girls to win them. It is all show, because Daniel is crazy about his wife, and any girl who plays along with him instantly becomes undesirable.

My mother hurried over to the door to move the chair, and closed it with a sigh of relief. Daniel stepped forward: "Rachel, uh . . ."

He was mumbling, staring at my mother.

She realized that he wanted to speak to me in private and she apologized profusely before vanishing out on to the terrace.

As soon as she left the room Daniel whispered, "I have to talk to you. But not here."

"What's it about?"

"Not here."

"I have a plane to catch . . . What's the problem?"

"Please."

His eyes were so imperious, so full of urgency, that I went to find my mother on the terrace. She dropped her towel with a gesture of total despair.

"Your father will never forgive you if he doesn't see you. *Aïsh benti*, wait for him!"

"It won't take a minute. I'll see Daniel out and then I'll come straight back."

"You will send her back to me, won't you?" she said, going up to

Daniel, who blushed to the roots of his hair and murmured, "Of course, of course," but his tone implied, "Sorry, sorry."

"I'm trusting you. And don't forget your promise about next Friday!"

"I won't."

He replied half-heartedly, nodding his head, incapable of saying goodbye for fear of hurting her feelings.

"What promise?"

"It's a secret between him and me."

The embarrassed smile that drifted on to Daniel's face sent me into a rage. My mother noticed my dark look and added, stammering, "I invited him for a couscous, with his wife and children."

"Why are you trapping him like this?"

"I'll come with pleasure," said Daniel in her defence.

My mother puffed herself up. So you see, said her expression, you see that your friends do appreciate us, and she hastened to add, "Wait there. Don't you dare leave, Daniel."

She came back with a box of cakes.

"For your sons," she said; and I was so ashamed of her generosity that I left without kissing her, without even looking at her.

Daniel was still thanking her when I reached the bottom of the stairs.

What must he think of us, this financier, I thought, my heart sinking: he comes here empty-handed and leaves again with cakes in a used ice cream container?

SHIN BET

The secretary opens the door a crack and is startled to see the cloud of smoke hovering in the room.

"You gave in, huh?"

"Just the one. It's not the end of the world."

"By noon it'll be the entire pack."

"Don't be such a defeatist."

The secretary laughs. Bar Tzion smiles. But a split-second later his smile has already faded, and his eyes are back on the document.

The secretary goes on laughing, alone, gazing at him admiringly. *Neshama*, she thinks, he does not have his equal in the entire country. They all say, Bar Tzion will eat you alive, you have to watch it with Bar Tzion. The entire country is afraid of him, even the reporters with their big mouths. Clueless twits! How can you be head of the Shin Bet and act all friendly like some vendor in Mahane Yehuda? Assuming vendors in Mahane Yehuda are friendly.

"The team is here."

"Give them some coffee."

"How long shall I make them wait?"

"Five minutes?"

"You're the boss."

Bar Tzion picks up the first batch of photographs. Three black-and-white prints that he spreads out on his desk. A puny man belted in a Nazi uniform is staring at the camera. His eyes are sunken; there are strands of hair combed over his forehead in an attempt to hide his baldness. It's not the sort of face you forget; it gives you the creeps. The face of a sadist, with long narrow lips, and as he stares at him Bar Tzion feels his throat tighten.

The second photo shows the same man surrounded by high-ranking officers, their thumbs in their belts, and in the background three SS soldiers are aiming their weapons at the sky.

In the last photo Bar Tzion comes upon a crowd in rags in a sorting area.

The man is standing in front of the crowd, with a pelisse thrown over his shoulders and his hands crossed behind his back. The shot is taken from an angle, three-quarters, and you can see his smile, like that of a hyena. Before him is a shapeless mass, trembling and docile, winding in a long queue among high snowdrifts.

Bar Tzion, distraught, stares at the women, children, old people staggering along the path that has become a vast sheet of ice.

He sees their bundles, the babies wrapped in shawls, probably dead.

There are crystals of snow on the mothers' eyebrows, and small clouds of vapour form at their lips, perfectly visible with the magnifying glass.

Behind the crowd, a train, a watchtower, the column of smoke from the crematorium. In front of them, four SS, watching over hundreds of people.

Bar Tzion feels sick to his stomach. He has never set foot in Yad Vashem, he hurries away when the old men begin talking. The stories make him sick; the extermination of the European Jews is one thing he absolutely cannot bear to think about.

His heart, his reason, cannot stand the shock of those stories.

The little he has heard sends him into a burning rage.

He knows nothing, he knows everything.

He needs no details. The number six million is enough for him to understand.

Bar Tzion shoves the three photographs to one side. He has seen enough, he thinks, it is time to go and join the team, to tackle the serious matters of the present. The only response to give the past is to verify the security in place to prevent terrorist attacks and infiltration.

He is about to stand up when suddenly he changes his mind and reaches for the second batch of photographs, this time in colour, taken with a zoom.

They all show the same old man, sitting in an outdoor café or walking down the street.

Forty-five years between the two batches, but Bar Tzion immediately recognizes the Nazi. A black suit has replaced the uniform. His body has filled out and he is now quite bald. At the age of seventy-five he ought to look as if butter would not melt in his mouth, had his lips not kept their contemptuous expression.

The secretary comes and stands in the door and calls to him.

"Ilan!"

She sees the look on his face and frowns.

"Is something wrong?"

His eyes focused on the papers on his desk, Bar Tzion is reading ever more hurriedly and suddenly he murmurs, "Oh my God, oh my God," then leaps up from his chair.

"What is it? What? What's the matter?" cries the woman.

In two strides Bar Tzion is at the door. He hurtles past his secretary, tears down the hall to the room where six young men, all information pros who speak perfect Arabic without an accent, are talking and laughing.

Silence falls over the room.

RACHEL

Daniel joined me out on the sidewalk. The air was thick as syrup. Children were on their way to school in their blue uniforms and I watched them, with the gaze of someone who knows she will be leaving.

"This way," said Daniel, pointing to the corner with a thrust of his chin.

I thought he was asking me to walk the short way to his car, and I followed.

"Are you familiar with the term *Versuchspersonen*?"

"No."

"You don't know German?"

"Well, no. What does it mean?"

"Literally, an experiment person. A fine euphemism to designate human beings who have been subjected to medical experiments in extermination camps."

"What exactly are you getting at?"

He unlocked the passenger door.

"Get in, Rachel."

I stepped back, and smiled, gesturing in denial: "I'm sorry, I can't. I promised my mother . . ."

"You'll see her this evening."

"Are you crazy? My plane takes off at noon."

"Would you go off and leave Elisheva in prison?"

He was watching me, breathing heavily. I was suddenly choking for air. Elisheva arrested? Elisheva? I do not know Daniel Luzzato very well, but I know he is not some sort of clown, above all not the type to go spreading rumours.

I climbed into the car without asking for any further explanation. Daniel tossed the box of cakes on to the back seat, where it bounced and fell to the floor. He turned the key in the ignition and pulled away from the kerb. The radio was blaring. He switched it off, mumbling an oath.

"Listen," I said, turning to him, "I don't know if you were there yesterday. But I swear to you that Elisheva is not to blame. It was my fault, and mine alone. I'm the one who will have to pick up the pieces."

He shot me a glance.

"What are you talking about?"

"The concert."

"On your life, forget the concert . . . This has nothing, but absolutely nothing, to do with music."

SHIN BET

It took only an hour for the reports Ilan Bar Tzion had requested to arrive from all over.

The men from inland security, placed on maximum alert, moved their arses to track him down, this criminal who was wandering around the Jewish homeland after trying to eliminate her people.

The team gathered in his office set aside all the other issues on the day's agenda.

The men were stunned to discover that the previous day, at nine o'clock in the morning, the assassin doctor from Majdanek had arrived, had come into Israel across the Jordanian border, under the identity of Manuel de la Serra, with a group consisting of thirty old-age pensioners of Venezuelan nationality.

Purpose of his visit: pilgrimage to the holy places. Length of stay: two days. With, as the high point, a visit to Jerusalem on Ascension Day.

They had a packed, ambitious programme.

In fact, it had been organized in such a way that they could drive virtually everywhere with the old people in the air-conditioned coach.

As soon as they entered Israel they went straight to the Dead Sea.

The pensioners had explored the ruins of the ancient Essene monastery at Qumran. Length of visit: one hour. Then they were taken to the oasis at Ein Gedi, where they were offered refreshments. Those who wanted to could swim in the Dead Sea, immerse themselves in the pools of sulphuric water, and buy creams made with minerals from the region.

"Do you think he needed a mud bath?" ventured one of the men.

His joke fell flat.

No-one had the heart to laugh.

The words *Einsatzgruppen*, crematoria and gas chambers entered the room at the same time as the Butcher of Majdanek.

"And then? What did he do after that, the swine?"

"At 2 p.m.," said Isaac, "the coach headed for Jericho for an evocation of Zacchaeus and Bartimaeus ... Who's that?"

"Go revise your classics! We don't have time for that, now."

"At 4 p.m., the group left for Galilee, through the Jordan valley."

"At six o'clock, visit of Nazareth by night."

"Let's have the map," Bar Tzion said in a low voice.

A map of Nazareth appeared on the wall.

With a pointer Boaz indicated the stops planned on the programme: the museum and the village of semi-troglodytic houses built at the time of Christ. Then, again with his pointer, he showed them the Basilica of the Annunciation.

Bar Tzion listened to the group's itinerary in silence, thinking again and again, he is in our country, he is wandering around among us, he dared, what is he up to?

"And where are they now?" Bar Tzion said.

"On the road for Jerusalem. Somewhere between Tiberias and Megiddo."

"Block the road."

"Which one? The one along the sea, or the one that goes through the territories, through Jenin, Sebastia and Ramallah?"

"Both. Put up ins and outs and check every vehicle. Find that coach. Stop that Nazi from entering Jerusalem."

Aaron got up and left the room.

Two maps appeared on the wall. The one on the right showed the road network between Tiberias and Jerusalem. On the left, the Old City of Jerusalem.

"Who organized the stay?" Ilan said.

"I'll find out."

"Find his name and bring him to me."

Noah reached for the phone.

"Do you think he's in on it?"

"I don't want to overlook anything."

Aaron came back.

"Both roads are on red alert. A helicopter will fly over the West Bank. Unless . . ."

"Unless what?"

"Unless the coach is already in Jerusalem. In which case, the security operation is pointless."

Bar Tzion's irises turned strangely dense, as if he were trying to visualize the coach, to find out where in the country it could be.

He spoke again, tensely, "Activate the Aleph Plan for the Old

City. I want men everywhere. At the gates. On the roofs. In the souk."

The men looked at each other, dismayed, without moving.

"What's the matter?"

"We're expecting a hundred thousand Christians for Ascension, Ilan . . ."

"All the more reason! I don't want any fuck-ups during the ceremony. Every neighbourhood must be searched with a fine-tooth comb. Get every available unit to control the sector."

The secretary motioned discreetly to Bar Tzion, three fingers folded, her thumb and little finger raised. The Prime Minister's principal private secretary was on the line.

Bar Tzion crossed the room, went into his office, slammed the door and glued the receiver to his ear. The Shin Bet boss was deeply upset, but his voice remained steady. He knew, from experience, that if you got carried away, your work suffered as a result. So he summed up the matter with clear, concise sentences.

"We arrest him and lock him up in the maximum-security block at the prison in Ramla," he concluded.

"No."

"What do you mean, no?"

"I refuse to have him arrested in Israel. Don't lose sight of him until he leaves the territory."

"But . . ."

"We'll decide later on an operation outside our borders."

Bar Tzion was choking. His wife's parents were survivors. He would never again be able to look them in the face.

"Why?" he said, clenching his teeth.

"We have priorities."

"That man was . . ."

"I know."

"But . . ."

"There's a time and place for everything, Ilan. Today, your mission is to protect the people of Jerusalem. Obey."

Ilan hung up, disgusted. How could he keep this operation a secret? How could he prevent journalists and photographers from getting wind of the story and spreading it?

One of the most dangerous Nazi war criminals was coming to Jerusalem and they were going to let him leave the country without doing a thing?

ELISHEVA

The room is still dark, but the whitening day slips through the half-open curtains.

Her eyes closed, her head against the cello's neck and tuning pegs, Elisheva is playing. Her body quivers, her left hand, light as a wing, shifts rapidly up the neck, and her vibrato is exceptionally fluid, rich with poignant musicality.

She played from memory to begin with, pieces from her repertoire, and then she went on to interpret the suites by Bach, as if Welwel were standing there by her side, guiding her tempo.

Curled up in the armchair where he spent the night, Carlos gazes at her, as her form grows lighter with the advancing day, first grey, then white, gradually taking the shape of a human being, with hair, hands, shoulders.

When at last her entire face emerges from the shadow, at the sight of her round irises, her small mouth, her very long neck, Carlos, although he knows her well, has a revelation. Elisheva is like a woman in a painting by Modigliani, the same melancholy, the dreamy strength, the bony frailty.

She is still wearing her concert gown, and it trails on the carpet, but she has removed her *caraco*. He knows she does not like to reveal her naked skin, her scars, her tattooed number, the torture from her past. Warmth and darkness compelled her to bare her arms, but there is more than that. Elisheva, thinks Carlos, is saying farewell to her music, the way a swan sings when it is dying.

During the night he could only guess at her movements as she played, but now she is visible at last. She bends her head to the instrument, she trembles and vibrates with it. When she stretches backwards, the instrument follows; when she sits forward again, the cello is cradled like a lover, like an adored child, and it sings to the touch of the bow as it comes and goes, untiring, enchanted.

Elisheva has been playing for a long time.

At first Carlos was worried about the noise, in the middle of the night, in the hotel. He expected to hear the phone ring, or a shout in protest, or a fist against the wall. There was nothing. The room must be soundproofed, he thought. And now when Elisheva stops playing, when at last she leaves her gesture suspended in the air, both hands far from the cello, Carlos tiptoes over to her.

He kisses her hair, embraces her, gently, as if he were afraid that his touch might cause her to crumble between his fingers.

And it is Elisheva who leans against him and rubs her head against his body.

So he puts his arms around her, crossing his hands over her chest that is icy with sweat. They stay there holding each other close, she seated, he standing, while he speaks to her in a hushed voice.

"How old were you when you first played those suites?"

"Twelve."

"And since then?"

"Occasionally. Rarely. They hurt too much."

"Why?"

"Because of the voices."

"Voices?"

She is silent, and he tries to encourage her, kissing her hair, a shower of kisses.

"What voices?"

"I'm so tired, Carlos."

He does not insist.

For a few seconds, they are apart, lost in their own thoughts, their spirits heavy and slow. It is as if they had travelled a long way together during the night, to the murmuring of Bach. They have never felt so good together, so close, eternity is opening before them, they could, why not . . . ? But no, it is impossible, they no longer have the courage, they have reached the edge of the abyss, now they must jump.

Carlos is the one to break the spell, as he tells her that the coach will soon be entering Jerusalem. They have to be at the car park before the Venezuelans arrive. That is the plan. Shoot the Nazi in the car park, like a dog, at the gates of Jerusalem.

"Already?"

Elsiheva feels dizzy. She had almost managed to forget.

Then suddenly she pulls herself together.

"Let me take a shower."

"How soon will you be ready?"

"Twenty minutes?" she says.

"Can I go down and buy some tobacco?"

She agrees: "Of course, of course," but feels something like a spasm, while her heart begins to beat wildly. She does not dare protest: don't leave me alone, not even for a minute, keep hold of me, I'm afraid. She merely squeezes his hand, while her soul bangs like a door forgotten in the wind.

Carlos goes out of the bedroom door and stops, mesmerized.

The corridor is crowded with a rapt audience, in pyjamas, sitting on the carpet or leaning against the wall. They have been listening to her playing, probably for most of the night. They are waiting, despite the silence, for the music to start again. No-one moves when Carlos walks past the numbered doors, stepping over these silent people still as statues, and he has the feeling he is disturbing them, destroying a mood.

The emotion of the audience scattered along the corridor follows him down to the lobby. He goes through the revolving door on to the square outside the hotel.

The street is deserted, the air is still cool. A crescent moon that has not yet melted hangs like a white comma in the sky, a suspended yod.

He has never seen such a luminous, peaceful morning. There are only a few passers-by, and no traffic. He buys his cigarillos, lights one, tells himself he has plenty of time to stop at his office on Rehov Mapu. It is only a short way, a few hundred metres, if that. He wants to pick up his post, and make sure everything is alright.

When he reaches the building he looks up at the sky and finds himself smiling, full of an inexpressible happiness. Like a pale, sparkling wine, the morning sunlight of Jerusalem is reviving him.

Suddenly the Spaniard notices three men standing in the entrance to the building and he stops, undecided, prepared to make a hasty retreat.

The men do not move.

Carlos strides forward, adjusting the strap of his bag on his shoulder. Don't be paranoid, he thinks. Who'd want to pick a quarrel with me? I haven't done anything yet.

RACHEL

I listened to Daniel, completely stunned, sweat on my brow. The more he told me, the more I was overwhelmed by remorse and worry and shame.

How could I have spent these three days without suspecting a thing? Elisheva, armed? Elisheva, a Nazi hunter? Elisheva obsessed by a desire for justice and revenge? What planet had I been wandering on? How could I have gone around without paying the slightest attention to her or to what she was planning?

Because if I had wanted to, I could have grasped it all, instinctively, a while ago.

Like a mysterious network, there had been words, gestures, looks, fragments of conversations, emerging one after the other, all coming back to me now, something I had overheard in a music room in New

York, or in her hotel room in Jerusalem. Misunderstandings suddenly became clear, why she arrived late, or laughed strangely.

I saw Amos again, his swollen eyelids, I saw Elisheva outside the walls of the Old City, her eyes burning with anger and her voice full of suspicion.

But I had preferred to ignore the signs, even though I boasted about being her daughter, about being closer to her than the child she did not have.

When Daniel at last fell silent I said, "Where are we going?"

"To the hotel."

"Because you think she'll still be there?"

"I hope so."

"O.K. Imagine we find her. Imagine . . . What do you want me to do? What am I supposed to say to her? She won't listen to me!"

"I think she will."

"I have no influence over her."

"At least say goodbye to her."

A fighter plane soared overhead and dropped behind the hills. The air trembled as if a bomb had exploded and the valley echoed with the sound of its engines.

EYTAN

Eytan is waiting in the dimly lit, dilapidated corridor of the Shaare Zedek hospital. Liora is in the recovery room, on a drip. The doctors have performed a Caesarean to try to save the mother and child. The baby, a boy, is alive, breathing feebly; he weighs only one kilo two hundred grams.

Although his chances for survival are minimal, he has been intubated and placed in an incubator.

Liora is still in a coma.

She has lost a great deal of blood.

She may live, or die; she may stay between life and death like a vegetable. The doctors do not want to give their opinion yet.

Eytan has to wait. And every passing second is as long as a century.

He listens. He places his cheek against the door he is not allowed to go through. Nothing. Not a sound. And this mystery pierces his heart. So much silence and rancour, so many betrayals and mis-understandings have come between them. Will he know how to win her back? Will he know how to make it up to her? And will his son, thrust from his mother's belly well before his term, know how to forgive his father, to prevent him from going away?

Eytan slumps on a chair with his head in his hands, and swears that if Liora survives he will be loving and faithful; he will be a husband. He swears that if his son survives, he will be an attentive, comforting father.

But there is Rachel. The part of him that fills with sunlight and music. And all his pledges fall to nothing, yet again. He wants, but he cannot. With either one.

On a slow, heavy backwash, the years rise to the surface.

He cannot deny that the moment he first saw Liora, in a circle of soldiers, he was captivated. There among the men's necks and shoul-ders he caught a glimpse, like a flash, of her thick woolly hair, her oval face, her skin as white as mother-of-pearl

He asked around, "Who is she?" and the guy next to him answered curtly, "The jackpot." This terse, resonant reply set him on a path and there was no turning back. The next day, he was running, elbows at his sides, towards the stadium, and he saw her again.

The female soldiers were exercising.

Officers and soldiers began to whistle.

The spectacle was edifying, as he recalls. For a few seconds, still at a run, his entire patrol, with their officer in the lead, voiced their admiration in one long clamorous shout that continued to rise even well after the women had disappeared. Like the others, he howled with excitement. He was easily influenced, like all young idiots; ready to join in the moment the rabble shouted.

Eytan did not even try to go up to her. He could tell she was looking for pretexts to come up to him, and he devised a strategy to avoid her. Until the day she threw herself at him, and he returned her kisses, thinking, basically, why not, since so many others have enjoyed her body, I'd be a fool to reject her.

Except that Liora was a virgin.

The spot of blood on the sheets, Liora's dazzled smile, and there he was stammering, stunned, "Why didn't you tell me? You've taken precautions at least, haven't you?" He can still recall the dingy hotel room, which had cost him half his wages, and the newspaper vendor shouting in the street.

At the end of the week, Liora introduced him to her father.

He can see himself outside the villa in Tel Aviv. The well-kept décor. Bauhaus architecture. One of those houses nestled on a bend in the HaYarkon river, opposite the park where branches of weeping willows fell in a cascade on to the steep pathways.

In the garden Eytan recognized generals, a few ministers with their wives and three big-shot television reporters.

One man stood out in the crowd, tall, bald, his face hidden by bifocals, a studied nonchalance about him. Instinctively, Eytan moved away from Liora. Why on earth had he accepted her invitation? He had no intention of letting the affair go any further. She was not the love of his life. Definitely not. He had nothing to fault her with; she was pretty, tender, cultured. But he was not in love. And yet, the moment Lipchitz started to walk towards him Eytan knew he would not get out of this. As if he sensed that he had belonged, since time immemorial, to this house and this man.

"Everything O.K., kids?"

Lithuanian, thought Eytan automatically, when he heard his accent.

Lipchitz immediately suggested a game of ping-pong. Liora tried to protest. Her father cut her short, scathing.

"He's big enough to refuse, isn't he? Go kiss your mother."

Guests were drinking wine, never taking their eyes off them. Eytan can still feel the anger that overcame him. His parents did not display that sort of casual style with his friends. Gershon would say something jolly; Noga would open the box of pastries. Here they sent you off to bat a white ball.

Lipchitz beat him in two sets, effortlessly. He was quick to hit the ball, and used wily tactics that obliged Eytan to run from one side to the other of the table. More than his sliced shots, it was his words that stung, his dubious jokes, full of innuendoes, as if Lipchitz were getting even: how dare he go up to his daughter, how dare he think he could ever be part of their clan?

"So, soldier! Out of breath? What unit are you in, already? Commando? Hey, we're well defended, then. Come on, here's an easy ball . . . Get it, lad, move your legs, come on! Go get the ball, go, go."

When Liora came to join him he was soaked in sweat, humiliated by two crushing defeats. His hands spread wide in a gesture of peace, Lipchitz wore a triumphant smile on his face.

"He still has a way to go, your friend."

"Stop it, Dad."

"Didn't I advise you choose your relations carefully?"

"What do you want?" Liora shot back. "A table tennis champion for a son-in-law? He isn't one! Get over it."

Lipchitz went pale. Liora had just trumpeted her intentions to all the high society gathered in the garden. A few bravos rang out, someone shouted, "Lucky in love, unlucky at games." Lipchitz handed his bat to a guest and led Eytan into his study.

There the engineer left him standing.

Eytan had not misread the situation. In the panelled room, to the ticking of a clock, the cross-examination continued, to see whether he could prove himself worthy of the cherished daughter. The conversation went on to harmless topics: the atmosphere in Eytan's unit, the meals at the cafeteria, relations among soldiers. Eytan answered monosyllabically. Lipchitz poisoned the conversation by slipping in a reference to bastards who used girls to advance socially. Eytan blushed

297

and protested. He had no intention of . . . He was not one of . . . Lipchitz gave him a cynical smile. No, of course not. Obviously. Liora's name and her father's position had nothing to do with it.

"But I don't give a damn," stammered Eytan. "Your name, your . . ."

Lipchitz swept his objections aside with the back of his hand. He had asked around. Mediocre studies, rebellious behaviour. Since then, of course, he had improved somewhat in the army. His superior officers said he was a good element. But then, once his military service was finished, what did he plan to do with his life? Study? He did not have his matriculation. A manual job? *Tsk, tsk* . . . Lipchitz's son-in-law? Nothing, then. Strictly nothing. There, he had been warned. He would not be living off Liora.

"Who told you all that?"

Lipchitz, clearly, looked down on him. He was a man with connections, after all. Any loving father, particularly of an only daughter, was duty-bound to be cautious, not to give his daughter to a yob, right?

"Well then, you can keep her," said Eytan, leaving the room.

Liora ran after him, her face on fire, screaming his name.

"What are you doing? Come back!"

He got in his car. Liora too. The ten minutes that followed were torture. He told her that it would be better for them to part, she clung to him, soaking his jacket with tears and snot, saying no, no, no. Great! So let her pay for the insult he had suffered at Lipchitz's. He had nothing to lose, anyway.

"Listen," he said hoarsely, "I liked you, I fucked you, let's leave it at that. Our relationship is just a fling, nothing more. Go reassure your father. Go tell him it won't go any further, that I don't want you."

He was staring through the dusty windscreen at the end of the residential avenue and he thought about Rachel, who would have ripped his cheeks with her nails and scratched his eyes out if he had dared to speak to her like that. But Liora was not Rachel. Liora only knew how to burst into tears.

"You're lying to me. It can't be. It's not true."

To destroy her hopes, he told her about Rachel. Besides, Rachel and he were practically engaged.

He reached past her and opened the car door.

"Get out, now."

Liora was sobbing quietly, her face hidden in her hands.

"And me?" she said. "Me? Don't you love me?"

That was all she could find to say. Her only claim.

"Get out."

Voices were calling from the garden. "Get out, they're looking for you."

Liora gave a stifled exclamation. "Drive on, please. Don't dump me here in front of them."

Lipchitz was standing behind the grille of the gate with a general and two reporters in his wake.

To escape the melodrama, Eytan nervously put the car in gear.

They had finished their conversation by the sea.

Three months later they were married.

Eytan took a diploma in electronics. Lipchitz, the better to control him, found him a position in a humdrum factory. Eytan was badly paid and had to do all the grunt work, but all things considered, there was no lack of money.

Lipchitz took care of the luxuries – travel, clothing, restaurants. He went on footing the bill for his daughter at the two most elegant boutiques on Dizengoff Street, and Liora came home with handbags, shoes and dresses that Eytan could never buy her. When he reproached her, she flung back, "My father loves me!" And insisted: "At least *he* does!"

Lipchitz also co-signed the purchase of the Mamila flat and paid for the rental of the Moshava villa. In short, the money his son-in-law brought in was mere pocket money.

★

Eytan lifts his pale face at the sound of hurried steps along the corridor.

The Lipchitzes are running towards him.

Eytan goes to meet them. He holds out his hand to Mathias. The man is at the end of his tether: he raises his fist and punches Eytan on the nose. Eytan staggers and lands in one of the chairs in the corridor. Ruth Lipchitz cries out.

Lipchitz holds her back with one hand, never taking his eyes off Eytan.

"You're not going to fight?" Ruth says, alarmed.

Lipchitz does not answer. Glaring at him, he waits for the young man to sit up. This hatred has always been there, ever since he first set eyes on him. Eytan, likewise, has never been able to stand the guy. At last they will come out with it, man to man.

"How do you plan to behave, now that you have a son?" Lipchitz says in a neutral tone.

Blood is flowing in a scarlet thread down Eytan's mouth and chin. Slowly wiping his nose, he stares at Mathias. Stares at him with a grave intensity, bitter and ironic, as if to say, I won't stoop so low as to hit an old man. Mathias Lipchitz looks flustered, tenses up, then finally swivels round, ignoring him, to greet Noga and Gershon.

Ruth Lipchitz seizes the moment to go up to her son-in-law. She takes a handkerchief from her pocket and reaches out to wipe his face.

"Ruth, no!" Eytan said wildly.

She quivers, finds the strength to say, "Forgive him. Anything to do with Liora and he cannot control himself. But you are like my own son. You are our son."

He can see her face very close to his, a strand of pearls from Eilat around her neck, her short, coppery hair, her thin mouth and clear gaze. She is a peaceful, maternal woman. The little she says is always mysterious, almost hypnotic. And she is as discreet as her husband is overbearing.

Eytan walks down to the end of the corridor, to the coffee machine, where Gershon, like an old polar bear, goes to join him with measured steps, his face expressionless.

Gershon puts a coin in the slot. He presses the button, and says in a dull voice as if talking to the machine, while the coffee drips into the cup, "Don't pay any attention to what Mathias did just now. He did it, it's done. Act as if it was me . . ."

"But it wasn't you."

"I should have given you a hiding long ago," Gershon said cautiously, his voice slow, as if he were entering a minefield. And he places his hand on his son's arm, still not looking at him. They have always communicated without having to spell things out, even before Gad's death. Gershon can count on that. And on the complicity of happier days.

Almost in spite of himself, Eytan now stares at the luminous buttons indicating chocolate, coffee, tea, tomato soup. He reads it over and over, chocolate, coffee, tea, tomato soup. He is about to burst. After these three days of crisis he has only one wish: to scream, to sob, to smash everything around him, this fucking machine for a start. He can feel the blood rising to his head, he is shaking, but Gershon's fingers are exerting pressure on his arm, growing ever stronger, checking his fury and reassuring him, bit by bit.

"It's all my fault, I know that."

"All of it? Don't exaggerate . . . In a couple, there are two of you."

Eytan gives a short, mad, unbearable laugh. Gershon takes a quick look at his son before turning again to the coffee machine.

"I've seen Rachel."

"You have?"

"I wanted to leave with her."

"You wanted?"

"I feel so lost, Dad."

"It's — it's a rough patch," says Gershon, hesitantly.

"No! I've fucked up my life."

301

"Wait until you're my age and then you'll see."

Gershon turns at last to look at Eytan. Eytan sees the bags under his father's eyes, his white eyebrows. His white moustache. His thick, almost mauve lips. And his heavy body, dressed simply, a body that was once strong and colossal and has now grown weak.

The son looks at his father, and Gershon tries to express his affection, without raising his brows, without smiling or talking, simply soaking in his gaze.

"Well?" murmurs Gershon.

Eytan looks down at the patch of sunlight edging across the tiled floor, with its message that time is passing, that he must make a decision.

"She's waiting for me . . . You see, I'm being open."

"She?"

"Rachel . . . What should I do?"

"What do *you* want to do?"

There is the sound of a murmur growing louder at the end of the corridor. A nurse has come out of Liora's room. Noga and the Lipschitzes surround her immediately.

Eytan rests his forehead on his father's shoulder.

"They say that torrents of water cannot extinguish love, that rivers cannot drown it."

"Water, perhaps not . . . But a child that weighs twelve hundred grams?"

For a long time Eytan does not reply. Then he finally says, his voice hoarse, "A child, yes."

Gershon embraces his son with all his strength. He knows that this is only postponing things, that his son will never completely overcome his childhood. But that's life, he thinks; that is also life.

"I haven't even had a chance to congratulate you! *Lehayim!*"

Eytan begins to float again. It seems to him that Gad is there with them, Gad is there whispering their slogan, from the old days: "Let's go fishing in Tel Aviv!"

ELISHEVA

Elisheva glances at her wristwatch. Carlos has been gone for over half an hour and he is not back yet. She took a cold shower, brushed her hair, dressed in white – skirt, blouse, safari jacket – without looking in the mirror: she is too afraid of her own image. With her pale complexion she looks like a ghost.

She lingers by the bay window, pointlessly, because she cannot see the street, only the hills and the walls.

And as she does not dare call the front desk to see if there are any messages, she paces across the room, empties the ashtrays, airs the room, puts the cello back in its case, checks her handbag and makes sure her papers are as they should be. If something happens to her, she wants everything to be found at once, she wants to leave things in order.

The envelope!

She almost forgot it.

With a few quick strides she goes through the door into Rachel's room; the bed has not been slept in. Empty like this, the room seems sinister. In a corner her suitcase is overflowing with hastily folded clothes; the cupboard doors are half open. What will become of Rachel? Will she turn into an arrogant, adulated musician? A lonely woman, consumed by failure? Elisheva would have liked to have seen her go through life, to lean on her arm in her old age, but that good fortune will not be given to her.

Elisheva smoothes the envelope with the flat of her hand before placing it in the middle of the bed.

When she returns to her room she tries once again to find an explanation for Carlos's absence. She imagines the kiosk closed, its wooden shutters held in place by an iron bar. Carlos must have had to continue as far as King George to find his cigarillos. She gives him a first deadline, then another as she glances at her watch. Then she lies down again, rigid, elegant, numb, the only music the ticking of the watch hands.

Ten minutes go by. A quarter of an hour. Carlos left nearly an hour ago. She no longer has any doubt. Carlos has lost his nerve. If only he had spoken to her about his scruples, she would have told him that she too was tempted to abandon, that she had also had moments when she thought, "What's the use?"

She cannot fault him for anything. He has helped her more than she dared hope. In the course of these three days he has been present, attentive, loving; he has watched over her, supported her. If she has managed to behave almost normally it is surely thanks to him, and him alone.

She dials the number of the combination safe and stares at the door as it opens with a click.

She slips her hand inside and takes out the gun.

It is a matt black colour, with finger grooves at the front and back of the grip. The hammer has vanished, replaced by a firing pin. The safety system, consisting of a double trigger, makes accidental firing virtually impossible. The weapon is so light that it makes killing seem like child's play.

Elisheva aims at the wall, lowers her arm, lifts it again, aims again. Yes, she can do it.

Yes, she will do it.

Ten times, twenty times, Elisheva repeats the same gesture, then she sits on the bed and lets the weapon slip into her skirt.

When she looks down at her zipper, she notices the words etched on the butt: Glock, 18C, Austria 9×19. An Austrian weapon to kill a Nazi.

Schweine, bleibt ruhig! Pigs, be still!

The words explode in her head.

She inserts the clip.

The white gloves, moving like claws towards her chest.

304

Elisheva shudders.

Not that image, no, not that image. She does not want to be carried away by her obsessions.

A last glance at her watch and she realizes it is no good. It is ten minutes to nine. She has left it too late. Their plan has failed. She will never find a taxi to get her to the appointed place in ten minutes. Because if the group left on time, the coach must be by the walls now, a long shining rectangle with two huge wing mirrors, an immense windscreen, the driver swinging his torso to gain the momentum required to turn the vehicle and manoeuvre it into the car park.

Elisheva grabs her bag, heads to the door, suddenly turns back: she is barefoot.

CARLOS

The room is windowless, the closed door is reinforced. A bare bulb dangles on a wire from the middle of the ceiling. The furnishings are basic, a formica table and two folding chairs made of wooden slats.

"So you organized the trip, Montana?"

"Yes."

"Why?"

"It's my work."

Carlos replies in a placid voice to the volley of questions, thinking only of Elisheva who, back in the hotel room, must be thinking he has got cold feet. What state of mind will she be in when she leaves the hotel? Has she too been arrested? He curses their bad luck, curses himself. What came over him, to want to make that detour by Mapu Street? His post! As if the post had the slightest importance on a day like today.

He does not dare to glance at his watch for fear of giving something away to the agent. He tries to reassure himself that this is a routine interrogation. Shin Bet knows something, but evidently not everything. Not everything. Otherwise the agent would have been rougher, more aggressive, or perhaps more kindly.

They went through the preliminaries very quickly – name, age, profession, date of arrival in Israel. The Shin Bet agent who has been staring at his I.D. card starts harassing him again.

"Do you know these tourists?"

"No."

"Not one of them?"

"They are Venezuelan, I'm Israeli. I haven't left the country since I got here, not once."

The man looks up and Carlos is sure that a camera is hidden somewhere in the room. People are listening to his answers and checking every one of his words.

"Who contacted you to arrange the stay?"

"A priest."

"What priest?"

"A priest in Caracas."

"He called you, personally?"

"Not me. My company."

"What is your profession?"

"I'm a guide."

"I thought guides did no more than lead people round on tours, not play at being organizers."

"I do both. I have to."

"Why do you have to?"

"Because I love Israel."

"That's not an answer."

"The priests . . ."

"You work only with the Church?"

"With the Vatican, yes."

"Are you a Jew or a Christian?"

"I'm both."

"How is that possible?"

"I'm a Marrano Jew, *cojones!*"

The Shin Bet man sits with his mouth agape at the gleam of defiance lighting the Spaniard's gaze.

"A Marrano Jew," he repeats, then quickly regains his self-control. He opens the top drawer of his desk, takes out a blue folder, and from the folder, a photograph.

"Do you know this man?"

Carlos leans over the table and pretends to examine the Nazi's face. And he thinks, *puto tiempo!* How did they find out? They're real pros, no two ways about it. I am proud of my country.

"No," he says curtly. "Who is it?"

"You don't know him?"

"No."

"You've never heard of him?"

"No."

"Think carefully. Take your time."

"No, I told you."

"He is one of the group you brought here."

"Never seen him. *Hostia!*"

"That's strange."

"I don't have any connection with the tourists. I only deal with their leader. I arrange everything with him directly."

"Why didn't you go and meet them at the border?"

"That's not my role. I sent someone else."

"O.K. Explain your role to me."

"I guide them through the Old City."

"You?"

"Me. *Me cago en la madre que te parió!*"

"Are you supposed to meet them today?"

"Of course!"

"What time?"

"Nine o'clock."

The agent looks at his watch, goes pale, looks up at the ceiling.

Carlos looks down at his watch. Nine ten. She's done it, he thinks, with a feeling of ineffable joy. It's over. He's dead.

"Where are you supposed to meet?"

"At Herod's Gate."

"Why didn't you say so earlier?"

"Did you leave me the time? With all your questions . . ."

Suddenly the reinforced door is thrown open and three agents burst in. Ilan Bar Tzion is with them.

"Get up. You're coming with us."

They push him, shove him in the back, he is surrounded by agents, running along the corridor, while orders explode into two-way radios. Calling all units, calling all units . . .

In the courtyard Carlos is thrust into the rear of an unmarked squad car. The door locks with a dull click, the car roars off, followed by five others with flashing lights. Bar Tzion, sitting next to him, dictates his orders into a transmitter. A voice crackling with static replies, "Sha'ar Haprahim . . . ? Got it. Let's go."

Bar Tzion throws himself back against the seat, pale, his pupils dilated. In a minute or two the coach will be surrounded, no matter how horrific the traffic is, the siren will open the way, yes, in a minute or two, the soldiers he sent will surround the coach, all the tourists will be caught in the net.

"I haven't figured it all out yet," says the Shin Bet boss in an altered voice, turning to Carlos. "But I promise you I am going to get to the bottom of this. And very soon. You'd better watch your arse if you had anything to do with this."

The radio crackles. A voice saying, sorry, sorry, the target is empty.

Bar Tzion shouts with rage. He calls for reinforcements, gives new orders. Split up and search the shops, the taxis, the warehouses. Go after the prey.

Carlos makes himself smaller against the seat, terrified. Where is Elisheva?

RACHEL

I rushed out of the elevator, down the hall, and opened Elisheva's door. The room was empty, but the slight untidiness was still full of her presence.

Her high-heeled shoes lay under the desk, her concert gown over the arm of a chair. Her clothes were still hanging in the wardrobe and the cellos were lying in their cases and had not been wrapped. Daniel had not lied to me.

We were not leaving.

I hurried into my room. In the middle of the bed there was a letter addressed to me. I tore open the envelope and in my haste nearly tore the message.

A photograph fell out, of me playing the cello in a room at the Juilliard.

I knew from my haircut and the clothes I was wearing the exact moment the picture had been taken. Elisheva's last farewell consisted of one order alone: work.

I ran back down to the lobby.

Daniel was talking to the doorman, a dignified old man with white hair. I lit a cigarette. I tried to follow their discussion.

"She took a taxi," said the porter. "I opened the door for her myself."

"The address? Did you hear the address?"

Daniel took some banknotes out of his pocket. The doorman pushed his hand away, shaking his head. He did not want any money.

"Last night, you see, I heard the angels playing . . ."

"What are you talking about?"

"There were a lot of people in the corridor outside her door. All the hotel guests, and staff as well, on the landing. We all took turns going up to her door. I could only stay for a few minutes. I'm not an

309

educated man, I don't know a thing about music like that. Still . . ."

"Right," said Daniel breathlessly. Then, pleading with him: "Where did she go? What address did she give the driver?"

The doorman shook his head. He had not heard, because there were tourists arriving, with all their luggage, and he had to help the young porter to put everything on the cart. But if that was all they needed, the taxi driver could give them the information.

"What's his name?"

"He's called Duddi, he's with the Hashalom company."

Daniel hurried to a phone booth to call the driver. I went into another one to page my brother. I needed to hear his voice, to have him by my side. His reaction was just what I had hoped for: "I'm on my way," he said, and I suddenly felt better for his promise. Then I wanted to get in touch with my friends, with Michael, Gabriel, Elena, Tamar and Nurit. I felt I had no right to hide the truth from them. We had all been Elisheva's students, we were all in her debt. I called Michael and in a few words I summed up the situation.

I hung up, in tears, and went to wait outside the lobby.

Daniel came to join me.

"Duddi is on his way," he said, squeezing my arm.

But we had to wait fifteen long minutes, and we jumped every time a car came up the ramp. Finally a driver got out of his car, slowly, pushing his dark glasses up on his head.

"So what's the problem?" he drawled.

I immediately liked him: solid, unshaven, swarthy, dark hair and eyes, with a fold of flesh like a rubber tyre around his waist, above his trousers.

Daniel shook his hand and said, "Thanks, thanks for coming," and the driver replied, "If I can help, why not, tell me." Daniel gave a brief description of Elisheva.

"Do you remember her?"

The driver smiled.

"Of course. Who could forget such a woman? She has an

incredible face . . . Don't worry. She's fine."

"Where did you drop her off?"

"Sha'ar Haprahim, Herod's Gate."

"Did she speak to you? Did she say where she was going?"

"I tried to chat with her but she didn't want to, no. The only thing I got was that she wanted to go to the Church of the Holy Sepulchre. I was surprised. She looked Jewish to me."

"The Holy Sepulchre," said Daniel, slowly. "That makes sense. Outside the church he won't be on his guard, she can shoot him there."

"What are you talking about?" asked Duddi, dumbfounded.

Daniel shrugged. I was wondering how he was going to explain his way out of this when he said, "Are you free now?"

"Yes, my friend."

"O.K., take us to the Old City. We'll save time that way."

We climbed into the taxi and Duddi took off, tyres squealing. Daniel looked very worried.

"The Nazi is old but he is still pretty powerful. Elisheva won't get him just like that," whispered Daniel to me.

"Is she in danger?"

"Yes."

I burst into tears. In a sort of nervous panic I had a vision of her body lying on the ground, her chest covered with blood. Words were spinning in my head. Majdanek. The great massacre. Six hundred survivors, three hundred woman and three hundred men who had to erase all trace of the slaughter, and Elisheva was one of them. Then the evacuation, to Auschwitz. Katya and Elisheva, holding each other up in the snow. Elisheva in the women's orchestra at Birkenau. Then the two young women arriving in Israel. And the Butcher.

Daniel looped his fingers through mine, unable to find the words to console me. Duddi tilted his rear view-mirror to meet my eyes.

"Hey, why the tears?"

His voice was gentle, sing-song, rolling over the r's and the sh's, filling all the words, comforting me. And suddenly I knew why this man's presence was so reassuring. He had the same voice as my father when he chanted his psalms at the synagogue, my father's tender voice, calling to God.

"Never mind! Sometimes it's good to cry," said Daniel.

"You should only cry for the dead. And your friend, your mother, whoever, the lady I dropped off, ten minutes ago, at Sha'ar Haprahim, she was alive and well. So don't go burying her too fast."

ELISHEVA

Elisheva is distraught as she scrutinizes the coaches parked outside Herod's Gate. Empty. All of them empty. She has come too late. Now she must go looking for him down the narrow streets, she must resign herself to hunting for him in the crowd.

She feels the sun burning on her back. And the weight of the Glock in the pocket of her safari jacket; she wonders if she will be able to confront the wretch, raise the revolver to the proper height. And shoot.

She catches up with some young believers on their way to school. Children! Carefree children! She follows close on their heels, without thinking. She just wants to imbibe their laughter, and forget the other children who rest in her memory, the ones the Butcher tore from their mothers with a wave of his finger, before his flunkeys carried them off to the lazaretto. The Butcher gave them a lethal dose – made them swallow or inhale it, or applied it to their skin. He measured their resistance, watched as they struggled against death. Some of them, at the last minute, were given an antidote. The Butcher administered it, not out of compassion, no, just to obtain a precise measurement of the key value of the mortal dose. And then . . . And then the child was sent to the gas chamber. He had outlived his useful purpose. He was fit for nothing now.

One of the schoolboys turns around and sees Elisheva, and he feels his heart tighten at the sight of her grey face, her distorted features.

Who is this witch? Why is she following them? The adolescent leans over to his neighbour, murmurs a few words. His friend glances back at her, warns the others, and the band of friends dissolves.

Lost in her memories, Elisheva does not notice their fright. She keeps walking straight ahead, her mind full of music, the music she used to play to herself to escape the pain, the music that was her lifebuoy, her beacon, her rope in the night. For months, years, she heard the organ music. Bach's Toccata. Because of the 35th psalm: Contend, O Lord, with those that contend with me, fight against those that fight against me.

But where have the notes gone? Who has stolen them? Only yesterday she knew the work inside out. The rest of the piece ... The rest ... The women whose fingers and toes and ears were amputated, who were enucleated, mutilated by the removal of their liver, their ovaries ... They had taken the rest of the piece with them ...

And suddenly Elisheva stops, as if she has been stricken.

The prisoners called the Butcher *Malah Hamavet*, the Angel of Death.

They said he ate the flesh of his victims, that he was a cannibal. To eat *Untermenschen*, is that a crime against humanity?

The sky is filled with cries.

Elisheva's hand closes around the butt of the Glock.

Soldiers, plain-clothes men, are stationed outside the shops, watching the flow of humanity heading toward the Christian quarter.

Groups of people come out of their hotels, step down from their buses in a steady stream.

Processions are converging from all over. They meet and turn down the Via Dolorosa, the ground shaking beneath their feet.

Pilgrims hand out prayer sheets. Bells are chiming throughout the neighbourhood.

The crowd is enormous. Whites, Africans, Asians, nuns, priests in homespun cowls; choirboys swinging censers. They stumble over each other, smile, marvel that they are all there together, in the narrowness of streets.

313

Elisheva huddles like a beggar at the entrance to the Holy Sepulchre. She sits on the stone steps, brings her knees up under her chin. Coins rain down at her feet. Her eyes on the crowd, Elisheva awaits the arrival of the cursed man.

Lord, Christ, Lord, Mary . . .

The pilgrims' fervent words trickle down to her, like the drops from a leaky tap.

RACHEL

Eight gates open the way to old Jerusalem. Seven, actually, because the Golden Gate, which the Jews call Sha'ar Harachamim, the gate of Mercy, was walled up on the orders of Suleiman the Magnificent, and bones were buried at ground level to prevent the Messiah from gaining access to the Temple Mount.

To enter the Christian quarter, the best way is to go through the Lions' Gate, which gives on to the Via Dolorosa. But Duddi explained to us that the road from Jericho, which leads to the valley of Josaphat, has been closed to traffic. He saw there were Jeeps, soldiers and road blocks. A *balagan*, he said. It must be a bomb alert, or the fear of an attack. The processions headed for the Basilica of the Agony and the Garden of Gethsemane have all been slowed down, and are being watched.

Daniel and I looked at each other in silence.

"What do you plan to do?" asked Daniel.

Duddi suggested we go into the Old City through the Damascus Gate, and he drove through the neighbourhood of Morasha, street by street, to reach Derech Shechem.

But there too we were trapped in the stream of vehicles. Tour buses from every hotel in town and the surrounding area were unloading their cargoes of tourists on the sidewalk, and the bus station for East Jerusalem with its wheezing old vehicles looked prehistoric.

At one point during the ride Duddi decided he would help us

look for Elisheva, and he called his company's switchboard. A man answered: "*Ay*, Duddi." "*Ay*, Yaacov, what's up?" "Nothing, and you?" "*Beseder*, everything fine my end . . ." Duddi told him he had an errand to run, and could not be reached for the next few hours.

Yaacov lost his temper.

"Oh no, oh no," he said, "this is not the day, the switchboard is overloaded with calls from tourists looking for a ride, you can't let them down . . ."

"Yes I can," said Duddi in his calm voice.

"Listen, Duddi, on your life, on your children, don't do this to me." And since Yaacov would not shut up, Duddi switched off his radio.

Duddi slowed along the sidewalk outside the Damascus Gate. I opened my door and bolted like an arrow toward the arcade. A religious holiday was a godsend for the illegal pedlars, and now they had set up trestles beneath parasols, where they sold cakes, drinks and religious souvenirs.

The crowd was dense, nonchalant, under the watchful eye of the soldiers, and I was jostled this way and that. As I entered the souk I bumped into a pastry vendor who was walking with a copper tray balanced on his head. He shouted at me in Arabic. I did not apologize. I know I should have, but I did not.

A wheelbarrow with huge wheels was blocking the path and I would have jumped over it if the driver had not swivelled it out of the way in time. I could hear the tradesmen shouting, I saw the green haze beneath the huge worn canopies, the carpets, necklaces, water jugs, a woman wearing a niqab; I inhaled the scent of *za'atar*, and mutton skin, and I went on running.

"Elisheva, Elisheva!"

I was shouting her name as I ran, and people gave me strange looks. Two believers murmured to me as I ran by – one was a *Tzedakah*, the other *Shechinah* – and it made me realize in the end that people thought I was suffering from Jerusalem syndrome; that I was prophesying the arrival of God.

315

A stitch in my side winded me. I was not even halfway there and I was already exhausted.

I stopped, completely out of breath, doubled over in pain. I looked behind me. No sign of either Daniel or Duddi.

By cutting through the Khan el-Zeit souk, I had thought I was taking the shortest way; and I said to myself again, in a few moments I will be in front of the Holy Sepulchre, and I'll speak to Elisheva. But I quickly realized my mistake: I was on the Way of the Cross that the pilgrims were following.

I started running again, covered in sweat; my shirt stuck to my back and there was a phrase going through my head like a refrain, an absurd phrase: "Elisheva was born in 1927." I could still hear it — stubborn, insistent — when I was stopped by a procession outside the Franciscan chapel.

People were converging from every little street and alleyway, chanting hymns and carrying crosses and torches.

I tried to push my way through, but the crowd was too dense, too fervent. Their backs and necks, that was all I could see before me. I was shouting, "Please, please," but I was like a mosquito before a roaring lion, my shout vanished into the incantations of thousands of voices singing, "*Hosanna, hosanna*," and verses in Latin.

Some people were weeping, others were beating their chests with their fists, and the paving stones resonated with the thud of their pilgrims' staffs.

Suddenly a humming sound rose above the clicking of prayer beads: "Our Father, who art in Heaven, *Notre Père, Pater noster, Vater unser, Abun D'Bashmayo, Padre nuestro, Abana El Aziz . . .*"

I saw I would never be able to get through, and I retraced my steps.

By way of Al-Wad and Al-Tuta, going around the Ethiopian Patriarchate, I managed to reach the last stretch of the Via Dolorosa.

I was mesmerized by the beauty of the ceremony. Ten priests dressed in homespun cowls, ropes around their waists, were slowly moving forward, bent to the weight of a heavy cross. Bishops and cardinals followed beneath a canopy. Behind them the faithful were carrying a Virgin in their outstretched arms. For a moment I forgot what I had to do, why I was there. And I was about to follow the procession when in the crowd I saw, jumping up and down and trying to force their way through, my brother Avner and his friend Ahmed.

I elbowed my way over to them, blessing the hotel doorman.

"Avner . . ."

We kissed, and the crowd swarmed around us, past us.

"*Hahla el yom*," said Ahmed in greeting. "A magnificent day."

"Are you alright? Bearing up?" whispered Avner. "I'm so sorry . . ."

"I don't want her to go to prison. She's suffered enough."

My brother raised an eyebrow.

"She?" he said so slowly that I felt my legs weaken and begin to give way beneath me. "Who is 'she'?"

"Elisheva."

He opened his mouth, not a single sound came out, and I realized he was talking about Eytan.

It would have been better not to have asked any questions. But I wanted to know, and Avner decided he ought to tell me what he had heard: the radio had announced the birth of Lipchitz's grandson.

There was an explosion in my head. What will become of me?

Ahmed leaned over to me: "*Shu badak?* What's wrong?"

The heart is a muscle, so Nurit had said, it can atrophy. I smiled, murmured, "*Safi*. Help me find Elisheva."

Ahmed said he knew a passageway through a house that he had used on several occasions. I heard his words, I understood what he was talking about, but a huge rock where waves were breaking one after the other had risen up between us.

I hunted in my bag for my pack of cigarettes. My hand closed around the pieces of my bow. I clung to them. This is what will help you out of this, I thought, your only salvation. Elisheva was right, music can cure you of anything.

317

Ahmed sensed there was something wrong. He nudged my brother with his elbow and whispered, "*Ahtak*, your sister . . ."

The rest of his words were lost in the cries of the faithful.

Avner took me by the sleeve and dragged me ahead. I wanted to be by myself, but I did not have the strength to say so. I followed my brother as he forced his way roughly through the crowd, we went through a carriage entrance, up some stairs, across a terrace where laundry was drying. I could see the roofs of Jerusalem, the domes of the mosques like two breasts facing the sky, one gold, the other silver, and I saw the television antennas, and the Jews who with their talliths on their heads were heading toward the Wailing Wall; I saw them dancing around the sepharim, because it was Thursday, and on Thursdays the books are taken out of the cupboards. And my life was draining away through a tiny pinhole.

We went back down into the street, into the crowd, searching for Elisheva, the angel of death, and the Butcher.

Prayers surrounded me, prayers and the flames of the large candles.

ELISHEVA

Suddenly he is there before her.

He is walking, surrounded by old people.

He is not wearing a uniform.

He is a civilian, he looks harmless, an old, unarmed man who has lost his henchmen and his dogs.

His face is white, wrinkled, as dry as ancient plaster. Only his eyes have not changed, a pale satin-blue, and in their depths, like a beast at the bottom of a well, lies the same sinister, intolerable cruelty.

Elisheva gets to her feet, her knees trembling.

The trembling spreads to her hands, her jaws. In fright, her hair stands on end. Her back against the chapel wall, she stares at the Butcher; she sees him walking towards her, as if in a nightmare, in slow motion.

Bach's Toccata. At the edge of the abyss, Bach. He sends for her. Play. The moment she falls silent, he threatens her, in a soft voice, threatens to cut off her fingers. Play. Play again. She plays. She is not playing for him. She is playing for her brothers, outside. For the entire camp, where the condemned walk, backs bent, diarrhoea flowing between their legs.

She whips the Glock from her pocket. She reaches deep inside for breath, and with her mouth open, and one hand on her breast, like a soprano, she screams.

"Heeeeeeenker."

The man stops short.

"Henker!"

The faithful surrounding the Butcher have seen the Glock, and the woman who stands there, gleaming.

The people stop, frozen.

Mouths close. Silence falls.

Elisheva screams, her finger pointing at the Nazi.

Silence washes like a wave over the crowd as they recoil, leaving an empty space around the Butcher.

RACHEL

Elisheva's scream wrenched me from my torpor.

"Henker!"

The people around me were pushing backward.

I was no great distance from her now, only a few metres, if that. But the tidal wave that had taken hold of the multitude risked carrying me with it to the end of the street, to the little alleyways, and I would no longer be able to reach her.

I was thrown against a wall, separated from my brother. I clung with all my strength to an iron bar fixed in the stone to keep from being swept away. People were turning on their heels, in a collective panic, taking refuge any way they could, in the shops, while others hoisted themselves on the grilles outside the windows or pressed themselves against the drainpipes.

A mass of people does not need to know the reason for danger, they will repeat their neighbours' gestures or behaviour to infinity.

There was an explosion of tear gas grenades.

Soldiers came running, emerged on terraces, raised their weapons, waited for the signal from their battalion commander.

A man shouted over a loudspeaker in Spanish: "*Párate, de la Serra! De la Serra*, don't move!"

There was nothing more I could do. Just stay there clinging to my spot. And abruptly I thought of the verse my father would say to me, *veharbo shelufa al yerushalayim*, and his sword is spread over Jerusalem.

I rushed forward, brandishing the bow, holding it by the heel. I elbowed my way, pricking people with the tip to let me through, and they jumped, moved aside with little cries, made animal-like by fear and anxiety.

I inched my way through the crowd, so slowly, but it was better than nothing, I was getting closer to Elisheva.

And suddenly I was there, right behind them.

She stood there and proclaimed, "Henker, you are dead!"

At that very moment, because the Butcher was walking toward her, step by step, completely calmly, a pilgrim screamed, "*Achtung! Achtung!*"

Elisheva froze.

Why did she not fire?

What was going on?

Then I understood. The fine membrane that had protected her from the past had just broken with the cry of *Achtung*.

Elisheva had gone back into the past.

"Fire. Fire! Elisheva!"

In tears, I was shouting at the top of my lungs.

"You are in Jerusalem! You are free!"

She turned to look at me. She saw me. I am sure she saw me, in a flash; and in the space of a second we said it all. We spoke of music, the sky, summer, love, warmth, beauty, we spoke of our love for Jerusalem, our joy in New York, the feverishness in the concert hall, we spoke of Bach, and Schubert.

When she fired, it was already too late. The Butcher had grabbed hold of her. She did not even struggle when he took her weapon, and aimed at her chest, point-blank.

A second later, she recoiled to the deafening sound of the gunshot.

"*Párate! Párate!*"

He let her fall to the ground.

I saw her fall, her legs folding under her, her body the shape of a broken cello.

All the music fell silent.

I threw myself on the Butcher's back. With all my strength, in a single thrust I stabbed my cello bow in his neck, up to the heel. I felt the viscous flow of blood on my taut fingers, heard the rattle as he died.

ELISHEVA

She falls back. Slowly.

Her body curls in an arch.

The steel entering her flesh, wounding her, like long ago, exactly the same.

Skin, flesh, muscles. Everything tears.

Her heart explodes.

The pain is so sharp that she cannot breathe.

She is going to the *Himmels Allee*, the Avenue in the Sky, to the gate in the hedge, all the way at the end of the women's camp, where the trees rustle in the wind, where everything is music, and she can hear the strains of Fauré's *Elegy for Cello*.

Glossary

Aba, Aba	Father, Father
Achtung!	Attention!
Adonai	Lord, God
agora	unit of Israeli currency. There are one hundred agorot to every shekel.
ahtak	sister
Aïsh benti	May my daughter live long
akbak lilak	May that happen
Allahu Akbar!	God is Great
anavim	grapes
Ani lo mevateret	I won't let anything go by
ashooma	shameful act
ashtana	wait
atzor	stop
aywa	alright; also slang for "yes"
balagan	mess
Baruh ashem	God be praised
bat zona	daughter of a whore
bekhavod	"In honour", which the Rabbi repeats as he walks to the tebáh (the reader's platform) to recite the Torah
beseder	in order; fine
bombón, mi	my sweet
börek, bourekas (pl.)	filo pastry stuffed with cheese or vegetables
bouzouki	Greek instrument, similar to a mandolin
busha	dishonour; shame
cariña	term of endearment; "cute little one"
Caudillo	ref. to General Franco
cojones	balls
conversos	Muslims and Jews who converted to Catholicism after the Reconquista
djellaba	loose-fitting woollen robe worn in the Maghreb
dybbuk	a lost soul invading a body, in need of an exorcism
Einsatzgruppen	S.S. death squads tasked with the mass killings of Jews and others
Elohim	Lord, God

Eretz, Eretz Isröel	land, Land of Israel
falafel	ball-shaped chickpea and fava bean fritter; *taamaiya* in Egypt
Falasha	Ethiopians claiming to be Jews who were forced to convert; formerly of Beta Israel
gilgul neshamot	reincarnation; the cycle of souls
goy	non-Jew, lit. "stranger"; in plural can also mean nations or peoples
grimoire	esoteric textbook of pagan origins
Habibi tfadal	Go ahead, mate
Haganah	the defence; Jewish militia forming the core of the I.D.F. after 1948
Haggadah	the telling; scripture (not holy) reciting the story of Passover
Hahla el yom	A wonderful day (greeting)
halal	food prepared according to Islamic dietary laws. Forbids the use of alcohol.
Hamdullah	Thanks be to God
Hannukah	Festival of Lights, from "to dedicate", celebrating re-dedication of the Temple after the Maccabees defeated the Assyrians
ha-olam haba	the next world
harissa	hot chili sauce used in North African cooking
Hassidim	ultra-orthodox Jews, spiritual and mystical worship; from "piety"/"loving kindness"
Hatati, hatati ya Rabi	I have sinned, I have sinned, my God
Haval al hasman	You're wasting your time
hevre	friends, mates, comrades
hora	Israeli folk dance
hostia	Spanish curse, also the name of the communion wafer
houya	brother
Inal a bouk	A curse on your father!
Inta min oun?	Where do you come from?
intifada	Arabic for "awakening"; commonly used to refer to the Palestinian struggle
Judío	Jew (Spanish)
Kabbalah	School of mystical thought based on rabbinic litera-ture. Originated in 11th-century Europe
Kaddish	a prayer chanted during mourning rituals
kalba	she-dog; can also be used derogatorily as "bitch"
Katel tini	You killed me
kawa	coffee
keffiyah	square-shaped head-cloth worn by men, popularized by Yasser Arafat
kelb	Arabic for dog

kelev	Hebrew for dog
khat	Arabic name for *catha edulis*, whose fresh leaves are chewed to extract the mild stimulant within. Very popular in the Horn of Africa and Southern Arabia.
kibbutz, kibbutzim (pl.)	agricultural (and sometimes industrial) collectives in Israel
Kibinimat!	What the hell!
Kiddush	blessing of wine, lit. "sanctification"
Kinnereth	the Sea of Galilee
kippa	also yarmulke, skull-cap worn by men in synagogues
kippur	atonement or expiation
kosher	food prepared according to Jewish dietary laws; forbids the mixing of milk, meat and wine. Similar to halal, its Islamic equivalent
ktoubot	marriage certificates
lamed	twelfth letter of the Hebrew alphabet
lavaliere	large cravat popular in 19th-century France, shaped like a bow
Lehayim!	"To life!"; a toast
Likud	lit. "the consolidation"; name of a right-wing political party
marabouts	Muslim hermits who maintain tombs, popularly believed to have supernatural powers. Soothsayers
Marranos	Spanish Jews forcibly converted to Christianity
mashub	Oh, right
mazel tov	congratulations, good luck
Me cago en la madre que te parió	I shit on the mother who bore you
mektoub	fate
mem	thirteenth letter of the Hebrew alphabet
meshuga	crazy
mesukan	dangerous
Mincha	afternoon Jewish prayer; lit. from flour offering in the Temple
Moloch	ancient Semetic god
moshav, moshavnik	Israeli agricultural settlement, non-communal; member of a *moshav*
Mossad	Security and special operations agency
narghile	water-pipe, also known as shisha
neshama	my soul (affectionate)
niqab	veil that covers all of a Muslim woman's face except the eyes
Nyet!	No!
oeil-de-boeuf	small oval window
Oy vez mir!	"Oh pain!"; Yiddish exclamation

pączki	Polish doughnuts; plural of *pączki*
Palmach	strike force; elite Haganah unit
parasha	portion; division of the Torah into sections
párate	stop (Spanish)
Purim	Hebrew spring festival celebrating the saving of Jews from slaughter by Haman, Grand Vizier under the Persian King Ahasuerus; told in the book of Esther
puto tiempo	"Fucking time" (Spanish)
rebetiko	modern Greek folk music, with a bouzouki player accompanying a singer
Rosh Hashanah	Jewish spiritual New Year, "head of the year" in seventh month
Sababa	Great
sabra	someone born in Israel
Safi	"O.K." or "Stop!"
Saha lik	Lucky you
schlepping	Yiddish slang for dragging or hauling an object
Sepharim	Jewish holy scriptures; plural of "*sepher*" or book
Shabbat	the Jewish Sabbath or day of rest
Shallah	Contraction of Inshallah, if God wills it
sharav	hot dry desert wind, blowing from the Arabian desert
shawarma	roasted meat wrapped in bread, usually with pickles and tahini
shechinah	divine presence (fem.); from "to dwell"
shema	Jewish "*fatiha*"; "Hear, O Israel, our Lord is God, Our Lord is One"
shezaphani hashemesh	"The sun made me brown" (famous verse of Song of Songs)
shiduh	Yiddish term for a matchmaking that results in marriage
shin	twenty-first letter of the Hebrew alphabet
Shin Bet	security agency reporting directly to the Prime Minister
shiva	seven days of mourning after burial.
Shnua adak?	What's that?
shofar	ram's horn, blown in the synagogue.
shoofooni ya nes	make a show of oneself
Shouf	Look
shtayim	"two" in Hebrew
shtetl	Yiddish diminutive of "town", usually referring to Orthodox communities in the Pale
Shu?	What?
Shu badak	What's wrong?
sovev ve mesuvav	"who surrounds and is surrounded"
stele	upright stone or slab with engraved surface

streimel	fur hat worn by married Jewish men
tallith	Jewish prayer shawl
Talmud, Talmudists	compilation of Rabbinic commentary and tales from second to tenth centuries; those who study the Talmud
Talmud Torah	lit. "student of Torah"; Jewish primary schools for religious education
Tfadal	Please come in; welcome
Ti-ye bari, adoni	Good health to you, Sir
Tishri	the month with the most holidays in the Hebrew calendar, including Rosh Hashanah and Yom Kippur
Torah	the five books of Moses
Tsahal	acronym for Tzva Hahagana LeYisra'el, the Israeli Defence Forces
Tzedakah	charity; from Hebrew "righteousness"
Untermenschen	subhumans or inferior persons
Valle de los Caidos	Valley of the slain
vav consecutive	feature of Classical Hebrew that allows for changing a tense with a single letter
Versuchspersonen	people on whom experiments were performed
Verus Israel	the true Israel
Voy	Yiddish exclaimation
wadi	valley with a dried-up riverbed; gully
weld hahalal	honest boy
ya'ani	Arabic equivalent for "you know"; can also mean both "oh well" and "not bad"
ya kebdi	my liver (term of endearment)
Yallah	"Let's go!"; can also mean "O.K."
Yallah, nou, sah!	Come on, drive!
Ya Rabi laziz	Almighty God
Ya Rabi, ya hanoun	O God, O Merciful
Yazi ad!	That's enough!
yekiri	dear, darling
Yesh gvul	There are limits
Y.H.W.H.	the personal name of God
yod	tenth letter of Hebrew alphabet
Yom Kippur	Day of Atonement
za'atar	savoury mixture of dried herbs (typically marjoram and thyme) and sesame seeds

Acknowledgements

This book would have been impossible without the friendship of Michèle Chiche, Hélène Cohen, Aviva Cohen, Denise Berrebi and Rachel Grunstein, who read the manuscript and whose advice enabled me to cut, eliminate and deepen both scenes and characters.

I would like to thank André Laks, Claude Torres and Ariel Sion from the Mémorial de la Shoah for the documentation on the presence of music in the death camps. And Claire Roch, who introduced me to Fauré's *Elegy*.

Thanks to Peter Black and Philip Selim of the United States Holocaust Memorial Museum for their answers to my queries regarding Majdanek and the Aktion Erntefest.

Heartfelt thanks to Corinne Mellul, François Sergent and Géraldine Amiel for the room in town where I had the peace and quiet to write for some time.

Thanks, finally, to Thomas Nolden for his encouragement and support.

And many many thanks to Bruno Flamand for his pencil marks, which were adroit, intelligent and always full of tenderness.

The translator would like to thank Ayelet Jospe-Ritchie for her help with the Hebrew transliterations.

CHOCHANA BOUKHOBZA is a novelist of Tunisian-Jewish descent now living in France. Her first novel, *A Summer in Jerusalem*, won the Prix Méditerranée. Her second novel, *Le Cri*, was a finalist for the Prix Femina.

ALISON ANDERSON's translations include Muriel Barbery's best-selling novel *The Elegance of the Hedgehog* and, for MacLehose Press, *The Breakers* by Claudie Gallay.